AWAY WITH THE PENGUINS

www.penguin.co.uk

Also by Hazel Prior

Ellie and the Harp-Maker

AWAY WITH THE PENGUINS

Hazel Prior

BANTAM PRESS

TRANSWORLD PUBLISHERS
61–63 Uxbridge Road, London W5 5SA
www.penguin.co.uk

Transworld is part of the Penguin Random House group of companies
whose addresses can be found at global.penguinrandomhouse.com

Penguin
Random House
UK

First published in Great Britain in 2020 by Bantam Press
an imprint of Transworld Publishers

Every effort has been made to obtain the necessary permissions with
reference to copyright material, both illustrative and quoted. We apologize
for any omissions in this respect and will be pleased to make the
appropriate acknowledgements in any future edition.

A CIP catalogue record for this book
is available from the British Library.

ISBNs 9781787630932 (hb)
9781787630949 (tpb)

Typeset in 11.5/15pt ITC Berkeley Oldstyle Pro by Jouve (UK), Milton Keynes
Printed and bound in Great Britain by Clays Ltd, Elcograf S.p.A.

Penguin Random House is committed to a sustainable
future for our business, our readers and our planet. This book
is made from Forest Stewardship Council® certified paper.

MIX
Paper from
responsible sources
FSC® C018179

1 3 5 7 9 10 8 6 4 2

For Jonathan

'I find penguins at present the only comfort in life . . . one can't be angry when one looks at a penguin.'

John Ruskin

1

Veronica

The Ballahays, Ayrshire, Scotland
May 2012

I HAVE TOLD EILEEN to get rid of all the mirrors. I used to like them but I certainly don't now. Mirrors are too honest. There is only so much truth a woman can take.

'Are you sure, Mrs McCreedy?' Her voice implies she knows my mind better than I do. She always does that. It is one of her innumerable annoying habits.

'Of course I'm sure!'

She clicks her tongue and tilts her head to one side so that her corkscrew curls brush against her shoulder. It's quite a manoeuvre when you consider the extraordinary width of her neck.

'Even the lovely one with the gilt edge, the one over the mantelpiece?'

'Yes, even that one,' I explain patiently.

'And all the bathroom mirrors too?'

'Especially those!' The bathroom is the last place I want to look at myself.

'Whatever you say.' This in a tone bordering on impertinence.

Eileen comes every day. Her main role is cleaning, but her domestic skills leave much to be desired. She seems to be labouring under the impression that I don't see dirt.

Eileen has a limited collection of facial expressions: cheerful, nosy, busy, nonplussed and vacant. Now she puts on her busy face. She bumbles around emitting a semi-musical noise like a bored bee, collecting the mirrors one at a time and stacking them in the hall. She is unable to close the doors behind her because her hands are full, so I follow in her wake, shutting them carefully. If there's one thing that I can't abide in life, it's a door left open.

I stroll into the larger of the two sitting rooms. There is now an unsightly dark rectangle on the wallpaper above the mantelpiece. I'll have to fill the space with something else. A nice oil painting with plenty of verdure, I think; maybe a Constable print. That would set off the Lincoln green of the velvet curtains. I should like a calming pastoral scene with hills and a lake. A swathe of landscape empty of human beings would be best.

'There we are, then, Mrs McCreedy. I think that's all of them.'

At least Eileen refrains from using my Christian name. Most young people these days seem to have abandoned Mr, Mrs and Miss, which, if you ask me, is a sad reflection on modern society. I addressed Eileen as Mrs Thompson for the first six months she worked for me. I only stopped doing it because she begged me. ('Please call me Eileen, Mrs McCreedy. I would be so much happier if you would.' 'Well, please continue to call me Mrs McCreedy, Eileen,' I replied. 'I would be so much happier if you would.')

I like the house much better now that it's lost the appalling spectres of Veronica McCreedy taunting me from every corner.

Eileen puts her hands on her hips. 'Well, I'll be putting this lot away, then. I'll bung them in the back room, shall I? There's still some space in there.'

The back room is excessively dark and a little on the cold side, not really usable as a living space. The spiders think it belongs to them. Eileen, in her great wisdom, uses it as a depository for any item I desire to be rid of. She is a firm believer in hoarding everything 'just in case'.

She heaves the mirrors across the kitchen. I resist the urge to close the doors as she goes back and forth, knowing this will only make life more difficult for her. I console myself with the thought that they'll all be shut again soon.

She is back five minutes later. 'I hope you don't mind me asking, Mrs McCreedy, but I had to move this out of the way to fit the mirrors in. Do you know what it is, what's in it? Do you want it? I can always ask Doug to take it to the rubbish tip next time he goes.'

She dumps the old wooden box on the kitchen table and goggles at the rusty padlock.

I choose to ignore her questions and enquire instead, 'Who is this Doug?'

'You know. Doug. My husband.'

I'd forgotten she was married. I've never been introduced to the unfortunate man.

'Well, I shan't be requiring him to take any of my possessions to the rubbish tip in the near or indeed distant future,' I tell her. 'You can leave it on the table for the time being.'

She runs her finger along the top of the box, stroking a clean trail in the dust. Expression number two (nosy) has now established itself on her face. She leans in towards me conspiratorially. I lean backwards a little, having no desire whatsoever to conspire.

'I've tried the padlock to see if there might be something valuable inside,' she confesses, 'but it's stuck. You need to know the code if you want to open it.'

'I am well aware of that fact, Eileen.'

3

She clearly assumes I am as clueless about the contents as she is.

My skin crawls at the thought of Eileen looking inside. Other people meddling is the very reason I locked it all up in the first place. There is only one person who I will ever permit to see the contents of that box and that person is myself.

I am not ashamed. Oh no, never that. At least . . . But I absolutely refuse to be led down that path. There are things contained in that box that I have managed not to think about for decades. Now the mere sight of it provokes a distinct wobble in my knee joints. I sit down quickly. 'Eileen, would you be kind enough to put the kettle on?'

The clock strikes seven. Eileen has gone and I am alone in the house. Being alone is supposed to be an issue for people such as me, but I have to say I find it deeply satisfying. Human company is necessary at times, I admit, but it is almost always irksome in one way or another.

I am currently settled in the Queen Anne armchair by the fire in the 'snug', my second and more intimate sitting room. The fire isn't a real one with wood and coal, alas, but an electric contraption with fake flames. I have had to compromise on this, as with so much in life. It does at least fulfil its primary requirement of producing heat. Ayrshire is chilly, even in summer.

I switch on the television. A scraggy girl is on-screen. She's screeching her head off, spiking her fingers in the air and caterwauling, something about being titanium. I hastily change channels. I flick through a quiz show, a crime drama and an advertisement for cat food. When I return to the original channel the girl is still caterwauling, 'I am titanium.' Somebody should tell her she isn't. She is a silly, noisy, spoilt brat. What a relief when she finally shuts her mouth.

At last it's time for *Earth Matters*, the only programme all week that is worth watching. Everything else is sex, advertising, celebrities doing quizzes, celebrities trying to cook, celebrities on a desert island, celebrities in a rainforest, celebrities interviewing other celebrities, and a whole load of wannabes doing everything they can to become celebrities (with a spectacular success rate in making fools of themselves). *Earth Matters* is a welcome respite, demonstrating as it does in manifold ways how much more sensible animals are than humans.

However, I am dismayed to find that the current series of *Earth Matters* seems to have ended. In its place there's a programme called *The Plight of Penguins*. With a gleam of hope I observe that it is presented by Robert Saddlebow. That man demonstrates that it is occasionally possible to be a celebrity for the right reasons. Unlike the vast majority, he has actually done something. He has voyaged around the world campaigning and raising awareness of conservation issues for several decades. He is one of the few people for whom I feel a degree of admiration.

This evening Robert Saddlebow is relayed to my fireside all bundled up and hooded, in the midst of a white wasteland. A flurry of snowflakes whirls around his face. Behind him is a clump of dark shapes. The camera homes in and reveals them to be penguins, a seething great tribe of them. Some are huddled together, others sleeping on their bellies, others waddling round within the group, on missions of their own.

Mr Saddlebow informs me that there are eighteen species of penguin in the world (nineteen if you count White-flippered Little Blues as a separate species), many of which are endangered. During the filming of the programme, he says, he has developed a massive respect and admiration for these birds – for the race as a whole, for each species and for every individual penguin. They live in the harshest conditions on the planet and yet daily take on challenges with a gusto and spirit that would put many of us humans to shame. 'What a tragedy it would be if any one of these species was lost to the planet!' declares Robert Saddlebow, fixing his ice-blue eyes on me from the screen.

'A tragedy indeed!' I say back to him. If Robert Saddlebow cares about penguins this much, then so do I.

He explains that each week he's going to pick a different penguin and show us the qualities that make the chosen species unique. This week features the Emperor penguins.

I am transfixed. Every year Emperor penguins walk some seventy miles across a desert of ice to reach their breeding ground. This is indeed a remarkable achievement, especially when you consider that travelling on foot isn't exactly their forte. They walk like Eileen, shuffling forward with a singular lack of grace. They look rather uncomfortable in their own skins. Yet their persistence is inspiring.

When the programme is finished, I pull myself out of the chair. I have to acknowledge this is not as difficult a task as it is for many others who have reached my mature years. I would even classify myself as sprightly. I am aware that this body cannot be wholly relied upon. In the past it was a faultless machine, but these days it has suffered losses in both elasticity and efficiency. I must be prepared for the fact that it might let me down at some point in the near future. Yet so far it has managed to keep going marvellously well. Eileen, with her habitual charm, often comments that I am 'as tough as old boots'. Every time she says this I'm tempted to reply, 'All the better to kick you with, my dear.' I repress the urge, though. One must always strive to avoid rudeness.

It is a quarter past eight. I make my way to the kitchen to get my evening cup of Darjeeling and a caramel wafer. My eye falls on the wooden box, still sitting unopened on the table. I consider twisting the combination on the padlock and taking a peek at what's inside. In an illogical, sadistic sort of way I'd like to. But no, that would be a foolish move. It would be like Pandora in the myth, letting loose a thousand demons. The box must absolutely go back to the spiders without my interference.

2

Veronica

The Ballahays

LIFE HAS JUST BECOME a degree more difficult. I tried to comb my hair into some semblance of order this morning, but the mirror in the bathroom wasn't there. I hurried back to the bedroom only to discover that that one has vanished, too. So has the one in the hall and the one in the living room.

I proceed with breakfast, none too pleased with this new and unreasonable state of affairs.

At nine o'clock Eileen lets herself in.

'Morning, Mrs McCreedy! What a lovely one it is, too!' She will insist on being exasperatingly cheerful.

'What have you done with all my mirrors?'

She blinks slowly like a frog.

'I put them in the back room, like you told me to!'

'That is absurd! How can I sort out my hair and make-up

without a mirror?' She really is an irrational creature. 'Would you kindly put them back before you do anything else?'

'What, all of them?'

'Yes, all of them.'

She produces a faint huffing sound. 'Whatever you say, Mrs McCreedy.'

I should hope so too. I don't pay her all that money for nothing.

I remember too late that a certain wooden box is still on the kitchen table and she's bound to want to interfere.

'You haven't managed to open it yet, then?' she says the minute she lays eyes on it, assuming this is by incapacity rather than by choice. 'I could probably get Doug to saw off the padlock with a hacksaw if you can't remember the code.'

'I do remember the code, Eileen. My memory is faultless. I can recall dozens of lines of *Hamlet* from my schooldays.' She does a quick rolling of the eyes here. She thinks I don't notice it, but I do. 'And I don't want some Doug of yours tinkering around with my box,' I continue. 'I'd be grateful if you'd see to those mirrors without further ado.'

'Yes, of course, Mrs McCreedy. Whatever you say.'

I watch as she drags the mirrors from the back room and hangs them up where they were before, muttering to herself.

Once the mirrors are back I set about tackling the problem of my hair. There isn't a great deal of it these days and it is startlingly white, but I like to keep it tidy. I don't relish looking at myself though. My reflection isn't a pleasant sight when compared to reflections of the past. Years ago I was really something to look at. People called me 'a true beauty', 'a stunner', 'a corker'. No vestige of that is left now, I observe as I scrape the comb over my thin strands. My skin has become papery and loose. My face is scribbled all over with wrinkles. My eyelids sag. My cheekbones that used to be so beautiful jut out at peculiar angles. I should be used to these repugnant physical flaws by this time, but it still galls me to see myself like this.

I do my utmost to improve matters with the application of lipstick, powder and rouge. But the fact remains: I am not fond of mirrors.

The wind cuts through me. It is that damp, feral variety of wind one finds only in Scotland. I huddle in my coat and pick my way northward along the coast path. I have always believed in the efficacy of a daily walk and I refuse to be put off by inclement weather. To my left the sea churns in slate-grey patterns and spits a wild, white froth out into the air.

My stick steadies me over the uneven turf and sand. I have brought my fuchsia gold-trimmed handbag, which is floundering tiresomely against my thigh. I should have left it on the hook in the hall but one never knows when one might require a handkerchief or a painkiller. I have also brought my litter-picking tongs and a small refuse sack. It is a lifelong habit of mine to pick up litter because of something my dear father once said. It is a small act of remembrance as well as a token gesture to atone for the chaos caused by the human race. Even the rugged pathways of the Ayrshire coast have been sullied by the carelessness of mankind.

It is no easy task wielding stick, tongs, sack and handbag, especially in this wind. My bones are beginning to complain at the effort of it all. I work out a way of angling my weight to lean into each gust so that it supports me instead of fighting me.

A gull screeches and dips through the clouds. I pause for a moment to admire the beauty of the tempestuous seascape. I have a particular liking for rocks, waves and wilderness. But something scarlet is bobbing up and down on the billows. Is it a crisp packet or a biscuit wrapper? My younger self would scurry down on to the beach, wade straight in and get it, but now, alas, I'm incapable of such things. The spray blows into my face and drips down it like tears.

People who litter the countryside should be shot.

I push back against the wind and battle my way homewards. I am flagging slightly by the time I reach the front gates.

The Ballahays boasts a substantial driveway and is surrounded by three acres of pleasant grounds. Most of the garden is walled, which is one of the reasons I like the place so much. Within these walls are cedars, rockeries, a fountain, various statues and four herbaceous borders. They are tended by Mr Perkins, my gardener.

I glance up at the house as I approach. An ivy-clad, late-Jacobean-style creation, The Ballahays is constructed from mellow brick and stone. With its twelve bedrooms and several creaking oak staircases, it is admittedly not the ideal home for me. Trying to keep up with its needs is a considerable task. It suffers from crumbling plaster and terrible draughts, and there are mice in the roof. I purchased it back in 1956 simply because I could. I enjoy both the privacy and the views and therefore have not troubled myself to move.

I step indoors, deposit the refuse sack and tongs in the porch and hang up my coat.

As soon as I enter the kitchen my eye falls on the box. That wretched box again. I had almost forgotten. I sit down at the table. I look at the box and the box looks back at me. Its presence permeates the room. It is impertinent; mocking, challenging me to open it.

Nobody could claim that Veronica McCreedy is the sort of person who fails to rise to a challenge.

I make myself do it. Twist the controls and line up the numbers one by one. You will note how perfectly I remember those numbers. One nine four two: 1942. Still engraved in my memory, even after all this time. The lock is stiff, but that's hardly surprising: it's been seventy years.

The very first thing that meets my eyes is the locket. Small and oval, a 'V' etched into the tarnished silver amidst a design of curling tendrils. The chain is fine and delicate. I run it through my fingers. Before I can stop myself I've snapped the catch and the locket springs open. My throat clenches and lets out an involuntary gasp. All four specimens are there, just as I knew they would be. They are tiny, as indeed they had to be to fit into such a case. They seem so tired and so very, very fragile.

I will not cry. No. Absolutely not. Veronica McCreedy does not cry.

Instead I gaze at them: the strands of hair from four heads. Two are intertwined, brown and auburn. Then there is the dark, dark, luscious sprig of hair that a long-gone version of myself used to take out and kiss so often. Tucked in next to it is a tiny wisp, so fine and light it is almost transparent. I cannot bear to touch it. I snap the locket shut. Close my eyes, steady myself and breathe. Count to ten. Force my eyes open again. I place the locket carefully back in the corner of the box.

The two black leather-bound notebooks are also there. I lift them out. They feel horribly familiar. Even the smell of them, the ragged scent of old leather combined with an echo of the lily-of-the-valley perfume I used to wear.

Now that I've started, I can't stop. I open the first book. Each page is packed with handwriting, eager loopy letters in blue ink. I squint and manage to read a few lines without my glasses. I smile sadly. As a teenager my spelling wasn't very good but my writing was considerably neater than it is these days. I close the book again.

Read it I must and read it I will, but if my past is about to suck me in I need to brace myself.

I brew a nice pot of Earl Grey and arrange some ginger thins on a plate, using the Wedgwood porcelain with the pink hibiscus design. I bring it all through to the drawing room on the tea trolley. I settle in the armchair by the bay window. I eat two of the biscuits, drain one cup of tea and pour myself another before I take the first notebook into my hands. I do not open it for a further five minutes. Then I put on my reading glasses.

And, like a window opening to sunlight and fresh summer air, it is there. My youth: tender, vivid, spread out before me. And even though I know it will hurt me three times over, I can't help but read on.

3

Veronica

The Ballahays

IF I WAS YOUNGER I would run. Run and scream and shout and break things. That is not and cannot be my way now. Instead, I sip tea and I cogitate.

I have read through the night and am in a state of shock. Having been fed my own fifteen-year-old voice solidly for hours, it feels as if part of that wilder, more vulnerable self has entered me. The sensation is odd and uncomfortable, like a scalpel slipping under my skin. For so many years I have denied access to those memories. Now, as if to make up for lost time, they've burst the floodgates of my mental fortress and will not leave me alone.

Along with the turmoil, a sneaky little question has entered my head. I ponder it over breakfast. I am still pondering it when Eileen arrives. It remains with me during my mid-morning walk, while I am trying to read Emily Brontë, over my salmon-en-croûte lunch,

13

during my post-prandial lie-down, while I am completing the *Tele-graph* crossword and while I am picking roses for the dining-room table. As I file my nails afterwards I am beginning to realize I'll have no peace until the question is answered.

I return to my bedroom. I have placed the diaries back in the box and padlocked it. I've removed the locket, though. It is now under my pillow.

I fish it out, take it in my hands and run the chain through my fingers again. I do not open it this time, but my thoughts dwell on that thinnest, palest wisp of hair. With considerable exertion I manage to barricade the tide of emotion once more. I force my brain into action.

The clock is ticking particularly loudly today. I dislike clocks but, like politicians and paracetamol, they have somehow made themselves indispensable in this world. I tear out my hearing aid. The tick-tock dies down. I am able to hear myself think at last.

By the time Eileen has finished her chores my mind is made up.

I go down to the kitchen, select a few items from the fourth-best china set and make a pot of good strong English breakfast tea. I insist on making tea myself. Nobody makes tea as well as I do.

'Sit down for a moment, Eileen. I believe there is something I'd like you to do for me.'

She plonks herself on a chair and mutters something.

'I do wish you would speak up, Eileen.'

'What have you done with your hearing aid, Mrs McCreedy?' she mouths back at me, madly gesticulating and pointing at her ears.

'Bedroom, I believe. Would you be so kind as to—'

'Of course.'

She gets up and trots out of the room.

'Door, Eileen!'

'But I'm coming back in a— Oh, never mind,' she yells, hurling the door shut behind her. She returns an instant later with my hearing aid in her hand, this time remembering to close the door in her wake.

I put the hearing aid in, then pour out two cups of tea.

Eileen sits down again and slurps noisily. I take a sip from my cup and gather my thoughts. My decision will deeply affect whatever small fraction of future is left for me.

I would not call myself a superstitious person. I will always walk under a ladder if a ladder is there to be walked under and I am quite partial to black cats, whether they choose to cross my path or not. But never in my life have I made a will. That, I have always thought, would be asking for trouble. Yet I'm aware that if I fail to make any provision, my wealth may well pass to the government or some equally undesirable beneficiary. Having reached mid-octogenarian status, I believe it is incumbent on me to consider the matter in some depth. It is quite possible that this mortal frame will hold up for another fifteen years. I may get a postcard from the queen to congratulate me on my hundredth birthday. Then again, I may not.

As far as I'm aware, I don't have a single blood relative alive in this world. But, having revisited the past, it strikes me that circumstances have not provided me with utter certainty on this point. It does not take much to create a new human being, after all. Not every birth is publicly celebrated and there must be thousands of fathers who have no idea they are fathers. Now that this small but undeniable doubt has manifested itself, I have become quite fixated with it. I am determined to find an answer. And I must pursue it without further ado.

Eileen is sitting across from me, her hands wrapped around her teacup. She is wearing her vacant expression. I observe that her hair is even wilder and curlier than usual. I do wish she would do something about it.

'Eileen, I have a favour to ask of you. Would you be able to use your internet contraption to find me a trustworthy and reputable agency?'

'Yes, of course, Mrs McCreedy, if that's what you want. What sort of agency were you thinking of?' She smirks into her tea. 'A dating agency?'

I am in no mood to pander to her foolishness. 'Don't be ridiculous! No, I need the sort of agency that unearths documentation regarding long-lost relatives.'

Her hands fly up to her powdery white face, her smirk replaced with wide-eyed curiosity. 'Oh, Mrs McCreedy! Do you think you might have some family out there somewhere?'

She waits, hungry for further information. I have no intention of telling her anything more. At my age I should be able to do exactly as I wish and not have to proclaim it to the world.

'So you'd like me to google for agencies. Family reunited sort of thing, you mean?' she asks.

'Something of the kind, yes. Use your googly doo-dahs or whatever means are within your power. It would have to be a very discreet agency,' I warn her, 'and one with a good reputation and track record. I would be grateful if you could make sure of that, please.'

'Of course, Mrs McCreedy. How exciting!' she declares.

'Well, exciting or not, I would very much like to investigate the matter. So I would be indebted to you if you could provide me with an address and phone number at your earliest convenience.'

'Not a problem, Mrs McCreedy. I'll do a search tonight, as soon as I get home. I'm sure I can find you some details. I'll bring them in when I come tomorrow.'

'Excellent. Thank you, Eileen.'

I flick the switch. The fake flames leap up in an instant orange blaze. Next I turn on the television for *Earth Matters*, my favourite programme, only to discover they have replaced it with a documentary about penguins. Come to think of it, I do recall having seen something similar recently. It will provide a welcome break from the pernicious thoughts that have been my company all day.

This week we are looking at King penguins. I confess, I am rather charmed by these singularly courageous yet waddlesome creatures. When the camera shows one of them losing its egg, which rolls down into a steep, inaccessible gully, I observe how the poor bird grieves, beak pointing to the sky in despair. It is really quite moving.

Robert Saddlebow talks passionately of the penguins' massive population decline in recent years. It appears to be due to environmental factors, but more research is needed.

I hate to think that these noble and attractive birds might vanish from the planet.

My father's words come back to me, words he spoke when I was sitting on his knee as a child, then on many occasions as I was growing up. I can almost hear them now, spoken in his earnest, gentle voice. 'There are three types of people in this world, Very.' (He called me Very.) 'There are those who make the world worse, those who make no difference, and those who make the world better. Be one who makes the world better, if you can.' I have met few people in my life who fall into the third category. I have myself done little in the way of bettering. I have chosen to interpret the three categories as *people who throw litter into the countryside, people who ignore litter* and *people who pick up other people's litter.* I have satisfied my conscience by means of tongs and refuse sacks. Beyond that I cannot see that my life has been useful in the least.

Now an idea is beginning to take root. It is perhaps feasible that my demise might be useful in some way. Unless it is proved otherwise, I must work on the assumption that I have no blood ties at all. It would be pleasing if I could make some small difference to the planet. The more I think about it, the more I am attracted to the idea.

By the time I perform my night-time ablutions I am bordering on the obsessive. Indeed, I cannot wait until a time when pen and paper might be handy. I take the nearest thing to write with, which, as I am in the bathroom, happens to be an eyebrow pencil. (Yes, even at my advanced age I am not immune to a little vanity. My natural eyebrows have dwindled to a few pathetic grey wisps, so most mornings I take the trouble to enhance them a little.) I use the eyebrow pencil and write the word 'PENGUINS' in the bottom right-hand corner of the mirror.

My memory is completely intact – I frequently recite passages from *Hamlet* to reassure myself of the fact – but if there is something I wish to keep at the forefront of my brain there is no harm in having a written reminder, in a place where I will see it.

Terry's Penguin Blog

3 November 2012

Shall I tell you something lovely about Adélie penguins? They have one rather romantic habit. A boy penguin will woo his girl with a gift: a carefully chosen, special pebble. How could she fail to be impressed? Not only this, but he'll also put on a fine display, throwing his head back, puffing out his chest and making loud braying noises – which, of course, if you are a female penguin, is totally irresistible.

With any luck he'll also have a shiny new nest already built by the time she returns from the sea. The pebble gift, in fact, represents more than loyalty and love. Pebbles are the most valuable currency at the moment because they're the key nest-building material. The penguins are not above theft, either. We've witnessed a few comical instances of penguins nicking pebbles from each other's nests when backs are turned.

Many of last year's couples are now joyfully reunited. On the whole, the Adélies are a faithful bunch. Occasionally, however, there's an issue.

For example, here's a penguin who interests us. Adélies generally look pretty similar, but you'll see from the photo why we always recognize this one, even from a distance. Instead of the standard white chest and tummy, with black covering everything else, he's almost entirely black. Just a few paler feathers in a patch under his chin. His mate, a normal black-and-whiter, was with him for the last four seasons. But where is she? Did she fail to get through the Antarctic winter? Was she eaten by a leopard seal? Or do we have a rare case of penguin infidelity? We'll never know. Whatever the reason, Sooty (we call him Sooty) is sitting there on his nest, very, very alone.

4

Patrick

At his flat in Bolton
May 2012

ON AND ON. EVERY single fricking song I've ever heard about loneliness keeps playing inside my head. It's driving me insane.

It's been two weeks. Two gut-wrenching, bloody, bug-mongering weeks and not a squeak from her. Man, after four years together you'd think she might provide me with some sort of explanation. But no, not Lynette. Took all her stuff and just rocketed out of my life. No note, no nothing. I hadn't done anything wrong as far as I could see, not recently, anyway. Not any of the things that normally wind her up. Forgot to put the recycling out? Nope. Left a snotty hanky in the bed? Nope. Licked my plate after dinner? Nope. It's not as if we'd had a row or anything, either. Not that day, anyhow.

I hadn't the foggiest what she was playing at, what it was all about. It was only when Gav told me he'd spotted the two of them hand in hand that the truth of the matter made itself clear like a wallop in the face. I did a bit of research, asking around at the bike shop, pub and any other hotbeds of Bolton gossip I could think of. I found out he's a builder, the guy she left me for. All muscle, apparently. Often seen at the chippy mouthing off about the Poles and Pakis nabbing our jobs.

Lynette, Lynette, Lynette! You stick a needle in my heart. What the hell do *you* want with a racist brickie? You, with your masters in anthropology and your designer jeans and your perfect Cleopatra haircut. You, with your work ethic and your positivity ethic and your just-about-everything-else ethic. You've turned your own moral compass upside down. You've exchanged your bulging book-shelves for bulging biceps. You, of all people!

Where does this leave me? OK, here it is. I've lapsed. You turned me into a health freak, Lynette, and got me into cooking all those fruity, vegetably, superfoody meals. Well, you probably don't give a flea's fart but in case you want to know, I'm on a diet of cake, crisps and beer. My own biceps, which I confess I was a little bit proud of before, are gathering a lovely layer of fat. As is my stomach zone. More blubber every day. Soon this lean, mean sex machine will be a walking lump of jelly. Thank you for everything, Lynette. Nice one.

Three weeks. Where did it all go wrong? Was it me? I guess it was. I know Lynette didn't like me taking over the cooking. She didn't mind having a gourmet dinner waiting for her when she got home from work but at the same time she did see the kitchen as her domain. It was she who bought the coffee machine and skillet and juicer; she who rang the landlord every time the dishwasher played up. Thinking about it, she was maybe a bit of a control freak. Or was it all my fault?

I guess there *were* rows. But I thought that didn't matter. I still reckoned she was the girl for me. I still fancied the pants off her. I still wanted to be with her.

I can't seem to shake her out of my thick skull. She's this living spectre that haunts the flat. One minute it's her head bent low over her Margaret Atwood novel, her hair sweeping down over the pages. The next minute it's her strident laugh echoing in the stairwell. The next it's the image of her teetering in high heels as she scatters fish food into the tank for our one pet, the goldfish called Horatio that she took with her. I've become a total headcase. Can't seem to snap out of it. I wouldn't have her back now, though. Not if she begged me. Not even if she stripped off all her clothes and covered herself in taramasalata.

I was seriously late for work on Monday, nearly half an hour. Crawled in with bags under my eyes, grime under my fingernails and a stinking hangover.

'Not getting any better, is it?' said Gav. That's so Gav. Not a word of reproach, even though the bike shop is his own business, built from scratch, and he cares about it like . . . well, it's up there with his wife and kiddos. And he can barely afford to pay me for the one day a week I work for him and it'll be all my fault if he goes under because of my sloppy behaviour.

'Sorry, mate,' I muttered.

'Just hate to see you like this, Patrick,' he said, putting a hand on my shoulder.

'Any repairs this morning?'

'Yeah, got a couple for you out the back.'

I slunk into the yard, glad of the prospect of oil and tyres and inner tubes for a bit.

But I spent the morning wondering if Lynette makes the brickie do that thing she used to make me do and if he's any better at it than I was. Does he find it fun or humiliating? Does she still flick back her seductive Cleopatra hair and laugh in that serrated, sexy kind of way?

My hands were getting the shakes, big time. Couldn't get the chain in place, it kept slipping and slithering away. Man, I needed some weed . . .

Some weed . . . Soon as the thought arrived it began kind of hen-pecking me. I'd have given anything, like *anything*, for a joint. My own stock got used up years ago and I don't exactly move in those circles any more. I guess there's Judith, though. . .

Four weeks. My landlord has kicked me out, of course. Well, I couldn't keep up the rent payments, could I? Not without Lynette's tidy bunch of wages from Benningfield Solicitors Ltd. I thought I'd be on the streets, but I guess I've been lucky. I've got this bedsit belonging to a mate of a mate of Gav's. Gav did some asking around for me. That's the kind of thing he does. He's churchy, but he's OK; his kindness is genuine. He doesn't inflict his religion on other people. If he did I'd be out of that shop as fast as you can say 'bicycle clips'.

My new home is up two flights of dingy stairs and the couple who live below me shout at each other all day, but hey, there's a sofa and telly. It's a bit of a dive but the rent's like, a fifth of what it was for the flat.

I'm still banging my head against walls, feeling shrivelled up inside. I suppose it's that insanely messy thing we call love. Must have loved Lynette even more than I thought I did.

Jeez, I hate brickies.

I met up with Judith (the ex who still speaks to me) on Tuesday. She was reluctant to part with any of her weed plants, but the combination of my dubious charm and a thick wad of cash did the trick. She had a new blue streak in her hair and was looking pretty good in a bony, greasy sort of way. We shared a spliff along with some chips and I thought we might sleep together for old time's sake, but no. She said she couldn't be arsed. She was more into girls now, anyway.

Oh well, I came away with some dried stuff in a jar and – because I know I can't afford to keep on buying it – a grow-your-own kit in the form of two nice leafy, pot plants. My babies. I've named them Weedledum and Weedledee (I think I must be missing

23

that goldfish more than I'm letting on). I've dragged the table in front of the windowsill and put them there, where they catch the early-morning sunlight. I've rigged up a high-power lamp, too. Pricey on the leccy, but needs must. I've got through a few of the dried buds already. It was bliss. You know how it is. The stress just melts away. But I'm not proud I'm going down this path again. And I'm going to have to ration myself until the plants have grown a bit.

I'm still a wreck. My flat's a wreck, my life's a wreck, everything I do is a wreck. I asked Gav on Monday why he hadn't sacked me.

'Haven't a clue, mate,' he said.

'You can tell me to sling my hook if you like,' I told him. 'I wouldn't hold it against you.'

'Well, I would do just that . . . except that you know everything there is to know about bicycles, you can fix things that nobody else can fix and . . . well, if I gave you two safety pins, a battery and a carrot you'd go and construct, like, a bloody Hadron Collider or something. Plus you're honest, you're hard-working and – at least until recently – you're totally reliable.'

'I'm losing it with the customers, though,' I tell him.

I can't muster up the patter any more. You know the sort of thing: *Hello, madam, what a lovely bicycle! What seems to be the problem? Oh yes, we'll have it fixed in no time. Of course I can show you how to pump up your tyre. No, don't worry. It isn't going to explode.* I seem to have lost the knack.

Wednesday. A day of nothingness. A narrow band of sunlight is creeping round the edge of the curtains. I think I'll go out the front this morning for a quick look outside before settling into my telly-watching day.

I head downstairs to the communal hallway. There's a letter sitting on the shelf where the guy in the bottom flat bungs all the post. My guts lurch at the sight of my name on the envelope. The letter must be from Lynette because I never get letters. Emails, yes, letters, no. But when I calm down and look properly I know it's not her. Lynette's writing is like a school teacher's: narrow, neat and totally upright as if it's trying to prove something. This writing is all on a slant. Copperplatey. In ink-pen, not biro. Very thin lines. Sort of careful but scratchy too, like marks from a cat's claws. The postmark is . . . God, I don't know. Looks Scottish or something. The letter was sent to my old address but it's been forwarded by my ex-landlord, I guess. I'm amazed he bothered.

I tear the envelope open. Just a few paragraphs inside, same old-fashioned writing.

Dear Patrick,

I trust you are well? I am writing with news that may surprise you, as it has surprised me. After some careful research from a reputable agency, I have discovered important information regarding my estranged son. I have obviously questioned the veracity of this information, but it seems that it is corroborated on several counts: birth certificates, censuses and other legal documentation.

My son himself was given up for adoption as a baby. He is, sadly, no longer alive, but, unbeknown to me and apparently quite late in life he became involved with a woman and had a child. That child, I am reliably informed, is you. Although you and I have never met it appears we have a very close blood tie: I am your grandmother.

You will doubtless deduce that I am no longer in the first flush of youth but nevertheless I would be most interested to meet you. I am able-bodied and quite prepared to travel to your place of abode should this suit you.

I look forward to your swift response.

With kind regards,
Veronica McCreedy

5

Patrick

Bolton
June 2012

WHAT THE HELL AM I supposed to do with this? A new granny? It's
not exactly what I need right now. It's hardly on my dreams-
come-true list. Especially bearing in mind she's the mother of my
dad and, well, let's face it, he's never been my favourite person. Not
after what he did to Mum.

I stomp back upstairs, screw up the letter and chuck it over
towards the bin. It misses and bounces on to the floor next to the
heap of dirty washing. There's no washing machine here. I'm going
to have to get myself in gear and find a laundrette sooner or later.

I've recorded some old *Top Gears*, so I watch them and then an
episode or two of *Who Wants to Be a Millionaire?* I like trivia. There's
no point gawping at all these programmes about death and depres-
sion and murder. It's not going to help you on in life if you're just
going to sit there getting heavy about stuff, is it?

I've successfully used up a third of the day without thinking about Lynette much, so that's got to be good. I stand up, stretch and go over to the window. The view from here is mostly stained brickwork and drainpipes. There's one tree but it's kind of bedraggled and nondescript. The sky is hanging murkily over the rooftops. After its brief appearance this morning the sun seems to have gone on strike again.

Weedledum and Weedledee are doing fine. There are some lovely little shoots just aching to be picked and dried and smoked. It's a beautiful thing. The plants smile at me temptingly.

'No, no, stop it. Not yet,' I tell them. I cross the room and pick up the crumpled letter on the floor instead. I uncrumple it slowly and read it again.

The woman's barking. What century does she think she's living in? *I have questioned the veracity of this information . . . no longer in the first flush of youth.* Is she taking the mickey? Can it be true that she's my actual grandmother? She seems to have done her research.

I've never made any attempt to find my dad. He's not worth the effort. I can't remember anything about him but I do know he didn't give a monkey's bum-hair about myself and my mother. Poor Mum. That nightmare . . . It sickens me and drags me down all the time.

I stand like a muppet staring at the letter from Veronica McCreedy. Family, you know; it's supposed to be a good thing, isn't it? But complicated. I'm already a mess. And at twenty-seven suddenly to be granted an incredibly formal and quite likely addle-headed granny – is it seriously going to help that much? I imagine not.

Still, I'm a tad curious. And you know what it's like with curiosity. It's like this worm that keeps nibbling away at you. It just keeps nibbling and nibbling until you can't help but give way.

What's the worst that can happen?

Veronica McCreedy hasn't thought to give me an email address or phone number so if I reply I'll have to send it snail mail. I haven't got writing paper but there's a jotter pad somewhere, I think. Yes, it's by the pile of books and mags, with a screwdriver on top of it. I put the screwdriver in my jacket pocket, then grab a biro and write a note. Brief and to the point:

OK. When do you want to meet? I'm free next week. Any day but Monday.

I add my new address and phone number at the top. If she's fully with it she'll notice. If not, who cares.

I know it's rude to write to her like that, but I'm actually pretty peed off with the woman. It would have been nice if she'd contacted me a bit sooner in life when I was, like, six years old and in desperate need of an adult to look after me. It might have saved a lot of people a lot of aggro.

I'll go out, get this reply in the post then pop to The Harp and reward myself with a beer. Maybe I'll give Gav a call. He could meet me there. I think I owe him one. His mum died a few months ago and one of his kids is ill and he's got me as an employee. He definitely could do with a pint or two.

The thought of a pint or two puts a spring in my step. I hurtle down the stairs again, the letter in my jeans back pocket. Outside, the air feels damp and grey. I jog down the street. Traffic booms past. I'm not thinking of much apart from beer as I go, but no sooner have I bunged the note through the postbox than I start to feel bad about being so blunt to Granny Veronica. She's an old woman, after all. She's probably fragile. It wasn't cool of me to come on all terse like that, even if her letter *was* bizarre.

I wonder if she'll respond. Part of me reckons she will. Part of me reckons she won't.

I start thinking (OK, maybe *hoping*) that Granny Veronica might be a sweet old biddy. I can picture her, all plump and rosy-cheeked and vanilla-scented. She'll have a glint in her eye and a bright, girlish laugh. Maybe she'll speak with a soft Scottish lilt. She'll bring me a home-made apple cake wrapped in a checked cloth.

As I stand at the bar of The Harp with my first beer (I'll call Gav in a mo), I'm getting into the idea. I'm even hatching a plan. I know what I'll do: I'll make a cake when Granny Veronica comes. Cake is cool. I can totally do cake. Cake-making could be the thing Granny and me have in common. We can bond over it. We'll compare recipes. And she'll tell me I've inherited her eyes and nose and her fondness for almond essence. And I'll tell her all about Lynette. And she'll be all sweet and sympathetic and grandmotherly. Sorted.

Granny's going to totally adore me.

6

Patrick

Bolton

I HAVEN'T A CLUE why, but I've woken up feeling better. I'm fizzing with new life and determination. I spring out of bed, scoop up the dirty clothes off the floor and push them into a polythene bag. There aren't any clean clothes left but I pull on my old Gorillaz T-shirt and my jeans with the ripped knees – they're marginally less stinky than the rest. God, I've let things go. It's pitiful. Time to sort myself out. I stick my nose in the fridge but there's nothing in there except half a pint of sour milk. I'll have to go without breakfast.

I launch myself into the communal hallway, down the stairs and out the front.

I'm in top gear. The traffic hasn't got busy yet and there's none of the bad-tempered honking of horns you usually get here. The sun's dazzling today and the leaves on all the trees look floodlit. Nice.

This is the start of a new life, a single but way more together new me. Lynette was right about one thing: if you don't look after your health, man, everything falls apart. I take deep breaths as I jog along the road, through the park then down the slope till I reach Tesco. I'm going to enjoy this.

The contents of my trolley: avocados, dates, shiitake and brown mushrooms, leafy salad, a lean cut of lamb, fresh mint, potatoes, apples, sunflower-seed bread, quinoa and (OK, I'm not an angel) my reward for it all: two six-packs of lager. I use my credit card, trying not to wince at the cost. If I'm lucky, my next benefit will be in just in time.

I stop off at the newsagents on my way home and get distracted flipping through mags. Then realize I've stayed too long and the meat might have gone off. I dash back homewards, my shopping bags banging against my legs. Up the stairs two at a time. My answerphone is beeping. I listen to the message as I bung the shopping in the fridge.

'Good morning, Patrick. This is Veronica McCreedy.' The voice doesn't have a Scottish lilt. It's very English. Clear cut and prissy. 'I am ringing to inform you that I am now at Edinburgh Waverley. I am due to arrive at Bolton at eleven seventeen and, assuming I can get a taxi without delay, I should be at your house at around twelve o'clock.'

Nothing else. Just that. Hell's Bells!

She might have given me a bit more notice. I glance at my watch. It's nearly ten now. And I haven't got the ingredients for the lemon polenta cake. I'm starving and a whole load less buzzy and keen than I was first thing. Still, if I'm about to meet my one living relative, I'd better get that cake made. Everything seems to hang on the cake. Cake might be my one chance to hit it off with this new granny of mine.

I zoom out again, banging the door behind me. All the way back along the street (the traffic is nightmarish now and the cars are in crazy honking mode), back through the park and down the slope to the supermarket. Hot and sweaty. I can definitely smell myself and it's not good.

I charge round, grabbing polenta, golden caster sugar, lemons and all that. I pick the shortest queue at the checkout but (just my luck) end up with the slowest assistant in the universe.

'Beautiful morning, isn't it, love?' she says, holding my bag of lemons in mid-air rather than scanning it. She's one of those people who can't talk and act at the same time.

I grunt and look at the lemons pointedly.

'They say it's going to rain this afternoon, though. Best make the most of it while you can.'

'Yup.'

'Polenta! I've often wondered about that.'

'Mmmm.'

Eventually we get through my six items. I'm about to stick my credit card in the machine when she stops me, waving a frantic hand in my face.

'You've forgotten your Clubcard!'

'No, I haven't!' I tell her.

'You mean . . . so you don't actually have a Clubcard?'

'Got it in one.'

'Oh! Can I interest you in getting a card? They're very good, you know. You get points on your shopping every time, then you get money back on some items. It soon mounts up.'

'Not now, sorry. I've got to dash.'

She pulls a face as if I'm the one who's being difficult and then (God help us!) slows down even more.

'Here's your receipt and here's your token,' she tells me, pressing a round plastic disc into my hand. 'Just pop it in one of the charity boxes on your way out.'

I duly post the plastic disc into the first charity box without reading which local PTA group or garden club it will go to. And at last I'm free to get back home and make the goddamn cake. I pant up the slope, swerving in jaggy patterns to overtake people on the pavement. They're all such bloody slow-coaches.

But, hang on a mo, what's this? Two people on the pavement ahead of me, wound around each other. The man with a great, square head and huge shoulders, the back of his neck deeply tanned. The woman as thin as a whippet. Designer jeans and a crisply ironed top. A perfect cut of Cleopatra hair. It's her. It's Lynette.

Straightaway there's this massive earthquake right inside my guts. It's like all my organs and intestines have suddenly decided to turn upside down and tie themselves in knots. My head screams. My feet stop pelting along the road. I'm stuck there, just stuck on the pavement gawping like an idiot.

Lynette! Lynette Lynette Lynette. All over him. The fricking brickie.

I stare until they disappear down the far end of the street.

Man, I'm in need of a joint. I leg it back to the bedsit, throw the shopping on the floor and reach for my rollies. Stuff them with dope and light them quick. Take deep drags and breathe the smoke out into the room. My hands are still shaking. Ash drops from the end of the fag on to the carpet.

There's a ring at the bell. Makes me jump. Lynette?

No, of course not. It'll be Veronica bloody McCreedy.

She's more than twenty minutes early. I don't believe in early. Lynette reckoned you should be early for everything, but c'mon . . . it's cool to be late. It gives people a chance to get ready for you. Twenty minutes early, that's totally not on.

I'm still shaking like jelly and I'm in no mood for small talk. What kind of a person is this McCreedy woman anyway, to give up her own son? I *mean* . . .

The bell rings again. I glance out of the window, just in time to see a taxi driving away. A woman is standing by the front door. Can't see much of her from here though, only the top of her head and a bit of white hair. A purple clip file and a large scarlet handbag.

I guess I can't leave her standing there, can I? She's an old woman.

I go down and open the door. She looks me up and down. Me:

spliff in hand, ripped jeans, crumpled T-shirt, hair a mess, face unshaven and my whole body reeking like a pig shed. Her: all dressed up smart in a starchy jacket and pleated skirt. Not quite twin-set and pearls, but almost. Her puckered lips pasted with vivid red lipstick.

'Patrick?'

'Yup, that's me.'

I guess you can't blame her for that look of horror. I almost feel sorry for her. I must be several rungs below the bottom of her worst expectations.

'Come on up.' I can't manage a smile. She follows me upstairs, her eyes taking in the battered banister and stained eighties wallpaper. I push open the door to the bedsit and wave her in.

'So this is where you live, is it?' Her voice is dripping with disapproval. The bag of dirty clothes has toppled over and emptied itself all over the floor again. The bed's unmade. The dope plants are there by the window in plain view. But do I care? No. All I can think about is Lynette and the brickie. There's no way I'm going to pretend that I'm something I'm not. Or make out I'm pleased that Veronica McCreedy is here.

I blow out a slow lungful of smoke. 'Do sit down.'

She removes a pair of underpants from the one armchair and lowers herself cautiously into it. She's clutching that expensive-looking handbag, the sort the Queen always has, scarlet and shiny. Apart from her ruby lipstick she looks much the same as other old people look. You know: white hair, hollow cheeks, sunken eyes. Family resemblance? Maybe something about the bone structure but hard to say. I reckon not.

I'm in such a bad way myself I'm almost relieved to note she isn't a sweet old biddy at all. She's the opposite. She's what Lynette used to call a 'trout'. Stiff, stuffy, formal. And no, she hasn't brought me cake. Hasn't brought me anything except a scowl.

Terry's Penguin Blog

10 November 2012

Survival is a tricky business. The creatures of the Antarctic have all evolved ways of coping with the hostile conditions here. Antarctic petrels produce a special stomach oil: an energy-rich food source during long flights, it's also a defence mechanism which they spray out of their mouths into the face of their predators. A tough hide is also necessary in most cases. Leopard seals have thick layers of blubber to protect them from the extreme cold. Penguins trap a layer of air under their feathers to keep them warm underwater.

Penguins must also manage for long periods without food. In the Antarctic winter, Emperor males survive an unbelievable four months without eating, keeping their eggs warmly balanced on their feet while the females stock up with food for the new chicks. Our own Adélies, much more sensibly, breed during November (the Antarctic springtime), when conditions are relatively easy. But they still have plenty of problems to contend with. Predators are plentiful. Ice and snow can be perilous. They need to be incredibly tough to survive.

7

Veronica

Bolton
June 2012

I HAVE DONE WHATEVER I had to do in order to survive. If this has made me hard or vitriolic, then so be it. I am what I am.

I must accept the fact that Patrick is what he is, too. But it is difficult to conceal my disappointment. I did not expect perfection. I did not expect affection, either. I know better than that. But this? I despair. It is yet another slap in the face from that cruel dictator commonly known as Fate.

How is it possible that this disgraceful, smeary, drug-befuddled creature could be my own grandson? Doesn't he know about the existence of soap and water? And his bedsit! I simply do not understand how anyone can live in this squalor. Even a rabbit would find it tiny. Even a rat would find it filthy.

I deliberately didn't give the boy much advance warning of my visit because I wanted to see how he truly lived. I'm already regretting my decision. He's had a good few hours to tidy up, yet he hasn't made the slightest effort on my behalf. It appears he hasn't been brought up to respect other people. No doubt his mother is to blame.

He turns his back on me entirely, stomps to the far end of the room and mumbles something I can't catch which sounds like 'flicking pickie'. Then he comes back and stands in front of me. He's smoking like a chimney. I have no idea what substance he is using to pollute the already fetid atmosphere and destroy both his lungs and his brain cells, but it certainly isn't tobacco. I examine him as best I can through the layers of grime that besmirch his features. His face has a structure similar to my own, with slightly prominent cheekbones and a strong jawline. He is a large lad with olive skin and messy brown hair (too much of it at the top and too little of it at the sides). His eyes are dark but apart from that I can't see any resemblance to the man I once adored. A sinking sensation gathers in the pit of my stomach. I should have steeled myself for this.

I steel myself now.

'So you reckon you're my granny?' No offer of tea after my long journey.

I'm tempted to say that this has been a most inconvenient and inexplicable administrative error and, in fact, no, I am not his grandmother after all; but I was brought up to be honest and truthfulness has become a habit. 'Yes, indeed,' I say. 'It appears to be the case. I have printouts of certain documents.' I take them out of the clip file to show him. The druggy stench intensifies as he comes closer and bends to look. 'Here is your birth record,' I tell him. 'You will observe that your father's name is entered as Joe Fuller. That is the name given to my son by his adoptive parents when they took him to live with them in Canada. Various other references also indicate that this is the same Joe Fuller. DNA tests can provide further proof if necessary, but I've been assured by legal experts that these references are one hundred per cent reliable.'

Patrick scarcely bothers to look, as if his long-lost family simply doesn't matter to him. 'I took my mum's name,' he remarks. 'My father didn't hang around for long after I was born. Less than a week, in fact.'

He seems to think I should apologize for this. I do not.

'So are you going to tell me what happened?' he asks unpleasantly.

'About your father?'

'Yes, my father, the guy who deserted me and my mum. Your son. You said you were "estranged" from him. How come?'

I refuse to descend to his level of rudeness. I provide the briefest sketch of the facts. 'I parted with your father when he was only a baby, just a few months old. Sadly, I have never seen him since. It was impossible to track him down – until it was too late.'

I tried so many times over the years. It was only in 1993 that I received any information, when that awful letter arrived at The Ballahays.

Patrick gives a noise like a harrumph. 'So when did he die?'

'My son died in 1987.' The words drop from my mouth like stones.

'Right.' He is unmoved. He goes to the window and comes back again, breathes a long line of putrid-smelling smoke into the air.

'How did he die?'

'He was a keen mountaineer,' I reply, tautly. 'He went mountaineering in The Rockies and was tragically killed falling down into a gorge.'

'Clever.'

I wince at his insensitivity. I am starting to loathe this Patrick. I go on, nevertheless. 'I never had any contact with the couple who adopted him. It seems they were unable to have children themselves. By the time of his accident they'd both passed away. A few years later some relatives of theirs – cousins, I believe – finally sorted through the family archives and discovered an old document that stated I was his birth mother. One of them, a woman living in Chicago, contacted me by letter to let me know what had happened. This was back in 1993.' I'd given up all hope of ever seeing my son by then but the last thing I'd expected was news of his death. The memory of that letter is still raw. 'She had only met him on a handful of occasions as they were far-flung geographically. She couldn't give me nearly as much information as I'd hoped. He died unmarried. He was, she wrote – and I had no reason to doubt it – childless.'

Patrick breathes smoke in and out again. His expression is inscrut-able. 'But now you say he was my dad.'

'Yes.' I know I'm glaring at him with ice-cold eyes. Rarely have I experienced such bitter disappointment. 'Recently it occurred to me that this cousin might have been wrong in her assumptions. I decided it was worth delving a little further – just to be one hun-dred per cent sure my son didn't leave any offspring. And, to my utmost astonishment, the agency uncovered all this.'

'And nobody over there knew about me?'

'It seems not. As you say, he left England again soon after your birth.'

My son, the tiny baby who used to wave his miniature fingers in the air, trying to clutch at my loose curls of hair; who cuddled into my lap and gazed up at me while I read to him . . . he became a man; he produced his own son. Did he search for me when he was in this country all those years ago? Or perhaps he didn't even know I existed? The cousin hadn't known he was adopted so it's possible he didn't even know himself. When we parted he was too young to remember me, and his Canadian parents might never have seen fit to enlighten him. I don't know, and it seems the man in front of me, my far from delightful grandson, knows nothing either. So many questions remain unanswered.

Patrick grunts. 'Seems like he conveniently forgot all about Mum and me.'

Who can say if he forgot? It does appear that he severed any contact with his partner and child. I have no idea why a man would do this. I assume my son had his reasons. Again and again throughout history men have deserted their women and babies. No doubt they'll continue to do so as long as there is life on this planet.

I can see Patrick's brain trying to grasp it all. I wish he'd sit down. He looks strained and hostile. He runs his fingers through his hair with one hand, still holding the cigarette in the other.

'So did you find out anything else about his life?'

'Yes, but only a little, from the cousin.' I tick off the points I'm prepared to tell him. 'He spent most of his life in Canada. He liked to do dangerous things such as skiing and parachuting as well as the mountaineering. He travelled a lot. He came to England for a brief spell in his early forties. During this time he will have met your mother and you were born soon after.'

'My daredevil father. My not-so-proud father,' Patrick mutters, and adds, 'My poor mother.' He screws up his face. Then he confronts me again.

'So what made you give him away when he was only a baby?'

Patrick is so blunt in his questioning, so accusatory. I feel my hackles rising. I resent having to justify myself to such a person. Still, I believe he has a right to know.

'I was very young.'

'And?'

'And unmarried.'

Patrick paces the room. 'Seems like deserting babies is a family trait.'

How dare he speak to me like that? I am his flesh and blood and I have travelled all this way to find him. I see now that this whole thing has been a mistake of colossal proportions. The history is too complex, the distance too wide. Patrick is what he is. I am what I am. We are very different animals.

I ask myself if I want this new-found relationship to go any further. The answer comes back sharp as a razor. I do not.

'How old were you when you gave birth to my father?' Patrick demands.

I am equally bald in my response. 'Too young.'

I observe something flashing in his eye. It could be sympathy, but I doubt it.

'And how old are you now?'

'Too old.'

'How old is too old?'

I note he didn't ask me how young was too young. I sigh. 'I shall be eighty-six on the twenty-first of June, which is next Thursday.'

He frowns. 'I see. And do you live alone?'

'Yes. I have a woman who comes in to help with the cleaning, though. Eileen. The house is rather too large and ramshackle for me to keep in order by myself.'

'Well, Granny,' he says. I cringe at the word. 'You've done all right for yourself, then.'

I bow my head in acknowledgement. 'It very much depends on your definition of all right. But yes, the house is worth a few million.'

He chokes and a shower of ash scatters over the carpet. I am immediately furious with myself. On no account should I have mentioned my wealth. Now he'll automatically assume he has a right to it. At least I didn't refer to the other few million that are sitting in various bank accounts accruing mountainous interest.

Patrick is unable to speak for some time and then doesn't seem to want to look at me, instead focusing his attention out of the window.

'So how come you got to be so rich?' he says to the drainpipes.

'I married. My husband was in the property business. I helped him with it for a while, before the divorce.' That is all I am prepared to share about myself.

It is my turn to ask questions, to grill Patrick as he has grilled me. I am far more civil in my approach, even if I fail to muster much enthusiasm. I establish that Patrick works just one day a week at a bicycle shop. Even this is solely because of the charity of a friend who is his boss there. For the rest of his income he scrounges off the government. He has recently split with his girl-friend. I can't say I'm surprised at this. What surprises me is that such a man can find a girlfriend in the first place. I dread to think what kind of a girl she was. I refrain from asking Patrick if he ever takes a bath. I feel in need of a good wash myself after being here, but I have absolutely no desire to see his bathroom.

Our conversation runs out of steam very quickly. I am increas-ingly anxious to extricate myself from this man's malodorous company. I'm quite certain I haven't missed anything by not mak-ing his acquaintance earlier. I ask him to call me a taxi as soon as it is polite to do so.

I am extremely relieved to get away.

8

Veronica

The Ballahays

'So I EXPECT YOUR grandson will be coming here to visit soon!' declares Eileen happily as she fixes a brush attachment on to the vacuum cleaner.

'I sincerely hope not.'

I couldn't avoid telling her about my visit to see young Patrick, but it was a conveniently summarized account. I have no wish to encourage further conversation on the subject.

'Really, Mrs McCreedy?' She pauses, eager to believe that my grandson and I must harbour feelings of affection for each other. 'You'd surely welcome him if he knocked at the door right now though, wouldn't you?'

I don't answer. It can be an advantage, being slightly hard of hearing. You can get away with not answering stupid questions.

Eileen shrugs her shoulders cheerfully. 'Well, I suppose that hoovering isn't going to do itself!' She drags the vacuum cleaner through the kitchen and into the hall, leaving the door open behind her.

'Eileen. Door.'

'Sorry, Mrs McCreedy,' she says and closes it behind her.

I finish my cup of tea and leaf through the gardening catalogue. I do little gardening myself these days except for pruning the roses, but I do occasionally order a set of bedding plants or a shrub. I have some specimen rhododendrons at The Ballahays of which I am particularly proud. Bright blooms help one along in life; I am convinced of it. Besides, Mr Perkins, the gardener (who has been with me for twenty-six years and is beginning to look a little mouldy) needs a few new projects to keep him interested.

I put on my coat and gloves and wander out. I breathe in the clean, sparse Scottish air. I am still feeling polluted after my visit to Patrick's disgusting abode.

The locket is currently lying under my pillow. I shall fetch it next time I am upstairs and put it back into the box. The box must return to the unfathomable depths of the back room. I shall endeavour to forget again what I have so painfully remembered. These things should never have been unearthed in the first place.

This evening Robert Saddlebow speaks from a penguin colony on a remote island in the South Shetlands of Antarctica.

'The Antarctic Peninsula is one of the most rapidly warming parts of our planet,' he informs me from a snow-speckled hillside. 'Over recent decades there has been a significant reduction in sea ice.'

'Oh, dear me!' I comment.

His rugged face becomes larger until it (rather pleasingly) fills most of the screen. 'Penguins are used by scientists as indicators of change within their ecosystem,' he continues. 'Any changes in their breeding performance or populations are likely to reflect changes in the Antarctic as a whole. So monitoring species such as the Adélies gives us valuable insights into large-scale environmental changes.'

'Oh, Robert, you are a tour de force! We ignoramuses need to know about these things,' I murmur.

He smiles. 'Adélie penguins are also particularly delightful,' he adds, as the camera pans out once more.

I wholeheartedly concur. The assembled birds fill the barren landscape with rambunctious life. The species is named after the wife of a nineteenth-century French explorer. In spite of their name, they do not come across as particularly feminine. With their sleek black-and-white outfits they have the look of stumpy little men in tuxedos. Adélie are one of the smaller breeds, only about twenty-eight inches tall. They have bright, intelligent eyes with white rims. Most appealing. After enjoying their antics on land, I am shown some superb footage of the birds swimming underwater, their tubby figures transformed into paragons of grace and balletic precision.

The programme also features a group of scientists who are living out there and studying the penguins. Robert Saddlebow interviews one of them, a German fellow called Dietrich. He calls himself a penguinologist. I don't take to his accent but I am impressed by the passion with which the man speaks. He asserts that although Adélies are not one of the *most* endangered species (not like the Northern Rockhoppers and the Erect-crested penguins) they fall into the 'near threatened' category. Moreover, this particular colony of birds has been dropping in numbers alarmingly over recent years and nobody knows why. A new field centre was built on the island seven years ago to try to get to the bottom of it and scientists have been studying the penguins in depth every season, but the funding has almost run out. When the programme was filmed there were only four scientists there trying to do the work of five. This year there will be three. Possibly after that the project will have to stop altogether, unless they can find further funding. His words seemed to nudge at something in my subconscious.

This Dietrich man has concern written all over his big hairy face. He gesticulates wildly. I would normally be unaffected by such a display of perturbation but Robert Saddlebow (I foster a degree of admiration for him) seems quite moved too. He professes his hope that the scientists will find a way to continue their invaluable work, shakes the man's hand and wishes him the very best of luck. The scene slides to reveal a handsome if rather stout penguin standing on a rock, drip-drying his flippers by holding them out at right-angles to his body. His eyes fix on mine, creating an eerie connection from him on his rock in Antarctica to me in my armchair in The Ballahays snug.

'If you'd like to know more about this community of Adélies,' says Robert Saddlebow's voice, 'please look up "Terry's Penguin Blog". It will provide you with regular updates on the progress of the scientists and the penguins on Locket Island.'

Locket Island? *Locket* Island? The word seems to set off a series of electrical currents along my neural pathways. A strange coincidence? Or an omen?

I switch off the television as the credits run. To avoid dropping off in the chair (which is an aggravation to the neck muscles) I head upstairs straight away. As I step into the bathroom I utter a gasp of amazement. There it is before my eyes: the word 'penguins' inscribed at the bottom of the mirror in brown eyebrow pencil. The reminder must have been very important for me to have resorted to an act of graffiti. This is interesting.

I take up the pencil again and add the words 'Adélie' and 'Antarctica'. And, as an afterthought, 'Locket Island'.

There is a penguin waddling towards me, wearing a locket around its neck. It is opening and shutting its beak as if it's trying to tell me something, but no sound is coming out. I am a carefree young version of myself complete with an array of chestnut curls blowing in the wind. But everything around me is white. White flowers, white trees, white feathers spiralling in the air. I step closer to the penguin, bending down to hear him. I can almost catch words, penguin words coming out from that beak, but then there is an interruption. A shrill ringing that hurts my eardrums.

I sit bolt upright in bed. I realize at once it is the phone that has disturbed my slumbers. I scoop my dressing-gown up from the chair and fling it round my shoulders, glancing at the clock: nine thirty at night. What cretin would ring at this hour? I stumble across the room and pick up the receiver. The voice at the other end is muffled.

'Just a moment,' I tell it and fumble to get my hearing aid in.

'Veronica McCreedy speaking,' I say when I am ready.

'Hello, Granny.'

I think I've gone barmy for a moment, then remember my unpleasant encounter with my new-found grandson. *Granny*. Ugh. Why does he have to call me that?

'Patrick,' I say, his name springing back to me in an instant. It is fortunate I am so on the ball and my memory is so remarkable. I am not convinced it was a good idea giving him my phone number, though. At the time it seemed a necessary formality and a courtesy, but I am now filled with misgivings that he is going to abuse my goodwill.

'Sorry I forgot your birthday. It was the day before yesterday, wasn't it?'

I consult the calendar I keep on the windowsill with each day's date carefully crossed off in red once it's finished.

'Day before that,' I tell him, not seeing why it's any of his business.

'Oh, so that would be . . .' He pauses, trying to squeeze some information from his drug-befuddled brain. ' . . . The twenty-second?'

'Twenty-first.'

'Twenty-first, then. And you are what, now? Eighty-eight, is it?'

'Try again.'

'Eighty-seven?'

'No, Patrick.'

'Eighty-six?'

I humour him. 'Very good. Well done. Brilliant. Exactly right.'

'Well, many happy returns for, um, the other day! It's . . . it's a fantastic innings.'

He is trying to be jolly and not succeeding very well. What an annoyance it is for him to have me in his life. What a relief it will be to him when I'm dead and gone.

'Did you do anything special?' he asks.

'Nothing. Eileen brought a cake.' He'll have no idea who Eileen is.

'Oh, that was nice. Eileen's the carer, right?'

'Certainly not! I have no need of a carer. I'm not entirely incapable of looking after myself. Eileen acts as my occasional assistant with the house and running of things.'

A slight pause. 'Ah! OK. Good old Eileen! Was it nice? The cake?'

'It was quite acceptable.' (It was actually a ghastly affair, all almonds and sugary pink icing. It tasted of tooth decay. As if I haven't got enough of that going on as it is.) 'Eileen's not a culinary genius by any means. But it was a kind gesture. She tried.'

'Unlike me,' my grandson says with atypical astuteness.

'You're trying now,' I point out, kindly.

'Very trying, I suppose.'

I am inclined to agree but don't let myself do it out loud.

'Look, I don't know how to say this, but it's been bugging me. I feel I . . . I feel we got off to a bad start, Granny. It wasn't like I was expecting it to be and I know I must've come across as a total arsehole – 'scuse my French. I was wondering if we could maybe, well – start over again?'

This piece of unpoetical unctuousness does not impress me and I glean at once that he has been thinking about my money.

'Very well,' I reply with studied patience.

There is an uncomfortable pause. 'How is everything with you?' I ask. Not that I particularly want to hear the answer – his life is made up of boorish trivia – but somebody has to say something.

'Oh, you know. The usual. Not a lot going on. Bicycles on Mondays. Rain. Bills. Cooking. Eating. The occasional job application that takes, like, for ever and gets me nowhere. But not complaining. Cheered on by visits to the pub and *Who Wants to Be a Millionaire?*'

'You do, presumably.'

A slight pause. 'Well, of course I wouldn't sob my heart out if a million pounds happened to come my way.'

I am affronted at the boy's cheek. He's hinting in the most unsubtle way imaginable. He must have worked out that I have no one else to leave my money to. That is to say, nobody who classifies as a family member. I have indeed given much attention to this quandary of late. It is a grave responsibility being in possession of so much wealth. There is the possibility of leaving everything to Eileen, who, for all her faults, has been assiduously loyal to me over the years, but she'd probably give it straight to Patrick anyway because her conscience would protest. She sings (if you can call it that) in a church choir and considers herself to be an upright and moral person.

There is another pregnant pause on the phone line.

You'd think Patrick might demonstrate some molecule of interest in his grandmother, but no. The conversation has already dried up. It is pointless to prolong the agony.

'Thank you for ringing, Patrick.'

I put down the receiver. Bitterness and anger flood through me. How dare he try to buy my favour by ringing in the middle of the night to wish me a Happy Birthday *three days late*. This, after he treated me so badly during my visit to his stinking abode. He was disrespectful to me and, more importantly, disrespectful to the memory of my son, his own deceased father. Evidently he's had second thoughts merely because the idea of my inheritance has penetrated his skull.

Let him dream about becoming a millionaire. Why should I reward depravity and sheer laziness? My not insubstantial hoard is being looked after by various banks and building societies at present. I shall have to contact my solicitor and make arrangements. They say that blood is thicker than water. That, unfortunately, is nowhere near the truth in our case. No, it appears that McCreedy blood runs much, much thinner than water. That boy needs to do something with his life other than fritter away my inheritance on drink, drugs or worse. I've decided. My legacy will be going towards a more worthy cause. There's no way Patrick is getting his grubby little fingers on my money.

9

Patrick

Bolton

I TRY TO SHAKE off that scratchy, uncomfortable feeling she's left me with. Hell, I did my best, didn't I? I didn't exactly *want* to phone but this inner voice kept on and on at me: *Just do it, mate. Just ring her.* So I forced myself. And I made a spectacular mess of everything, as usual. I had a go at being contrite, but got confused over dates. Days of the week, man: I never know which is which. Mondays are work-days, that's sorted, but the other days all merge together in a kind of blob. Anyway, I managed to offend Granny V by getting the date of her birthday wrong, then dug myself even deeper into a hole by overestimating her age. She was positively bristling down the phone at me. If there was a gold medal for sarcasm she'd win it. I felt so stressed I went and said 'arsehole'. Then I started blathering on, saying anything to make it sound more like a normal, relaxed conversation between granny and grandson. And then somehow the subject changed and got on to me wanting to be a millionaire, which was totally bizarre and irrelevant. I hope she doesn't think I was hinting or anything.

At least I tried. I think I've earned myself a beer. It's still early – only about 10 p.m. – so I text Gav, then head out. He's usually up for a pint once he's got his kids to bed.

He's already at the bar of the Dragon's Flagon when I arrive. We get some drinks in and wedge ourselves into a corner.

'How's things, then, mate?' he asks after the first glug or two. 'Any better?'

'Think I've turned a corner, yeah.'

'Good man. So you're finally over Lynette?'

'Sorry, did you just swear?'

'Right, I get you. We won't mention the L-word.'

I suppose it's a good thing I saw her and the brickie like that. It was a total ouch to the heart and the timing could hardly have been worse but at least it's done. There's no two ways about it: Lynette's out of my life now.

'Tell you what, though,' I say to Gav. 'Newsflash: I've got myself a new granny.'

Gav always makes you feel like what you're saying is important. He listens in encouraging silence as I describe everything: my dire first meeting with Granny V and my crap attempts to make amends on the phone. When I mention that Granny V lives in a mansion in Scotland he gives a low whistle.

He swirls his beer round for a minute. 'You know what I think?'

'No. But you're about to tell me.'

'OK, mate, right you are. I know you two didn't exactly hit it off, but I reckon it's worth trying again with this Granny Veronica. She's your only family, after all. Given time, you could become something special to each other.'

I grin. 'You haven't met her, mate. She's a cold, cold fish. She'd make an icicle look warm and fluffy.'

He grins back at me. 'OK, I'm getting the idea she's not exactly cuddlesome.'

'Hell, no.'

Then his face darkens. 'But, seriously, mate, you should keep making an effort. The older generation are kind of . . .'

He's struggling to find words so I give him a few options. 'Boring? Selfish? Mean?'

'No, I wasn't going to say that. They've got this different take on things because they've been through so much. They're not just full of wrinkles, they're full of . . . *stories*. And so often we don't bother to appreciate them till they're gone.'

He's sounding a bit choked up. He's still hurting after his own mum's death. I'd forgotten about that. His mum was loaded, too (not as much as Granny Veronica, of course, but doing nicely, thank you). She never thought to help Gav out with all his financial problems, though. Even when his eight-year-old daughter got cancer.

Gav was besotted with his mum in spite of it all.

The conversation's getting too heavy for both of us, so we leave it there and get into talking about bikes. He's thinking of upping our stock of top-end electric bikes. We don't do much top-end at the mo. It's too risky.

On the way home I have another think about Granny V. Gav's right, of course. I need to keep trying.

There seem to be dead socks everywhere. The floor's littered with them. I gather them up and bung them in the polythene bag. I'll take them to the laundrette straight after work. I keep trying to get back on track otherwise I'll just slither back to where I was before I met Lynette, and I don't want that. So I'm in the process of giving the flat a major overhaul. Over the weekend I finally changed my sheets, hoovered the carpet and scrubbed the grime off the inside of the oven.

I've started trying to get back into shape, too. Yesterday I cycled long miles into the countryside and made myself a good, healthy dinner in the evening: lemon chicken and steamed French beans with sautéed potato. What's more, I ate it without switching on the telly. I listened to music instead. Sixx:A.M.'s 'This is Gonna Hurt'. Stabbed my potatoes to the rhythm and lacerated the beans. It was ace.

I've made that lemon polenta cake. You don't go wasting expensive cake ingredients, do you? I could take the train up to Scotland this week and deliver it into Granny V's hands, but I can't quite bring myself to do it. She hates me, I'm sure, and I'm finding it pretty difficult to like *her*. I keep thinking about the way she gave up her own baby, and how that might have affected the whole of my dad's life – and how differently things might have ended up for me, as well.

But still, I shouldn't have spoken to Granny the way I did.

I stroll over to Weedledum and Weedledee and give them a quick water. The cake is sitting on the table, next to the plants, wafting warm, cakey, lemony smells through the flat. The mere sight of it is making me feel guilty.

So I make a decision and take it into work with me.

'Cake for you, Gav,' I mumble as I dump it on to the shop counter. 'Just to say . . . you know. For the support. For everything.'

I'm not good with words at the best of times, especially when I get a lump in my throat like this.

'Patrick, mate!' he cries, all smiles. 'You shouldn't have.'

'I should. I've been behaving like a right plonker for weeks,' I say. 'Take it home to your missus and kids.'

I don't manage to say sorry in so many words, but I think he gets it.

After work (a much better day: *Madam, I'm happy to tell you your bicycle is now in perfect working order*) I make that long-awaited visit to the laundrette. I'm on my way back to the bus stop now with a bag full of clean clothes. Coldplay is rippling through my headphones and I can't help head-banging a bit, you know how it is. I must look a right prat. I'm crossing the road and skirting a big puddle when, out of nowhere, this massive lorry roars up and nearly goes smack into me. It swerves just in time, horn honking, brakes screeching and all. Nearly gives me a heart attack.

The driver is a bald man with a red face. He swears at me through the windscreen. I mouth 'Sorry, mate' to him and carry on.

I'm kicking myself for saying 'Sorry, mate'. Yes, I should look before crossing, but he was seriously over the speed limit. I make a V sign at the back of the lorry as it zooms down the road. I'm way too late for the guy to notice.

Makes you think, though. If I'd been killed, would anyone care? Gav, maybe. Yes, Gav would be genuinely sorry. Judith (the ex who still speaks to me – 'You're a nice guy, Patrick, just an awful boyfriend') might shed a tear. Lynette? I don't think she'd give a damn, not now she's got brickie boy. Anyone else? Granny McC? Somehow I don't think so.

I reckon Granny will live for-bloody-ever. Longer than me, anyway. Especially the rate I'm going. And when I do get myself run down, my guess is she won't even notice. That carer woman of hers will be all clucking with sympathy and Granny V will go, 'Eileen, would you kindly desist? I am extremely busy arranging napkins.'

When you nearly die, your life is supposed to flash in front of your eyes, isn't it? Well, that didn't happen with me, all I got was angry driver glare. But now I seem to be getting a kind of delayed reaction. Bits of my childhood keep pinging into my brain while the music drums in my ears. I'm getting flashes of my five foster families. Five, no less! They ranged from the seriously strict to the unbelievably lax. I remember being locked in my room at the Millards' place just for swearing. I remember Jenny and Adrian Fanshaw lecturing me about how lucky I was. I remember going through the Gregsons' wallets and helping myself. It was shameful but I couldn't help it, I needed the money for drugs. I was a kid with issues.

I did all right on the whole, though. There was always food, there was always shelter, there was an education of sorts. There was a certain brand of cautious love. None of those guys counted as parents, though.

At seventeen I started working for Charlie, a local mechanic. I quite liked taking cars apart and putting them back together again. Charlie was decent. I stayed with him for four years, until he went bust. Then I was jobless for a bit, then did a spot of gardening for a couple of toffs, then got together with Judith, then split up with her again.

After Judith came Lynette. I first saw her when her car broke down and she was standing in the street manically punching numbers into her mobile. She looked stressed (not any old stressed; short-skirted, hair-tossing, lip-pouting stressed – *sexily* stressed) so I offered to help. I'm OK with cars and had her bonnet up in no time. Managed to sort it for her.

Lynette fell for my manly griminess – that's what she told me later anyhow. She wasn't grimy herself. Far from it. She was the opposite of Judith in every way. Well turned out, well read and well intentioned. We moved in together quite quickly. That is to say, I moved in with her. She was renting this big, smart flat and working as a solicitor. She tried to 'save' me, which . . . well, it kind of semi-worked. She got me into healthy eating, anyway. Never thought I'd get hooked on broccoli, but I did! And for a while I got clean off the drugs. I transferred my addiction into running and cycling. Bought myself a good second-hand bicycle from Gav's and, while I was at it, got myself a job there. Lynette said it would do as a stop-gap but I'd have to get something full-time sooner or later. I'm still waiting for that to happen.

Anyhow, Lynette is history now. I seem to have ended up with a curmudgeon of a granny instead. How bizarre is that?

I find it hard to get my head round the fact that Veronica McCreedy is the mother of my dad. I don't give him a lot of thought, to be honest. I know sweet Fanny Adams about him, anyway. I remember once or twice when I was a tiny kiddo pestering Mum about who he was 'cos my friends at nursery school all seemed to have dads and where was mine?

Mum's answer was always the same: a quick, harsh 'You have no dad'. Followed by a speedy change of subject. Only one time she added: 'If he'd stayed, it might have been different.' She never said that again, though.

Mum and me were in a caravan first of all. Well, a clapped-out old camper van that was parked up in a disused bit of scrubland. Later we moved into a council house, but I don't remember much about it except that Mum had wedged old newspapers into all the cracks to keep out the draughts. It didn't really feel like home.

Mum tried lots of jobs but they never lasted long. She was always up and down, I remember. One minute singing gaily, the next in floods of tears. When I was six, shortly before she decided life wasn't worth living any more, she came into the bedroom while I was busy building a castle out of bricks. Her shoulders were slumped and her cheeks were wet. 'Patrick,' she sighed. 'My darling boy, I'm sorry about everything. Sorry I'm so useless.' I had no idea what she meant. To me she seemed to be doing fine. She fed me, clothed me, got me to nursery school and all that. But I guess it must have cost her too much, both in money and energy. Looking back, I can see she sacrificed things. Her social life, for one. She didn't *do* friends. She must have been lonely. She did her best to hide her unhappiness from me but, wow, it must have been huge.

Because one day she left me with a babysitter, a woman I didn't know at all. I remember the babysitter giving me sausages and beans that night and getting fretful, looking at her watch. Then she spent a long time on the phone. She put down the receiver and dialled more numbers. Her voice sounded increasingly desperate.

She started saying to me, 'Don't worry, Patrick, I'm sure she'll be back soon,' and then it was 'I'll just pop you to bed. Mum will be back in the morning.' And then, when morning arrived and there was still no sign of Mum, it was 'Right, Patrick. We're going for a little drive.'

I was passed on to some more people I didn't recognize, who took me by the hand and told me I had to be a brave boy. Mum wouldn't be back for some time yet. Later they told me it was looking like Mum wouldn't be coming back at all. And later still I found out she had put stones into her pockets and walked into the sea.

I get to the bus stop and stand there with the commuters and shoppers. They all look like they've got their act together. Self-worth, that's what it is. That guy with the suit and tie, holding a black umbrella. I bet he and his wife and kids all go out for a Thai meal every Saturday night. And the couple holding hands. They can't wait to get home to peel the clothes off each other. And that woman with the dyed-blond hair is texting her partner, saying, 'I'm on the way home. Be there in twenty.' And sticking lots of xs at the end.

Being single again makes me listless. I'm totally over Lynette, but I have to admit she dominated every single fricking corner of my life. I never had the chance to dwell on depressing thoughts when she was around. Now that she's gone, life seems to have filled up with this cold, creepy silence. I feel like a beer bottle once all the beer's been drunk. Not needed. Worthless. Empty.

Terry's Penguin Blog

21 November 2012

Penguins are feisty and stubborn. They never give up.

For example, there's our lonely black penguin, Sooty. He is still sitting on that nest, patiently waiting, hoping beyond hope that one day his princess will come.

Then there's this bold character you see in the photo. The penguin in question (which may be a he or a she – it's hard to tell but I reckon it's a she) decided she wanted to climb up a very steep iceberg. Who knows why she decided it was so important? Anyway, nothing was going to stop her. I watched as she crawled up a near-vertical slope, made it halfway to the top but then slithered back down all the way to the bottom. She collapsed on her side, feet and flippers splayed out at undignified angles. Undeterred, she scrambled to her feet straight away. She looked up towards the summit. No way was she going to let that slope defeat her. She stuck both flippers out on either side for balance, waddled up a little way, skidded, waddled some more, fell on her front, got up again. The last bit of the iceberg was particularly steep. She stuck her beak in the snow and used it as a grapnel to pull herself up. Not dignified but it worked. She finally made it to the top, and I have to admit I clapped when she got there. She did look smug.

You have to admire that kind of persistence.

10

Veronica

The Ballahays
July 2012

I SHALL HAVE TO muster a quite extraordinary quantity of determination. But that is always the case if you want to achieve anything at all in life.

I remember when I was a child I expected hugely wonderful things to simply fall into my lap. Many people suffer from this illusion, I believe. They carry on expecting the wonderfulness to turn up round the next corner nearly the whole way through. In my case, however, that expectation died early. At a particular moment, about seventy years ago, all my dreams evaporated into thin air. Everything since then has been simply a marker of time. Life has been a trail of insignificant events, spooling uselessly along, forgotten the minute after they happened. Appointments with the doctor, dentist, optician, paediatrician. Standing in the queue at the supermarket. Instructing Eileen regarding laundry. Instructing Mr Perkins regarding petunias. Sleeping. Reading. Crosswords. Flower-arranging. Tea.

I have bothered to keep going merely out of habit. Yet those diaries have given me a sharp prod. They've reminded me of something I'd forgotten: my former spark. Ever since reading them this inner voice has been taunting me. *You used to be a human dynamo,* it whispers. *You used to throw yourself at things. You used to rise to any challenge. But have you actually done anything, anything at all of worth, in the last half a century?*

I must try to do something before it's too late. Not just something with my money but something with my life, whatever dregs are left of it. Naively I had hoped that the discovery of a new family member would provide a solution on both counts. I was wrong.

I need to find an alternative; a mission, something that inspires me. There are, alas, few things on this planet that match that description.

One has presented itself recently, however. As I clean my teeth, I glance up from the basin. It is still there, admitting no doubt, spelled out in my own writing across the mirror.

'Why not?' I ask my reflection.

Veronica McCreedy looks back at me with fire in her eyes.

Eileen is wearing a hideous pink-and-white-checked overall. She has a distinctly bleachy aura.

'Did you want me to clean the bathroom mirror, Mrs McCreedy?' She has come downstairs, it seems, specially to present me with this question. I am, at this moment, busy hunting for my reading glasses, which have gone missing again, as is their wont.

'Really, Eileen, need you ask?' I reply. 'It is your job to clean whatever needs cleaning.'

'Yes, I know that, but there seems to be a message written there in brown pencil. I wasn't sure if it was important. Something about a locket, an island, somebody called Adele and . . . and penguins?'

I do not like her tone. It is that half-concerned, half-amused voice that she uses when she suspects I might be finally succumbing to dementia.

'Though this be madness, yet there is method in't,' I quote. 'That is from *Hamlet*, you know.'

'Yes, I'm sure it is, Mrs McCreedy. But what about the writing on the mirror?'

'The writing on the mirror is merely a reminder,' I tell her. 'Pen and paper are never at hand when one requires them, so I was using my ingenuity, as needs must.'

'A reminder?'

'Yes. Not that I am in the least likely to forget, of course. My memory is entirely reliable and one hundred per cent intact.'

'So you keep saying,' she mutters.

I glare at her. 'You may clean the rest of the mirror apart from the corner with the words written on it.'

'Right you are. So . . . so it's a reminder of what? – if you don't mind me asking.' She is wearing her nosy expression.

I sigh. I *do* mind her asking, if truth be told, but unfortunately I am going to have to take her into my confidence. Worse still, I am going to require her assistance.

I inform her that I am planning to take a trip to the South Shetlands.

'The Shetlands!' she cries, giving an exaggerated shiver. 'Goodness, Mrs McCreedy! You are full of surprises. What a strange holiday destination! But at least you've decided on the *South* Shetlands. Not quite so cold as the north ones, I imagine.'

'No, Eileen.' I am going to have to explain it to her in words of one syllable. 'The South Shetlands are a completely different group of islands, not the ones near Scotland.'

She is wearing the nonplussed expression now.

'They are in the Southern hemisphere,' I inform her.

'Oh well, that's all right then. They'll be a lot more like it, I should think,' she grins. 'Nice and exotic. Full of golden beaches and palm trees, no doubt. I thought you'd gone crazy for a moment there, Mrs McCreedy!'

She is still in need of elucidation. 'The South Shetlands are in Antarctica,' I tell her.

It takes some time to convince her that I am serious, along with many assurances that, yes, I am absolutely in possession of my marbles.

When this Herculean task has been completed, I ask if she would be willing to use her computer know-how to send an email to the field camp where Robert Saddlebow stayed on Locket Island.

'I believe you can find the correct address by means of a blog, if you use your googly whatsit?'

'Oh, I see. Yes, Mrs McCreedy, quite likely I can. Websites do usually have a contact option. It should be possible, if you're really sure that's what you want.'

'Have you ever known me not to be sure about anything?'

'Well, no, Mrs McCreedy, but . . .' She mumbles something I can't catch. People nowadays never speak clearly enough. However, I do not ask her to repeat it. I feel fairly certain I am not thereby losing any great gems of wisdom.

Once we have located my glasses (they have somehow ended up on top of the fridge) I write down all the details on a piece of paper because I have found this is the best way to convey precise instructions to Eileen. She knows I am absolutely in earnest whenever I do this.

My mind returns to the penguins. I have charged myself with an important and worthwhile undertaking. I am feeling rather pleased.

11

Dear Scientists,

Having recently watched Robert Saddlebow's television programme featuring your project I am deeply impressed by your research into the Adélie penguins of Antarctica. As a keen admirer of your mission to protect the species – and as an advocate of conservation in general – I have decided that, should your work prove to be as invaluable as it currently appears, your research is likely to inherit a considerable sum of money as defined by the terms of my will. I am therefore intending to visit your site in the near future to furnish myself with further information and to ensure that your work is worthy of such a substantial sum. I shall bring provisions and necessities with me, but I will require a bedroom for three weeks (preferably en suite) and would wish to join you in your studies and penguin observations as much as is convenient.

Yours faithfully,
Veronica McCreedy

Note
Hello. I am Eileen Thompson (Mrs) and I'm Mrs McCreedy's daily helper. Mrs McC has asked me to send you this message because she doesn't do email. Mrs McC is pretty good mentally but she does often change her mind so I'd not worry too much and take it all with a pinch of salt if I were you.

Best wishes
Eileen Thompson

Dear Mrs Thompson
Thank you for your email. I would be grateful if you would forward this reply to Mrs McCreedy with our compliments. Many thanks and warmest regards, Dietrich Schmidt.

Dear Mrs McCreedy
We are delighted to have your support and very pleased that you are interested in our work concerning the Adélie penguins.

However, conditions in the camp are cramped and extremely basic with few facilities. We have little in the way of hot and cold running water, let alone an en suite bedroom. Whilst we would be delighted to meet you, we would be unable to host you as you suggest.

I am attaching a fact sheet about Adélie penguins which may be of interest to you, and of course any contribution towards their protection, now or in the future, would be more than welcome. With many thanks for your interest.

Dietrich Schmidt
Penguinologist and head of the Locket Island team.

I'm sorry, Mr Dietrich, to bother you again, but Mrs McC has insisted that I email you again with this message.

Yours, Eileen

Dear Mr Schmidt,

Thank you for your prompt and efficient reply. As I mentioned before, your project will benefit by an eventual seven million pounds, assuming I am satisfied with my stay at your research centre. I have now booked my flights to King George Island and my passage thence by boat with Blue Iceberg Ferries. I shall arrive at Locket Island on 8 December at 8.30 a.m. I would be most grateful if you could send one of your helpers to pick me up and escort me and my luggage to your research centre. Please do not concern yourself about my needs. Having lived for the last fifty-three years (out of my eighty-six) on the west coast of Scotland I have developed a certain toughness and can easily put up with uncomfortable conditions. Eileen has looked up temperatures on your island and tells me that during your Antarctic summer they hover around freezing point, which is not significantly lower than December here in Ayrshire. I shall, of course, pay for my food and lodging while I am with you. A luxury apartment in London, I am reliably informed, costs approximately £400 a night to rent. I shall therefore pay you at a rate of £400 per twenty-four hours of my stay. As you mention conditions are basic, I have no doubt this will more than cover your expenses and any inconvenience of having an extra person residing at your research centre. I am happy to cover any other unforeseen costs involving my visit. I will bring with me all my necessary medications and any creature comforts I need.

I am indebted to you and look forward to my stay.

Yours sincerely,
Veronica McCreedy

Dear Eileen

We are alarmed and concerned at Mrs McCreedy's most recent email. While we are extremely grateful for her magnanimous proposal, we cannot host her for three weeks. We are, in fact, not in a position to host anybody, let alone a person of advanced years. Although we have very occasional visitors on Locket Island this is not a tourist destination, and we are busy every day with our surveys and research. I do not doubt that Mrs McCreedy's intentions are generous and the money she promises is startlingly so, but please could you impress upon her that her plan is simply not practical.

With kind regards,
Dietrich and the Locket Island team

Dear Mr Schmidt,

I'm very sorry. I really thought Mrs McCreedy would change her mind. She usually does, but this time she seems quite stuck on it. It's no good trying to stop her doing anything, it only makes her even more determined. But please don't worry. It's true she is very tough. And ninety per cent of the time she is very on the ball, so I'm sure it won't be a problem. It's only for three weeks.

Dear Eileen

Does Mrs McCreedy have any relatives we could communicate with by email? We cannot, of course, prevent her from coming, but would certainly not wish to be held responsible for either her health or her happiness.

Kind Regards,
Dietrich

Dear Mr Schmidt
She has only a grandson in Bolton, but they don't see much of each other. Here is his email address if you want it.

Dear Mr Patrick (McCreedy?)
I expect you are aware that your grandmother, Mrs Veronica McCreedy, has booked a flight to Antarctica with the express wish of visiting our camp. This concerns us greatly. She is welcome to come and look round the field centre for an hour while she is here, but I would ask you to explain to her that a three-week or even overnight visit will not be possible, due to our lack of facilities.

Although it is always good when somebody shows concern for the future of our penguins and our scientific mission, we would be very aggrieved should anything untoward happen to her while she is out here. Mrs McCreedy's helper, Eileen Thompson, has assured us that she is 'on the ball' ninety per cent of the time, but that ninety per cent may not be enough. I really think your grandmother can have no idea how tough it is here – the cold in itself would be a grave danger to anybody in advanced years, no matter how healthy they are.

I sincerely hope that you are able to dissuade her and explain the reasoning behind the fact that we cannot allow a prolonged visit.

Kind regards,
Dietrich Schmidt (penguinologist) and the Locket Island team

Dear Patrick McCreedy
I am writing again as, having received no reply to my last email, I am concerned that you didn't receive it. Please could you contact us regarding your grandmother Veronica McCreedy as a matter of urgency.

Dear Eileen

We have attempted to contact Mrs McCreedy's grandson without success. Please could you inform Mrs McCreedy that we will be unable to host her on her visit to Antarctica but we wish her a very pleasant holiday.

Dear Mr Dietrich

Sorry you didn't manage to get through to Patrick. I don't think it would have worked anyhow. Mrs McCreedy is very set on the idea of going to see you and your penguins. I can't change her mind, I'm afraid. She's really quite independent and stubborn. When you meet her you'll see. I'm sure everything will be fine.

Best,
Eileen

12

Patrick

Bolton
November 2012

THIS WEIRD THING HAPPENED recently. I had an email in my inbox from some organization called penggroup4Ant. I don't get many emails, so I was intrigued. I wasn't going to risk anything, though. The fact is I had a massive problem last month because of opening a message from somebody I didn't know. My computer got the wobblies big time. Greg at the computer store took three weeks and £250 to sort it out. Never again, man. So I assumed this penggroup4Ant was spam and deleted it pronto. But the next week, lo and behold, another message from penggroup4Ant. I deleted it again.

Anyhow, this evening I'm in the process of making myself a con carne. I've just finished slicing chillies when I get this phone call from Granny Veronica's carer – or whatever you call her. The busybody called Eileen. Burbling on and on about some plan of Granny's to go on a long voyage. I didn't wash my hands before answering the phone and the chillies are making my fingers sting. I could do with ending the call quickly but this Eileen doesn't stop for breath. Her voice gets higher and higher.

'Mrs McCreedy's got a fixation about it. It's all to do with something in a box she found. She hasn't been the same since. I know she can be a bit erratic at times, but this is very worrying. Sorry to trouble you with it, but you're her grandson and, really, I'm at my wit's end. I've never seen her so keen about anything. And I expect you've realized it about her already – she's an unstoppable force. She's completely set her heart on going to Antarctica. And it's no good my trying to argue. You know what she's like. If you say that she can't do something it only makes her all the more determined to do it.'

'Hang on a mo. Whoa. Slow down!' I cry. 'You're saying Granny is going to *Antarctica*?'

'Yes, that's what she's planning.'

I burst out laughing.

There's a shocked pause from Eileen, then: 'You have to try and stop her. Please.'

This is getting surreal. Granny McC was OK mentally when I saw her, but I'm no expert. Either way, I can't believe Eileen thinks it has anything to do with me.

'Well, she's a free agent I guess.' I shrug my shoulders even though she can't see me.

'You have to do something!' she pleads. I've never met this Eileen woman but I picture her as a squat, angsty sort of a person in an apron, wringing her hands.

I'm baffled. Antarctica? I know money's no problem for Granny, but Antarctica? Not exactly your normal holiday destination.

'Why Antarctica?' I ask.

'Penguins!'

'Penguins?'

'Penguins!'

I wait for further information. Eileen doesn't need extra

71

prompting. 'She's got messages about penguins written all over the bathroom mirror! And she made me contact the penguin people. She saw this TV programme about penguins. She's obsessed with penguins. She wants to save them. But before she saves them she wants to see them.'

'I'm sorry. You're not making sense at all.'

There's an impatient huffy sound down the phone. 'She's gone and made me get her a ticket for the flights and ship and everything. I thought it would be OK but the scientists say it isn't. It really isn't. You can't just go there. But she thinks she can. She thinks she can save the penguins from extinction if she . . . well, it's to do with money . . .'

Eileen's voice suddenly goes fainter as if she's realized or remembered something.

'I just thought you might be able to stop her,' she mutters.

'Why the hell would she listen to me?'

'Because you're her grandson. Her *one and only* grandson. You have to try!' she wails.

It's hard to reason with her. 'What does it matter if Granny goes or if she doesn't?'

'The scientists!' Eileen gasps. 'They say conditions are impossible. For anyone, let alone an old lady. She made me send them an email saying she was going out there, but they emailed me back saying she mustn't. She really mustn't. Then she made me send them one back saying she was going to *anyway* and not to worry, but clearly they *are* worrying. I gave them your email address. Haven't you heard from them?'

The penny drops. Penggroup4Ant must be the scientists, trying to contact me, assuming I might be able to sway Granny in some way. I can't help having another little chortle.

'This is no laughing matter,' Eileen scolds. 'If something happens to her while she's away with the penguins I'd never forgive myself!'

Eileen must be fond of Granny. I have to say I'm actually developing a sneaky bit of admiration for her myself all mixed up in the dislike. You have to admit it, the woman's got gumption.

'Eileen,' I say. 'Calm down. I'm sure it'll be fine. She's not going for long, is she?'

'Three weeks!' Said in a tone of total despair.

'Well, tell you what I'll do. I'll email these scientist guys and say we'll do our best. You can make sure she has plenty of warm clothes and, er, pills . . . and whatever else she might need, can't you?'

'Yes, yes, but will you call her and try and persuade her not to go?'

My phone calls to Granny are not known for their success rate. There's only been the one so far and, let's face it, it went spectacularly badly.

'She's already got the tickets, you say?' I ask Eileen.

'Yes.'

'Well, there's no point then, is there? By the sounds of it, she's off to the other side of the world, whether we like it or not.'

Terry's Penguin Blog

6 December 2012

Penguins travel in many different ways. Most people think of a penguin upright and waddling, and that is how they'll sometimes get about when on land. Their tough feet have a kind of natural crampon which helps them move over snowy and stony terrains. But they're not stupid and they also know how to exploit the slipperiness of the ice. Often they'll flop down on their bellies and toboggan along at high speed. Tobogganing penguins always make me smile. I snapped this one while I was at the colony this afternoon. You'll see how the flippers are tucked into its sides and the feet stick out behind, propelling it forwards with the occasional push. The laws of physics do the rest.

Of course, much of a penguin's life is spent at sea. Perfectly streamlined, these guys dive in and out of the waves with flawless timing, flippers acting as a combination of fin and wing. Under the water, they are real masters of movement. They swoop, soar and perform incredible acrobatics. They can stay underwater for fifteen minutes without a breath, then they'll shoot out from the surface in a great arc like a dolphin. Sometimes they grab a breath before the next underwater sortie or sometimes they'll carry on porpoising in and out of the waves. It's a magnificent sight. It really does look like an act of pure joy.

13

Veronica

I USED TO ENJOY travelling. I have mixed feelings about it now. My late ex-husband whisked me away to several exotic destinations when we were in the first flush: San Francisco, Florence, Paris, Monaco and Mauritius. It was tolerably pleasurable at the time but, alas, those memories have been tainted by what happened in the relationship afterwards. I have not bothered with travelling at all in recent years. I have no issue with the actual flying. It is more the close proximity of so many people that disturbs me.

The tickets are called E-tickets. I previously thought that the E stood for 'ether' (which I've been led to believe is the substance through which these messages travel) but Eileen tells me this is not the case. Apparently it stands for 'Electronic'. A great number of things these days begin with an E, or alternatively an I. The I-words are ubiquitous: I-phones, I-players, I-pads, I-tunes, I-don't-know-where-it-will-end. Everyone is obsessing about 'I'; nobody has time for anyone or anything else.

My tickets were ordered by phone from the travel office in Kilmarnock. They confirmed them by email via Eileen and sent the tickets also by email via Eileen, who has printed them out and given them to me. Why they have to make everything so complicated I will never understand.

Eileen accompanies me in the taxi to Glasgow Airport. With her assistance, I have prepared for my expedition as well as it is humanly possible to prepare. We have calculated everything down to the last decimal point and wedged everything into my suitcases down to the last corn plaster. Bearing in mind the emphasis those scientists put on the 'basic conditions', I have packed a sprinkling of life's little pleasures, to wit: a tin of loose fresh Darjeeling, some peppermint creams, my three favourite handbags and a couple of bars of ylang-ylang and pomegranate soap. I have also invested in the best cold-weather outfits that money can buy: long-sleeved Merino wool vests with matching long johns, an assortment of corduroy and waterproof trousers (I prefer skirts but have regretfully concluded they are not practical for Antarctic conditions), cashmere double-knit jumpers, thick woollen cardigans and a rather grotesque 'Dynotherm' hooded down jacket in a shade of scarlet that matches my second-favourite handbag. Footwear is a special kind of boot that rejoices in the name of 'mukluk'. These mukluk creations are unsightly but apparently ideal for extreme conditions. They are well adapted (so the internet has informed Eileen and Eileen has informed me) for icy and rocky terrains. They will be accompanied by thermal socks, of course.

I have also brought my locket with me. This was a last-minute impulse. As I am headed for Locket Island it seems appropriate. I am currently wearing the locket against my skin, under my layers of clothing, just as I used to do. Whimsical as it may seem, I feel it enables me to draw on some of that young energy and drive I once had.

Eileen and I alight from the taxi. The airport is full of over-packaged and overpriced products and people in uniform who call me 'dear', which is most infuriating. I am many things, but I am certainly not a dear.

As we are in good time Eileen insists that we stop to have a coffee together in one of the noisy cafe areas. I have just selected the only table that is free from other people's detritus when, to my shock, I discover a tall, scruffy young man is standing right in front of me.

'Hello, Granny!'

This is unexpected. 'What in the world are you doing here?'

He darts a shifty glance at Eileen. 'A little bird told me that you were heading for the frozen South. So I thought I'd come and see you off.'

'Why?'

'Well, you took the trouble to come and see me a while back. I thought it would be nice to . . . er, do the same.'

Eileen is beetroot-coloured and trying her hardest not to look like a traitor.

'I thought you'd be pleased, Mrs McCreedy,' she mutters.

I would hardly say 'pleased' is an accurate description of what I am experiencing right now. Whatever possessed the boy? Is he trying to ingratiate himself into my favour in order to borrow money? Does he think an excessive gesture like this is likely to earn any points in his favour?

'I really admire your pluck, Granny, in travelling so far,' he babbles, as if reading my thoughts. 'And I thought you deserved a . . . er, family send-off because it's such an epic journey.'

I survey him. I perceive in his eyes an honest desire to please. Perhaps I have been a little hasty in my judgement.

Eileen buys coffees and we force them down whilst embarking on a stilted conversation. I can at least report that Patrick has made more of an effort than the last time I saw him. None of his clothes are ripped and they look relatively clean, although they are in very poor taste. A word is scrawled across his T-shirt that looks like 'Spikey' but could be almost anything. Why do people have to walk about with advertising written all over themselves? And I will simply never understand the trend for jeans with waistlines that sink halfway down a person's nether regions. At least he isn't smoking drugs. They wouldn't allow that here.

Patrick asks me if Antarctica will be cold at this time of year and continues to pose other such inane questions. He also makes a few attempts at penguin jokes, most of them extremely poor. Both he and Eileen are manifesting a strained, worried kind of jollity.

'Are you sure you're going to be all right, Mrs McCreedy?' whines Eileen, wrinkling her brow.

'Of course I am,' I tell her with considerable sternness. 'Even if I'm not, what does it matter?'

'Oh, don't say that, Mrs McCreedy! Of course it matters!' Her eyes are brimming. She can be absurdly sentimental at times.

The three of us finish our unpalatable coffees and make our way to a waiting area. The chairs are too close together but they are screwed to the floor so nothing can be done about it. I settle down, walling myself in with my hand luggage. It is a poor deterrent. Within two minutes a family of five, complete with grizzling children, infringe on my personal boundaries by sitting suffocatingly close.

'I've put all your pads and meds in the blue holdall with the smalls,' Eileen informs me. Her voice is far too loud.

'Yes, yes, I know.' I have no desire to talk about pads and meds at this precise moment. The family of five have expressions of delight plastered all over their sticky little faces.

Patrick consults his watch. 'Soz, you two, but I've got to get the bus back straight away or else I have to wait another one and a half hours.' He looks at me uncertainly. 'I'll say bye-bye then, Granny.'

'Goodbye, Patrick.'

He looms in as if he is about to hug me, then, I am glad to say, thinks better of it.

'Take care. Um . . . bye!' and he's gone.

Eileen stays until it's time to board. She can't stop herself going over my schedule dozens of times and pointing things out to me as if I am an idiot. Various little men are booked to meet me on and off flights and help with luggage. Eileen insisted.

'If you can, will you let me know you've arrived safely, Mrs McCreedy?'

I nod. I don't wish to burden her with any extra worry. 'I'll send a postcard if such a thing is possible.'

'Or maybe tell that nice Dietrich man to email me?'

'As you wish.'

'Oh, Mrs McCreedy, if only I could come with you! I did ask Doug about it, but he just laughed. And he reminded me I don't ever fly. It makes me go wobbly and sick.'

'I neither want nor need you to come with me, Eileen,' I reassure her kindly.

'Please look after yourself, Mrs McCreedy, won't you?' she whimpers.

She will make such a meal out of everything. I keep my eyes firmly focused ahead.

In view of my grandson's unexpected appearance I have come to a decision. Slowly and clearly I spell out to Eileen some very specific instructions regarding a certain wooden box. She puts on her nosy expression but refrains from bombarding me with questions.

'There is a little something for you in a Manila envelope and a tin with tulips on the lid that I have left on the hall table,' I tell her. As she will be without employment for three weeks I have left her the three weeks of pay. Plus a family-sized tin of her favourite chocolate marshmallow biscuits. 'Now, Eileen, I'm sure you have things to do. Be off with you!'

'Have a great time, Mrs McCreedy!' she murmurs, dabbing her eyes with a limp piece of tissue.

'Goodbye, Eileen.' I watch her wide back disappear through the crowds. I turn, boarding card at the ready, and go through to the Departure Lounge.

I am glad of my scarlet Dynotherm jacket. It is bracing out on the deck and the wind stabs my face like needles.

The flights were cramped but mercifully punctual. The assorted staff who'd been booked to look after my needs played their part with efficiency (I should think so, too – we paid plenty of extra money for them) although tending to obsequiousness, particularly the last. It was a relief to be off aeroplanes and board the ship yesterday. I far prefer the open sea.

Already I have seen a humpback whale spouting a jet of water, seals floundering on rocks and a few bedraggled penguins grouped on the shores of some of the islets.

I am out early today. There is little of interest in my compact but well-equipped cabin, so I have decided to brave the cold. The sky is composed of slowly moving patterns in marbled grey. Vast icebergs sail on the surface of the water like elegant sea monsters. Gulls wheel overhead. The waves slap at the ship's side. The water is fragmented, chinking with ice crystals. I gaze out as the whiteness becomes whiter.

I am so absorbed that I jump when I hear a voice at my shoulder. 'Cool, isn't it?'

It is a portly man of about half my age wielding a large amount of photographic equipment. I nod my acquiescence, not sure if 'cool' refers to the temperature or the marvels of the scenery.

The man sidles up and messes about with his lens. My instinct is to move away, but I was here first. He seems to want to converse with me and assumes I wish to converse with him also.

'Hey, look at that!' he cries as we drift closer to an iceberg sculpted like an archway. I do not need to be told what to look at. The man is failing to look at it properly himself, he is too busy focusing his camera on it. 'Yay! It's a beauty!' Click, click, click.

'You don't take any photos!' he comments, incredulous.

'No,' I reply. 'I would rather look at something with my eyes unhampered by a wall of cumbersome machinery.'

'Ouch,' he says. 'That stung!' Then he adds, 'But y'know, it's a great feeling to be building up a collection of fabulous memories for the future.'

'I'm not in the business of building up memories for the future,' I inform him. 'The present will do.'

In spite of his tiresome chit-chat I feel light-hearted at the sight of these wondrously barren icescapes.

Tomorrow I will arrive at my destination. A childlike excitement is rising inside me. It is a very long time since I've had an adventure.

14

Veronica

Locket Island, South Shetlands, Antarctic Peninsula

Locket Island appears to be a mountainous affair. The shoreline is jagged in some areas, smooth in others. The ship gradually comes to a standstill. Alongside us is a narrow spit of blackened volcanic beach streaked with snow. Frozen pools and runnels reflect the pale light. I cannot see any penguins.

I am the only passenger scheduled to get off here and there is no sign of the others. There was a so-called 'funanza' last night, a dreadful affair with loud music, alcohol and people crashing about, so they are doubtless recovering from their excesses. By good fortune my cabin was far away from all the drunkenness and debauchery, so I was able to sleep soundly and am feeling quite fresh and energetic this morning.

The man who acts as my on-board assistant is a dark-skinned, sharp-eyed creature with little English. I tell him to place all my luggage on to the small Zodiac boat that will transport us to land. He gesticulates and mutters under his breath but does as he is bidden. He helps me on to the boat with a steady hand, which is just as well.

As we approach on the lapping waves I spot two figures on the beach. My man helps me out of the boat again and starts unloading the luggage. It is a relief to feel land under my feet, albeit rough and stony. With mukluks and the help of my new polar walking stick, I can negotiate the terrain very well, avoiding the slippery coils of coloured seaweed that festoon the rocks.

The two figures walk over to greet us.

Both of them are in thick parka jackets. The man steps forward. He's just my side of forty, stocky with sprouting thick brown hair, a beard that resembles a scrubbing brush and a firm handshake.

'So . . . welcome! I am Dietrich. You made it, Mrs McCreedy.' His voice is a combination of warmth and worry. His accent is pronounced.

'Of course I did. I said I would. You are German,' I add.

'Austrian,' he answers tetchily.

'I'm Terry,' says the girl brightly as she takes my hand. I knew there was a Terry on the team (the one who writes the blogs, Eileen told me) but I'd assumed Terry was a man. This Terry is in her mid-twenties, I'd say, with a pasty sort of face, blond shoulder-length hair and glasses. Her smile is a little timid. 'We saw the message from your helper to say you were due here on the ship today. We're . . . well, we're glad you made it. We weren't sure if you'd come.'

'Why ever not?' Assuming Eileen sent those emails, I would have thought I had made it abundantly clear I was coming.

'Well, no offence, but I don't think you quite realize how hard things are here. I'm sure you are very healthy and able, but even we – and we're used to basic conditions – find it hard at times.'

'Basic conditions', yet again! 'Let me be the judge of that,' I say.

The two of them look at each other, mentally conferring; you could spot it a mile off.

Dietrich consults his watch. 'The ship is due to depart again in three hours, Mrs McCreedy. Why don't you take that time to look around here? You'll see what we mean, I am sure. Nobody will think any the less of you if you change your mind. After you've seen everything I suggest you return to the ship, enjoy its relative luxury and travel to a more suitable destination for the remainder of your holiday.'

'I have come all this way,' I tell them, 'to spend time with the penguins. And that is precisely what I am going to do.'

The Locket Island field base is situated close to the shore. It doesn't take long to get my luggage there with the help of the foreign grumpy man and Terry and Dietrich, who have brought a sled.

Terry sweeps her arm forward, indicating a kind of shack made of breeze blocks that sits on a plain of stone and ice. It is not a thing of beauty. 'Home!' she declares.

On top of the snowy bank behind the shack there are a few rudimentary metal windmills slowly turning against the mottled sky. It seems a sacrilege that anything has been built here and I am not impressed by these ugly man-made welts on the pure white face of nature. But I suppose needs must.

'We have solar power, but those supplement it,' Dietrich explains. 'Together they generate enough for our various electrical devices.'

'Where are the penguins?' I ask. I had expected there to be swarms of them all round the centre.

'Not here, but not far away. See that big slope of snow? The other side of that is their nesting ground. We'll go out and visit them as soon as you've had a rest.'

Terry pushes the door open and leads the way inside. We shed our coats and my cases are deposited in the large central room. My man murmurs something to Dietrich, then backs away and disappears.

I decline Terry's offer of coffee. I indulged in tea and croissants shortly before leaving the ship. Instead I devote my attention to examining my lodgings.

There is a propane heater against one wall, a few chairs and a sizeable table. The room also contains an extraordinary amount of clutter that isn't quite normal household clutter. Many items hang from nails: pans, spoons, plastic tags, nets, goggly things and hooky things. I couldn't say what they all are, but presume they must be penguin-relevant. A tangle of electrical wires sags from the ceiling in a rather alarming manner. The shelves are stacked with faded tins and packets along with an assortment of natural debris – lichens, bits of bone and eggshell, feathers and fish skeletons. I am glad to note there are a couple of books, too.

'We can never bring out as many as we'd like, but we've accumulated those over the years,' explains Dietrich.

'Not that there's much time to read them,' Terry sighs. 'Now, I'm sure you'd like to put your feet up for a while, Veronica.'

I do hate it when people equate old age with incapacity. I have been cooped up without any exercise on aeroplanes and then a ship for the best part of three days. Moreover, I have been out of bed for a mere two hours, yet they expect me to lie down again already.

I oblige them by sitting on a hard chair for fifteen minutes, then arise and stride about the room, eager to demonstrate the plenitude of my energy levels.

I notice a few pen-and-ink drawings stuck on the walls, none of them very good.

'Dietrich did those. Aren't they wonderful!'

I cannot, however, partake in Terry's enthusiasm. The drawings all depict anthropomorphized penguins. There's a penguin choir singing, a lone penguin sitting on an iceberg wearing a flat cap and dangling a fishing rod, and a group of penguin children playing on swings. Without exception they are utterly ridiculous.

Dietrich coughs by way of apology. 'It's my little hobby. I draw them for my children whenever there's a spare moment. I email copies to keep them and my wife entertained. Terry insists that I put the originals up here.'

Terry smiles. 'Well, it makes it homely,' she says.

'This place was purpose-built only seven years ago,' Dietrich tells me. 'It's in the prime position for penguin watching. They mostly come past here on their way from the sea to the nesting ground, or rookery, as we call it.'

'Rookery?' That is a very contradictory name for a penguin nesting ground, if you ask me. Rooks are rooks and penguins are penguins.

Dietrich is keen to tell me about the project. 'Our centre is a good size, as you will see. It was built to accommodate five scientists throughout the year, and the first year it did just that. See, we have bunks in here, here and here.'

He opens the doors quickly so I can't register which room is going to be my bedroom.

'But now it's just the three of us,' he continues. 'And we're only here because we agreed to do it for exceptionally low wages. Mike is the other scientist, and he's out with the penguins at the moment. He's due back later.'

'So you three are busy trying to work out the reasons for the penguin decline?'

'Yes. We were determined to give it one more go. We have a little lab in here where we can conduct a few tests on samples. That's Mike's job, mostly. We have a computer room, too. We need it for inputting our data and sending it back to the number-crunchers in Britain. We have intermittent internet access. Better than nothing.'

'But only one actual computer,' Terry adds. 'Our other one packed up a few weeks ago. The computer room is always in demand.'

Dietrich beams. 'We try not to fight over it.'

I dislike anybody making jokes about fighting. Fighting is no laughing matter.

I frown at him. 'Would you kindly show me which room is to be my bedroom?'

I observe the flicker of deceit that passes between the two of them. 'We'd better show Veronica the facilities first,' says Terry, gently levering me towards the smallest room you've ever seen. 'We have the luxury of a toilet, but no bath or shower, I'm afraid. Not much in the way of hot water, either.'

The sink is largish. The toilet is a collection of buckets and a hard foam seat positioned high enough to fit one of them underneath it.

Again Terry and Dietrich exchange a furtive little look. The toilet, it appears, is their trump card.

'Splendid!' I declare, banging my stick on the ground. I will admit that age has inflicted a few disadvantages upon me but they are certainly not insurmountable. It will take more than an incommodious washroom to put me off. 'An excellent lavatory. And where is my bedroom, please?'

'I'm very sorry, Mrs McCreedy,' replies Dietrich, looking guilty. 'We have been extremely busy and it isn't made up for you yet—'

'Well, in that case I should like to see the penguins without further ado.'

Apparently Dietrich must supervise the unloading of food supplies from the same ship that brought me here (it passes Locket Island every three weeks en route to the more popular tourist destinations, enabling the scientists to replenish their larder). Terry therefore acts as my guide.

'Are you wrapped up warm?' she asks. 'I hope you have thick underwear on. Frostbite is a horrible thing.'

I give her a long look. I do not like being taken for an idiot. I am encased in three thermal vests and long johns under my woolly jumpers and the fleece-lined trousers Eileen bought for me. My Dynotherm coat set me back three hundred and twenty-five pounds. I can scarcely move, I am so trussed up.

We step outside. The sun has rolled out from behind the clouds and we are met by a blaze of white light. I tread gingerly forward in my mukluks, prodding the snow with my stick.

Terry mistakes my slowness for unfitness and tries to take my arm. I shake her off. She herself is carrying a vast amount of equipment as if it were light as a feather. She has no idea how lucky she is to possess such strength. But then I could have done it too when I was her age.

The snow is so bright I can hardly look at it, even through my anti-glare sunglasses. We struggle up the slope. It is neither steep nor far but I am taking my time. I stop regularly to examine the landscape. A range of porcelain-blue mountains rises off to my right. They exhibit a slight dichotomy of character, being smooth as glass in some places and craggy in others. Glittering streams of meltwater ribbon through the rocks. The lower slopes are startlingly colourful. They are lit up with lichens in lime green, yellows, pink and fiery orange.

As we reach the top, Terry points.

'Look this way first,' she says. 'You'll see why it's called Locket Island.'

In the distance is a narrow loop of land that stretches all the way around a semi-circular lake. Beyond it is the sea. With its oval form and this natural aperture, the mapped version of this island must resemble a locket in shape.

'Now look this way.'

I do. On the flat spit of land below us I see a mosaic of darker shades against the paleness. It is a vast company of small waddling bodies. As we come nearer something akin to excitement starts gathering in the pit of my stomach. Suddenly I am walking faster.

'What is all that pink stuff?' I ask Terry.

'I'm afraid it's penguin poo. Otherwise known as guano.'

'Oh!' They seem to be living in a swamp composed of their own excrement. It is disgusting.

'Well, you didn't expect them to be all clean and cartoony, like on the Christmas cards, did you?'

In a way that is exactly what I'd expected. But my disappointment is quickly dissolving into excitement again. These aren't pretty illustrations in a book but real living creatures, spectacularly three-dimensional and unashamedly physical. Here they are, bold and bright, getting on with life in a big, bustling community. Messy, noisy, reckless, pulsing with life and energy. I feel immensely privileged to be here, seeing them in the wild, in their black-and-white, slightly comical brand of glory. Despite the prevalence of guano it is indeed a marvellous sight. Their raucous calls fill my ears. But now I have a problem with my eyes. They seem to be stinging intensely and beginning to water. It must be the cold. I blink the moisture away.

There are penguins everywhere. Some are preening, some lying on their bellies asleep, some seem to be gossiping together. Others are just standing there stoically staring into space. En masse and individually they have it all worked out. They don't seem the slightest bit perturbed by our presence.

My sense of smell has considerably diminished over the last few years but the stench of fish is extremely pungent. A slimy, earthy sort of odour.

Terry swings a small camera off her shoulder. 'I always take a few snaps,' she says. 'You never know when you're going to capture that perfect pose.' She crouches down near the edge of the cluster of penguins. A few turn their heads and look at her.

'They have no fear of humans,' she explains. 'Which is extremely handy for us.'

'Excellent!' I say, stepping closer to a little huddle who bear some resemblance to a posse of diminutive youngsters having a cigarette break. I want to examine each of their expressions and try and work out their characters, their raison d'être. I am seized by a desire to be close to them. One of them seems to be equally fascinated in me and ducks his head a little in what I take to be an expression of greeting.

We contemplate each other for a while then the penguin resumes conversation with his companions. Terry clicks away with her camera while I roam along the outskirts of the crowd, delighted by each and every penguin. I don't notice the cold at all. Then suddenly Terry turns the camera towards me.

'Don't!' I screech, lifting my arms to cover my face a split-second too late.

'Oh, sorry,' she says at once. 'It was just a moment. Your face. Your expression. You looked totally mesmerized. Uplifted. Like a different person.'

This, I note, is hardly complimentary about the way I normally look. But there's something about Terry that makes it hard to take offence.

'Don't worry,' she assures me. 'I won't use it for my blog or anything.'

'Oh, yes, I recall Eileen saying something about a blog.'

'It doesn't have a huge following but it's growing, thanks to the Robert Saddlebow programme. I put photos up there and tell the world what we're doing.' She fiddles with the camera for a second then holds it out to show me the picture of myself.

I look like an old woman in the snow.

'Wonderful, isn't it?'

I don't see it at all.

'Wow, it would be amazing if I *could* put it up on the blog,' Terry comments, viewing it again. 'It's so unusual. Having you out here would grab loads of attention.'

Then she snatches a look at her watch.

'Oh my God! We have to move. The ship's going to leave in forty minutes! The others'll go crazy if I don't get you back in time.'

15

Veronica

Locket Island

THE WALK BACK IS exceedingly slow. I seem to be having problems with my stick, which becomes wedged in crevices no less than three times and is difficult to pull out again, even with Terry's help. Then I need to sit and rest on a rock for ten minutes. When I say 'need to', I may be exaggerating slightly. In fact I'm revelling in the pure, unpolluted quality of the air and feeling uncommonly energetic. The rock, due to my ample wadding, is not as uncomfortable as you'd expect. Terry gesticulates wildly and talks at me. My hearing aid isn't functioning well so I have to keep asking her to repeat herself.

I confess to a little gloating by the time we finally arrive back at the field centre. Terry and I witnessed the ship sailing away just as we reached the top of the slope. Terry was fretful about it but there wasn't much she could do.

'So you will have to stay now, Mrs McCreedy,' Dietrich comments as we take off our coats. 'The next ship doesn't come for a full three weeks.' He is looking far from thrilled.

'Well, it's not as if we don't have the space.' Terry shrugs. 'I'll tell you what: Veronica can use my bedroom while she's here. It's the warmest. I'll move into the cabin room.'

My suspicions have been confirmed. They never intended me to stay in the first place. However, as the girl is prepared to sacrifice her own bedroom for my comfort, I will not make a fuss about it.

'You sit down and have a cup of tea while I sort my stuff out,' she says. 'I'll only be twenty minutes. Then you can move in properly and unpack.'

'I must confess I am surprised you're not more prepared. I did give you ample notice about my visit,' I point out, somewhat icily.

Dietrich stands up. 'I'll make tea,' he says, and goes to put the kettle on. 'You liked the Adélies, then, Mrs McCreedy?' He is civil, oh so civil.

'I did indeed.'

After I have carefully closed all the doors that have been left open in the building I lower myself into the only chair that has a cushion. It looks marginally more comfortable than the others. The cushion is battered and a putrid shade of orange. Still, it is better than nothing.

At this moment the front door opens and a young man walks in. He is wearing the ubiquitous parka jacket. He is of a slight, wiry build and has a long chin and intense, steely eyes. The eyes focus immediately on me, slide across to Dietrich in an accusatory manner then back to me.

'Hello.' His voice is not welcoming.

'Allow me to introduce Mike. Mike, this is Veronica McCreedy,' Dietrich tells him. 'She is staying,' he adds in a measured tone.

Mike peels off his outer layers and carefully hangs them on the peg. He slowly exchanges his mukluks (I am interested to note he has them too) for a pair of plimsolls. Then he crosses the room to shake my hand.

'Excuse me if I don't get up,' I say. 'I am recently returned from my first trip out to see the penguins.'

'Mrs McCreedy was not back in time to return to the ship,' Dietrich informs Mike. I really do not like that accent of his, and I do not like his attitude, either.

'I wasn't intending to return to the ship anyway,' I remind him sharply. He passes me a mug of tea. The mug is chipped and the tea tastes like tar.

'I'll have one too, if you're making, Deet,' says Mike.

He takes a packet of biscuits from the shelf and offers me one without bothering to put them on a plate first. They are digestives, very plain indeed. I accept one graciously.

We sit in silence over our tea and biscuits for a few minutes.

'Anything unusual today?' Dietrich asks Mike.

Mike shakes his head. 'Not really. I saw Sooty again. Still sitting hopefully on his nest.'

'Sooty is our local eccentric, Mrs McCreedy,' Dietrich tells me. 'A penguin who is almost completely black all over.'

Before I can pursue the topic any further, Terry emerges from her bedroom, her arms full of bulging polythene bags and bedding. Immediately the atmosphere lightens. She seems to have this effect on people.

'Oh, hi, Mike! You've met Veronica, then.'

He nods. 'Yes.' The 'yes' is short and laced with disapprobation.

'The room's all yours, Veronica, whenever you're ready,' she chirps.

'Excellent,' I reply.

We've consumed a sloppy and tasteless meal comprising bits of unidentifiable meat floating around in ready-mix gravy with resuscitated potatoes and carrots on the side. Mike (or is it Mark? I forget) was this evening's chef.

Terry rolls up her sleeves. 'My turn to do the washing-up!'

I offer to help with the drying. It's an opportunity to quiz her.

Over the dishes she informs me that it is Dietrich who runs the project, although he tries to ensure every decision is democratic. He is the 'penguinologist' who has devoted his whole life to studying the birds. According to Terry, he has a lovely wife and three children back in Austria. He misses them more than he lets on. Dietrich is a 'real gentleman' who would 'do anything for anybody'.

No matter what Terry says, I can't help being wary of Dietrich. Unlike anyone else here, I've lived through the war. These things make you realize there's a monster lurking in all of us. *One may smile and smile and yet be a villain.* I shall give this Dietrich a wide berth.

Mike (Mark?) is, I'm told, 'a great guy', although he hides it well. His spiky manner is a habit that he has long cultivated, almost like a hobby. 'We take it with a pinch of salt,' Terry comments, with a wry smile. Young men, I have observed, are always desperate to prove themselves one way or another. Being acerbic is, no doubt, Mike's perverse method of trying to demonstrate his toughness, masculinity, etc etc. It is utterly pathetic, but there you are. Terry informs me that he is the expert on biochemistry and enjoys nothing more than testing bits of bone and guano for their mineral content. He has a girlfriend back in London who nobody knows much about. He's rather cagey about her.

'And you?' I ask Terry. 'Are you attached to anyone?'

There's a sweetness behind her smile. Even a tough nut like me can see that.

'I'm attached to a lot of people and a lot of penguins,' she answers, tucking a strand of pale hair behind her ear. 'But I classify as single.'

I peer at her. I register that, if only she would get a proper haircut and apply a bit of make-up, she could be very pretty indeed. Her skin is monochrome but unusually flawless. Her features are neat and pleasing. Behind those unflattering glasses her eyes are a wide expanse, the colours of sea and shingle.

'Why do you have a man's name?' I ask.

'Well, it's really Teresa,' she answers, screwing up her face. 'But I don't like that.'

'Why ever not?' I ask. I would have thought it infinitely preferable to 'Terry'. She could hardly have picked a more unattractive word. 'Teresa is a pleasant enough name.'

She is adamant. 'I've always been Terry.'

The scientists have left open the door of the computer room and the door of the lab. I conscientiously close them both and then head for my bedroom. My body is tired and demanding to be horizontal for a while. I stretch out on the lumpy bed. Terry has made it up with abundant duvets and blankets, but it is still lumpy. I am not one to complain, however.

Seeing the penguins was a joy but also somehow a shock. Their bright beady eyes, their pudgy bodies, their characterful flippers and feet. The admittedly disgusting yet simultaneously satisfying smell of them. Their cacophony of trumpeting, squawking and braying calls. The way they sometimes walk single-file in a line along a penguin highway; the way they scoot and slide across the snow. The way they waggle their bottoms, shake their feathers and preen. Their whole outlandishly gregarious approach to life.

It is hard to believe I am actually here. At last I am doing something interesting and important. I think about all those penguins, a hundred times realer and truer than they'd been in my imagination. At this precise moment, notwithstanding the inconvenience of the other human beings, I feel surer than ever that this is where I want to bequeath my money.

It promises to be a most interesting three weeks. I feel an onrush of self-approbation. It is indeed laudable that I made the effort to come. Pleasant, penguiny images drift around inside my head.

. . . I can hear a soft murmuring of voices. I don't know how long I've been asleep. It takes me a moment to realize where I am, then reality filters through and spreads a smile on my face. I am in Antarctica, my aim to embark on a final, great adventure and to thoroughly enjoy it; my mission to help the Adélie penguins. I feel the warm metal of my locket touching my skin. It all makes perfect sense.

This hut has thin walls. I catch the word 'Veronica', said with some acidity. I believe it is Mike's voice. I sit up, reach for my hearing aid, put it in and turn the volume up to maximum.

Now Terry is speaking. 'But she *is*,' I hear her say, as if disagreeing with something somebody has said. 'You should have seen her face when we went out earlier. She was transfixed by the sight of them. It's more than just a whim.'

'I don't care. Three weeks is a hell of a long time.' Mike, again. 'We're under no obligation to keep her here. We were more than clear in all our communications that she shouldn't come. Yet she's foisted herself upon us without anyone's permission. It is rude and it's manipulative. A total lack of respect and a total lack of common sense.'

There's a small silence.

'She said she'd pay for her accommodation. About ten times more than it's worth,' Dietrich points out.

'I'll believe that when I see it!'

'But if she really is going to donate a serious amount towards the project,' Terry mutters. 'Like, *millions*. Can we afford not to?'

'Even if it's true, we're not going to see most of that money until she's dead, I gather.' Mike does indeed have more than his fair share of spikiness. His voice is full of hard edges. 'Although, how long can it be?' he muses. He laughs. The other two don't join in. 'She seems pretty sturdy, I'll grant you,' he continues. 'She may last another decade. And I have to say I'm not prepared to wait and kowtow to her, all for money that may or may not materialize. By the time she's kicked the bucket, the penguin project will be long gone.'

At this point I find that my eyes are stinging severely. The second time today. Normally they cause me no problems whatsoever. I hope this is not the beginning of some visual ailment. I manage to find a handkerchief and give them a quick dab, then put my ear to the door again.

'In any case, how could we get any work done with her around?' exclaims Mike. 'She'd drive us insane. We're friends and fellow scientists but in this environment even *we* find it difficult not to kill each other!'

There's a ripple of knowing laughter here like the acceptance of a well-explored truth.

'You're right there,' Dietrich answers. 'It's a miracle we're still talking to each other.'

'But maybe a bit of fresh blood is exactly what we need,' Terry urges.

'Yes, that's all very nice, but the fact is she's an old lady.' Mike again. 'Old ladies don't belong here. They should be surrounded by radiators and fitted carpets and daytime TV. I vote we send her away straight off.' I realize at this point that, no matter who speaks with which accent, it isn't Dietrich who is the enemy. It is Mike.

Terry is clearing her throat. 'Easier said than done, Mike.'

They lower their voices and I can't catch the murmurs that follow, which is extraordinarily frustrating. But then Mike's voice is raised again. 'We're quite within our rights to turn her away. I'm sorry, but we have to get rid of her somehow. While she's here we have responsibility for her, and I for one am not happy about that.'

'I'm worried too,' confesses Dietrich. 'If she gets ill we can't possibly give her the care she needs.'

'Come on, give her a bit longer, will you?' pleads Terry. 'We can't send her away yet. She's only just arrived and—'

'—And we already hate her,' says Mike.

16

Patrick

Bolton

BOLTON JOB CENTRE: NOT exactly a bundle of laughs. In fact, it's one of my least-favourite places on the planet. I'm on my way back from there now. My benefits will be cut off unless I show some kind of token effort at finding work. I guess there are heaps of things I *could* do, but without qualifications on paper I haven't a hope in hell. In an ideal world I'd find something that fits round Mondays at the bike shop. But is that ever going to happen? Let's face it: big, fat No.

The only possibility up on the boards today was a job monitoring trolleys in a supermarket car park. Apparently you needed good communication skills and spatial awareness and the ability to think on your feet. What? To push trolleys into a trolley bay? There's an online form to fill in with about thirty-five questions and you have to send in a covering letter and CV on top of that. And when you've done all that they'll no doubt ask you to climb to the top of Everest whilst balancing a phoenix egg on the end of your nose. Jeez. No wonder people prefer to leech off the state.

'Would you like to apply?' the starchy woman behind the desk asked me in a robotic, I-don't-care-either-way voice.

'I'll think about it,' I said.

Well, I've thought about it and I really don't want to think about it any more. I trudge back along car-honk avenue feeling useless and gloomy. A right Eeyore. It might well be time to assault the Weedledum and Weedledee jar. I'm not cheered by the idea, though, because I thought I was doing all right and it shows I'm still a fricking weakling.

I'm about to go up to the flat when my eye falls on this package waiting for me in the hall. Loads of stamps on it – it must have cost a bomb to post. What the . . . ?

I think for a moment it must be for the downstairs neighbours, not me. I double-check. Nope, it's not for the caterwauling couple. It's my name on there, my address.

Lynette? The thought knocks the breath out of me for a second. Fact: I'm 100 per cent over her. But who else is there who'd send me anything? It must be her, mustn't it? She took some of my crap with her, like the battery charger and headphones. Maybe she's had an attack of conscience and decided to return them?

The parcel isn't from Lynette, though, I can see that. It's not her writing. Could she have got the brickie to write out the address for her? She's the world's expert in getting people to do stuff for her. Maybe brickie boy is acting as, like, her *secretary* now. Not very likely, though. I doubt he can even write. Anyhow, this looks like a woman's writing. It's a very rounded, squat sort of writing in blue biro.

I heave the package upstairs and rip it open. Inside all the brown paper and string is a battered box, pretty heavy. It's got an ancient, woody sort of smell. It has one of those padlocks you have to know the code to unlock. How weird is that?

Then I see the folded-up bit of paper. I unfold it.

Dear Patrick,
I hope you are well.
Mrs McCreedy (your grandmother) asked me to send this to
you before she went. I know it's locked but she said to send it
anyway. She said please to keep it safe. You can't open it – you're
not allowed to open it – unless you get the code. And she said
you won't be getting that at the moment.
Nasty weather, isn't it?

Yours,
Eileen

I'm beginning to wonder if Granny needs to be under lock and key herself. It's all getting more and more surreal.

What the hell could be inside the box? Something that belonged to my father? Or some family heirloom from the sixteenth century? A Victorian set of napkin rings? An antique stuffed squirrel?

I wish I'd found out a bit more about Granny the two times we met. I'm kicking myself now for being so bogged down in my own problems.

I try twisting the dial of the padlock into a few number combos but none of them work. I could always get out the toolkit and saw it open anyway. I shouldn't, but you know how it is with curiosity . . .

No. I'm going to do what Granny V wants. If she's determined to be mysterious, that's fine by me. Maybe all will be revealed when she gets back from Antarctica. I wonder how she's getting on.

I shove the box under the bed.

17

Veronica

Locket Island

'Help yourself, Veronica.'

It is my first breakfast here. Mountainous supplies of hot food are on the table: bacon, eggs, baked beans, hash browns and toast. The emphasis is on quantity rather than quality. Every item is of the colourless and defrosted variety. The scientists are tucking in as if it is manna from heaven. Presumably such elephantine helpings are necessary to set everyone up for the day. I pour myself out a mug of tea from the pot and take a sip. It is revolting. Somewhere in my luggage I have a supply of fragrant Darjeeling. I will have to dig it out.

The air is full of unexpressed resentment towards me. I transfer a slice of toast, some yellow mush masquerading as egg and a leathery-looking slice of bacon on to my plate. Then get straight to the point.

'I haven't paid for my accommodation yet. I'd like to settle it immediately after breakfast. I am proposing to pay you considerably more than I suggested in my email.'

I watch the incredulity spread across their faces.

'Pay *more* than you suggested for your accommodation?' repeats Dietrich.

'Yes.'

They gawk at me. Mark – or is it Mike? – sniggers. 'Why? It's hardly five-star!'

'I know. But I'd like to contribute something substantial straight away, so as to assist you with the project. To help the penguins.'

Dietrich frowns. 'I'm not sure we can allow that, Mrs McCreedy. The fact is—'

I interrupt him. 'No arguments.'

Terry looks from me to Dietrich and back again. 'That's unbelievably generous of you, Veronica.'

I catch Mark's eye. He looks annoyed, as though he thinks I am engaged in some kind of bribery. Which I undoubtedly am. I can see that he's mustering himself again to give me a dismissal speech. He seems to have taken it upon himself to be the one who decides, even though it should be Dietrich.

I pick at my food. I am having some difficulty eating this morning. I had very little sleep last night. My mind was too busy turning things over. I tidy my unpalatable bacon and egg to the edges of my plate, making the waste look as small as possible. It's always a bad idea to look ungrateful.

'Terry, I've been thinking about your doo-dah.'

Her eyes widen. 'My doo-dah?'

'I am no fool, young lady. I know you and Dietrich and Mark want me to depart speedily and leave you in peace.'

'Not Mark. Mike,' the discourteous man puts in pointedly. I ignore him.

'But if I stay here for the full three weeks it will be mutually beneficial. I can spend time with the penguins, which is my one last wish upon this earth. As for you, you'll receive ample money for my lodgings and, in due course, my entire inheritance to ensure the continuation of your project. In addition, Terry, you may feature me in your bloggy thing if you so desire.'

Terry's face lights up. 'Oh, *that* doo-dah,' she says.

'I am no great advocate of social media gimmicks,' I continue, 'but am prepared to have you put my photograph up there, do an interview or whatever else you might require of me. For publicity, as you seem to think it will make a difference. For the future of the penguins.' Seldom have I been so magnanimous about anything.

'Oh, thank you so much, Veronica!' cries Terry. 'That would be wonderful! You can provide that human-interest angle that's lacking at the moment. It'll really help!'

She turns to Mike (not Mark) with an I-told-you-so look. His face is like thunder. He puts his knife and fork together with a loud clink, gets up quickly and leaves the room.

Veronica McCreedy is not one to be overcome by the machinations of small-minded people. I experience a delightful stab of victory.

Terry is to be my guide again today. She climbs into her weather-proof clothing at lightning speed and waits for me. I am rather slower due to the disadvantage of stiffer, eighty-six-year-old limbs. The others have long gone by the time we're ready.

'What exactly are they doing?' I ask.

'We each have our own area to cover. We check the nests and mark where they are. We do counts and weigh some of the penguins. And we monitor which ones have returned from last year.'

'How do you know which are last year's penguins? Do you put rings on their legs like pigeons?'

'No,' she informs me. 'Penguin feet are too thick and fleshy for that. It's been tried in the past and they get infections where the rings rub the skin. No, there's a metal armband thing that goes over the flipper. Each armband has a number so we can recognize penguins we've seen before.'

As soon as I step outside, the air seizes my lungs. It is most invigorating. Sunlight glances off the snow in a joyous dance of silvery whites. I have my sunglasses on and the lilac scarf Eileen gave me. I also have my second-favourite scarlet handbag in case I should need a handkerchief or painkillers. And my stick, of course. I manage the slope with speed and alacrity.

Terry seems impressed. She has a little more pink in her cheeks today and is wearing a hat with dangly tassels coming down over each ear. It is not a good look.

'You are young,' I observe. 'Don't you find it a trifle isolated here on an Antarctic island with just two peculiar men for company?'

'I actually prefer to have lots of space around me,' she replies. 'It's unusual but that's the way I am. I realized it first years ago when I went to Glastonbury Festival with a bunch of mates. I liked the mud and I liked the music; I didn't mind *at all* the smelly portaloos and the cold nights in the tent that everyone else moaned about. But what I couldn't hack were the crowds. I felt overwhelmed and suffocated.'

'Really?' Perhaps we have more in common than I thought.

'Really. Don't get me wrong. I do like people, I like them very much. I just can't cope with them in huge quantities. I'm so aware of all those emotions, all those plans and dreams and longings. All those *agendas*. It's like this massive overload to my system. I know other people like the buzz of it, but I find it too much.'

My interest is piqued. 'So large numbers of people are intolerable. Large numbers of penguins, presumably, are a different matter?'

'Oh yes!' she enthuses. 'You can't ever have too many penguins. They've got a different sort of energy to humans. It's more fundamental and earthy. They don't agonize over things. They don't have issues.'

'I don't like humans en masse either,' I confide. 'But, unlike you, I also don't like them individually.'

'Oh?'

'Have I shocked you?' I ask.

'No,' she replies. 'I'm sad that's how you feel, though. Maybe you've just met the wrong people. Or maybe somebody did something to make you feel that way?'

I scowl at her. I have no wish to talk about the manifold tragedies of my life. I'm well aware that, to a person like Terry, I am living proof that money doesn't make you happy. Comfortable, certainly. Healthy and long-lived, yes, if you are lucky. Happy? Hardly.

We pause at the summit and I take in the view. The mountains are grouped in the distance, white-capped and majestic. Their south-facing slopes are draped in ragged shawls of snow. The half-moon lake glints the palest turquoise. The fine line of land beyond is just visible, dividing it from the sea. In the foreground the rocks flaunt their gaudy emblazon of multicoloured lichens. Every tuft and fibre stands out in the morning sunlight. The snow is patchy here; packed into every nook and cranny, gathered in frills against the stones, winding through the gullies.

'Is it these sunglasses or are there tinges of pink and amber in that snow?' I ask.

'No, it's not your sunglasses. It's a coloured glow made by microscopic algae. Pretty, isn't it?'

We approach the penguins and the sounds of chirps and caws slowly filter through the air. The thousands of miniature figures are outlined with fine threads of gold in the sun's rays.

'Makes you glad to be alive, doesn't it!' Terry exclaims, swinging her camera off her shoulder as we arrive at the bird colony.

The penguins exude joie de vivre. I understand what Terry means. In spite of their noise, their smell and their excessive swampy guano, I already like penguins much more than I like humans. Today the birds seem to be involved in some kind of tribal dance, moving their heads up and down, marching to and fro and gabbling to themselves and each other. They pick up pace and some of them go down on their tummies and slide along the ice. Their flippers are outstretched, their beaks pierce the rush of oncoming wind. They look insanely happy.

Terry rushes towards them, insanely happy too. 'It's such a beautiful morning, I'll just start with a few photos.' She clicks away. Every so often she turns the camera on me.

'Smile, Veronica!' she calls. But she needn't tell me. I'm smiling anyway.

Terry spots a banded penguin in the distance and passes me the binoculars. I gaze through them intently. The penguin doesn't seem remotely perturbed by the encumbrance on its flipper but it does look rather a tight fit.

'Doesn't it hamper their swimming?'

'Not at all. And it doesn't hurt them either, before you ask.'

'I'm relieved to hear it. I'd have my doubts about supporting you if I found out you were in any way causing them hurt.'

She nods. 'Quite right, too!'

We wander through the aisles of penguins. Terry records facts about the returning couples in her notebook while I appreciate the view. In between her scribbling she points out a few other local residents. They all look like gulls to me, but apparently one is an albatross, several are skuas and one is a storm petrel. Terry hands me the binoculars again and I examine the storm petrel as it wheels through the sky, trying to make out its markings.

Suddenly there's a loud squawk and a sharp jabbing sensation in my leg. I drop the binoculars in shock and let out a sharp cry. A penguin is at my side, flippers lifted in indignation, beak poised for further action. Before I can do anything else it gives my shin several more hard pecks then fastens itself, hanging on below my knee like a pair of pliers. My flesh feels the pain acutely through the waterproof trousers and long johns.

'Off, off, off, you little bugger!' Terry yells, grabbing it with both gloved hands. At once it lets go of my leg, only to attach itself to my second-favourite scarlet handbag. I screech and use all my might to shake the bag. The fierce little creature won't let go and is dragged around in circles, feet flying. Only after the leather has been ripped beyond all hope of repair does it relinquish its grip and stumble off drunkenly.

'Oh, I'm so sorry!' Terry gasps. 'Are you all right?'

'I'm . . . I'm fine. Just fine,' I lie. 'And it's not you but the penguin who should be saying sorry.'

'I know it can be pretty painful when a penguin goes for you, even through lots of layers of thick clothing.'

She stoops and starts rubbing my leg gently.

'Don't!' I bark at her.

'I thought it might ease it. We can put some ointment on back at the base, but obviously I can't examine the bruise or expose it out here. How bad is it? Do you want to go back?'

'I'm fine.'

She wrinkles her brow. 'You don't look fine.'

'I just need a painkiller. Can you help me get this thing open?' I ask, shoving my ruined handbag at her.

'Oh, what a shame. Your, um . . . your beautiful bag!'

She slips off her gloves for a second to unclip the fastening and extract my tablets. She offers me a sip from her water bottle to wash one down.

I am furious with the penguin, who has hotfooted it back to the colony and merged with his fellows.

'Why did he do that?' I demand. 'Why?'

'It's . . . well, feistiness. Call it natural high spirits. It's the two- and three-year-olds you need to watch out for. They're too young to breed and haven't got much to do apart from flirting, fighting and trying to prove themselves. He's just an arrogant teenager.'

'I see.'

I still feel injured, both literally and metaphorically.

Terry attempts to reassure me. 'I don't know why it picked on you. It could just as easily have been me.'

'Well, it's quite normal,' I tell her. 'Everyone takes an immediate dislike to me.'

She jolts her head round to look at me. 'Oh, don't say that, Veronica!'

'Why not? It's true.'

She is too honest a girl to deny it.

18

Veronica

Locket Island

Terry insists on escorting me back to the field centre, apologizing non-stop all the way. I maintain a dignified silence.

She helps me off with my mukluks and leads me to the chair with the cushion. It has become my chair.

'I'll get you a cuppa for the shock, then we'll have a proper look at that leg.'

'As you wish.'

I am presented with a steaming mug of the unpleasant tar-flavoured liquid they call tea.

'You've left the kitchen door open,' I tell her.

'Does it matter?'

'I'd be grateful if you would close it.'

She shrugs her shoulders, goes and closes the door then comes back. I allow her to peel off my waterproof trousers and long johns enough to expose the wound. It is purplish and unsightly but not unduly serious. She dabs it with TCP from her first aid kit and puts on a plaster. Already the pain has abated.

'Well, I think you'll live.'

'No doubt I will.'

'Perhaps you need to rest?'

'Perhaps I do.'

She tries to help me to my room. I shake her off. I do not require help. She lingers, full of concern.

'Please go out and do your important penguin work, Terry. I shall be fine here. I need to be by myself.'

'Are you sure you'll be OK?'

'Absolutely.'

She looks undecided. 'To be honest, I do need to do some work. I've fallen behind a bit . . .'

'Then go.'

'I'll be back in a couple of hours. Please relax. Make yourself at home. And help yourself to anything you want.'

I do hate it when people fuss.

It is a relief when she leaves. I stretch out on the knobbly bed. I am still seething inside. This whole Antarctic escapade is a disaster. It has become abundantly clear that the scientists don't want me here and, to my bitter disappointment, neither do the penguins. Ungrateful birds! I *had* thought – nay, I had been *sure* – there was a kind of destiny for me in this ends-of-the-earth place . . . but it is of no matter.

My anger slowly dissolves, leaving a sense of deflation. My bubble of penguin-induced beneficence has burst. I am in need of fortitude.

I pull myself up again and take another painkiller. It is an apt reminder of all the other bitter pills that I've had to swallow. My past threatens for a second to overrun my thoughts. I wrestle it out and focus on the present problem.

I have gone off penguins.

It is a woman's prerogative to change her mind.

Doubtless there are plenty of other noble causes worthy of my legacy.

'Hi, Veronica. So sorry, did I wake you up?'

I am disorientated for a moment then realize it's Terry popping her head round the door.

'No. I merely settled into a recumbent position since there's a dearth of comfortable chairs around here.' I bring myself slowly into a more vertical posture.

The anxious demeanour is still disfiguring her mouth and forehead. 'How are you doing? How's your leg?'

'It is completely recovered, thank you.'

'Thank goodness. What a thing to happen! I'm so sorry about that rude penguin.'

'For goodness' sake, stop apologizing!'

'Can I get you anything?'

'No.'

'Well, in that case, I'm going to spend a little time in the computer room. I need to input today's data on to the system.'

She vanishes.

'Terry!' I call.

'Yes?'

'Door.'

'Door. OK. Sorry.' She closes it and I am left in peace.

She knocks on it only a few minutes later.

'Veronica, an email has arrived for you. I've printed it out. I thought you'd like it straight away. Here.'

She puts a sheet of paper into my hands before retreating once more.

I embark on a hunt for my reading glasses. After going through both my ruined scarlet bag and my rather less good but at least unvandalized fuchsia-and-gold handbag without success, I delve into my suitcase. I discover the tin of fragrant Darjeeling in its depths but no reading glasses. The tea is some consolation, however. I wander into the kitchen and boil the kettle. By good fortune a 'Brown Betty' teapot is lurking at the back of one of the cupboards along with a tea strainer. I brew myself a pot. In spite of the tragic lack of teacups and consequent necessity of using a chipped mug, the taste of real tea is a welcome boost. On my first sip, I feel the McCreedy determination flowing back into my veins.

As I put the mug down again I spot my reading glasses on a shelf where I must have left them earlier whilst examining the books. I settle myself in my chair to read the printout of Eileen's email.

Dear Mrs McCreedy

I had two emails, one from Mr Dietrich and one from the blog bloke Terry saying you'd arrived all right so I've stopped worrying. I hope you are well and not too cold. I hope your corns are not giving you too much trouble. It must be nice to see the penguins. I don't know much about them but they are my nephew Kevin's favourite bird. He has a cuddly penguin, navy and white that he is very fond of.

Here the weather is quite dull. I am finding it harder to fill in the time with you not being here, but Doug (my husband, in case you don't remember) says I should get out more. I think he might only be saying that because he doesn't want me around the house. He says I hum too much.

Anyway, it would be good to have some news every so often and to know that you are happy. Perhaps the nice scientists can get another email to me if you tell them what to write.

The biscuits are very good.

All the best,
Eileen

Well, I shall be giving Eileen plenty to do again shortly.

I am draining my second mug of Darjeeling when Mike and Dietrich enter together.

'Ah, Mrs McCreedy. How was today's outing?' Dietrich asks politely.

'Not the greatest success,' I inform him, looking over my glasses. 'I was attacked.'

'Attacked?'

'Yes, indeed. A penguin decided to vent his fury on both my shin and my second-best handbag in a very uncalled-for and aggressive manner.'

'Oh. That's not good.'

'No.'

'Did Terry . . . ?'

'Terry has sorted me out. TCP and a plaster.'

Dietrich has so many whiskers it is hard to decipher the facial expression underneath them. But his 'Good' sounds genuine. Mike, on the other hand, has pasted a falsely sympathetic expression to his face. It does little to conceal the underlying sneer.

'Penguins are wild creatures, Veronica. We have to remember that.'

'We certainly do,' I reply with feeling.

'You don't look very happy,' he observes, lowering himself into one of the plastic chairs. 'It's not too late if you want to go back home, you know.'

'In fact, I was going to ask you about that.'

He looks at Dietrich then back at me, the sneer becoming more apparent and blending with pleasure at the prospect of my departure. 'There's no ship for another three weeks. But what we can do is to radio the Crisis Management Team and see if they'll help. They're normally reluctant to send a helicopter out unless it's an emergency, but maybe, if you're prepared to stump up for the costs involved . . . ?'

'Money is not an issue,' I assure him.

'In that case, it should be possible, Mrs McCreedy,' says Dietrich, his tone modulated to sound neutral. 'I can look into it straight away.' He digs in his pockets and pulls out a small black contraption that I presume is a radio of some kind.

They are in an indecent hurry to be rid of me. Mike smiles wolfishly. 'Locket Island isn't such a cushy number after all, is it, Veronica?'

I take exception to the way his voice curls as he says my name. I do not deign to reply.

He can't resist pushing his point further. 'We did all try to warn you. But – with respect – you would insist on having it all your own way, wouldn't you?'

Respect, my elbow! He knows no more about respect than an aardvark knows about St Paul's letter to the Ephesians. This insufferable man is trying to belittle me, to pooh-pooh my decisions. How dare he!

'I think you'll have to admit it, Veronica: this is no tourist destination.'

'And I am no tourist!' I spit the words out at him.

'Maybe not. Not entirely. But you're not a scientist either. You haven't had any training, and only thoroughly trained scientists are equipped for any long-term stay on Locket Island.'

I am conscious of my locket as he says these words, its smooth silver hanging against my chest under my thermal vest. I'm aware of its contents, quietly whispering messages into my heart.

'Well, I wish you a pleasant journey back home,' Mike concludes with blatant insincerity.

Dietrich, who has been silent during this display of rudeness, starts pressing buttons on his radio. I stop him with a sharp gesture. 'Who said I was going home?'

Mike throws his hands in the air. 'You said that was what you wanted!'

I view him coolly. 'No, not at all. That is *not* what I want. You have completely misunderstood. I was merely reviewing my options. I can assure you my mind is made up.' If it wasn't before, it certainly is now. 'I am staying here for the next three weeks, whether you like it or not.'

And I shall persist in helping those wretched penguins, whether they appreciate it or not.

It is the cantankerous Mike's turn to cook supper. His efforts are lamentable. Sausages the texture of wire wool, sprouts that have failed abysmally in any attempt to be green, mashed potato from a packet and gravy that resembles mud in both colour and taste.

I push the sprouts about my plate. The atmosphere is somewhat strained.

Terry, who was not a party to the conversation earlier, seems to think I am being sniffy about the food.

'Sorry we can't provide any fresh vegetables, Veronica.'

'Don't keep apologizing for what isn't your fault.'

Mike seems to think I am implying the poor quality fare is *his* fault.

'Considering the chronic state of our food stock, a cranky cooker and a shortage of time, I don't think I did so badly.'

I frown at him. If there's one thing I cannot abide it is people who are always moaning.

Everyone looks as though they are trying to think of something to say to fill the silence that follows.

'You consider this to be hardship,' I comment. 'Your generation is used to easy access to any food, food from all over the world. But I remember a time when bread was hard to come by, most people had to dig up their back gardens to plant potatoes, and anything resembling a sausage was a luxury. This meal would have been considered a banquet.'

Dietrich winks at Mike. 'There you are, Mike. A compliment!'

'Yeah, right,' he replies.

The silence resumes. My hearing aid magnifies the sounds of discontented chomping.

'I believe I shall go out *on my own* to look at the penguins tomorrow,' I announce. 'I have no wish to get in the way of your scientific studies, and I can remember the way to the colony.'

Mike splutters. 'Not a good idea.'

'Why not? You don't need to wrap me up in cotton wool. I am quite capable of looking after myself,' I reply tartly.

'If you stay here, you play by our rules,' he insists, glaring at me. I glare back. I can out-glare any young upstart.

Terry turns towards me with a conciliatory air. 'We'd feel better if you went with one of us, Veronica. The weather seems mild at the moment but it can turn quickly and things can get nasty. And the three of us have experience of what to do in an emergency. I'm very happy to accompany you. If that's OK?'

I am galled by her suggestion. My chief desire is solitude. However, it appears that compromise is called for yet again. 'Very well,' I say.

'I'll tell you some more about the penguins as we go. And perhaps we can get some footage for the blog.'

'The blog. Always the bloody blog,' mutters Mike.

Terry pretends to throw her sausage at him. That makes him smile at least.

Terry's Penguin Blog

12 December 2012

Take a look at this lady. I think you'll be impressed. She's our new arrival, she loves penguins so much she came all the way from Scotland to Antarctica, and she's – wait for it – eighty-six years of age! Now that's commitment for you.

Veronica's her name. She'll be staying with us at the Locket Island field centre for the next three weeks and we can't wait to see how she settles in.

As you see from the photo, she's already out there, enjoying the view of five thousand Adélie penguins. She'll be getting to know all their little ways . . . and ours.

She has already digested plenty of knowledge about the Adélies. She knows, for example, that their favourite dish is the tiny shrimp-like crustacean known as krill, and that it's the Antarctic springtime at the moment, which means massive changes lie ahead for the birds. Many of them are sitting on their nests now, ready for new life to begin.

Veronica commented that the stony nests didn't look very comfortable or very warm. She has a point, but we must remember the penguins themselves are lined with layer upon layer of fat. They also wear coats made of super-specialized insulating feathers. Cold just isn't an issue for them the way it is for us.

Talking of which, in case anyone is worried, Veronica is fighting fit and very well equipped for her stay here. Her quantities of weather-appropriate clothing are only matched by her quantities of determination. She is going to need both.

19

Patrick

Bolton

I GOT AN EMAIL from those Antarctica penguin people today. Some guy called Terry saying he thought I'd like to know Veronica is all right and sending me a link to a blog. After breakfast I logged on to have a butcher's. Straight up there was a photo of Granny V, and I have to say I was fricking flabbergasted. In the photo she was smiling, actually smiling! She looked *ecstatic*, like she'd seen a throng of angels or something. But it wasn't angels. It was penguins. A great mass of them all around her, a kind of ocean of stumpy black-and-white figures. And her, all togged up with a fluffy-hooded scarlet jacket, with her big shiny handbag as well, all blazing reds against the snow. Blazing red lipstick to match. So you couldn't miss that smile.

Clearly, Granny V likes penguins. Shedloads.

I grabbed a coffee and read the blog. 'Take a look at this lady,' it said. That Terry guy sounded impressed. He almost made Granny

V out to be a miracle-worker. I guess she must be on her best behaviour.

It's funny. I keep pushing Granny V to the back of my mind but she keeps resurfacing. That day she came to the flat I was nowhere near ready for all this sudden long-lost-relation stuff. I blame Lynette. The shock of her being wound round brickie boy was the only thing in my head that day. There wasn't space for anything else (timing, man; it's fricking vital). But when I saw Granny at the airport I wasn't thinking of me-me-me quite so much and I got this weird feeling, as if the first time we'd met I'd been missing something. Like her harshness was a kind of coat she wrapped tightly round herself so nobody could see what was underneath. Even Eileen.

I've missed a hell of a lot of Granny V's life. Will I ever catch up with her properly? Is it too late? What is she like, I mean *really* like, underneath all the war-paint and stuffiness? What on earth possessed her to go all the way to Antarctica, to be with penguins?

I wonder more and more about my dad, too. Joe Fuller. He's her son. He's our missing link, the middle generation, the thing that cements us (like it or not) together – yet neither of us ever got the chance to know him at all. I've always had him down as a lump of slime because of what happened to Mum. But maybe he didn't know what he was doing, maybe he had issues. You don't know anything about other people, do you? Even the ones you know well, you don't really have much of an idea about what makes them tick.

Now, suddenly, I wish I knew more. Any info would be good. What he ate for breakfast, what he watched on telly, if he was into trivia like me, or mechanical stuff like me. He was a mountaineer, so I guess he must have been an adventurous kind of guy. Maybe he got that from Granny.

That family who adopted him, surely they must be able to fill in some details? The parents are dead and there weren't any brothers or sisters, but the cousin's still alive, as far as I know, in Chicago.

Maybe I can get in touch with her. Or maybe I can track down my dad's mates. Assuming he had any.

I wander over to the window and stare out at the drainpipes.

Granny must be keen to know about her son too, mustn't she? She took the trouble to locate me, after all. But she's not internet-savvy. I could help her. When she gets back from Antarctica we should meet up and talk about it. I'm hungry for everything she knows, right from the moment she gave him up for adoption.

Why the hell did she go and do a thing like that? I didn't get anywhere near to the bottom of it. Man, I wasn't even halfway down, I was too busy pratting about on the surface. When Granny V comes home, things'll be different. I'm going to get digging.

The phone is ringing when I get back from my jog. Panting like a dog from the last lap up the stairs, I pick up the receiver.

'Still nasty weather, isn't it!' a voice says, as if we're continuing a conversation we started earlier.

'Um, who is it?'

'Eileen Thompson. You know. We met at the airport.'

'Hi there, Eileen. What can I do you for?'

'Well, you see, I've just had an email from them. Them in Antarctica. The Terry one, actually.'

'Oh yeah. Me too. Did you see the blog?'

'Yes, yes, I did. Mrs McCreedy looked very nice, didn't she? Very smart, I thought.'

'Yes, very, er . . . colourful.' I pace the room, flapping cool air up my T-shirt with one hand, holding the phone to my ear with the other.

'But did Terry tell you the other thing?' she says.

'Which other thing, Eileen?'

'The other thing about Mrs McCreedy. She's been bitten by a penguin!'

'What?'

'Your grandmother. Bitten. By a penguin.'

'Right-oh.' I'm not sure if I'm meant to be worried. I have to admit I'm not that familiar with penguin bites. 'It's not fatal, I presume?'

'No, no, not at all! The Terry scientist says Mrs McCreedy was rather put off by it, though, and nearly decided to come back home. But she's OK about it now. And I had a brief note from Mrs McCreedy herself as well, which was emailed to me via Terry.'

'This Terry bloke seems to be acting as Granny's skivvy, doesn't he?'

'Yes, I suppose he does. But I'm very relieved somebody's looking after her. She can be a bit . . . well, you know. She's not as young as she used to be.'

I smile. Eileen's a gem.

There's a minuscule pause down the line then an abrupt question: 'Have you opened the box?'

Am I imagining it or is she hoping I have?

'The box? The one you sent? You told me Granny had said not to – so, no.'

'Ah, yes. Just wondered. You see, I do worry about her, Patrick. She's got used to having nobody around her, except me, and she doesn't, you know, *let me in* much. I mean, she lets me into her house, of course – she has to do that – but she never lets me into what she's thinking or feeling. Then there's this thing I read in Doug's *Daily Mail* yesterday . . .'

She pauses for dramatic effect. I think I'm meant to be impressed by her current affairs savviness. She definitely assumes I'm on total tenterhooks about what she's going to tell me next.

'Go on,' I say.

'It was all about old people and loneliness.' Her voice becomes a confidential whisper. 'It said what a bad thing that is, the not communicating. Wait a moment. I've got it here.' Another pause and the sound of pages turning. 'Yes, here it is! "*A new study . . .*

blah blah blah . . . *confirms the heavy toll that loneliness can take on your health* . . . blah blah . . . *Not sharing thoughts and opinions with others increases your risk of dementia by 40 per cent.*" Forty per cent!'

'Dementia?' I'm amazed. 'Granny V seemed spot on both times I met her.'

'Oh yes. She is, she is! I didn't mean to alarm you. Please, that's not what I meant *at all*. But sometimes there's a . . . a little blip. A tiny memory blip. And I wonder if she's needing more in the way of family and friends, to stop her getting worse. That's why I'm so very glad she's got you, now, Patrick. And the nice Terry man. And penguins.'

20

Veronica

Locket Island

'I THINK ALL THIS fresh air is doing you good, Mrs McCreedy,' says Dietrich (who is the only one who doesn't call me Veronica. He has evidently been well brought up). 'You're looking well.'

'Thank you, Dietrich.'

'Don't you think she looks younger, Mike?'

The unaccountably disagreeable Mike makes a low noise in his throat which is open to interpretation. I choose to take it as confirmation that I am indeed looking younger. Not that it signifies in any way whatsoever.

I am surprised about Dietrich. Terry's support is natural, desperate as she is to improve this blog of hers. The support of Dietrich, however, is most unexpected, bearing in mind he is both a foreigner and a person of the male gender. I have the distinct impression he has conducted a consultation with himself and decided to give me the benefit of the doubt.

As for Mike . . . well, we tolerate each other. Had it been up to him, I would have been ejected from their company by now – although quite how they would have done it, I don't know. Possibly they would have simply turned me out into the cold. It wouldn't be the first time in my life that has happened.

Mike persists in leaving doors open constantly. I know he does it just to rile me.

Due to immense forethought and consideration, I started getting muffled up and mukluked a while back. I am therefore already poised at the door by the time Terry has got her parka on. She grabs her cameras, notebooks and a handful of penguin tags. She is wearing her unsightly woollen hat with the dangly tassels. Her blond hair pokes out from beneath it, limp and untidy.

'You're obviously not bothered about fashion and style,' I comment.

She bursts into a ripple of laughter. 'Thank you, Veronica! You're not impressed with my image, then?'

Politeness demands that I pussyfoot around the truth. 'Well, I absolutely understand that Antarctica demands certain compromises when it comes to style. So I'll admit the possibility that back in England you may be a glamour puss . . . but I somehow doubt it.'

She giggles. 'You're right to doubt it,' she admits, then adds, 'but who needs designer handbags when you can have a guano swamp and five thousand penguins?'

I glance down at my own designer handbag, which (due to the demise of my scarlet one) is my third favourite, the fuchsia one with gold trimmings. I am about to answer sharply then realize she didn't mean it as a jibe at all; the reference was entirely random.

We set off together. The snow squeaks and crunches beneath our feet.

The girl beside me is so different to how I was at that age. She takes herself for granted, blithely heedless of the years of possibilities stacked up ahead of her. It doesn't occur to her that they can all be wrecked by a single step in the wrong direction. I hope she does more with her life than I did. But she is already doing more, isn't she? For the first time I start wondering about Terry. Her presence is quiet but there's a definite sense of purpose about her.

'What's your background, Terry?' I ask out of genuine interest. 'How did you come to be out here?'

'Oh, there's nothing special.' She is more focused on the landscape, the chance of sighting a seal or a rare bird, than she is on the question. 'I've always been a nature buff.'

'Tell me more.'

'Well, I was totally fascinated by birds as a child. Wildlife in general but birds in particular. I spent my teenage years sitting on rocks, wading up rivers or standing in the middle of marshes staring through my binoculars. My friends must have thought I was such a bore.'

At least she'd had friends. Unlike me, she has probably always been easy to like.

'After school, I took a degree in Natural Sciences,' she continues, 'then a masters in wildlife conservation. I worked at a local nature reserve for a while and in my free time did a lot of volunteering for conservation charities. I spent a few summers tracking seabirds in the Outer Hebrides.'

If you are interested in something these days you simply go ahead and do it. Such opportunities didn't exist when I was young. Not for a woman, anyway. Envy, sour and cloying, rises in my throat. It is difficult to swallow life's multiple unfairnesses.

'I never expected to get this job when I applied,' she continues cheerfully as she stomps up the slope. She's warming to her theme now. 'But every day I'm just so grateful that I did! I love being here, love the challenges and the hardship and all the funny little things that happen. I love the team. We're not perfect but we're strangely close. And, of course, it's a dream come true to work amongst penguins.'

We've reached the top. Her pace slows and with a sweep of her arm she encompasses the panorama. A gauzy lavender-coloured mist hangs low over the mountains. Ice crystals glint from the dark recesses in the rocks. The population of penguins is spread out below us, a multi-piece jigsaw detailed in black and white.

'This place,' she goes on, 'it gets right into your heart and soul. It changes everything. The way you see the world and yourself, the way you think about it all.' She looks at me suddenly. 'You find that, too, don't you, Veronica?'

I don't know how to answer. I suspect she may have a point. Neither I nor my handbag have been attacked since my first unfortunate experience. Indeed, my initial delight at seeing the penguins has returned. It is with great pleasure that I look forward to my daily encounters with these small, flippered life-forces.

Yesterday I witnessed a wondrous thing for the first time: an Adélie chick in the process of hatching. First the egg wobbled and there was a faint tapping from inside. Then the tip of a tiny beak appeared. A sticky little creature followed, uncrumpling itself, lifting clumsy feet to clamber out of the shell. It was grey, fuzzy and somewhat dazed-looking. I wasn't the only witness, of course. The penguin mother was waggling her head about to view her new baby from every angle. They nuzzled each other affectionately. Then the little one craned his neck to look round his mum at the scene beyond her. He was all agog at finding himself in a universe made up of shining stones and snow.

I am glad I didn't let the obnoxious Mike push me into leaving Locket Island. This definitely beats writing out shopping lists for Eileen or giving Mr Perkins instructions about the perennials. I am proud to note, as well, that the physical limitations of old age have not turned out to be too great a burden. I have risen admirably to the challenges of Antarctica.

Terry knuckles down to work. She dives in to grab the penguins one by one and suspends them in a weighing bag. Some of the birds struggle and peck but she is very deft at avoiding beaks and claws. She records statistics in her notebook. Every so often she pulls out her camera and takes a snapshot. I enquire whether the photos are part of her research.

'It's partly that, partly for my own pleasure and partly for the blog,' she answers.

'You're very keen on this blog of yours, aren't you?' I comment drily.

She nods. 'Social media is the best way – virtually the only way – to influence minds, to make people care.'

I wonder if this can really be the case. I am wholly ignorant about the machinations of social media, but I have observed that the media in general wields tremendous power. When Robert Saddlebow presented a programme about the ozone layer a few years back everyone suddenly noticed what had been staring them in the face for decades: that humans are destroying the planet not only for wildlife but also for ourselves. A few people even started to act upon it.

If this social media gimmick can make people care, then it may not be such a bad thing after all.

I view the penguins fondly. Terry takes a snap of me.

'You look like a queen, with all her subjects gathered around her.'

I rather like this idea.

As I am musing, Terry starts up again. 'Don't get me wrong, Veronica, but I'll confess I'm surprised that you should want to leave your millions to a project on Adélie penguins. I'm very glad, and oh so grateful, but I can't help wondering . . . You have a grandson, don't you?'

'I do,' I reply. My enthusiasm plummets at the thought.

'Patrick, is it?'

'Yes.' I am uncomfortable with her probing. I did not come here to be probed.

Terry releases a penguin and it scoots off, first upright and then plopping on to its tummy to slide across the snow. 'So, if you don't mind my asking . . . is there a problem? I mean, the normal thing is to leave your money to members of your family. Sorry if I've overstepped the mark, but I can't help being a bit curious.'

I sigh. The fact of Patrick's existence is like a persistent fly bashing itself against the window of my consciousness. The more I try to forget it, the louder it seems to be. I have no wish to discuss it and my normal modus operandi would be to change the subject. But there's something about the presence of penguins that makes me more relaxed, more unguarded than usual. If Terry needs an explanation, then I can give her one. 'Patrick and I barely know each other. I don't think of him as family. We only met for the first time a few months ago.'

'Oh?'

'Yes. And it was all most unpleasant. Although I had travelled some way and gone to considerable trouble to make his acquaint-ance, he was far from friendly. He has made a few paltry attempts to make up for it since, but I am not impressed with his pecuniar-ily induced advances. Besides, he is a lost cause.' I then deliver what is commonly called the punchline. 'Patrick is on drugs.'

Terry is shocked, just as she should be. 'Oh, I'm sorry to hear that, Veronica. Have you any idea why?'

Why? I haven't given any consideration to this question. I would have thought the answer was self-evident. 'Just your common or garden degeneracy, I believe.'

Terry's face displays a species of half-smile but her eyes are pensive behind those unattractive glasses she wears.

'If you barely know him, perhaps he's been through hard times he hasn't told you about. Maybe that's why he turned to drugs?'

This hadn't occurred to me. I am not accustomed to delving into what causes other people to behave badly. If truth be told, I am not accustomed to considering other people very much at all. In my experience, it usually leads to inconvenience and aggra-vation. However, Terry has forced a snippet of memory to the forefront of my mind: a few words that Patrick mumbled about his mother. He didn't go into any specifics. And I was too angry at the state of his abode, his personal hygiene and his rude manner to make any further enquiries. Now I begin to wonder if Patrick is shaped by some tragedy that happened in his past. Perhaps, like me, he does not choose to share his history with the general public.

'So, is he on *hard* drugs?' Terry asks.

'I have no idea how hard or soft they are. It was something he smoked. It smelled disgusting,' I answer.

'Probably just cannabis,' she says. 'It could be a lot worse.'

'Hardly!' I snort.

I turn my attention back to the penguins, but Terry has stopped weighing them and I can feel her eyes on my face. Then she says in a measured tone, 'Cannabis is legal in a lot of places these days. It's had bad press, but it does have quite a few medicinal uses. As a scientist I can assure you it has benefits as well as downsides.'

'Really?' I look at her sceptically.

'Oh yes! It can be used to treat multiple sclerosis and to ease the awful side effects from chemotherapy, for example. In some cases, it's actually less harmful than painkillers.'

This is not at all what I was expecting. I grip my handbag tightly. I am aware of the packets of paracetamol and aspirin that are tucked into the inside pocket. Surely these are morally far superior to cannabis? But Terry doesn't seem to grasp my horror of drugs.

'I'm sure Patrick has his reasons for smoking dope,' she insists.

'No doubt,' I say in a voice that makes it clear the subject is closed. But her words have given me cause for reflection.

21

Patrick

Bolton

'Eileen, why are you ringing me?'

'I've had another email from the Terry one.'

'Right-oh.'

'With a letter from Mrs McCreedy copied in.'

'Great. Any news?'

'She's doing well. The penguins are having children.'

I smile. I sense there's more. 'Anything else?'

'Mrs McCreedy mentioned in her letter that she'd sent an email to you, too, via Terry. Have you got it?'

This is interesting. An actual written communication from Granny V? I'm thinking it must be an explanation about the box.

'I haven't checked my emails today,' I tell Eileen.

She clicks her tongue impatiently. 'I think it's something important. I think it might be . . . you know. You'd better check right away. I'll wait.'

She's not going to put the phone down until I've done it. What is it with me and pushy women? I wearily get out the laptop and bring up my emails. Yup, there's one from penggroup4Ant. I skim-read.

'Yes,' I tell Eileen. 'It's very short. The message from Granny is even shorter. Not really a message. Just numbers. I guess it must be the combination code for the box.'

'Oh, I've been wondering and wondering what could be inside that box. You see, it was after she opened the box that she started to get so . . . so very *peculiar*, you know.'

'Ah, was it?'

'Yes. All this business with agencies and then going to visit you and then suddenly rushing off to Antarctica to save the penguins. Are you going to open it now?'

Nosy or what!

'Yup, will do,' I tell her and ring off.

She'll probably ring back later to talk about the weather and *Oh, by the way, what did you find inside the box?* Still, her heart's in the right place.

I crouch on the floor and drag the box out from under the bed. Eagerly I twist the numbers into place. The padlock clicks open.

There's nothing but a couple of scruffy old black books inside. No title or anything written on the front of them. I open up the book at the top. Every page is tightly covered in handwriting, very neat. An old-fashioned slanted script in blue ink, similar to Granny's writing but softer, fuller. It seems to be the journal of a teenage girl from way back. The entries start in 1940. Looks like I'm in for a bit of time travel.

I sit on the bed and start to read a few random entries.

Saturday, 20 July 1940
Shepherd's Bush

Am I unusual? I think I must be. I went out today for a wander and everyone seemed to be staring at me – again!

131

I've noticed it more and more ever since I 'put on another growth spurt' as Mum calls it. All the boys have eyes on stalks, and the girls goggle at my features as if they want to steal them.

I sneaked a glance at my reflection in the greengrocer's window as I passed. There I was, floating above a heap of apples, my chestnut curls streaming out from under my wide-brimmed hat. I looked slim in the mulberry taffeta dress that Mum said was impractical (she made it for me anyway after a lot of begging). I do love the way the dress hugs my waist then washes around my legs in waves. Not like the neat, straight-down skirts that all the other girls are wearing. The only thing spoiling the image today was the box on a string I have to carry everywhere. It's dreadfully plain. I hope I never have to wear the hideous black gas mask inside. I transferred the box to the other side so I couldn't see it in the reflection. It's amazing how happy you can be if only you focus on the right things.

Everything was looking idyllic, all honey colours in the sunshine. A wooden hoop rolled past me in the street, chased by a gang of children. Women stood in queues, gossiping about the meat rations, comparing what was in their baskets. You wouldn't know that half of them spent the night cowering in shelters, the wailing of air-raid sirens in their ears.

I walked home through Ravenscourt Park and found Tufty tied to the railings. He thumped his tail up and down the moment he saw me. I don't know who owns him but they leave him there for hours most mornings – a vile thing to do to a sweet little Scottie dog. I desperately want to take him home, but Mum and Dad say no. His cruel owner had left him in the hot sun today, so I untied him, took him a little walk, let him cool off in the lake, then tied him back to the railings a bit further on, in the shade of a nice, fat cedar tree. He was bouncing around with joy.

What will his owner make of it when they find him a few feet on from where they left him, and soaking wet? Hahaha!

There's talk of stripping the railings out because the iron is needed for war weapons. I wonder where Tufty will get left if that happens.

A crowd was gathered round the bandstand. The band was honking out a familiar tune and lots of the audience sang along, bobbing their heads. A few couples were even dancing on the grass. The music kept blasting inside my skull all the way home. I can still hear it now.

Later

Gosh, when I wrote earlier I'd no idea that everything was about to change. As soon as I'd finished the diary entry I ran downstairs, singing at the top of my voice: 'Doing the Lambeth Walk – Oi!'

Mum called out: 'V McC! Pipe down, won't you? You gave me the shock of my life!'

I jiggled and pranced into the kitchen, still singing, and came to a sharp standstill on the 'Oi' right in front of Dad. He was on the spindle-back chair smoking his Woodbine, today's paper on his lap. He grinned.

'Dad, Mum, will you teach me the Lambeth Walk?'

They go to dances nearly every week. They know all the steps.

'Not now, Veronica,' Mum answered from her place by the stove. 'My hands are all floury.'

'Dad, will you show me?'

But Dad's smile had vanished. 'Well, Very . . .' (He's the only person in the world who calls me Very. I love to hear that word spoken in his warm Scottish accent. Unfortunately, I haven't inherited it. My voice is posh English, like Mum's.) 'I'll show you the Lambeth

Walk if you'll do something for us,' he said. 'Don't pout, now!'

Maybe I was pouting, just a little. 'It's going to be something horrid, isn't it, Dad? It always is these days.'

Mum and Dad have changed recently. A heaviness often settles over them and I hear them earnestly discussing things late into the night. But then on other days they're full of frantic brightness, as if they're helping themselves to as much fun as they possibly can, before it runs out.

Dad put his cigarette in the ashtray and held both my hands in his. 'You're growing up too fast, Very,' he said. 'Much too fast.'

Dad has the kindest face you could ever imagine but it was all criss-crossed with worry lines. Mum abandoned the stove, walked over and sat down next to him, wiping her hands on her apron.

I stuck my chin out.

'Well?'

'Well, you know how you always wanted to go and live in the country?'

'Are we moving house?' I asked.

'No. We can't do that. At least, not as a family.'

'We both have work to do here,' said Mum. 'It's more important than ever.' Mum has recently trained to drive ambulances. She enjoys it much more than the dull domestic work she's always been tied to before. We can all see that. Dad's proud of his job, too. He fought in the last war but is too old to fight in this one. He's become an ARP warden instead.

I didn't like Mum and Dad being so serious. I was in the mood for dancing.

'There's an opportunity for you to go up to Derbyshire,' Dad said.

'What? Why?' Plenty of children are being evacuated from London. It's happened to Dinah and Tim down the road. But it wasn't going to happen to me. Or so I thought.

'You know why, Very. It's so much safer there. And we've had an offer from your Great Aunt Margaret. You can stay with her.'

'Oh no! Not Aunt Margaret! Anywhere but there!'

Mum sighed. 'I know it's not ideal. I'm sorry, sweetheart, but otherwise you'd be staying with a complete stranger. And Aunt Margaret has been so, so kind to offer.'

'I hate this silly war!' I cried.

'We all do,' Dad said. 'But it won't be as bad as you think. You'll only be with Aunt Margaret at weekends. The rest of the time you'll be in your new school, St Catherine's. Before the war, the school was in York, but all the pupils have been moved to Dunwick Hall. It's an enormous country house with towers, almost like a castle.'

I've seen buildings like that at the pictures. Mansions with mob-capped maids shaking sheets out of the windows and sometimes a handsome young man on horseback galloping through the grounds. It may be all right. I'm not happy about leaving Mum and Dad, but they're both ridiculously over-protective. They still treat me as if I'm a child. I'm fourteen, for goodness' sake!

I looked from one face to another. They hadn't made the decision lightly.

'All right, then. I'll go.'

I could almost see how they started breathing again.

'Now, Dad, you have to teach me the Lambeth Walk. You promised.'

He stood up and took a slow, exaggerated bow. 'May I have the honour of this dance, young lady?'

'Absolutely!' I crowed. Together we paced out the steps across the kitchen floor.

Mum took off her apron and hung it on the hook behind the door. Then she slipped upstairs.

Later this evening she came back down, as I was writing this at the kitchen table. Her eyes were all red and swollen.

Friday, 16 August 1940
On the train to Derby

I'm not looking forward to seeing Aunt M again, but at least I have the locket. Dad gave it to me and I love it. It used to belong to his mother. It has a V etched into the silver amongst a design of curling leaves, a V that stood for Violet. Now it stands for Veronica. I treasure it above everything in my luggage – above my mulberry dress, above my favourite book on animals and even above my precious, precious ration of chocolate.

As yet there's no handsome prince so I insisted Mum and Dad each gave me a strand of hair to put in the locket. I can tell my new school friends that they're locks of hair from two young Romeos and I haven't decided which one to favour with my love.

I thought of getting a bit of fur off Tufty to put in the locket too, but there wasn't time with all the rush this morning. I hope he'll manage all right without me.

'Don't worry, Very,' Dad said as he and Mum kissed me goodbye. 'Everything will work out fine. Be strong!'

I certainly will be strong. I'm always strong. But I do feel a little nervous.

What will my new life be like? Will I meet boys?

Aunt Margaret is a hazy figure in my memory. From what I recall, she isn't the type of person to let anyone of the male gender come within a mile. This is unfortunate, but I expect I can find a way around it.

Friday, 16 August again, in the evening
Aunt Margaret's house in Aggleworth

As I stepped off the train at Derby station I was greeted by a meagre figure in a brown coat and headscarf. Aunt Margaret reminds me of a hawk, what with her beak-like nose and heavily hooded eyes. She leaned in to kiss me but didn't quite make the full distance, instead kissing the air an inch from my cheek.

'You've changed, child,' she commented in a thin voice.

'Good,' I returned. Already there was hostility between us.

The conversation on the bus to Aggleworth was dreadfully strained. Aunt M scrutinized my face while she asked after Mum and Dad. She tutted more than once at the answers. Her shopping basket sat on her lap throughout the journey. She clutched its handle with wrinkled, white-knuckled hands.

The village of Aggleworth is reasonably pretty but too grey. Most of the houses are squat and stone-built, roofed with slates. I've only met Aunt Margaret at a handful of family weddings and funerals and I'd never been to her house before. It turns out to be spacious but very drab. The only decorations on the walls are embroidered hangings of Biblical quotations: God is our refuge, etc etc. There's a wireless in the living room, but Aunt M says she only ever listens to religious programmes and the news. I'm already feeling bereft of music.

My bedroom is a small, low-ceilinged room under the eaves, with a Virgin Mary painting above the washstand. The Virgin was pouring superiority down on me, so I turned the picture round so that she's facing the wall. Much, much better.

The only redeeming feature of the bedroom is that the window looks out on to a patch of garden. I've just spent a whole hour at that window, watching birds fly about the three apple trees. I know their names from all the country walks with Dad. Greenfinches, blackbirds, flycatchers, thrushes, robins, blue tits, great tits, ravens. I wish I could ride on their wings and fly back home.

Thursday, 29 August 1940
St Catherine's School at Dunwick Hall

Life is so different now. Early on Monday mornings I travel to school on the horse-drawn milk float. I travel back to Aunt Margaret's house on Saturdays by the same method. The float picks up several other girls on the slow, clopping route through the villages. It's driven by a Mr Bennet, who is mild, middle-aged and very civil. At each stop he doffs his cap to us after offloading the milk bottles, making us all giggle.

From a distance Dunwick Hall looms huge and ghostly, its squareness relieved by two rounded towers and even a few battlements. The grounds are rather thrilling, too: a green enclave in the wilderness of the Derbyshire hills, with cedars, oaks and towering chestnut trees.

The house itself is full of marble fireplaces, diamond-paned windows and creaking oak staircases. The valuable stuff is all put away, but it's still a grand old place. I've written to Mum and Dad and told them about the mermaids carved into the banisters, the sparkling chandeliers and all the other beauties of Dunwick Hall. I didn't mention that I'm desperately homesick.

Nor did I mention the dearth of handsome princes. I would have been quite prepared to compromise but there aren't even any standard-style boys. Plenty of schools have started acquiring both genders due to wartime reshuffles, but St Catherine's prides itself on its untainted femaleness.

Apparently our headmistress, Miss Harrison, is forever reassuring anxious parents (who despair of the current lax morality) that their daughters, at least, will remain untainted. Untainted!

Schoolwork doesn't present much of a problem. My favourite lessons are geography, mathematics and science. I seem to absorb new information without making much of an effort. Sometimes I answer the teachers' questions too quickly. Then they glare at me as if I'm being insolent, while my schoolmates make faces. I don't think they like me much.

I share a dorm with five other girls, who know each other well. It's sometimes hard to understand what they're saying because of their broad accents. Most of the girls in this school go about in flocks. They stare at me.

On my first day, I passed two schoolmates in the corridor and noticed them jab each other in the ribs. 'Who does she think she is?' sniggered the one with the broad face and upturned nose. Her friend, a skinny, freckled girl with slanting eyes, shrugged her shoulders and whispered back something I couldn't catch.

Sometimes I wonder if being such a noticeable individual is a good thing, after all. No one else has long, loose, untamed tresses. Their hair is pinned back or tightly curled. They're all trying to emulate the Gracie Fields look. They roll their eyes at my smock-like blouse and flowing skirt. I hold my head high. I refuse to be cowed by them.

I do feel disappointed, though. Instead of the luxury lifestyle a castle like this should provide, only bleakness seems to be on offer. The school food is dreadful, too. The other girls trade boiled sweets amongst themselves but they never offer any to me.

Sunday, 15 September 1940
Aunt M's

Summer is merging into autumn. We've had some expeditions into the surrounding countryside, students and teachers rambling together, baskets over arms. We picked flowers to be sent to the wounded soldiers in the hospitals and scoured the hedgerows for blackberries and rose hips. Rose-hip jelly is supposed to be good for topping up the vitamins.

I was told off the other day for not finishing my food. It was some sort of potato pie but it tasted vile. The teacher, nasty Miss Philpotts, was going to make me eat it so I accidentally on purpose tipped the plate on to the floor.

'Oh, Veronica! What an awful waste!' she cried. I was given extra sums as a punishment.

'Waste' is a word I hear again and again. Several times I've seen a girl in tears because her cat or dog has been put down at the vet's; apparently it's a 'waste' to give food to pets. It's horrible. Why should animals be killed because of humans' stupid fighting? I hope beyond hope that my friend Tufty at Ravenscourt Park is all right. I ask Mum and Dad about him every time I call, but they say they haven't seen him in ages. I can't bear to think that my little waggy-tailed friend might be dead.

Most of all, the word 'waste' is used when there's news of people – young people, old people, families – killed in the bombings. 'What a terrible waste of life,' the teachers say.

Weekends are awful. It's hard to put up with Aunt M's scrutiny and all her dreary religious homilies. Today, like every other Sunday, we went to church. I sat on the hard pew and wondered what God is playing at.

Mum and Dad normally ring once a week to tell me about London life, the neighbours, the progress of the

potatoes and cabbages they've planted in our tiny garden
where roses and irises used to grow. Sometimes they
mention planes, explosions and showers of shrapnel. They
don't have a telephone in their house so they ring from the
ARP office in Shepherd's Bush. Aunt M's phone is in her
hallway and she listens in to any conversations, which
means I can't say anything private. So last weekend I used
the phone box on Aggleworth Green and rang Dad at the
ARP office. When I heard his gentle voice, everything came
pouring out of me: how boring it is at school, how nobody
will befriend me, how much I loathe Aunt Margaret and
yearn for home. He was quiet. I could picture his face full
of sympathy. Dad understands.

This afternoon it was Mum's turn.

'I'm so sorry you're unhappy, my darling, but this is the
reality of wartime. We must count our blessings.'

'Count them? I can't think of any at all!' I moaned, not
caring if I sounded like a drama queen.

'Don't say that! You know there are plenty,' Mum
scolded. But she's incapable of being harsh. 'I'm sorry about
Aunt Margaret. I know she's not much fun, but she isn't
used to having anyone else in her house. She probably
finds it just as difficult as you.'

I suppose Mum's right. She's good at thinking about
other people; much better at it than me.

She went on: 'Dad and I have managed to find
something that might cheer you up. Every Saturday
afternoon there are dance lessons in Aggleworth village
hall, a fifteen-minute walk from Aunt Margaret's house.
Would you like to learn how to dance?'

'Yes!' I shrieked down the phone the minute the words
were out of her mouth.

How I long to dance!

And at the lessons there may be boys . . .

Saturday, 21 September 1940
Aunt Margaret's

Unbelievable. I've started dance lessons and THERE ISN'T A SINGLE BOY! I should have guessed because the whole thing is run by church workers. We have to partner up with each other, taking it in turns to be the man. There's only an old gramophone and a limited selection of records.

Oh well, it's still good to move to music. We're learning the quickstep, waltz and foxtrot. I don't want to boast but I honestly think I'm the most graceful in the class. The other girls are so slow to pick up the steps.

At least they're friendlier than the ones at school. Last Saturday I walked back part of the way with a girl called Queenie. We were arm in arm and laughing gaily and I thought she might become a friend, given time. But then an old man stopped us in the street. He was really cross. 'Don't you know there's a war on?' he demanded.

I was very put out by it. I said to Queenie: 'Lorr, everyone keeps saying "Don't you know there's a war on?" I'm so sick of the phrase. Of course we know. We could hardly miss it!'

But Queenie had gone quite cold and sullen. It seems that nobody is allowed to enjoy themselves any more.

22

Patrick

Bolton

I CAN'T GET OVER it. Why has she let me into all this? It's the last thing I'd expect from somebody like her, total trout-face and iciest ice queen on the planet. There's no doubt about it, Veronica McCreedy is not your everyday, common or garden grandmother. First disappearing off to Antarctica and then sending me her teenage journal. Why the hell would she do either of those things?

I can't believe the withered old crone I know is the same person as this crazy, gorgeous fourteen-year-old. Young Veronica was one hell of a snobby madam, for sure, but it looks like she had a big heart back then. She cared about animals at any rate, and she loved her parents. Seems like what she really needed was friends.

I don't know what to make of it. All these feelings keep firing at me. Like the feeling I shouldn't be eavesdropping on this girl's thoughts, even if the adult Veronica *has* OK'd it. And the feeling that I'm tuning in to her loneliness. And the feeling that I've been given some kind of rare opportunity . . . but I'm not sure what exactly.

There's a letter tucked into the pages of the diary, written in spidery letters across old, browning paper. I pull it out.

Dearest Very,

We have such good news! You have probably already opened the package we've sent with this letter. Yes, it actually is what it says on the jar. Strawberry jam! I wish I could see your face now, Very! How long is it since you've tasted such sweetness? We knew you'd be pleased. Have it all to yourself or share it with your friends, whatever you want. It comes from my cousin in Australia. He sent it over when he heard about the sugar ration, a special treat for us all. He also sent a pot of black treacle. But I hope you don't mind, I have kept that back for your mother. We are both well, but not getting as much sleep as we'd like. There is still anti-aircraft fire through the night, but we take flasks into the Anderson shelter and tuck ourselves in with blankets. We play whist or Ludo when it's too noisy to sleep. We look after each other as well as we can. Mum is still loving her ambulance-driving. She comes home with dreadful stories of people with missing limbs and blood spouting everywhere, then manages to cook dinner. She's discovered a recipe for glycerin cake. Not as bad as it sounds! I wanted to post you some, but she says it would be off by the time it reached you. You know Mummy! Always practical!

ARP work is much the same. People take stupid risks sometimes but keep up their morale amazingly well when you consider everything that's happening.

I hope you are keeping up your own morale, dear girl, and that the dance lessons are helping. Mum sends love and says she will write next time. We both hope that you are working hard and enjoying the almost-castle. We think of you every day, Very, and we look forward to hearing all your news. Do write soon.

Your ever-loving father

Friday, 4 October 1940
Dunwick Hall

Dad truly is the best dad in the whole world.

I've just ripped open the parcel and have the pot of jam in my hands. 'Have it all to yourself or share it with your friends.' Typical of Dad to assume I have friends. He can never grasp that I'm simply not popular. I'll confess I've cried a little. I wish this stupid old war would end and I could go home.

I've just taken the lid off, stuck in a finger and scooped out a mound of sticky red paradise. I'm letting it sit on my tongue. I'm trying to make it last, resisting swallowing for as long as possible. The taste is exquisite. Strawberries and summer and pure joy.

But I mustn't eat any more. I have a plan.

Saturday, 12 October 1940

I was feeling light-headed as I jumped down from the milk float and ran to Aunt Margaret's house this morning. Aunt M looked nonplussed when she answered the door. She didn't even recognize the young lady in front of her. Then she suddenly did.

'What in the name of all that's holy has happened to you?'

'I'm just keeping up with the others,' I said, brushing her cheek with a dutiful kiss.

My new haircut accentuates my high cheekbones and delicate jawline. My hair sweeps up from my brow in a great chestnut swathe and nestles behind my ears in short, glossy coils. Everyone says how much it suits me. It's especially good when I complement it by staining my lips deep red. Lipstick isn't available, of course, but beetroot juice is almost as good. They grow beetroots on Janet's farm.

Yes: I have a friend. No: friends, plural! Janet, the broad-faced, upturned-nosed girl who sneered at me at the beginning, classifies as a friend now. So does her sidekick, Norah, the one with the freckles. I had to surrender most of my strawberry jam, but it was a small price to pay.

Janet says I make her laugh. She especially likes it when I play tricks on the teachers. Like when I put a blob of glue on Miss Philpotts' chair last Wednesday . . .

It was Janet and Norah who suggested the haircut. I somehow think they weren't expecting me to come out of it quite so adult-looking and alluring.

'What is the world coming to!' Aunt Margaret exclaimed on the doorstep. 'I pray for you every night, Veronica, and look what you've gone and done to yourself!'

She believes that fashion and corruption go hand in hand; one is scarcely possible without the other. I tried to explain. 'There's nothing wrong with the way I look, Aunt Margaret. They were making fun of me before.'

They still do, actually, and they still think I'm a prig, but at least I fit in more than I did.

Before bed Aunt Margaret made me go down on my knees in front of the wooden cross in the drawing room. She knelt beside me. She read a few prayers from her old black prayer book and finished, as always, with the Lord's Prayer.

'Lead us not into temptation but deliver us from evil. Think about those lines, Veronica. While your father and mother are working in London and our brave men are fighting in the fields, think about those lines. Think about them and stay away from bad influences.'

'Yes, Aunt Margaret,' I answered, good as gold. 'Of course I will.'

Of course I will not.

Monday, 21 October 1940

Hooray! I don't have to go back to Aunt M's every weekend any more. Janet has invited me instead to her home, Eastcott Farm. It's only three miles away. Norah already goes there every weekend. Like me, her home is some distance away so she only goes back in the holidays.

First thing on Saturday morning the three of us were picked up by the farm cart at the park gates. I was so excited! The cart was pulled by a lovely dappled horse. Janet's father and older brother are away, working in the air force, so the cart was driven by Janet's other brother, Harry. He's sixteen. He's large and clomping, with the same wide face as Janet, but his nose is all right. His ears stick out too much and his skin is bad, but apart from that he's quite nice to look at.

The route to Eastcott Farm winds through green pastures and hills dotted with sheep. The road eventually turns into a wide track with twisty hawthorns on either side. Harry was shouting at the horse and flicking the whip over its neck to make it trot faster.

'Don't hurt it!' I shouted at him.

'I'm not. It don't feel a thing,' he said. 'C'mon, you lazy beast!' he added to the horse.

'Stop showing off, Harry,' Janet scolded. 'We don't need to get home any quicker. It's lumpy and bumpy enough as it is!'

When we got off amongst a sprawl of farm buildings Harry's eyes were roving all over me. I stared right back at him.

Janet and Harry's mother, Mrs Dramwell, came out in her pinny to greet us. She isn't just broad in the face but broad everywhere else as well. Her hair is rather grimy but she seems nice enough.

She invited us in and gave us mugs of hot milk but didn't sit down herself. I know from Janet that things have been hard at the farm since her dad left. Two land girls stay there and a prisoner-of-war is sent daily from the camp over the hill for the hard manual labour. Otherwise it's just Mrs Dramwell and Harry trying to keep the food production going. So we girls helped all we could. It was tiring but good fun. I've learned how to milk a cow! Dad and Mum won't believe it when I tell them. I fell about laughing at those udders to start with (they were so huge and floppy), and I couldn't believe I had to squeeze them to get milk out. But after Janet showed me how I managed to do it.

Later she took us to see the pigs. I'd never seen an actual pig before. They were sweet but very, very dirty, all grubbing about in smelly muck. One piglet had fallen into a kind of rut thing and couldn't get out. It was really upset.

'Poor little thing!' I cried.

'Why don't you go in and get it out?' Janet said, amused that I cared so much.

I hopped over the fence.

'You can't do that!' screeched Norah.

'Watch me!' I said. I worked my way through the sea of pig muck and hauled the little creature out of the rut. He squealed and wriggled. I gave him a big kiss on the snout and set him loose. How we all laughed!

I was in such a mess afterwards. My shoes, socks and the hem of my skirt were all encrusted with stinky mud. I had to scrub them and leave them to dry by the stove and borrow some clothes of Janet's in the meantime. The piglet was happy, though.

Monday, 28 October 1940

I'm just back from my second weekend at Eastcott Farm. Janet's brother, Harry, fetched us and took us back in the cart again.

'So what do you like to do with yourself, Veronica?' he asked when I got down at the farm. He said my name with a slight sneer, but then Janet and Norah do that, too. It seems they can't help it.

I told him I like drawing and science, but my chief love is animals. This didn't seem to be the right answer. So I asked in turn what he likes doing.

'Well, when there's time off from the farm I make models of aeroplanes,' he answered. 'Just out of bits of old junk I find around.'

'He's obsessed with them,' Janet told us.

'They're all very good, very clever,' Norah put in, keen that I should register she was here first. 'Will you show us them again, Harry?'

Harry led us to a small back room that smelled of wood and glue.

'That one is a Wellington. It took me ages. This is the one I'm working on at the moment.' He picked up a model gingerly. 'It's a Spitfire. You can hold it if you like.'

I took it and held it up to the light. It was carefully cut out from old tin cans, matchsticks and nails bent to shape. I could appreciate the ingenuity, but it's not my sort of thing. I prefer pigs. I saw, however, that it was important for him so I pretended to be interested. Janet pretended to yawn. Norah was pretending the hardest. She was pretending to be absolutely fascinated. I passed her the precious object. Norah looked as if she'd been given the crown jewels.

'Marvellous, absolutely marvellous!' she repeated again and again. I'm laughing my head off now, remembering it.

Tuesday, 29 October 1940

I can't believe I was happy only yesterday. I'm so stupid, so clueless.

I'll never be happy again.

I'd give anything to be back there, stuck in yesterday for ever.

How can I face anything? How can I go on? This happens to other people. Not to me.

God oh God.

23

Patrick

Bolton
December 2012

SHE'S UPSET, REALLY UPSET. I don't like it.

I'm kind of creeped out, too. That guy, Harry. Could he be my grandfather? Is Harry's blood running in my veins? As I pull on a clean shirt I look over at my reflection in the mirror. You couldn't say my face is broad, not really; and my skin isn't too bad. Still, I could have got those things from my mum's side. Do my ears stick out a lot? Hard to say. I turn my head about, trying to make it out.

That thing with the model aeroplanes is exactly the kind of thing I'd be into. It's weird. I don't know what I'm hoping. I'm not warming to Harry much, but it's clear he fancies the pants off Veronica. I have to say I'm rooting for her. I hope she doesn't rush into things. She's way too young.

This whole thing is getting under my skin. But I can't carry on reading because it's time to go to the thing at Gav's. Whether

I like it or not, Granny V's teenage life will just have to go on hold. Needs must.

Gav seems to have got the idea I'm in need of company. At least, I presume that's why he invited me to dinner. Gav's a star to be thinking of me when he's got so much stuff going on in his own life; it must be a fricking nightmare dealing with grief for his mum *and* worrying about his daughter both at the same time.

To be honest, I'd be much happier meeting him down the pub for a pint. I'm not blessed with great social skills and I'm hopeless at dinner party chit-chat. Still, there'll be kids there. I find kids much easier to talk to than adults. There's no pressure to be cool or anything with kids. They just accept you as you are.

I cycle to the address. Gav's place is third along in a terrace of mushroom-coloured ex-council houses. A stack of bicycles against the outhouse is a giveaway I've come to the right one. They've made an effort with the front patch of garden. There's a neatly trimmed hedge, some flower beds and that.

When I ring the bell the door is opened by a little girl in a red dress with ladybird patterns all over it and shiny red sandals to match. She has huge eyes but no hair. A faded blue cloth is wrapped tightly around the top of her head.

'Hi there!' I say.

'Mum!' she shrieks. 'He's here!'

Without waiting for an answer she takes my hand and leads me through the hall and into the sitting room. 'You are Patrick,' she tells me, 'and I am Daisy. This is the sitting room. This is my dad, but you know him already from bicycles.' Gav leaps up from his chair and squeezes my hand but can't say anything yet because Daisy is in full flow. 'This is my brother, Noah, but you don't need to take any notice of him' – here a small boy with his head in a comic lifts a hand and waves it in my direction but doesn't look up – 'and this is my doll, Trudy, who is my daughter – not my real daughter, actually, but she is like a daughter to me and I look after her.' (Trudy the doll, a big-headed, bulbous-eyed thing, is clearly more important than Noah the brother.) 'The only other people left for you to meet are Mummy and Bryony. They're in the kitchen, making the pudding look nice and drinking wine. Mummy *and Bryony*, that is: both of them.' She's very emphatic.

'Oh, right. I've met your mum before,' I tell her, recalling the waif-like woman who sometimes appears in the shop when Gav's forgotten something. 'But Bryony?'

'Bryony's a friend,' Gav explains with a bit of a sly grin. 'We invited her, too, because she's been at a bit of a loose end lately.'

'Bryony's very, very pretty,' Daisy tells me. Her eyes wander across my face, taking in my features. 'And you are quite handsome,' she eventually decides.

I feel a bit daunted at the prospect of this Bryony. More than a bit, to be honest. I get tongue-tied in the presence of attractive women. I revert to teenagerdom in a way that isn't good.

Without warning, Daisy makes us all jump by shrieking, 'Mum! Patrick is here and you're keeping him waiting. You shouldn't do that. Are you and Bryony coming any time soon?'

There's laughter from the direction of the kitchen. 'Yes, dear! On our way.'

Gav's wife steps into the room and gives me a peck on the cheek. She's as thin as ever and her face seems to be collecting lines too quickly for her age. 'I'm so glad you could come, Patrick. I'm afraid dinner's going to be a bit basic. I had to make something the children will eat.'

'No probs,' I say, pushing my gift of cheap plonk into her hands.

She moves aside and I see a dazzling smile attached to a little oval face. As introductions are made I register that, yes, Bryony is *very* pretty. Her eyes are luscious and lashy, her hair is cut in a sleek bob. It shines in lots of different tints of copper and gold whenever she moves her head. She's made an effort with her appearance. She got herself sparkled up with a sparkling necklace and little sparkling earrings. She's wearing a floaty (almost see-through) top and tight black skirt that doesn't reach her knees. Nice legs.

Over toad-in-the-hole and peas, I learn that Bryony is a divorcee and she's working at the local museum. Her hobbies are tennis, ancient history and felting. She promises to make a felt giraffe for Daisy. She's a hell of a lot nicer than me, more intelligent than me and more interesting than me.

In spite of all this, I somehow can't get myself to be that interested in *her*. I keep thinking about Granny's diaries. Is Harry my grandfather? Did he love Granny V? What exactly happened between them? And why was she so upset on 29 October 1940? I just want to get back home so I can read more.

After the meal Daisy and Noah are anxious to show the visitors their three guinea pigs. Bryony and I are led out to the back garden. Daisy scoops the guinea pigs from the hutch and they are passed round, one by one.

'Cute, aren't they?' says Bryony, cradling one of the furry guys. 'Do you like animals, Patrick?'

'Yup. Err, yes, I s'pose.'

Daisy beams at us. She seems to be expecting me to say something more but my head is empty of ideas. A total vacuum. She waits a little longer, then takes the guinea pig back from Bryony crossly and declares: 'So you two'll have to get a guinea pig when you get married.'

I'm now wishing the earth would swallow me up, but Bryony doesn't seem the least bit rattled. 'Daisy, you're slightly jumping to conclusions!' she declares with a ringing laugh.

Bryony only lives down the road and Gav has made me promise to walk her home.

I don't mind much. She's pleasant company. When we've said goodbye to our hosts I trot down the road with her, wheeling my bike on the other side. We talk about Daisy. Bryony says what a shame it is she's so ill and what a brave little girl and how amazing she is and for that matter the whole family is amazing. I agree. It doesn't take long for that conversation to run its course. Next up we talk about the safety of different neighbourhoods and how she's normally quite happy to walk the streets on her own at night but as Gav was so insistent . . . I say it's a pleasure (A *pleasure*! I'm using my shop-speak now) and it's not far out of my way in any case. There's an awkward pause and our footsteps sound loud.

'I gather you recently split with your girlfriend?'

'Yes,' I admit. 'Lynette, her name was. She left me a few months ago without warning.'

Bryony makes a sympathetic sort of noise. 'So hard when that happens. It took me two years to get over my husband leaving. Almost as long as the marriage!'

'You don't say!'

I wonder vaguely what her husband was like. An idiot, I bet. She deserves better.

She seems deep in thought as she walks by my side. I'm wondering if she's going to invite me in for a coffee and what I'll do if she does. Coffee isn't tempting but what comes after might be. Is it going to be a longer night than I'd expected? How far do I go? How far does she want me to go? How far do *I* want me to go? And am I wearing clean underpants? All sorts of performance-related anxieties are beginning to circle like wolves.

We've almost reached her door. The renewed silence is getting unbearable. I grasp around in my headspace for something to fill it.

'I've been reading my grandmother's diaries,' I say at last.

'Oh, how intriguing,' she answers politely.

'She was, like, beautiful when she was younger. Really beautiful.' I wonder whether to add 'just like you', but decide against it. Too corny.

I stop and she stops, too. I face her in the street, under a lamp post. 'Bryony, I'm going to ask you something, and I'd like you to be honest with me.'

'Of course I will, Patrick.' She looks like she's in a state of preparation, her features deliberately calm but all ready to arrange themselves into an appropriate reaction.

We view each other for a moment in the lamplight. Then I just come out with it. 'Bryony, do you think my ears stick out?'

She looks startled. This isn't what she was expecting. 'Why, no, not especially. They're quite nice ears.'

There's some hope, then.

We carry on walking.

'Well,' she sighs as we come to the steps of number sixteen. 'We're here. And . . . I still like your ears.'

'OK, great.'

She fumbles in her bag for the key. When she's found it she plays with it, looking up at me. Am I supposed to kiss her? Is it a good idea? I can't quite make it out. She does look alluring. Her eyes are all twinkly like her jewellery and the edge of her hair gleams red-gold in the dusk. Her lips are full and slightly open. I could just go for it. I'm thinking right now that she looks like she'd be up for it. But am *I* up for it? Man, I must be crazy! What's wrong with me? It's bloody shameful, not to grab a chance like this.

I can't exactly say what excuse I've got. It could be that I'm not over Lynette yet. But I don't think it is. Jeez, I'm not right in the head, mate. Here's this gorgeous, sexy woman, available, waiting for me to make a move. But no, nothing's going to happen between me and Bryony. Because do you know what I'm going to do? I'm going to head straight back home and get on with reading my granny's diaries.

Terry's Penguin Blog

14 December 2012

Penguin couples have really got their act together. As Veronica pointed out to me today, they seem much more organized than many human couples. They don't waste any time. Once the eggs are laid, the females will return to sea for a few weeks to feed while the males egg-sit. Then, during early December, the couples take it in turns to incubate. After the chicks have hatched, again the mother and father take turns in their roles of watching over their young and finding food.

It's incredibly heart-warming to see the penguins cooperating. Here are a few snaps of Veronica at the rookery, admiring the dynamics of Adélie family life.

24

Veronica

Locket Island

Dear Mrs McCreedy,

It's very great to see the pictures of you on those blogs. You look well and very stylish and not too cold. I hope your corns are OK and the penguins are well.

I saw some Penguin biscuits in Kilmarnock Stores yesterday and thought of you. I didn't buy any, though. I haven't got through the lovely marshmallow chocolate biscuits you left yet. I'm trying not to eat too many at once. Doug (my husband) says it won't do my figure any favours. I know he's right, but I do like sweet things so much.

We have been learning a new song in the church choir, lots of Lord Lord Lords and an Amen that goes on for two and a half pages. It's very hard to keep track of.

The weather has been quite sunny here recently, but frosty every morning and bits of snow. I call in on The Ballahays every day to water the houseplants and check up on things like you told me to. On my way out yesterday I saw Mr Perkins with a wheelbarrow full of compost and I said to him how it feels strange and empty without you, and he said yes, Eileen, it does, doesn't it.

I hope you are eating well.

Yours,
Eileen

I cannot think why she bothers to send these emails when she has nothing of any interest to say. However, as Terry has gone to the trouble of printing it out for me, I read through the message briefly before tossing it into the wastepaper basket.

The evening is quiet and still. Mike is absent at the moment, analysing blood, bones or faeces in the lab, no doubt. Dietrich is seated at the table, shading in one of his drawings with a pencil: two penguins dancing a tango, he has informed me.

Terry has returned to the computer room. She spends longer in there than anyone, typing penguin information into databases and working on her blog. I wonder if Patrick will have read it and if he is interested in the slightest. I wonder if he has looked at the diaries.

Dietrich pushes his pens to one side and stands up with an air of purpose.

'Have you finished your drawing?' I enquire politely.

'No, not yet. But it's my turn to cook tonight.'

He grabs a few tins from the shelf and looks at them with a doleful expression. He disappears out to the 'larder' then comes back with a nondescript hunk of meat that might have been any body part from any animal.

'Should be defrosted by now,' he mutters.

'Can I be of any assistance?' I ask. Terry is the only one I have helped with domestic tasks so far.

'Well, that would be nice,' he replies, startled and pleased at my offer. We proceed to the kitchen. Standing next to him by the worktop I notice that, in addition to facial whiskers, he has many hairs sprouting all over his neck. It is rather like standing next to a bear.

'Perhaps if you could stir this for me?' He upends the greenish contents of a tin into a pan and hands me a wooden spoon.

I dutifully stir.

'Tell me, Mrs McCreedy, do you think Terry's OK?' he asks out of the blue.

I am taken aback. It never occurred to me she could be otherwise. 'Of course she is. I suppose you feel responsible for her happiness in some way, do you?'

'Being in my position, I can't seem to help it,' he replies.

'You're fond of her, aren't you?'

'Oh yes. Very much. Her and Mike, both.'

A smallish growl escapes from my throat. How could anyone possibly be fond of the ungallant Mike?

'They are a great team,' Dietrich continues, laying into the meat with a cleaver in a slightly desperate fashion. 'It's important that they're coping all right. Eight months is a long time to be in a place like this with so little human interaction. When it all ends I am lucky that I have my wife and children to go back to. Mike has his girlfriend. But Terry? She doesn't have that special person. And her family don't really get her. She's all about the penguins.'

'I believe you're right. Terry would go to any lengths to ensure the future of the species. Seldom have I observed such passion and such commitment.'

Dietrich beams. 'That is exactly what I think. She's always doing extra work behind the scenes. And she's so great with people, too – even Mike and me. There's not many who could put up with us two for so long.' He adds: 'It's great that she's got you for company for a while.'

'You flatter me.'

'No, I mean it.'

He pauses, cleaver in mid-air. 'You and I are older than the others, Mrs McCreedy, and we can see all this from a different perspective.'

A dry laugh rattles in my throat. 'You're hardly a decade older than them. Whereas I am five or six decades their senior.'

'You have the edge on me, yes,' he admits. 'But I expect, like me, you find that ageing brings at least one advantage, Mrs McCreedy. Don't you find that, as the years pass, you become less obsessed with yourself – and you care about other people more? As you get older, it's as if your capacity for love grows.'

I am silent. I have not found this to be the case at all. Quite the reverse.

25

Veronica

Locket Island

THERE ARE RAISED VOICES issuing from the lab. All three of them.
I am on my way back from the woefully inadequate facilities; I
always retire to bed long before they do, and, as it is nine fifteen,
I have already completed my ablutions, donned my dressing-gown
and removed my hearing aid. Nonetheless, such is the volume of
the argument that I cannot miss a few phrases. A 'For Chrissake!'
from Mike; a 'No, my mind is made up,' from Dietrich; a 'Please,
let's not argue,' from Terry, all in amongst a cacophonous jumble
of other words. I pause to try and glean more but it seems that
the dispute has drawn to an end. Dietrich emerges from the room
and passes me with nothing more than a polite 'Good night, Mrs
McCreedy.' Immediately afterward I hear the distant voice of Ella
Fitzgerald filtering through the closed door of his bedroom.

I return to the lounge to pick up my glasses. I linger at the
bookshelves, pondering the merits of a Sherlock Holmes tome for

my next read. It is, alas, a paperback, but it might provide me with a little mental stimulation.

Terry enters, an unusual crimson bloom in her cheeks.

'Oh, hello, Veronica. Nice dressing-gown.'

'Thank you, Terry.'

She doesn't sit down.

I continue my examination of Conan Doyle's work, but she is an unquiet presence. She blows on her glasses and rubs them ferociously. Then she lets some air through her teeth with a loud hiss. After which she shakes her head quickly as if trying to rid herself of a troublesome midge.

'Whatever is the matter?' I ask, pushing Sherlock back between Christie and Dickens.

She mumbles something indistinct. I am not going to let this go. 'Fetch me my hearing aid, will you, and then tell me all about it.'

She pulls a face, but trots off, returning a moment later with the aid. Once it is in and we've settled in the lounge with a mug of tea each, she confirms what I had suspected all along: the problem is Mike.

'Why am I not surprised?' I exclaim.

She frowns. 'I know he's a bit funny towards *you*, Veronica. There are reasons for that. But he's never been horrible to *me* before. Normally we get on so well.'

The implications here are not lost on me. 'Excuse me a moment, Terry, but, if there are "reasons" for him being "a bit funny" towards me (as you so generously put it), would you be so good as to explain what they are?'

'Well,' she replies slowly, 'I *will* tell you, as it'll help you understand. You might remember we had another scientist with us last year, and for the past few years?'

I do have a vague recollection about it. They never talk about this fourth scientist, though.

'His name was Ryan,' Terry informs me. 'He was funny and

clever and full of ideas, and he was practical, too. He was the one who fixed our plumbing when it went kaput, who installed the generators and the reverse osmosis plant. Even more importantly, he was the great communicator, the great liaiser who waved his magic wand and procured funding for the project. A certain amount was arranged from the Anglo-Antarctic Research Council, enough for a six-year project – but we all knew we needed more time. There were so many significant ups and downs in the Adélie numbers on Locket Island in those six years, more than anywhere else. Ryan promised us that he was on the case. When the project first started looking wobbly, he said it wouldn't be a problem, his personal contacts would step up their contribution. In fact the opposite happened. They withdrew their contribution altogether. And what did Ryan do about it? He left us. He deserted the project and went off to a cushy number tracking seabirds in Iceland.'

I would never have considered tracking seabirds in Iceland to be a cushy number, but then my knowledge of such things is limited.

'It was a grim time for all of us, but it hit Mike worst. Mike was close to Ryan. He'd put all his faith in him, only to be totally let down. So you see, when *you* came along promising all this extra money, Mike wouldn't let himself believe it would happen. He couldn't bear for us all to have our hopes raised again, only to be crushed. That's why he's been odd with you. It's only because he cares about the Adélie project so much.'

Terry persists in believing the best of people. I, however, am underwhelmed by her explanations. I clear my throat pointedly. 'I believe several thousand pounds of my money have already been transferred by Eileen from my account to the Locket Island Trust to pay for my three weeks' accommodation. Isn't that enough to show him I am in earnest?'

She shrugs. 'Well, I think he's beginning to realize. But he doesn't like being proved wrong.'

She isn't stupid.

'So what is Mike's issue with *you*?' I enquire. 'What was all that squabbling about tonight?'

A variety of emotions cross her face then she seems to make up her mind. Further revelations are imminent. I feel rather pleased that she considers me a suitable recipient of these.

'Well, the fact is that Dietrich is handing over a task . . . to *me*,' she confides, with some pride. 'He wants me to take over all communications with the Anglo-Antarctic Research Council. It's a huge responsibility, especially now that the future of our project is in the balance. And if (it's a big if) we can somehow carry on our research, Deet has said he's planning on dividing his time up differently, spending more of it in Austria with his family. As he won't be here so much, he's asked if I'll take the helm in two months' time. He's asked me to be head of the Locket Island team. I said yes, of course.'

'Ah!' This is indeed a revelation. I take her hand warmly. 'Congratulations! It is no more than you deserve.'

'I'm looking forward to it, the challenge of it all,' she acknowledges with a wide smile. 'But I think – well, I *know* – Mike's a bit upset he won't be getting the job.'

'Undoubtedly,' I reply. 'You have what he wants. It's called envy. I have seldom suffered from it myself, but I do remember being around people who were quite severely afflicted. One of the symptoms is nasty behaviour.'

'It does seem to be.'

There may well be an additional cause for Mike's unpleasantness. Terry has no idea that, despite her unkempt appearance and lack of style, she is in possession of considerable charms. Indeed, somebody of an appropriate age might find her rather an attractive prospect. Bearing in mind he has a girlfriend back in England, it may well be that Mike is in denial about the way he feels towards Terry.

'Now Mike's picking holes in everything I do,' she says crossly.

I reach out and lay a hand on her arm. 'It's his problem, not yours. He'll get over it.'

'You're right, Veronica. Of course he will.'

I can hear a roaring in the hills. The air has acquired a ghostly grey tinge. Wildly tousled clouds chase each other across the sky at an alarming rate. The penguins seem uneasy, stumping about in close circles and huddling up together.

A sudden gust of wind blows my hood down and plays havoc with my hair.

'Right, that's it. We're going back to base,' exclaims Terry, setting a befuddled bird down on the ground. It straggles off and plumps itself back on its nest. Terry starts to pack up her penguin scales and camera.

I consult my watch. I'm getting used to the fact that it never gets properly dark here and the sun travels backwards through the sky. I still find Antarctic timescales disorientating, however.

'It's only twelve o'clock!' I protest.

'I know. But that's a storm on its way.'

I glance towards the mountains. They're veiled in a swirling mist. The roaring is becoming louder by the minute.

Terry pulls out her radio and speaks briefly to Dietrich and Mike on it.

'Yup, we're all agreed. Quick as you can, Veronica.'

We march up the slope. By the time we are at the top specks of white are flying in our faces. We're both panting. I am thankful it's all downhill the rest of the way to the field centre. I have to be reasonably careful, though, due to the risk of slipping. Mukluks are good, but the ground is unforgiving when you fall. I've only done it once here so far and still have the bruises. I have no wish to repeat the experience.

We arrive at the field centre unscathed. It isn't long before Dietrich and Mike join us.

Dietrich crouches down to light the heater. 'Let's get this thing going and hunker down.'

'A day in the lab for me, then,' declares Mike, taking off in that direction and leaving the door unclosed behind him. I close it.

'Probably a good idea, Mrs McCreedy. That'll stop any draughts,' comments Dietrich.

Terry aims herself towards the kettle. 'We may be stuck here for some time, Veronica. Best find yourself a book or something.'

I bypass Sherlock Holmes once more and choose something more topical: *Scott's Antarctic Expedition: The Worst Journey in the World*. Once I have located my glasses, I accept the mug of tea from Terry and settle into my chair . . .

. . . Two days later I am still sitting here. We haven't been able to venture outside at all. It is mind-numbingly tedious and suffocatingly claustrophobic. I miss the earth, the air, the sky. I miss the penguins. I can't stand Mike any more, can't stand Dietrich. At times I even can't stand Terry.

The Worst Journey in the World does little to make me feel better about it.

26

Veronica

Locket Island

WHEN DIETRICH FINALLY DECLARES it is safe to go out again we
tumble through the door, all four of us slightly hysterical with relief.
The scenery has changed, the contours of the land softened by an
extra feathery coating. A pristine lace skirt has gathered all around
the field centre. The ground has become a series of deep undula-
tions in whipped-cream whites.

We stretch and drink in the fresh air. The three scientists frolic
and whoop in the snow. I, too, feel greatly uplifted but I refrain
from whooping or frolicking.

Mike has evidently accepted that Terry is to be his boss in the
near future. At least, I presume that is why he is putting a handful
of snow down the back of her neck. She retaliates by scooping up
as much as she can manage and rubbing it in his face, hard. They
all shriek with laughter.

But it's already time to return to business. It seems that one of the power thingumies has suffered from storm damage. Dietrich drags a ladder from round the back and props it against the smaller of the two wind turbines.

'Up you go then, Mrs McCreedy!' he calls to me. I grant him a smile. Fit and able as I am, we both know there will be no ascending of ladders as far as I am concerned.

'I'll go,' Mike volunteers and in no time he is at the top. His good mood rapidly evaporates.

While he is raining swear words down on us, Terry and Dietrich each get a shovel and start digging a pathway up the slope. The snow is far deeper in some areas than others. 'It's treacherous when you can't see which are which,' Terry comments.

I am impressed by the way they are both applying themselves. She is not afraid of hard graft, that girl.

A visit to the rookery is out of the question until the issues have been resolved, so I wander back inside and make myself a Darjeeling. I note that the scientists have left all the inside doors open again. I diligently shut them.

Half an hour later Mike appears in front of me, dishevelled and sulky.

'We have a problem on our hands, Veronica. The generator is bust and can't be fixed. Which means we have to rely on just the one.'

'How very tiresome,' I comment.

Unfortunately he hasn't finished. 'I'm afraid we're going to have to cut down our energy usage,' he explains. He assumes an expression of authority. 'That means boiling the kettle less, for starters. From now on you are strictly limited to four mugs of tea a day.'

I blanch. This is a travesty indeed. 'Isn't there anything else . . . ?'

'Terry is cutting down on her computer blog time, Dietrich on his CD playing and I'm going to do less work with the light on in the lab in the middle of the night. We can't compromise on heating or any electricity needed in penguin research, but we need to be economical with everything else. Clear?'

What an unpleasant man! He doesn't know the meaning of the word 'apology'.

'Surely, in this age of space travel, there is some means of repairing a simple generator?'

'No, there isn't,' he says bluntly. 'I haven't got the right tools.'

I am severely tempted to quote a certain proverb regarding a bad workman and his tools, but I resist. Instead I content myself with giving him a hard stare.

I always feel my feathers are ruffled after any dialogue with Mike. The Darjeeling soothes my spirits. I must appreciate every last atom if it is to be rationed in the future.

It is wonderful to see the penguins again but devastating to observe many small rounded corpses amongst them. The scene prompts a sharp twist in my chest, just underneath where the locket lies.

The living penguins continue with their riotous activities, bravely ignoring the graveyard elements of their community. Despite the losses, new life is blossoming everywhere. Tiny wobbling heads are emerging from eggs throughout the colony. I manage to recover my equanimity by focusing on the antics of a particular Adélie chick. This one is quite charming. He is a fat, fuzzy child running around in tight circles as if chasing an imaginary butterfly. He is delighted with himself and the world.

A huge, winged shadow glides across the snow. I look up and follow the path of the bird, recognizing it as a skua. It dips down into the community of penguins, snatches the very chick I was watching and soars upward again. I gasp in horror. The poor baby penguin is a struggling silhouette against the hard blue sky.

'Let go, let go, you brute!' I shriek at the skua, but my cries are in vain. The chick's feet kick out for a second, its neck twisted sideways, then it dangles like a rag from the skua's talons. A second skua wheels in and together they rip the baby bird limb from limb.

My whole body is shuddering in shock. My eyes return to the colony, seeking out the parents, conscious of their pain. I have no idea which penguins they are; they are anonymous in amongst the seething mass of black and white.

Terry's voice startles me out of my reverie. I am cradling a (now extra-precious) mug of Darjeeling while she messes about with a stack of penguin tags across the other side of the room.

I adjust my hearing aid. 'Did you say something?'

'You seem sad. Is something wrong, Veronica?'

I didn't realize it was that obvious.

'Wrong? No,' I answer. No more than usual, anyway.

Her brows are drawn together, her eyes searching my face. 'I know something's troubling you. You can talk to me, you know, Veronica. About anything, in confidence. Things can get to you out here, I know that. Feelings become kind of raw, kind of exposed. But it does help to talk.'

'Does it?' I very much doubt that.

'I won't tell anyone if . . . if it's something personal. And, for what it's worth, I'm not in the habit of judging people.'

A human being not judging another human being? That'd be a first.

'You don't talk much about yourself,' she adds. 'I'd like to know a bit more about you.'

She settles in the chair next to mine with the air of a person who won't give up. It is an attitude that reminds me of someone.

Yet at the moment the legendary McCreedy fortitude seems to be crumbling. My limbs weigh me down and everything I attempt to do is a Herculean effort. My brain feels worn out, too. At times it seems to me that I'm trying to realign things that simply can't be realigned. I would have thought that by now I'd shaken off the past, but ever since I read those old journals I have been acutely aware of it all. It's still there inside me, stronger than ever, a growing presence like a canker. It is expanding all the time, putting pressure on all my vital organs and poisoning my bloodstream.

I have allowed myself to believe that coming out here might provide some sort of cure or antidote. I have certainly enjoyed being among the penguins. But it isn't enough. I am beginning to realize that nothing will ever be enough.

'It's all a big waste,' I mutter, more to myself than to Terry. 'My life. All a huge, painful, inexplicable, pointless waste.'

'I'm sure that's not true, Veronica,' she cries, reaching a hand out to me that I pretend not to see. 'I bet you've done loads of amazing things.'

'Amazing? Hardly.'

Events happened and I responded to them quickly and impulsively in my own way, right or wrong. Then time passed, grinding onwards, year upon year, decade upon decade, silence upon silence. Like the layers of earth and rock and ice that have formed over the surface of the earth. Who would know or care that a fire is burning deep down, right at its core?

'Is it something about Patrick?' Terry asks.

'Patrick?'

'Yes, that's the name of your grandson, isn't it?' She has a good memory.

'I suppose, biologically speaking, he *is* my grandson,' I acknowledge.

'And so . . . you must have children . . . had children? A child?' I register all the patterns and strands of blues and silver-greys in her wide eyes.

'No. Not really. Not properly,' I tell her.

She looks slightly spooked. 'I don't know what you mean. You're a dark horse, Veronica.'

She's been kind to me. Perhaps I owe her an explanation.

'It was the war . . .'

I stop. I can't go over it, say it out loud, however much she wheedles. Life is a careful balance of what you let out and what you hold in. In my case, it is largely about holding in. Holding in is the only way of holding together.

Anyway, why should I tell her anything? What business is it of hers?

'I'd like to rest now.' I heave myself up and head for my room. I close the door firmly behind me.

27

Patrick

Bolton

I ARM MYSELF WITH a Guinness before reading on. I wonder whether a spliff might help, too, but decide against it. I'm trying to stop smoking altogether. I might even return Weedledum and Weedle-dee to Judith, then the temptation won't be there any more.

It's late, but who cares? I pour out the Guinness, stretch out on the bed and open the diary once again.

20 November 1940
Aggleworth

I haven't written in here for so long. I couldn't. Even now it all keeps crashing round and round in my head. Crazy little details. The 'Headmistress' sign on the door. Miss Harrison's grainy skin. Her small, darting eyes. The tight roll of hair on the nape of her neck that she kept poking and prodding. And Aunt Margaret, ghostly white, standing beside the desk. So stiff.

When I was summoned I just thought they'd found out about my stealing Miss Melton's chalk. I even felt a flicker of hope that maybe I'd be sent back to London as a punishment. But no. Instead came that news – terrible, hideous, unthinkable . . .

Oh Mum, oh Dad. You said everything would be all right. You promised.

I wanted to scream at Miss Harrison and Aunt Margaret that they were lying, that it couldn't possibly be true. Dad and Mum wouldn't . . . they couldn't . . .

They love me so much. They'd never do this to me. They'd never let themselves get killed, no matter how many bombs fall out of the sky, no matter how much all the rest of the world breaks and bleeds and burns.

Miss Harrison, prodding at her stupid bun again: 'They are at peace now, child. You have to accept that.'

I hate Aunt Margaret more than ever but I shall never forget what she said as I sank to the floor. 'It's selfish to cry, Veronica, because they are with Our Lord. Tears show weakness. They would not want you to cry.'

I heard an echo of Dad's voice, his kind, firm voice. His words the very last time he set eyes on me:

'Be strong.'

I bit the inside of my mouth, teeth clenching into flesh so hard I could taste the blood.

I WILL be strong, Dad. For you. I will NOT CRY.

Not then. Not now. Not ever.

1 January 1941
Eastcott Farm

So much time has flown away. I am still here: Veronica McCreedy, one of hundreds of wartime orphans wrestling with cruel fate, trying to make sense of it all. Now I must turn the page for another year.

1941 finds me here at Eastcott. I've been staying over Christmas because Janet offered (and who'd want to spend Christmas with Aunt Margaret?). The Dramwells have been kind. They even gave me a present, a bar of soap. Janet said it was in case I got mucky with the pigs again. I do go out to visit them often, and the cows. The animals are my friends. But Christmas isn't Christmas without Mum and Dad.

My New Year's Resolution is to be stronger than ever.

I woke up at midnight last night. Janet and Norah were both asleep. I slipped out of the bed the three of us share when we're here and tiptoed barefoot to the window. I opened the locket and carefully took out the two strands of hair, the only threads linking me to my loved ones. They lay in the palm of my hand, in the white band of moonlight, looking so peaceful. I lifted them and brushed them against my cheek, trying to catch a whisper of Mum, a whisper of Dad. The reality of loss is hard to grasp. Mostly it's like a story I'm reading that can't possibly be true. Then realization comes in a blast of splinters, sharp and cruel, and my heart breaks all over again.

28 January 1941
Dunwick Hall

It is horribly cold. We have to factor in extra time to break the layer of ice on the water before we can wash every morning. I hate the long, shivering wait in my nightdress with the other girls. The mornings are so dark, too. Darkness is hard to bear.

To try and counteract all this I make myself very, very loud and lively. 'Manic,' Janet and Norah call it. I don't rattle on and on about my grief and they've got no idea how I hurt inside. Just as well, because I don't want to talk about it. I grasp the company of my two friends because it helps blot out everything else. I laugh a lot, I'm rude to the teachers and break any school rules I can.

We've started to study *Hamlet* in English. Hamlet and I have a lot in common. We are both bereft and a little crazy. Like him, I 'put an antic disposition on'. I understand Hamlet and Hamlet understands me.

A lot of weekends I'm at Eastcott but some of them I have to go back to Aunt Margaret's. Thank goodness Aunt M still lets me go to dance class on Saturdays. Music is a lifeline. I lose myself in the stately waltzes and merry foxtrots. The rhythms cheer me, and dark thoughts melt away amongst the rippling harmonies.

The rest of my time in Aggleworth is bleak, though. As well as church on Sundays, Aunt M gives me endless horrible lectures. She drones on and on, saying Mum and Dad are in heaven now, watching me. I must do my best to get there, too. The way Aunt M says it implies that this will be tricky and poor old God will have to be extra merciful to let me in.

23 April 1941
Dunwick Hall

Sunlight streams in through the diamond-paned windows and our school expeditions into the countryside have started again. We fill our baskets with primroses. Later we sit and line boxes with moss and pack them with flowers to be sent to the hospitals for the war-wounded.

I spend lots of time at Eastcott these days. I'm getting to know Janet's brother, Harry. You couldn't call Harry good-looking, but he has his own sort of rustic charm. He's big and strong and can be quite funny. He shot a rabbit on Saturday and I didn't like that, but later Mrs Dramwell

served it up as a rabbit pie and I have to admit I ate some.
One can't be too fussy about food these days.

On reflection, I've decided I do like Harry. The future
may be worthwhile, after all.

22 June 1941
Eastcott Farm

I'm fifteen now but I feel so much older. When I look in the
mirror I think I look a lot older, too. Older than Janet and
Norah, anyway.

It wasn't Harry who came to collect us from Dunwick
gates yesterday, but a tall, dark man in a brown uniform
with flashes of yellow.

'Hi, Giovanni,' said Janet. 'These are my friends: Norah
and Veronica.'

'H-hello, Janet, h-hello, Norah. H-hello, Veronica,' he
answered with a wide smile and exaggerated 'H'. He
pronounced my name syllable by syllable: 'Verr-on-ee-cah'.

Janet explained as we climbed up into the cart:
'Giovanni is our new prisoner-of-war. The old one was
rubbish so we asked for another. You're from Italy, aren't
you, Giovanni?'

He nodded gleefully.

Behind Janet's gossip and the trotting horse hoofs, I
could hear him saying 'Verr-on-ee-cah. Verr-on-ee-cah'
over and over to himself throughout the journey. When
we arrived at the farm he took a handful of fresh grass
from the verge and offered it to the horse, speaking to it
gently in his own language, stroking its nose. I like
Giovanni.

When we arrived, Mrs Dramwell said we could have a
treat, what with my birthday and to say thank you for all
our help with the cows and everything. A picnic for us
girls. Harry came with us and we cycled to a viewpoint at

the edge of Eastcott Farm. You can see the crags of the Peak District from there. The air was balmy and loads of flowers were out: pink campions and foaming white cow parsley all along the edges of the track.

We had our picnic in the shade of an ancient oak. There was a freshly baked loaf, home-made potato pies, pickled onions, apples and ginger cake. Harry lounged at my feet and passed me everything, even though I was quite capable of reaching for it myself.

I caught Norah swivelling her eyes towards me whenever Harry spoke, to see my reaction. She knows Harry admires me.

It's nice to be admired, I must say. Might I be capable of falling in love? That might be rather agreeable.

To be honest, I think I'm due a bit of agreeableness.

I do need something to keep me going. There's a gaping hole in my life and I feel as if my soul will be sucked down it unless I can plug it with something.

12 July 1941
Eastcott Farm

At last it's happening. I'm all flurried and flushed. The plan is for us to cycle to the station and then take the train into town together. Just Harry and me. The picture house is then only a short walk away. Harry assures me it is an extremely naughty thing to do, so I'm game.

'It'll be easy to keep it a secret from my mum,' he said. 'I'll tell her I'm off to meet my pals and she'll assume you're upstairs with Jan and Nor.'

Janet thinks the whole thing is hilarious. Norah isn't so taken with the idea (I wonder why!). They've arranged my hair in big curls fastened with thousands of pins. I am wearing my poppy-red cotton dress and I've borrowed Janet's best beige jacket to go over it. We don't have stockings but Janet has drawn a line down the back of my legs in brown ink so it looks as though I'm wearing them.

I'm just writing to fill in the last ten minutes before I go. It's rather exciting. Mrs Dramwell is sewing downstairs. I shall slip out of the back door any minute now. I'm ready.

Monday, 14 July 1941
Dunwick Hall

I don't know who to talk to. There's nobody. Only you, as ever, my dear diary. Only you will listen to my woes and absorb them into your sad white pages.

This is what happened on Saturday night.

I met Harry as arranged outside the back door at Eastcott. He'd made an effort to slick down his hair, but it unfortunately made his ears seem to stick out even more. He'd brought only one bicycle with him. The other one was broken, he said.

'But you can squeeze behind me while I pedal. You're not frightened, are you?'

Of course I wasn't. I climbed up behind him on the seat and we were off, gathering speed fast. My poppy-coloured skirts flew in the breeze. I clung on to him and felt his muscles rippling through his shirt. And felt his pleasure at my body pressing into his back.

'My Aunt Margaret would have a fit if she knew!' I cried.

On the train people eyed us disapprovingly, trying to work out our ages, but nobody addressed us. I regaled Harry with stories about Aunt M's stinginess.

'I thought you was a snob when I first met you, Veronica,' he told me, 'but you're not. You're a good sport.'

The film was an adventure starring Jimmy Cagney. Harry didn't seem to want to watch at all, though. His arm kept stealing round my shoulders. I quite liked it at first, I even leaned in to him a little. My heart was pounding out new rhythms. I could feel the locket hanging against it, making me more and more desperate for love. Harry nuzzled closer and closer.

But then he put his face up to mine and started to kiss my lips. I recoiled. His breath was pungent, like boiled onions. I couldn't bear how his skin was so pimpled and coarse.

'Don't!' I hissed. 'I want to watch the film.'

On the way out he made a lunge for me again. His hands pawed at my body. I sprang away.

'No, Harry. I don't like it. Get off me!'

'What? You hot me up then suddenly turn frosty? That's not very nice.'

On the train back we were silent as stones. I was dreading the cycle ride. I kept racking my brain for another way I could get back to the farm or the school . . . and there wasn't one.

18 July 1941
Dunwick Hall

Oh that this too, too sullied flesh would melt, thaw and resolve itself into a dew . . .

Hamlet completely expresses it all.

It's horrible. Janet won't speak to me. She won't even look at me. She turns away pointedly whenever I sit next to her. Instead of sharing corned beef sandwiches like we used to, she stuffs them into her own face. Norah gives me the cold shoulder, too, of course.

Harry must have told them I seduced him or something because the school is rippling with ugly rumours. My schoolfellows now delight in labelling me a whore.

There's no way I'm going to condescend to tell my side of the story if the people I thought were my friends won't even listen.

I'm all churned up inside and don't know what to do. I hate Harry's guts. How could he do this to me? I think up all sorts of imaginary conversations and ways of getting my own back, but I can never put my plans into operation because I never see him. There are no more invitations to Eastcott Farm.

Sometimes I think the injustice is driving me insane. Nobody in this world will stand up for me. I wish, wish, wish I still had Dad and Mum. At night I bite hard into my pillow. It is the only way to avoid howling my heart out.

Saturday, 19 July 1941
Aunt M's house

This morning I stood outside the school gates, waiting for the milk float, apart from the cluster of other girls. Janet and Norah were waiting too, ignoring me.

When the Eastcott cart clattered round the corner I couldn't help looking up at the driver. But it wasn't Harry. It was the Italian prisoner of war, Giovanni. 'Verr-on-ee-cah!' he cried. I traded a brief smile with him. It was sweet how he remembered my name. Then I noticed that Harry was there, too, in the cart. He helped his sister and Norah up with exaggerated gentlemanliness. All the while he studiously avoided turning his head towards me. I stuck my nose in the air.

I caught the tail end of a phrase from Janet: '. . . no right to act so high and mighty, the dirty slut . . .'

I bristled. As Giovanni drove the cart off down the road I saw Harry pointedly place himself next to Norah, put his arm around her and give her a long, lingering kiss on the lips. Both of them looked back at me to see my reaction. I stood there alone, quivering with rage.

Sunday, 20 July 1941
Aggleworth

When I set off to my dance class yesterday I was exhausted from the pounding emotions of this last week. The warm sun on my face felt brutal, reminding me there's no warmth to be had from my fellow humans any more. Thank heaven there's still dancing.

I was striding fast to get to the hall when I saw two figures walking ahead. One was pushing a wheelbarrow full of vegetables along the road. He was wearing a brown uniform with yellow flashes. As if he sensed my gaze, he turned and looked round. It was Giovanni.

He recognized me immediately and bowed so low that his mop of hair flopped over his eyes.

'Hello,' I answered, imitating his style with a mock curtsy.

'*Bella!*' he cried. His companion urged him onwards, but he stopped for a further moment to pick a flower and lay it on the road before continuing.

The two men had turned a corner and disappeared by the time I reached the flower. I picked it up. It was just a dandelion, but oh how I loved that dandelion! It was brilliantly yellow and vibrant, defying anyone to dampen its ardour. I stroked its petals and then placed it carefully behind my ear.

The dance lesson dragged much more than usual. Afterwards, instead of heading straight back to Aunt M's, I wandered in the direction of the open-air market. I meandered among the stalls until I saw him behind a mountain of vegetables.

His face lit up. It wasn't at all the face of a desperate and down-trodden prisoner. He looked cheerful and lively. Suddenly I realized he was the most handsome man I've ever met.

Giovanni's eyes are deep brown and vivacious and fiery. His nose is noble. His hair is unkempt and there's stubble on his chin but it's nice stubble that suits him. He is well built; tall, fibrous and strong. Whichever angle you view him from he is utterly enthralling.

'So they let you out on your own, do they?' I asked him, fascinated.

'Oh yes, now they do. The people in these stalls next to mine make sure I do not run off with the money.' He addressed the oldish man in the striped apron selling meat cuts next to him. 'I do not run off with the money, do I, Mr Howard?'

'No, you don't,' replied Mr Howard with a grin. 'I hoard all the money for your vegetables, that's why. And return your takings to Mrs Dramwell when I see her at Eastcott on Monday.'

It is amazing that a POW is granted such freedom. Mr Howard and Giovanni seem to be on very good terms.

'Do you want to buy any vegetable?' asked Giovanni. 'See here I have the lovely potatoes. And the very fine beetroot. And the tomatoes most splendid. I am thinking you must like a very splendid tomato?'

'I certainly would like a very splendid tomato!'

I tipped the coins into his hands and he immediately passed them to Mr Howard.

I wondered whether to bite into the tomato right there but decided against it. A spray of red juice and seeds over my face would hardly look attractive.

'Also I would like . . .' I pondered, viewing the produce, 'something for my Aunt Margaret. What would you recommend, Giovanni?'

'What sort of a thing does she like?' he asked, looking at me and the vegetables in turn.

'I don't know what she'd like. But I know what I'd like to get her. Something very, very old and very, very un-delicious,'

I answered. 'What is your oldest and most un-delicious vegetable?'

His laugh was open and joyful – yet intimate, as if we were partners in crime together.

'How about this old, wrinkled turnip?' he suggested.

I smiled. 'Absolutely perfect.'

Sunday, 27 July 1941
Aggleworth

I've started to crave Saturday afternoons so much! Not for the dance lessons but for the trips to the market afterwards. Giovanni must know I come especially to meet him. He picked flowers again yesterday; meadowsweet, wild roses, and lots and lots of dandelions. He presented the bunch to me across his vegetable stand with a flourish. Mr Howard busied himself and pretended not to see.

I decided to bestow on Giovanni the greatest honour. 'Giovanni. I know my name is difficult for you. In the future will you please call me Very?'

'Very? Why, yes. I will! Very lovely, Very beautiful, Very Darling You!'

I purred. Very Darling Me! If only we could find some time alone together.

Sunday, 3 August 1941

There is much to tell.

Firstly, I am in love. How could it be possible not to love Giovanni, the finest and best-looking man in the world? And no, I don't give a fig that he classifies as the enemy. This war is so, so absurdly pointless anyway.

Yesterday I didn't even go to my lesson, I just went straight to the market to find him.

'You do realize I'm missing my dancing to be with you,' I told him.

'Ah, that's a shame. I do not want to stop any girl from her dancing. Especially you, Very. To see you dance – now that would be truly glorious.'

I gave a little twirl in the street. He clapped enthusiastically.

'Perhaps we dance together?'

He stepped forward and took me in a dance hold. It was beyond wonderful. I started to melt into his arms right there but then Mr Howard intervened, tapping him briskly on the back. 'No, you'd better stop there, Giovanni. There are limits, young lad.'

Giovanni let go of me.

He whispered in my ear. 'I heard there's a dance in the hall tonight.'

'Could we do it?' I whispered back, thrilled at the prospect.

'It's not easy. I will not be allowed in because I am the prisoner. But if I sneak away from the farm it's possible . . . We two can maybe meet behind the hall? We might hear the music. We might dance together then?'

I loved the fact that it was so difficult but he was willing to try anyway.

'I'll be there,' I promised.

In the evening I told Aunt M I was going to bed early with a headache. It was easy to tiptoe out without being heard. The air was warm and heady with the drifting scents of roses and wild honeysuckle. I ran all the way.

He was there. The moment he stepped out of the shadows I swooped across and flung my arms around him. I couldn't help myself. Shocked, delighted, he covered me with rapturous kisses. It was paradise.

A swell of music rose from the hall. Giovanni and I danced together in the dirt and dusk behind the back wall, where nobody could see us. It felt so close, so passionate, so gloriously reckless.

'Very!' he whispered. 'My Very. You make me so alive!'

'Me too!' I breathed him in, the earthy, manly scent of him. Every cell in my body rejoiced in the intimacy of the moment.

He looked even more handsome in the silver wash of moonlight that encircled us.

'They can black out every lamp on the earth, but they can't black out the moon and stars!' I whispered.

'No, they can't, Very,' he said, 'and they can't black out the light I hold in my heart for you.'

But all at once the band started playing a different tune. I stopped dead.

'What is it?' Giovanni asked. 'What's wrong, Very? This tune, it is good. Is happy. But you . . . you are not happy.'

A sigh came pouring out from my depths. I leaned heavily against the gate. It was the Lambeth Walk.

Giovanni enclosed me in his arms again. 'You are yet more beautiful when you are sad,' he told me.

He held me for a long time, kissing my eyes, my nose, my hair, my mouth. I felt rigid, holding my feelings in, tightly, oh so tightly.

Then I told him. I told him about Mum and Dad. How Mum used to plait my hair and tell me stories, and how Dad used to put the hearth-rug over himself and growl and pretend to be a bear and we laughed together until the tears rolled down our cheeks. About how we imagined my future together: Mum said I was going to be a writer, but Dad said I was going to be a famous explorer. About how we huddled under the stairs when the air-raid siren started, and how they were never afraid of anything. How Mum always went out to drive ambulances and help injured people even when it was dangerous. How Dad had been so sad at the prospect of another war when he'd only narrowly survived the first one. How they both treasured me above everything. How nobody, nobody treasured me now.

Finally I told Giovanni how they'd both been crushed to death as our home tumbled in pieces on top of them.

Giovanni listened; stunned, silent.

When I'd finished he stroked my hair back. I didn't want him to look at me. My face felt ugly and contorted.

'And yet you do not cry,' he said.

'If I start I shall never stop.'

He planted his mouth on to mine. It was an urgent connection as if he was trying to siphon away all my pain.

I extricated myself. I stared straight into his eyes.

His eyes; dark, full of understanding.

'Giovanni, I want you.'

'I want you, too.' It was almost a whisper, almost a whimper, as if he was trying to resist it.

I looked around and saw the sloping roof of a barn silhouetted against the sky.

Everyone seems to think I am a whore anyway, so why not?

'Now,' I urged. 'We have to seize this moment.'

I took Giovanni by the hand and pulled him over the moonlit fields towards the barn.

He asked if I was sure.

Yes.

Yes, I've never been so sure about anything in my life.

28

Patrick

Bolton
December 2012

I CLEAR MY THROAT. 'Tell me honestly,' I say to Gav, 'do you think I look a teeny tad Mediterranean?'

I've persuaded him to come for a swift after-work pint at the Dragon's Flagon. He looks at me curiously. 'Maybe a little bit Italian, for example?' I add. 'My nose, perhaps?'

'Let's see you in profile.'

I turn my head.

'No, I'd say not,' he says. 'It's not a Roman nose. Longish, but not Roman. Your skin's quite brown though. It's got definite undertones of olive.'

'OK. Right. Thanks.'

'Do you *want* to look Italian?'

'Do I?'

'I'm asking *you*, mate!'

God, I don't fricking know!

'I think those diaries are getting to me,' I tell him by way of a reply.

'Mmmm?'

'Because I grew up without any parents, this granny thing is kind of important.'

Saying that out loud makes me realize the truth of it. And the diaries are quite a revelation. In a way, history has repeated itself. Like Granny V, I lost both parents pretty early on and had to learn to fend for myself. But then, most of my foster parents were OK. Young Veronica didn't have anyone like that – she only had that awful religious nutter of an aunt. And she didn't have drugs to fall back on. Man, it must have been grim. No wonder she went off the rails a bit, no wonder she tried to find love wherever she could.

I never knew my dad at all but it's clear Veronica doted on hers. I lost my mother when I was six, which was horrendous, but I guess in some ways it's even worse when you're fourteen. You've got all that love built up over the years, all those hugs and conversations and things you do together and then all of it's just snatched away. Harsh. It must have done stuff to that poor kid's head.

'So you think you might have some Italian blood?' Gav asks.

'Looks like it's a possibility. But then . . .'

Veronica only went out with Harry the one time, but I'm not clear how it ended. She didn't go into any detail in the diary about the cycle ride home. She wasn't a happy bunny about it, though; that much is obvious. He didn't . . . Surely he didn't . . . ? Shit. No, he can't have. She'd have written it down . . . wouldn't she? I've only been skim-reading, skipping some of the long, boring bits about school, but I'm sure I haven't missed anything that big. Still, now that horrible doubt has entered my thick skull, I'm going to have to race through the rest of the diaries to find out what I can.

I slurp down the rest of my pint in one go. 'Soz, mate, I'm going to have to dash.'

My pulse has gone fricking crazy.

I'm being ridiculous.

It *must* be Giovanni who's my granddad – mustn't it?

Terry's Penguin Blog

18 December 2012

Adélie penguins are endlessly curious and endlessly busy. Today Veronica and I were followed around by one particularly inquisitive character as we were marking out nests. Not yet of an age to have his own family, his interest seems to have been piqued by our activities. Here is a photo of him and Veronica watching each other. As you can see, she's holding her handbag well out of his reach.

Elsewhere, nature is taking its course, couples are copulating, eggs are being laid and the first chicks are emerging. What a riotous community we have here on Locket Island!

29

Veronica

Locket Island

I GAZE OUT OVER the vast, rippling, black-and-white sea of Adélies. Everywhere I look there are interactions between penguin and penguin. Each one seems so at home in his community. They fit in a way I have never fitted with my fellow humans. Once again I feel all too conscious of my past.

Sometimes memories gather dust in the back crevices of your mind. Sometimes they hover over you like shadows. Sometimes they come after you with a club.

I wonder, now, about Giovanni. Is he still alive, out there somewhere? Even after all these years I can see him quite clearly in my mind's eye. I remember his hands, large and a bit roughened but with a touch so sensitive to my needs. I can almost feel again the faint stubble on his cheek, his lips on mine, youth against youth, a thousand nerve endings awakened, craving more.

At the time I couldn't have imagined a stronger force. But biology dictates so many things. Is my whole personality nothing more than a peculiar cocktail of chemicals? Moreover, is love just a series of biorhythms, a collection of electrical impulses to the brain? An excess of hormones? Maybe, under certain conditions, this alchemy we call love is intensified – intensified, for example, by such things as a long summer full of bright sunshine, a youthful rebelliousness and the extreme tragedies of war. It may be so.

What would have happened if we'd been allowed to stay together, Giovanni and I? Would it have continued to be such an all-encompassing magnetism? Or was it merely the madness of the times, the very fact that a relationship between us was forbidden, that made me so hopelessly in love with him? I am old enough and cynical enough to know that this may be the truth of the matter.

He might not have survived the war. Or he might have returned to his own country, as most of the POWS did. It is conceivable he is an old man now; crooked, wrinkled, perhaps smoking a pipe, perhaps wandering in a Mediterranean olive grove. Does he ever wonder about the English girl he loved so long ago? Even in his wildest imaginings it will not occur to him that she is in Antarctica with three young scientists and five thousand penguins.

I could, when I return to Britain, employ the agency to look him up, to find him as they found Patrick. Do I have a long-neglected duty there as well?

No. If Giovanni survived the war and if he'd wanted me, he would have come back for me. He would have found a way. I have already opened up a great can of worms by revisiting those diaries, by seeking out my grandson.

My thoughts turn to Patrick. What is the nature of the man behind the layers of grime and fug of drugs? Is it possible I have judged him too harshly? His behaviour at the airport was in stark contrast to that of our first encounter. Had I not been so preoccupied with my imminent departure on this Antarctic odyssey, and had I not been so shocked by his sudden appearance, I would have focused more clearly on the boy.

Now I have entrusted my past to him, in the form of those teen-age diaries. I need never have shown them to another human being, and I am somewhat surprised at my decision to follow this course of action. Indeed, I squirm at the thought of him reading them. Yet somewhere beneath the layers of horror there's an undeniable sense of relief that at last I have shared my story. My impulsive side must have recognized that need within me.

Will he read, I wonder? Will he understand?

'You seem deep in thought, Veronica.'

'Is there a law against it?' I ask tersely.

The sky is seeping blue into mauve, mauve into inky grey. Terry and I have been out for hours. There are still humps of penguin carcasses at regular intervals, mummified by the ice. I try not to look at them.

The living penguins waste no time in grief or self-pity. They are too busy. More and more chicks appear every day, comical little creatures, a stubbier, fuzzier version of their parents. The adults take it in turns to go out to sea for food. Each comes back with a dilated paunch and feeds the baby with regurgitated krill in a thrusting beak-to-beak movement. The first chicks are larger now and venture beyond their nests. They toddle through the puddles and mud, squeaking continually.

I espy one very tiny figure who is limply skirting the edge of the community. The chick is sooty-grey and bedraggled. It seems to have lost its way. It's making slow progress, wandering a few paces then stopping to look around. It arches its head upwards, then sideways, viewing the other penguins with an air of neediness. They continue with their day-to-day business: gossiping, arguing, wriggling about on their nests, presenting and accepting regurgi-tated fish. But this one seems isolated and afraid.

'Where are its parents?' I ask Terry.

'They're probably dead. Taken by a seal or trapped in an ice-chasm or something. It doesn't look like they're coming back, anyway. They both wouldn't have left it, it's too young. Poor little thing!'

The chick stumbles up to an adult who is sitting on a nest. The adult pecks it away.

'It won't survive long,' Terry says. 'Starvation or the cold will finish it off pretty soon.'

'Is there nothing we can do?' I ask, dismayed.

'Sorry, Veronica, but no. It is our policy not to interfere. Nature is tough, sometimes.'

'Your *policy*?' I enquire, imbuing the word with scorn. I detest policies. People are forever constructing policies to cover a general purpose, then they get trapped by those policies and become slaves to them; they feel they must obey them in every situation, blindly ignoring common sense or kindness. This policy is a prime example of such absurdity.

'Yes, our policy,' answers Terry. 'Human intervention has harmed wildlife beyond belief. It's best to let nature sort things out. Otherwise we might cause more harm than good.'

I try to suppress my exasperation. 'And would we be able to save this baby if it wasn't for your precious policy?'

She shakes her head sorrowfully.

This is not a proper answer and I am not going to let her get away with it. I repeat my question.

'Well, I suppose if we took the hatchling in and fed it there'd be a faint chance it might survive,' she concedes. 'But that's theoretical. It might grow dependent on us, which isn't what we'd want. The whole idea is to support the penguins in the wild, in their own habitat, not make pets of them.'

I try to digest this. It feels unnatural, like trying to digest a rusty nail.

She drifts away and starts filming two parents feeding fish to a chubby toddler penguin. My eyes remain riveted on the orphan.

He (I am already thinking of it as 'he') totters first in one direction and then the other. I am transfixed, as if I'm connected to the baby penguin. I feel his feelings: the cold, the confusion, the loneliness, the loss. He assumes help must come from somewhere soon . . . yet it doesn't.

I march up to Terry. My voice is a strident blare, belying the lump in my throat.

'Terry, unless we do something to help that little one I refuse to appear on your blog any longer.'

Terry lowers the camera. She looks anxiously into my face. Her eyes are searching, as if she doesn't quite understand me, as if I've done something out of character.

'You really care, don't you?' she says at last. 'It's no good being sentimental, Veronica. Seriously, it doesn't do to worry about individuals. Nature chooses which ones live and which ones die. I'm sorry, but that's the way it is. Try to forget that chick and focus on all the happy penguins.'

She has asked me to do the impossible. At this moment all the happy penguins do not interest me. It is this one lost soul who commands all my attention. He is drooping, actually drooping now. His flippers hang by his sides. His beak points to the cold earth that will soon be his grave.

I don't believe Terry is unreasonable. She has just been brainwashed by a couple of stupid men. Perhaps even they will see sense if I can approach it from a different angle, if they think they can get more funding that way. I'm not above exploiting human greed.

'If you managed to save this little fellow and put photos of him on your blog, surely everyone will like him. He's so . . .' I clear my throat. 'You'll get *far* more positive publicity than if you abandon him.'

Terry is motionless. I can see thoughts flashing across her consciousness, possibilities beginning to shine in her eyes. 'Well, as far as the publicity goes, you do have a point. There aren't many things in life as cute as a baby penguin. I guess the public would be bound to warm to him.'

'Absolutely!' I cry. 'And they're so much more likely to contribute money towards the project if you have a cuddly little mascot.' I wait while she continues to process the pros and cons.

'I very much doubt we can persuade Mike and Dietrich. But I suppose it's vaguely possible. I suppose we can try.'

'If we can, then we must.'

I will say this for myself: I am good at getting my own way.

Terry puts her load on the ground. 'I'll see if I can get hold of the little fella.'

We edge our way towards the chick. He turns his head towards us, registering no fear. Terry makes a swift dive, seizes him by the feet and beak and tucks him under her arm. The bird gives a miniature squawk and a feeble flutter of alarm, but submits almost immediately. Terry gives his neck a gentle stroke. It seems to calm him. I approach and stroke him too. He is no bigger than a teacup. His down is soft as cotton wool.

'We'll do everything we can for you,' I tell him earnestly. 'I promise.'

Terry looks at me sideways with a little smile. 'We'd better take him back to the camp,' she says. 'I'll radio Dietrich and Mike and ask them to meet us there. I won't say why. Hopefully it'll be easier to convince them if they actually set eyes on the poor creature.'

30

Veronica

Locket Island

As TERRY PREDICTED, THE recalcitrant Mike is completely closed to the idea.

'You've brought us back here for *this*? Have you gone completely cuckoo?'

Dietrich is equally firm. 'No, Terry. We said we wouldn't.'

Terry pushes her glasses up her nose and unzips her parka slightly, revealing the small, fluffy little package that is snuggled inside. 'I know, I know, but look at him, guys! There's no harm in trying. And I know loads of people would agree, people across the world who read my blog. This little chick could actually become the face of what we're trying to do.'

'A tame penguin? A *domesticated* hand-fed penguin? Hardly! We're scientists, Terry, in case you'd forgotten. We're environmentalists. We don't believe in human interference – at any cost. Isn't that right, Dietrich?'

'That's what we agreed,' nods Dietrich.

The baby penguin pokes its beak out, then its whole head. Unaware of its predicament, it surveys us with big round eyes. Its beak opens but no sound comes out. It tries again and manages a plaintive sort of piping noise.

In spite of himself Mike bends his head to look at the chick. In spite of himself he puts a finger out and strokes it on the head.

Is it conceivable that the uncharitable Mike is melting?

'Terry, you're unbelievable!' he says in a voice that isn't a compliment but isn't absolutely rigid either. He looks up again. 'I'm surprised at you. You know the answer has to be no.'

I open my mouth to say something, then think better of it. I battle with strong feelings just as I used to do in the past when they threatened to overcome me. I know that self-control, if I can find it, will be my best ally in this situation. Success is more likely if I can achieve invisibility. I observe Mike and Dietrich. There was a time when I could easily have got my way. An opening of the eyes a little wider, a pouting of the lips and any man would have been at my beck and call. Now whatever I do seems to have the opposite effect. My only remaining power is in my purse and even that can't work in this particular instance.

But Terry – she could win them over. If only she would take off her glasses and flutter her eyelashes a bit. She'll never master the direct challenge as I did at her age, but I'm sure she could muster a coy persuasiveness of her own. Alas! She has no idea. She is wrinkling her brow in a most unappealing manner.

'Come on, Deet, just think! It would give us a chance to study a juvenile in so much detail from close at hand.'

'You're not being logical, Terry,' answers Dietrich. 'We don't need that sort of information. We're studying the survival of the whole species. We haven't the time to watch over and cater for the needs of a single penguin.'

'Yes, but . . .' she peters out.

He shakes his head. 'Sorry, Terry. We've got more important stuff to do.'

The chick droops its head feebly as if it understands its own lack of importance. I swallow fiercely. Only I, Veronica McCreedy, unpopular, interfering old bat, am willing to help it. Once more I am filled with a strange, desperate sensation. It is so strong I want to scream in the faces of Dietrich and Mike. I want to knock their heads together, make them see that a species *is* its individuals. That individuals are what matter. It is men like these who cause wars, where thousands of peace-loving individuals are sacrificed for a so-called 'noble' cause. History looks back and says this side won and that side lost, but the reality is that nobody wins. And what about the thousands of men and women and children who are butchered in the process? Does nobody care about them? Each one of them matters. Each and every one.

And this individual penguin matters, too. He does to me, anyway.

The chick lifts his head again. He is so young, so friendless. At this moment nothing on earth is as vital to me as his safety.

Terry sighs, plainly upset too. Having carried it home and shared her body heat with it, she has begun to bond.

'*Please*, Dietrich.'

He tugs at his beard in a stressed manner. 'I'll tell you what. We'll put it to the vote.'

Mike takes it upon himself to summarize the situation in his own abhorrently prejudiced way. 'So: do we hand-rear the bird, staying up half the night, becoming exhausted and emotionally attached and making it totally dependent on us? Or do we let nature take its course?'

'Let the baby die, you mean,' I put in.

'*The baby*? It's not a human, Veronica,' Terry reminds me.

Dietrich holds up an impatient hand. 'OK. Enough! We know the facts. Who's for trying to look after the chick here?' he asks.

I raise my hand immediately. Terry raises hers, too. Nobody else does.

Mike scowls. 'Veronica isn't one of us. She can't vote.'

Dietrich ignores him. 'And who's for putting it back outside?'

Mike sticks his hand up. Our eyes turn to Dietrich. Very slowly he raises his hand, too.

'I'm sorry, you two. I know he's sweet, but we simply don't have the time or the resources.'

'Exactly! Couldn't have put it better myself,' says Mike.

A flash of anger glints in Terry's eyes. 'What *is* this – boys against girls?'

She turns abruptly and heads towards the door with the penguin still poking its head out of her parka.

I follow her out. 'Where are you going? What are you going to do?'

'Kill it.'

I can't believe what I've just heard. 'What?'

'I'll bang its head under a stone. It's the kindest, quickest way. Better than leaving it to a long, lingering death by starvation.'

I am aghast. 'You can't do that!'

'I don't want to, believe me, Veronica. I don't want to *at all*. But I don't have a lot of choice. The men have spoken,' she replies bitterly.

I pull her back. 'Yes, indeed, the men have spoken – but need you jump to attention? You're soon to be the boss of proceedings here. Why not practise some leadership and simply insist.'

'We'd need everyone's backing to save this little guy,' she answers in a resigned tone of voice. 'And even I can see it's not the scientifically sensible thing to do.'

I am losing her. She starts to walk away.

'No!' I shriek.

'Veronica, please don't make this any more difficult. I'm sorry. I was wrong to let you hope.'

'You were *not* wrong. I'm not having that. Scientifically sensible,

202

is it? Well, science can go to hell. Science can cut off its own nose to spite its face and disfigure itself in any other way it deems appropriate, I don't give a fig.' I'm getting worked up now. 'Sad, sick, cruel bastards.'

'Veronica!'

I throw my stick aside and stagger slightly, then regain my balance. '*You* may be a scientist but *I* am not, as Mike rightly points out. So give me the penguin.'

She gawks at me.

My hands are outstretched towards her. 'Go on. Give him here. I shall look after him myself.'

'Veronica, you can't do that.'

'Yes, Terry. Yes, I can. I mean it. I've made up my mind. I shall do whatever is necessary, whatever it takes.' Even if it is the last thing I do upon this earth. 'You may, of course, help me if you like,' I concede. 'Not as one of the scientists, but as a friend.' I've surprised myself with that last word.

Terry's glasses are a little steamed up. Her mouth puckers. She stretches out her fingers and strokes the chick's head. Then, in the speediest of movements, she grabs him in both hands and thrusts him towards me.

'Your penguin, your responsibility?'

'Quite!' I say, accepting the little one and holding him against me. He moves feebly, a tiny bundle made up of flippers, feet and fluff. He rests his head on my chest and seems to relax into me. My heart feels as though it's expanded. Now that I'm holding him I realize – quite unreasonably but with a force I can't deny – that it will be utterly impossible to let him go.

Terry watches. She blinks away a tear. Then she picks up my stick, presents it to me again and leans in towards me.

'I'll help. Of course I will,' she whispers. 'As a *friend*!' She smiles a wicked smile. 'Veronica, how the hell do you do it? You just made me go against all my logic and all my training.'

'And go *with* all your natural kindness.'

'You are a force to be reckoned with.'

'I know.'

She strokes the chick again. 'Please don't be too upset if he doesn't make it.'

'If he doesn't make it I will know, at least, that we have tried,' I tell her. It is not trying that I find unforgivable.

'What shall we call him?' she asks.

A name whisks across my consciousness. But I am quite unable to utter that name. It is another name that springs, unbidden, to my lips, a name that has kept on surfacing in my consciousness of late. Before I can stop myself, I've said it out loud.

'Patrick.'

31

Veronica

Locket Island

'HE CAN STAY IN my room,' I tell Terry decisively as we head back inside. 'We'll make up a little nest for him.'

'You go ahead and settle him in, Veronica. I'll see what fish I can find in the storeroom. We'll need to get some food down him as quickly as possible.'

The baby penguin nestles into me. His feet hang limply, his head flops against my chest. I carry him back through the lounge, whispering sweet nothings and ignoring the disgruntled faces of Mike and Dietrich as I pass. Just before I close my bedroom door behind me I catch Dietrich saying to Mike: 'Leave her be. The poor bird will probably die in any case.'

I cuddle 'the poor bird' close to me.

'You are *not* going to die,' I assure him. He doesn't respond.

Where can I put him? I lower him gently on to my bed while I think. He stays put in a semi-recumbent position, his eyes half closed. My empty suitcases are stacked against one wall of the room. I stoop down, causing my back to creak a little in protest, lift the smallest of the cases and place it, open, on the bed, near the foot end. I pad it out using my turquoise woollen cardigan with gold buttons. I place the fluffy orphan inside. He collapses at once on to his belly. A trace of pinkish fluid trickles out from his rear end.

'Don't worry about the cardigan,' I tell him. 'I have it in two other colours.'

He doesn't look remotely guilty. If I could read penguin expressions (and I believe I can) I would say he was manifesting sheer bewilderment. He's as floppy as a rag doll. It is indeed hard to believe he isn't some sort of soft toy. I sit next to him on the bed, stroking his soft down, trying to soothe him. Later I will go out and gather some stones, shells and lichen to make him feel more at home.

Terry comes into my bedroom carrying a bowl of pungent-smelling pinkish mush.

'Oh, I see you've already sacrificed a cardigan,' she notes. 'We could've given him an old blanket.'

'It doesn't matter in the least. What sustenance have you brought for him?'

'It's tinned tuna. I've warmed it up and mashed it with water . . . I hope he'll like it. It'll do him good, anyway, if we can somehow get it down him.'

She perches on the bed next to the suitcase so that we have him between us.

She takes a small syringe from her pocket. 'From the lab. Let's give this a go, then.' She fills the syringe and waves it about in front of his beak. He shows little interest. He is still in a state of collapse.

Does he, in fact, *want* to live? I ask myself. I automatically assumed that he did, which was very wrong of me.

'As I feared,' Terry comments. 'We're going to have to force the issue.'

I scrutinize the plate of revolting mush. 'I hope we're not going to have to regurgitate it for him.' At this point I begin to question where are the limits of my affection for this needy creature.

'Come on, Patrick!' Terry coaxes.

The chick shows no interest in the food, however, and continues to look fragile.

'Come on, Patrick! Patrick, come on!' I urge.

Terry gently prises open his beak with her finger and thumb. Before he has time to protest she has released several drops of the mixture down his gullet. She closes his beak again and holds it closed. Little Patrick wriggles and flails about, then gulps. We watch the lump in his neck travel down, the bolus of food safely on its way to his tummy. For a moment he looks affronted that we have taken such a liberty. But suddenly he seems to put two and two together: he is hungry and this is edible, therefore the whole undignified affair must classify as a good thing. He opens his beak wide in a clear indication that more is required.

Terry turns towards me with a triumphant grin. 'Well, that's the first hurdle sorted!'

I clap my hands together in glee. 'Tremendous! Oh, Terry! Well done!'

'It was nothing,' she says modestly, as she rests the bowl on the bed. She hands me the syringe. 'So, he's your chick. You do it.'

I need no further encouragement. I extract a generous amount of the fishy mush and release it into Patrick's open beak. He swallows it more eagerly this time. He opens his beak again.

We take it in turns to feed him. When he has eaten well, Terry and I shake hands.

'Thank you, Terry.'

'Thank you, Veronica. I'm glad you insisted. He's well worth the trouble. Aren't you, little Patrick?' she says to our new charge.

Already he seems stronger. I'm sure I can see a spark of determination has kindled in his bright eyes, a dogged willpower. He *does* want to live. He's going to give it his best effort. He's keen to defy the odds.

I'm not the only stubborn one around here.

I still go out to the penguin colony to be amongst the other birds every day, but only for a short time. Patrick the Penguin has become my chief concern. I now know the location of all the different sorts of fish at the field base. In addition to tuna, there is frozen cod, herring and fish fingers. Once they are defrosted I remove the skin, bones or batter as required, warm them in the oven, mash them carefully with water and serve them straight into Patrick's beak with the syringe. It is a rare and satisfying feeling to be of use to a fellow creature.

Terry is going to try and source some krill for him as well, because this (in regurgitated form) is what he'd be eating in the wild. There are fisheries on some of the islands. 'I wouldn't normally have dealings with them,' she has informed me. 'I feel a bit ambivalent towards them because overfishing is one of the big threats to the penguins' future. Still, if we can help our Patrick . . .'

Patrick's strength is building day by day. He spends much time snuggled up in the turquoise cardigan in the suitcase, which is now on the floor. He likes to play with the cardigan's gold buttons. I think he is amused by their roundness and shininess, as any child would be.

He is able to waddle about on my bedroom floor and make short forays into the lounge. He is, of course, incapable of opening a door himself, and doesn't grasp the concept of knocking. If he wants to go through he will wait, pressed up against the door. This alarms me because he is in danger of being squashed should somebody suddenly open the door from the other side. It nearly happened once with Dietrich. I suggested that to avoid this we should always call out 'Penguin clear?' before opening. However, people cannot be trusted to remember.

Terry says it's vitally important he doesn't develop agoraphobia and we must let him wander about the field centre. For this reason I've accepted the fact that most of the doors inside the building will have to remain open. Initially I found this trying and stressful but I'm becoming accustomed to it. Penguin Patrick takes full advantage of his freedom and wanders at will.

Unfortunately, Patrick, like his namesake, has no comprehension of basic hygiene. Little accidents occur all the time and require the application of strong detergent and a mop. If Eileen were present this duty would be allocated to her, but as the three scientists are out for most of the day, the responsibility is mine. I don't relish heaving a bucket of water around but needs must. Astonishingly I find that I rise to the challenge without the slightest trace of resentment.

Even more astonishing is the fact that my baby penguin seems to have taken a liking to me. If I lift him on to the bed he will crawl into the crook of my arm and press up against me. I am aware that any baby creature will seek something warm to cuddle up to, but I cannot help but be wholly delighted that the something, in this instance, is me.

The dear creature doesn't even mind when, if his nether regions become mucky, I scrub him in the basin. He seems to think it's a kind of game. He bobs his head in and out of the water and opens and shuts his beak in a charming manner. Then he gives his whole body a shake, sending scattered droplets through the air. I scold him gently for making me wet, but it's impossible to be angry with him.

Terry still shares feeding duties with me but she is out for much of the day. She always rushes into my room on her return to see how Patrick is doing. Sometimes she measures and weighs him. Often she takes photos of us together for her blog.

'Have you noticed,' I asked her over supper last night, 'that he recognizes his own name? He stretches his flippers out and widens his eyes whenever we say the word "Patrick". And sometimes opens his beak, too?'

'Yes, I've noticed,' she answered. 'Well, we do use his name *a lot*.'

'You sometimes call him "little sausage",' I point out. 'But that has no reaction. It's the name "Patrick" that he recognizes.'

'He doesn't know it's his name,' Mike insisted with his usual acerbity. 'You've heard of Pavlov's dogs?'

'It does ring a bell,' I replied.

'Ha ha. Very droll.'

Dietrich takes it upon himself to expand. 'Pavlov always rang a bell before feeding his dogs, as you'll remember, Veronica. The dogs quickly began to associate the sound with food, so that, after a while, merely ringing the bell caused them to salivate in expectation. It's probably similar with your Patrick. Baby penguins have very refined hearing. They can detect their own parents' calls amongst the deafening furore of the rookery. You are Patrick's substitute parent, and you say his name every time you feed him. It's not surprising he's come to recognize the word so quickly.'

Mike nods. 'It is merely a primal response.'

Mike is committed to concealing any hint of softness in his character. He calls Patrick 'that bird'. Right from the outset he was very sure that my baby penguin was going to die – and we all know that Mike doesn't like being proved wrong. Yet sometimes, when he thinks nobody is looking, I catch him holding out a titbit of food for our new resident. And on his face is that rarest of things: a fond smile.

Terry's Penguin Blog

26 December 2012

Well, it has been some Christmas this year! We made a token gesture towards celebrating: a pretty decent Christmas dinner and fun in the evening with board games and some carols, courtesy of Dietrich's CD player. But the major news is that we now have our very own adopted baby penguin! He has lost both parents – sadly a common occurrence out here on Locket Island. While we wouldn't normally consider nursing such a young one under our own steam we do have an extra pair of hands at the moment and Veronica was very keen to help him. It will be interesting to study his behaviour and monitor his progress.

The chick (we've named him Patrick) is a gutsy lad. He was a mere 510g when he arrived last week but since then he has almost doubled in weight. You see him here with Veronica being fed his own Christmas dinner: a formula made from krill and herring. He's up for anything and didn't mind (for the sake of the camera) wearing a party hat – unlike Veronica!

As a rule, we never interfere with the lives of Adélies. But Patrick the Penguin is an exceptional case, and he seems more than happy in Veronica's company. I think you'll agree this bond is quite remarkable.

32

Patrick

Bolton

RIGHT, WAS THIS GIOVANNI guy a one-off? Did he get her up the duff? Did he turn out to be a scumbag? And is she going to spill the beans about what happened with Harry? I grab the diary and flip through, reading entries on and off, searching for answers.

> *Friday, 15 August 1941*
> *Dunwick Hall*
>
> A few girls stay here for the holidays and I'm one of them.
> I only go back to Aunt M's at weekends (and that's only
> because she feels she has to make some gesture towards
> keeping an eye on me, else God will be cross). Miss
> Philpotts and Miss Long, two very tiresome teachers, are
> here the whole time at Dunwick Hall supervising us, but
> I've found ways of eluding them. Because elude them I

212

must if I'm to meet up with my Giovanni. The Saturday trysts at the market are no longer enough. I play the teachers off against each other, telling one I am ill, the other that my aunt has requested my presence in Aggleworth. I leave a trail of confusion in my wake. They're too lazy and stupid to work out that I'm actually sneaking out to meet my lover.

This new episode of life is unlike anything I've experienced before. I'm swimming in a wild, bright ocean of magic. I am gloriously, thrillingly, whole-heartedly submerged in love!

Luckily, Giovanni is trusted at Eastcott Farm to take the cart out on his own. He's good at finding pretexts so he can meet me at prearranged places and times. Once I'm out of the school gates I walk miles down the country lanes to reach the secret rendezvous. I select only the most romantic places, mapped out from my journeys in the milk float. Sometimes it's under a spreading oak, sometimes inside a hay-scented barn, sometimes beside the daisy-strewn banks of a brook. Sometimes we can meet for only a matter of minutes to share kisses and whispered words across a fence. If we miss each other we leave love letters under stones, marking them with a single plucked dandelion.

The harder it is to reach Giovanni, the more passionately I seem to want him. I dream and fidget my way through the knitting and cleaning chores and dull studies that Miss Philpotts sets for us. At mealtimes I don't even try to talk to the other girls. I live only for the next sight of Giovanni.

Last time we met I hid behind a tree to watch his reaction when he thought I wasn't coming. He did look crestfallen . . . until I started singing. How his eyes sparkled then!

'Very, you are here! How splendid!' he cried, wrapping me in his arms.

I love his funny use of English, especially his constant use of the word 'splendid'. I've started using it obsessively myself.

'It would be very splendid if you would kiss me again.'

'It would be very splendid if you would unbutton my blouse.'

'It would be very splendid if you would slowly but firmly put your hands here and here.'

He is always happy to obey.

When I feel Giovanni's flesh on my flesh the war and the hurt and the hatred all dissolve away. We are together and nothing else matters.

Monday, 25 August 1941
Dunwick Hall

Giovanni and I managed to meet up for a whole afternoon yesterday while Aunt M was at a church meeting. We wandered through a grassy meadow dotted with dandelions – our flower. Some were blazing yellow but many had turned into dandelion clocks. As we walked hand in hand, thousands of fluffy seeds were blowing on the breeze like confetti in the streaming sunlight. I took the opportunity to ask Giovanni about his life.

Giovanni was born in 1923, which makes him eighteen (three years older than me – although he thinks the difference is less because I've told him I'm seventeen). He is close to all his family, but especially his mother.

'When I was called up, Mama cried, big wailings and tears like the sea! That made the leaving home even more harder for me.'

Hearing that made me remember my evacuation from London and the sight of Mum's red, swollen eyes. I pushed the memory out of my head and asked Giovanni if he enjoyed the army.

He said that, once he was used to his new life, he enjoyed joshing with his fellow soldiers. But he'd felt very clueless about warfare. He'd been given such minimal army training before being sent to Libya with his platoon.

I tried to imagine it. I have no idea where Libya is.

'Were you scared?'

'I was.' He pulled up a dandelion and blew the white tufts into the air. 'I was scared of killing somebody and scared of somebody killing me.'

But the British Army had swooped in and captured the whole platoon before he'd had a chance to fire a single shot. Together they were sent first to a POW camp in Egypt, then to London, and then they were finally dispersed throughout Britain. The camp where he ended up is based in a Nissen hut some fifteen miles from Eastcott Farm. It houses a couple of hundred prisoners from different parts of Italy.

'I thought life as a prisoner would be bad, bad, bad. But it is not so hard. Your country has lost many men, many workers. For labour they use the women much more than before, but it is still not enough. England needs extra hands. So look! We Italians are prisoners but if we work they agree to pay us. In cigarettes, in tokens for food, in small pieces of freedom. So what do you think we said when they asked if we would cooperate?'

'You said yes.'

'Some of my Italian friends believe Mussolini will one day shoot them if they agree, so they said no. But these men are sent to work in supervised gangs anyway. I said yes – and so now I get to stay at Eastcott Farm and I get some freedom . . . and I get these very splendid extras.' He stroked my cheek with a tender finger. 'Your face,' he said in wonderment. 'Your beautiful, beautiful face.'

It was too ridiculous but I was purring all the same.

When we'd finished kissing I asked for a lock of his hair. I'd brought scissors specially. I snipped off the hair

and tucked it carefully into my locket with the hairs from
Mum and Dad.

Giovanni seemed quite touched and overcome by my
gesture.

'Will you come and live with me in Italia, Very, after
the war?'

I gazed at him as he stood there, the feathery dandelion
seeds floating all around him like dancing fairies.

'Yes,' I said. 'Absolutely.'

'Oh, Very, my dear darling!' he cried, whisking me up
in his arms. '. . . But maybe you want to stay in your own
country?'

I made a face. 'Not in the least. Oh no. Far from it.'

'Then I will show you the splendid piazzas and
fountains. We'll wander in the shade of the olive trees—'

'What are olive trees?' I enquired. I should become more
informed if I am to live in Italy one day.

'Olive trees? Of course they are the trees that grow the
olives!'

'But what's an olive?'

'Oh, Very, my lovely, there are many, many sorts of
olives. They are green or black or purple, this big' – he
showed me – 'and they are both sweet and bitter. They
taste like sunshine and earth and . . .' He paused for a
moment. 'They taste like youth.'

I slapped his chest. 'I do love you so splendidly much,'
I said.

Thursday, 4 September 1941
Dunwick Hall

It is term time again. That doesn't matter. I am still
adept at escaping from Dunwick Hall. But I'm worried.
Today I skipped Geography to be with Giovanni; I
dashed down the lanes to the edge of the spinney where

we'd arranged to meet and there was no sign of him.
I waited for half an hour at least. No message either.
I looked under every stone in the area to be quite sure. I
know it's not always easy for him, but I feel cross
anyway. It was raining and my hair was plastered to my
cheeks by the time I got back. I feel very weary and
upset by it.

Tuesday, 30 September 1941
Dunwick Hall

Dread. All I feel is dread. Dread, like rancid liquid, rising
higher and higher every day, filling my every thought. I
haven't seen him for weeks. He isn't at the market on
Saturdays any more. Mr Howard isn't there either, so I
can't ask him. Giovanni knows where I live, knows
where Aunt M's house is. Surely he'd find a way of
contacting me if he really tried? Does he not love me any
more? Has he met somebody else? Has he fallen for one
of the land girls at Eastcott Farm? I never bothered with
them, but I think one of them was rather pretty. I know
so little about men.

No. I cannot, will not, believe that my beloved
Giovanni has been unfaithful to me. Has he had some
kind of accident, then? Is he – can he be – dead? My heart
screams at the mere possibility. I have made myself
imagine his death in every gory detail, though, to prepare
myself for the worst. Not knowing is the hardest. I could
try asking Janet, but she hates me now and I'm sure she
wouldn't tell me.

Giovanni, where are you, where are you, my love? I miss
you so much I feel sick.

Saturday, 11 October 1941
Aggleworth

'When sorrows come, they come not single spies, but in battalions.'

At last I found Mr Howard at the market this afternoon. He told me Giovanni's camp has been requisitioned for other war work and all the prisoners have been moved on.

'I'm sorry, miss. I don't know where they've gone.'

I don't know what to do with this misery. I have no idea if I shall ever see my Giovanni again.

I am so tired. Utterly tired and depleted.

Friday, 31 October 1941
Dunwick Hall

I've noticed something and it scares me. Although I am eating hardly anything, my tummy has begun to swell.

I am a woman now. I should have realized sooner.

What would Mum and Dad have thought of me? Would they be horrified and ashamed? Still, it's their fault that this has happened. Why did they have to leave me? Why? And now Giovanni has left me, too. Everyone leaves me.

Today I opened up my locket to throw out the three strands of hair inside. I started to empty them out of the window of the dorm – but then I grabbed them back just in time. As soon as they were safe inside again I had to run to the lavatory. I was violently sick.

I've heard that the way to do it is to sit in a hot bath and drink gin, but there are no hot baths available at the school or at Aunt Margaret's, and certainly no gin. On Saturday I planned to steal the communion wine from Aggleworth church, hoping that might do the trick. But the bottles were under lock and key in the vestry.

The only other way must be to hurt myself. Every morning and night I lock myself in the bathroom and pound my stomach with my fists until I can't bear the pain any more. It hasn't worked so far. The baby is determined to stay glued inside me.

Wednesday, 10 December 1941
Aggleworth

What will become of me? I can't imagine. I'm a prisoner here in my bedroom at Aunt M's. I can only allay my fears by writing, so I will write everything that happened today.

It all began this morning, when I literally bumped into Norah on my way to the maths class. As we bounced off each other I automatically clasped my tummy. She glanced down then up at my face and she knew in an instant. Full of fury, she flew at me like a wild cat. 'Harry said you tried it on with him but he didn't do it. He's lying, isn't he? Isn't he?'

She pushed me against the wall. 'You and he did it together, didn't you, you little minx? And now you have his bastard inside you.'

I was so shocked at her venom I didn't reply.

Norah poked a finger in my face. 'You couldn't stop yourself, could you?'

Her freckles seemed to swarm over her flushed skin. My refusal to answer drove her madder still.

'You won't be so pretty by the time I've finished with you!' she cried, hurling her fists out. I fought back.

Through the violent slappings and scratchings that followed I could hear a clip-clop of shoes up the corridor. Then Miss Philpotts' voice. 'Girls, girls. Stop that! Stop it AT ONCE!'

She wrenched us apart. We glowered at each other, panting. Norah's nose was bleeding and her hair had fallen out of its net. I could feel deep scratches down my left cheek.

Miss Philpotts marched us up the stairs to the headmistress's office. Miss Harrison looked up from her desk, scandalized at our appearance. 'I am appalled, girls. What have you got to say for yourselves?'

'I'm very sorry, miss,' Norah moaned as she clutched a reddening handkerchief over her nose. 'I couldn't stand by and do nothing. I got angry because of' – she left a pause full of accusation and self-righteousness – 'what she did with my boyfriend.'

The headmistress turned to me.

'This is not sounding good. Veronica, what have you got to say for yourself?'

I held my head high, ignoring my stinging cheek. I decided to stick to my strategy of saying nothing.

Norah cut in. 'With respect, miss, look at her. She don't know what to say and I can tell you why: because she's pregnant.'

The headmistress's voice became louder and shriller. 'Can this be true, Veronica?'

I could hardly deny it.

'You are fifteen years old! A mere girl. How could this possibly have happened? It is unbelievable – preposterous!' Her voice rose to a shriek. 'Pregnant at fifteen! Fifteen! You disgust me, Veronica McCreedy. We have done our utmost for you under very difficult circumstances. Yes, you have suffered such terrible loss, and times are hard, but this is no way for a decent girl to carry on. Where is your sense of loyalty – to this school, to the memory of your parents, to your poor elderly aunt who has had to care for you?'

I was supposed to feel all remorseful and humble. I didn't, though. I felt defiant.

'It is impossible for you to stay at this school,' she went on. 'You have brought shame on us all. I will phone your good aunt and ask her to come and fetch you at once.'

'As you wish.'

Norah glared at me, her eyes glittering with hatred.

They phoned Aunt M but she didn't come to fetch me. Instead I was instructed to make my own way to her house. I had to walk forty minutes to the bus stop, then wait an hour for the bus, then walk the length of Aggleworth.

When I arrived, my great aunt was at the door.

'Do not set foot inside this house.'

'Please, Aunt Margaret. I'm tired.'

'Tired? Tired? And whose fault is that? I knew from the minute I set eyes on you that you were not to be trusted. Despicable, ungrateful girl. Dirty, disgusting, wicked girl, to do such a thing, to bring shame on the memory of your poor parents. To bring shame on me.' She went on and on in a great tirade. She'd phoned Eastcott Farm, apparently, trying to press Harry into marrying me, which, of course, he wouldn't.

'I have no intention of marrying him, either,' I declared. 'Did nobody think of asking my opinion?'

'He vows that the baby you're carrying isn't his. He told me in a manner most uncouth that he refuses to bring up the child – and he used another word here that I don't care to repeat – of another man. He swears he never touched you. Look me in the eyes and tell me: is the father Harry Dramwell?'

'No.'

If I hadn't wrenched myself from his grasp and spat in his face that night, it might have been. But it wasn't Harry and I'm glad of it.

'Heaven forgive you, girl! How many men have you been seeing? If it wasn't him, then who was it?'

I hurled the words in her face. 'A man ten times better than Harry. A man I love with all my heart. And you don't need to worry, Aunt, because after the war is over we're going to live abroad and get our baby right away from here.'

221

Our baby. I'd never said it before. Those words seared into my heart.

Raindrops began to fall heavily on to my hair and shoulders. Aunt M grudgingly moved aside to let me in.

'Who is he?' she asked.

'He's a soldier.'

'But how in the world could you have met a soldier?'

I sank into a chair. 'There is nothing either good or bad, but thinking makes it so,' I murmured. But the quote was completely lost on her.

'You will not eat a thing, Veronica – not one thing – until you have told me.'

I've already lost so much. There didn't seem to be anything left I could lose.

'My lover is a fine man, a noble man,' I answered, my voice sharp as needles. 'He was fighting for his own country.'

'A German?' she asked, with a quick intake of breath.

'An Italian.'

Her features distorted into a battlefield of reaction. I've never seen such silent rage.

I ache for Giovanni. If only I could talk to him, feel his arms around me again, everything would be all right.

Thursday, 11 December 1941
The Convent

While I was writing yesterday my aunt was making phone calls downstairs. An hour later an Austin 7 pulled up outside the house.

I was allowed to take a few things: my diary, my locket and my clothes. As I got into the car, the driver (a short, dumpy woman in sober woollens) looked me up and down. 'You are lucky we had petrol,' she commented, as she started up the engine.

'Lucky, am I?' I said quietly.

Aunt M didn't come out to wish me goodbye.

My new home is a prison of pristine white walls, hard chairs, crucifixes and ticking clocks. There are no mother-and-baby homes in the area, apparently, so Aunt M consulted her church contacts and found this convent where the nuns are willing to look after me for the time being. Perfect for Aunt M. She will feel she has done the right thing. Her conscience will be unburdened of me and now she can continue to lead her dull life in peace.

1 January 1942

Another year begins. Who would have thought I'd be pregnant and living in a convent?

I don't like it here.

At school I was treated like a child. Here I am treated like a dog. The sisters view me with revulsion. They skirt around me when they are in the same room and avoid any physical contact as if they'll be sullied by touching me. I'm supposed to feel shame, but my spirits rise up and rebel against it. I feel only anger.

I'm forced to attend a service in the little chapel every morning. I stand when I am required to stand, sit when I am required to sit and kneel when I am required to kneel. But nobody has power over what goes on inside my head. I have only one prayer: that my Giovanni will come back and find me and take me away with him to Italy.

The service is dull, but at least it's some relief from the relentless working hours. I am made to scrub floors and work in the laundry, washing, wringing out and pegging up the nuns' habits. The work makes my hands red and raw. I'm constantly exhausted. A scrawny, sour-faced woman called Sister Amelia has been put in charge of me. She does little to hide her distaste for the job.

'Why do I have to do this for you?' I demanded yesterday, up to my elbows in soapsuds.

She clasped her hands together with an air of tired patience. 'The mother superior, who is wise and generous, has decided on what is most beneficial for you. She knows that often the material world reflects the spiritual world. Cleaning work will help purify your soul.'

'I haven't got a soul,' I retorted.

'Never let me hear you say such a thing!'

'I haven't got a soul. I haven't got a soul, I haven't got a soul,' I chanted to the rhythm as I slapped wet clothes against the washboard.

I have made myself yet another enemy.

I don't miss Aunt Margaret or my schoolfellows or my lessons. But I do miss the meagre amount of freedom I had before. I miss the open countryside. I still miss my secret trysts with Giovanni, and I miss Mum and Dad more than ever.

Friday, 24 April 1942

I don't write much more in here, do I? What is the point? I'm only writing now because I'm bored and I wish it was all over.

I don't have to do laundry any more. I'm confined to a small, dark room. An alternating trio of nuns visits to make sure I am still alive. They bring me a diet of white bread, powdered eggs, stew and brown broth. They keep constant watch and check that I don't wander from the bed. I've tried to open the window but it is locked and the key has been taken away. They seem bent on keeping fresh air and daylight out of the room.

My body is no longer my own. It's a vehicle for a new force that nobody can stop. My skin stretches round the bulbous creature that is expanding inside me. No matter which way I turn, I can't get comfortable. When I manage to sleep I dream of Dad and Mum and my beloved Giovanni and they are slipping away from me down a great landslide. I wake myself calling out to them. I will not be weak, though. I will not cry.

Outside the closed walls of my current life, war rages on. There's never any word from Aunt Margaret.

I don't feel like myself any more. I don't feel like a human being at all. The growing presence in my belly sucks all life from me. I try to imagine the bump as a little person with a future stretching out ahead, full of promise – but I can't. I just want it out of me, a separate entity, and then I might be able to think again.

Monday, 4 May 1942

I'm not alone in this world any more. I'm a mother! I have a tiny, beautiful baby to love. If only my own mother was here to see him! And Dad. Dad would have adored him. And Giovanni. I can imagine him holding our little son aloft, his eyes sparkling with pride. How I wish he was here.

The blood and pain were truly terrible. Earth-shattering. I don't want to remember that now, though, because now everything is different. He is here: a new life, my very own boy. Red-faced, wriggling, but perfect in every way. I marvel at his tiny fingers and tiny toes, and each time I look at him I'm shocked by an onrush of extreme love. It's a different kind of love from any I have ever felt. It is fierce in its intensity . . . and yet so tender it's almost painful.

'You are . . . you are sort of rubbery . . . and so strange . . . but you are delicious!' I whisper to my baby. He gurgles back at me.

I have decided to give him an Italian name, but I only know two: Giovanni and the name of Giovanni's father.

'Enzo. Are you an Enzo?' I've just asked him. His hands
are punching the air in excitement. I fancy he enjoys the
staccato sound of the word.

I've managed to locate the pair of scissors that Sister
Molly used to cut the umbilical cord. I have gently cut off a
few wisps of Enzo's dark hair for my locket.

There, right beside your daddy's hair, little Enzo. You
will meet him one day, my darling Italian boy. I'm sure
you will.

1 January 1943

Another year has ended, another year begins. I am sixteen
and still live here in the convent. Enzo and I do all right.
We look after each other. More than that; we delight in
each other. I am never lonely now.

'It's you and me against the rest of the world, my little
darling,' I whisper to him, 'until your daddy comes. Just
until your daddy comes . . .'

The nuns don't take much notice of Enzo. I am
working again in the laundry, and I keep him close. Most
of the time he wriggles and giggles in his cradle or reaches
up his little arms and makes patterns in the air as if
playing an imaginary violin. I set him on the floor
whenever I can and watch him crawl around, exploring
everything. When he laughs I laugh with him. When he
cries I hold him against my heart until he is happy again.
When he soils himself I use masses of fresh, damp cloths
to clean him and make him spotless. His nappies give me
extra washing work, but I am far happier serving him
than those stupid nuns.

I abandon the laundry often to rush over to take my
Enzo in my arms and rock him. I sing 'You Are My
Sunshine' or any song that comes into my head, and he
loves it. He puts his little fingers around my thumb and

holds on tight or grabs at my stray coils of hair. I only get half the amount of work done that I did before.

Poor Enzo didn't have any toys at all but now I have made him a puppet out of an old sock. I stayed up late one night sewing a cat's face on to it, a face with a big smile and woollen whiskers. Whenever I put the puppet over my hand and make it miaow Enzo shrieks with joy.

I have also discovered there's a library at the convent. It's mostly religious books but there are some classic novels too, which I love. In the evenings I read *Ivanhoe* aloud, rocking my son on my lap. He gazes up with his big, dark eyes and cuddles close, soothed by my voice. Then I tell him everything about his handsome daddy and how the three of us are going to live in Italy together one day and eat splendid olives.

33

Patrick

Bolton

WHAT? THAT'S IT? THERE'S nothing more. Just a load of blank pages.

I can't believe it. Why did she suddenly stop? I'm totally baffled. It seems like she loved that kid, seems like she was bonkers about him. Yet I know that at some point she gave him up for adoption. What the hell . . . ?

It all keeps spinning round and round in my head. I'm going to have to meet up with Granny V when she gets back from Antarctica and see if I can get her to tell me more. I don't understand the woman at all.

34

Veronica

Locket Island

SOMETHING IS HAPPENING TO my shrivelled old heart. After seven decades of inaction it seems to be waking up again. I can only attribute this to the constant presence of a small, round, fluffy penguin.

Indeed, I adore Penguin Patrick far more than I should and far more than I am prepared to admit. Our joint care of him seems to have brought me closer to Terry, too.

It is the evening of Boxing Day. I only have a few more days on Locket Island before I must depart for Scotland and leave them both. Terry is sitting next to me on my bed and little Patrick is draped over my knees, both flippers outstretched. We have just given him a dinner of mashed fish fingers and his expression is one of sheer bliss.

Terry picks up the empty dish. 'I suppose I'd better go and do something useful.'

'No, don't go yet!'

She puts the dish down and looks at me curiously.

I'm experiencing a completely novel sensation: a wish to open up, to both Terry and the penguin. I decide to humour myself. What is there, after all, to lose?

I start in slow, measured tones and carefully structured sentences. I speak of things that I never imagined would pass my lips. I tell my audience of two all about my evacuation to Derbyshire, to Dunwick Hall; tell them of Aunt Margaret, of my so-called friends, Janet and Norah, of the terrible death of my parents. I tell them about Harry and about Giovanni. I reveal my teenage pregnancy and my consequent banishment to the convent.

Patrick shuffles, intrigued that I am talking so much. It is a most unusual state of affairs. He rolls on to his side so as to view me with one eye. His feet slither off my lap and Terry, who has subconsciously moved closer, gently lifts them and places them on her knees, so that he is bridging both of us.

I do not look at Terry while I am talking. It is easier that way. Instead I fix my eyes on my little penguin chick, stroking his chest absently with one finger. I derive some solace from his face, so young and eager.

The next part is hard.

I never thought I'd share with anyone what happened about my baby. Yet somehow now, in this field centre on Locket Island in the Antarctic Peninsula, in the company of a bespectacled scientist and a diminutive penguin, I do. It's as if, regardless of me, the narration has acquired its own current and cannot be quelled until it has reached its conclusion.

I talk of Enzo. In short, splintered, ice-cold words that can't express the tiniest fraction of what he meant to me. What he means to me.

'The twenty-fourth of February 1943, Enzo was in his cradle, fast asleep. I was busy boiling soiled cloths when I heard them.

Jovial voices, strong, with a foreign twang. Talking about looking at some specimen herbs before they finished their visit. Sister Amelia was ushering them down the corridor to the courtyard garden. I'd left the laundry door open to let out the clouds of steam. Stupid, stupid me, to leave the door open . . . to let them see him . . . If I had only closed that door . . .'

I gather myself together and continue. 'Their faces, peering in. A man and a woman, much older than me. Declarations of surprise and delight when they saw my little Enzo, sleeping there snuggled up in his blanket. They asked if they could hold him. I grudgingly said yes. How could I know? How clueless I was then! They scooped him up and cooed over him. His mouth puckered into a smile, a lovely smile, a smile they gazed at for too long. Then two weeks later . . .'

I am right back there, in the past: 11 March 1943. A sixteen-year-old mother, scarred but strong. Still full of hopes and dreams, despite everything that has happened. Fire running through my veins. A little weary, though, this afternoon. Busy putting nuns' habits through the mangle, winding the handle slowly, watching as the drums go round, streams of water pouring out into the bucket. My mind is on Enzo. Sister Amelia has taken him to the study because a doctor is here to examine his first, new teeth. For some reason I feel uneasy. I lower the pulley of the rack and spread the habit out to dry. I do the same with a second habit, then a third, then a fourth: a row of damp black shadows hang before me. On the fifth I begin to worry that all might not be well with Enzo's teeth. By the time I reach number nine he still hasn't been returned to me. I'm starting to panic. I abandon the heap of sodden habits, the mangle and the rack. I pelt through the convent and rush upstairs to the study. Silence, an empty desk and blank walls. I dash back down again, my feet hammering on the stairs. I run slap bang into Sister Amelia in the hall.

'Where is Enzo?' I hear myself demand in a tight, shrill voice.

She shakes her head slowly. Her fingers lock together round the silver cross that dangles on her chest.

I stare at her, crazed. 'What have you done with him?'

Then she tells me.

My screams echo down the corridor. My baby.

My baby.

35

Veronica

Locket Island

'Oh! Oh, Veronica!'

Jolted by Terry's wailing, Patrick the Penguin slithers towards the floor. He lands elegantly on his feet and starts waddling about, sticking his beak into things.

'How could you bear it?' asks Terry. 'To have your own baby taken away like that?'

How do you bear anything?

'I had no choice,' I reply. 'The nuns said it was for the best. They believed they were doing the right thing. In their eyes, the fact that the visiting couple desperately wanted a child was a God-given opportunity. They had been wondering what to do about us, anyway – they couldn't look after us for ever and I wasn't in a position to care for a baby on my own. I had no money, no job, no husband, no prospects. My son had gone to a good, Christian family, they assured me, and he would have a much, much better life than he could ever have with me, a disgraced teenager. They may have been right, for all I know. In those days everything was very different. More different than you can possibly imagine.'

Terry has no idea what it meant in the forties for a girl to have a baby when she didn't have a husband. Your life was ruined on every level. The shame attached itself to you and you could never shake it off. It became a part of you, like leprosy. People wouldn't want to touch you. They would cross over the road rather than have to speak to you.

'But those nuns tricked you!' she cries indignantly.

'Because they knew I'd never, never – not even if it killed me – let my baby go otherwise.'

I am conscious of my locket hanging heavy against my skin. In the caverns deep inside me something is struggling like molten lava, trying to find a way out.

Terry listens, appalled, as I outline my life after Enzo was taken away. How I managed to break loose from the convent and stumble on with life, getting a job in a local bank, working my way up. How I silently grieved for years on end. I kept my past well hidden. Nobody had any inkling about what had happened to me. I shunned any contact with the people I'd known before or during the war. I never set eyes on Aunt Margaret again.

I tried so many times over the years to locate my son, but adoption legislation in those days made it impossible for a birth mother to trace her child. Besides, Enzo's new parents had changed his name and made an agreement with the nuns to keep their own identities hidden. I believe money was involved, but in any case the nuns absolutely refused to share any information with me. Even when I applied to the same convent ten years later they claimed to have lost the details of the family he'd gone to. I treasured the hope that Enzo himself, once he'd grown up, might eventually find a way to contact me, but that never happened. My twin hope was that Giovanni would return for me one day. If he was still alive and still loved me, surely he would come and find me? As a married couple, our chances of locating Enzo would be much stronger. But the years passed, and both hopes, starved of information, withered and died.

Yet pallor and skinniness seemed to suit me just as much as rosy-cheeked enthusiasm had done. I attracted a great deal of male attention. I recoiled from it all. I gained nothing except the reputation for being a cold fish.

There was, however, one man who didn't give up. A proud conqueror of many women, he set his sights on me the very first moment he saw me. It was obvious from his whole demeanour when he walked into the bank that day, and he found excuses to come back and flirt every day subsequently. Never in all my years at the bank had I seen so many pointless financial transactions.

'Hugh Gilford-Chart was a charming, forceful, good-looking man,' I tell Terry. 'He was powerful in more ways than one, a well-known property magnate. And he flattered my vanity. He didn't give two figs about my brusque manner and constant refusals. He actually seemed to like them. Anyway, he showered me with compliments. And compliments are always nice.' I wasn't immune. To have a man so interested in me despite my disregard for his feelings was undeniably gratifying. By that time it had been twelve years since I'd seen Giovanni. I knew that he was never going to come back for me.

'I wasn't in love with Hugh, but I was drawn to him. When he proposed to me – along with champagne, diamonds and the offer of an immediate trip to a swanky hotel in Paris – well, it wasn't difficult to decide. I accepted. I certainly didn't expect a perfect marriage, but I appreciated the security he offered.

'He improved my life in countless practical ways. I acquired a plush lifestyle, a number of household staff, holidays in exotic places. I took an interest in my husband's work as well. I managed to educate myself, reading about money, investments and properties. Seeing that I had shrewd business acumen, my husband put me in charge of the rural side of his company. My chief role was buying country cottages and letting them out to tenants.

'Unfortunately, my husband loved all the ladies, not just me. A year into the marriage he had his first affair. I knew about it at once. He was slovenly about covering up his tracks and she left lipstick stains and lacy suspenders all over the place. She was his secretary. It was such a cliché. I was sickened by it, although not wholly surprised. After he'd tired of the secretary, my husband's affairs were as numerous as woodlice in a rotten log. I became fed up with it and eventually, after eight years of tolerating his lies and infidelity, I filed for divorce. With my experience at the bank I knew every last detail of his financial affairs and I did well out of it. I was able to keep on many of the rural properties.

'I have since sold most of them. That's how I came by my millions,' I inform Terry. 'I've invested money wisely over the years and I spend very little on myself.' I classify it as little, anyway. Although I spend far more than, say, Eileen. Or Terry.

'I was never tempted to marry again.'

Terry's eyes are two clear pools, brimming with sympathy. 'I can't say I blame you.'

'Years later I did receive some news of my son. A cousin of the adoptive family tracked me down. But it was only to inform me of his death.'

I remember the day so well. Checking the post and getting that three-page letter that summarized Enzo's life, or the life of Joe Fuller as he had become. Learning that he had died in a mountaineering accident and there was no possibility of ever getting to know him.

Terry is blotting her eyes with the end of her sleeve. 'My heart just goes out to you. You've been through so much! But you – you never cry, Veronica.'

'No.'

It's quite true. I have not shed a single tear since the day Aunt Margaret told me crying was a weak thing to do. I didn't want to be weak. I still don't want to be weak. I have always despised weakness.

'But *never* to cry! I would have thought it's impossible. How do you manage it?' Terry asks with a loud sniff.

'Years of practice,' I tell her. 'Years and years.'

I resume. 'The letter informed me that Enzo had no children of his own and I had no reason to doubt it. But it recently occurred to me that an adoptive cousin might not have known this with absolute certainty. I took it upon myself to double-check. And that's how I discovered my grandson, Patrick.'

The other Patrick stops in his tracks and turns to look up at me again, recognizing his name. I reach out my hand to him. He sidles up and rubs his head against my fingers. I am glad of the touch, glad of the small spiky beak and tousled baby fluff.

'You must have been so thrilled to discover a grandson, after all this time,' Terry exclaims, determined to find a ray of light at the end of my tale of woe. She wants so much to believe my grandson and I are in happy-ever-after land.

I don't respond to her comment. An odd clamminess is coiling under the surface of my skin. It chills me like a winter mist.

I need to be alone.

Patrick the Penguin is sleeping peacefully. One foot is lifted slightly and propped against the side of the suitcase. His chest rises and falls with each breath, a gentle penguiny snore gurgling in his slightly open beak.

I straighten slowly. Everything has changed. The past has resurfaced. Memories of my father, my mother, of Giovanni, and of my precious baby Enzo burgeon painfully in my consciousness. My baby boy, who I never found again, who was taken away before he learned to say my name, who died before he even knew I wanted him.

How I ache for them, for what could have been. Each of them snatched away from me too, too soon. I feel as if I am being strangled from the inside.

This room is much too small. It is claustrophobic. Oppressive.

Not far away there's a vast community of Adélies waiting for me under endless fathoms of polar sky. The penguins can help, I am sure of it. They have a brand of ancient wisdom that transcends the confused strivings of the human race. I need to get out and be with them. Just me, Veronica McCreedy, and the elements and five thousand penguins. Nobody else.

Dietrich is in the computer room. I can hear Terry and Mike talking in the kitchen. I silently struggle into my jacket and mukluks. I grab my stick. I can't be bothered with a handbag this time. Treading with utmost softness, I sneak out.

A chilly wind whips fragments of snow up into my face. I walk as fast as I can to put space between myself and the field base. I don't look back. My breath is short. Puffs of steam rise on the frozen air. I force myself on, up the slope, leaning heavily on my stick with every pace.

My face is numb. It is colder than I have ever felt it before. The sky is low, simmering with murky patterns. The wind becomes fiercer and fiercer as I go on. It batters against me, whistling around my ears. But I'm driven by an inner force that's equally fierce. I need to see the penguins, to be alone at last with the penguins. I put one step in front of another. Again and again and again. Somehow, in spite of my protesting lungs, I arrive at the top of the slope.

And there they are, laid out before me: a huge, undulating mass of life, a black-and-white realm of mothers, fathers, couples and babies.

I descend and walk amongst them in the dusky flurries of snow. Some lift their heads to look at me but mostly they carry on attending to their own business. Sheltering together, feeding together, arguing together, sleeping together.

That is it, I realize. That's the thing that gives their life purpose. That 'together' that has been so lacking in my own life. All that I possess is encased in silver and hanging on the end of a chain, under my thermals, pressed against my skin. Four strands of hair.

A hurricane of grief sweeps through me. And suddenly I'm wailing with the wind and spouting hot tears of sorrow. They burst out of my depths in a violent, gushing torrent. I never dreamed I had so many tears stored up inside.

It has become hard to breathe. Inside my ribcage something strange is happening. There's coldness like a huge mountain of ice beginning to shift. Then, without warning, the inner block cracks and splits right across the centre. Pain scythes through me. I let out a sharp cry. The pain gathers momentum and will not stop. I feel the ice shatter into a thousand needle-like shards. Wrenching my body apart.

I crumple on to the ground.

36

Patrick

Bolton

I WOULDN'T NORMALLY SWITCH on my computer on a Monday morning before work. Not at 6.30 a.m. But my sleep patterns have gone crazy. The couple in the flat below are screeching at each other and clomping about, which isn't exactly conducive to a good rest. Plus I can't stop thinking about Granny V.

I thought there'd be something more in that diary. Something about what happened to baby Enzo – *my father*, baby Enzo. The guy I got my skin tone from, and who knows what other traits? I know Veronica gave him up for adoption, but it doesn't make sense. From the diary it looks like she totally adored the socks off him. And she's not a wimpy kind of girl, not the sort that would be persuaded into it by those nuns or anyone else.

The whole wretched thing keeps banging around in my brain and what with all the noise from downstairs there's no way sleep's going to be an option. So I'm sat up in bed trying to distract myself by surfing the internet. I've explored a few interesting websites on electric circuits and LED lights and I've watched a couple of YouTube vids about the structure of bridges. It's nearly time to get up.

I check my emails before logging off, and what do you know, there's one from penggroup4Ant. I wonder if there's been any more penguin attacks on handbags. Or maybe something about Granny V's latest mission, the little penguin she's adopted. But it's something I wasn't expecting at all, and suddenly I feel a bit sick.

'What's wrong, mate?'

There's me, thinking I'm smiling and looking cool, but you can't get much past Gav. I tell him about Granny V.

'Bad?'

'Yup. Seriously bad. Like, the end.'

He puts a hand on my shoulder. 'I'm so sorry, mate. That's rough. Just as you were getting to know her, too.'

That's pushing it a bit. I was hardly getting to know her. I'd met her a sum total of two times. I'd got right inside her teenage head, though, reading those diaries.

'She's stuck in polar regions with three scientists and five thousand fricking penguins for company. What a way to go!' I'm trying to make a joke of it but neither Gav nor I are laughing.

'Harsh,' he says.

I drag the sandwich board outside the shop and set it up then come back in to see what's on today's repairs list.

'Are you going to go out there?' Gav asks.

I look at him blankly. 'What?'

'Are you going to go out there? To Antarctica, to say goodbye to her.'

'We've scarcely said hello yet,' I point out. What a bizarre idea. Me, in Antarctica!

241

'Well, it's not such a bizarre idea,' he says, reading my thoughts. 'She *is* your grandmother. And your only living relative.'

'C'mon, mate. It's hardly practical. Three reasons: (a) she wouldn't want me there, (b) she'd probably not last out till I got there anyway, (c) cash-flow won't allow, and (d) I can't stand the cold.'

'That's four reasons, mate.'

We get through the morning in the usual way. A family of five comes in, wanting to know if there's going to be an offer on electric bikes any time soon (there isn't). We sell a few bits and pieces. A lad comes in who's lost the key to his bicycle lock and wants a new key that fits rather than buying a new locking system. It takes a long time trying to explain to him that the whole point of locks and keys is security, so no, the same make of key won't fit into his old lock. Even if this was the case, we don't sell them separately. I am beginning to lose the will to live so Gav steps in. Very diplomatic, is Gav.

I manage to concentrate on and off; mostly off, to be honest. I wish I could have said something to Granny, met her one more time in person, just to say . . . Well, I don't know what I'd say, but I'd say *something*.

'Still thinking about your granny?' Gav asks as I take my sandwiches out the back for my lunch break.

'Yup, I guess. I keep wishing I'd known all this other stuff about Granny V sooner. And wishing I had a few more answers, now that I know which questions to ask. And wishing she was nearer so I could, like, make things better between us before . . . you know.'

'So you *do* want to say goodbye?'

'I would if I could,' I admit. 'But, like I said, cash-flow and that. I can barely cover the rent. The journey out there must be at least a grand.'

'But you'd go out all the way to Antarctica if you had the funds? Even though you hate the cold?'

I nodded. 'Reckon I bloody would, you know. As you say, she's my only family. I've just found her and I'm about to lose her. There's a hell of a lot more to her than I realized. And I kind of feel like we have unfinished business.'

Gav takes a long look at me. 'Patrick, mate, forgive me for being insensitive, but there's a bright side to all this. Looks like you might be about to become a millionaire.'

I won't say the idea hadn't crossed my mind. But I'd bundled it out again because, well, it all seemed pretty far-fetched, to be honest. Anyway, I wasn't going to count chickens.

'You reckon Granny's going to leave me her millions?'

'I do.'

'Come off it, mate. She hates my guts.'

He shakes his head. 'I think not. You made the effort to go and see her at the airport, didn't you? I bet she was touched by that, even if she didn't let on. And she sent you those diaries. They were all locked up, you said, with a padlock and code, so they're clearly not something she bandied about all over the place. Then she sent you the code. Nobody else has read those diaries, mate, not even her trusty carer, you told me. C'mon, Patrick, it's obvious she's going to leave you her money!'

I suppose it does make sense when he puts it like that. Holy shite! Me a millionaire is even more bizarre than me in Antarctica. I give a little leap in the air with the thrill of it. Gav puts his hand up to be slapped and I give him a high five.

The moment doesn't last long, though. I hate to think of Granny V dying out there in the cold.

'Listen, Gav. I kind of do want to go and see her. I don't suppose there's any way you'd be prepared to . . .'

'What, mate? Spit it out.'

Money's such a bind. I can't be sure of anything. Granny V is eccentric and impulsive, I know that much. It's possible she's left me her dosh, but on the other hand she might have gone and left it to an orphanage or something.

The words come tumbling out of my mouth. 'You wouldn't, er, consider lending me enough for the air fare, would you?'

He gives me a slap on the back. 'Of course, mate. Thought you'd never ask!'

God, what am I playing at? Am I a complete muppet? If the orphans get Granny's inheritance, how am I ever going to pay Gav back?

'Maybe you want to think about that answer,' I find myself saying.

Gav's not having it. 'No, you're all right, mate. In fact the timing couldn't be better: my mum's inheritance has just come through. I'd like to make good use of it.'

We argue back and forth. I seriously don't want to be in Gav's debt in the event that Granny V doesn't leave me a penny. He's an unstoppable force, though. Says I can pay him back any time within the next twenty years. In instalments or whatever. Says in the great scheme of things it isn't that much. Says he owed me big time anyway because the bike shop would never have survived without me. He's stretching a point here.

As he speaks, I'm quite getting into the idea of zipping off to Antarctica. Beginning to see myself as a bit of a hero. Me, Patrick the Brave, embarking on a valiant quest to bring peace and harmony to the troubled soul of an old woman. But then I remember something.

'Hang on a mo, mate, what about young Daisy? Shouldn't you be spending this money on the latest treatments for her? If anything can be done to make her better, that's a hell of a lot more important than sending me off to the other end of the planet.'

He won't hear of it, though. There isn't a treatment Daisy can have beyond what she's already having, apparently.

I still feel bad. 'If not a treat*ment*, how about treats?' I hate to think of Daisy missing out because of me.

'Daisy has tons of treats. And there's plenty of money to buy her more. Just shut up, will you, and get that flight booked!'

I'm not going to argue any more. I'm going to make things right with Granny Veronica.

Antarctica, here I come!

37

Veronica

Locket Island

I AM A MISSHAPEN collection of little dots. Every little dot twinges and stings, sore and raw. I'm under a great heap of blankets, but I'm cold, so cold. Husky breath comes in shallow gasps, fighting to find its way in and out of me.

A woman is fussing around.

'Look, Veronica, here's our penguin chick come to see you. He seems to get bigger and bouncier every time I set eyes on him. He's doing brilliantly.'

I try to prise my eyes open. Through the thin slit of vision the light burns torturously bright. I can make out shapes, but everything has blurry edges. A small, fuzzy grey figure is waddling about the room. I want to stretch out and touch it, but I can't. My eyelids won't stay open any more either. The shutters come down over the brightness again.

'And you're doing brilliantly as well, Veronica.' My lids flicker open long enough to register the woman. She looks familiar. She has limp, blonde hair that spills over her shoulders, and glasses that magnify her sad blue eyes.

She is a liar. I am not doing brilliantly.

She speaks again with forced jollity. 'We've got a surprise for you, Veronica. Your grandson is coming! All the way to Antarctica. Just to see you.'

The words float around, slowly circling each other. Then all at once they crystallize into something solid and I can grasp their meaning.

I know where I am and what it's all about. This is a young woman who has a man's name, a woman I like, one I've come to think of as a friend. Terry. Yes. Terry: scientist on Locket Island, Antarctica. What was it Terry said? The echo of the words is still in my brain. She said that my grandson is coming to visit.

My grandson! God in heaven! I must be even worse than I thought. I open my lips and try to say 'Tell him not to bother,' but the words are stuck at the back of my throat and refuse to come out.

So this is what dying is like. Who would have thought it would be so frustrating and boring? I'd like it to be over, but no doubt it will drag itself out as long as possible, just like life. How extremely tedious.

Something groans. It's me.

I feel a hand stroke the hair back from my brow.

She speaks softly, close to my ear, her sentences short and spaced out, following a trail of disjointed thoughts. 'He should be here soon. We'll have to make up another bed. I hope he doesn't mind cramped conditions. We'll have to make do, somehow. It'll be so nice to meet him, though. I'm looking forward to it . . . I think. I wonder what he'll make of it all.'

I wish she'd stop talking. I wish she'd pick up my baby from the floor and let me stroke his fluffy head instead. I'd very much like to touch him again before I die.

'You must try and get better, Veronica. For your grandson.'

My grandson? Oh. Him. I think I remember something about it. On a mad whim I got Eileen to send him my diaries. Was that terribly unwise? My brain hurts if I try to separate out the strands of thought. Didn't somebody say he was coming? If he does come, I'll be flabbergasted. I'm flabbergasted he's even thinking about it. Maybe it's some misunderstanding.

A voice is rambling on in the background. 'I was thinking how confusing it'll be to have two Patricks at the camp. We could call them Patrick One and Patrick Two, I suppose. But maybe our fluffy little sausage should change? What do you think, Veronica?'

I don't care in the slightest but am quite unable to say so.

'What can we call you, sausage?'

She pauses, mulling it over. I'm starting to drift into oblivion. All these Patricks and numbers and sausages are somewhat trying.

Terry pipes up again. 'I know! I've got it. The book on your bedside table is *Great Expectations*, and we have great expectations for our little sausage. So we should call him after the main character in the book. We should call him Pip!' Her voice changes as she turns her head and addresses the stumpy character on the floor. 'Would you mind if we called you Pip from now on?'

There's a response from the corner of the room, a brief high-pitched fluting sound that is almost, in itself, like the word 'pip'.

'I'll take that as a yes, then!' I can hear affection in her words.

It's brought things into focus again. Sausage is a penguin. Patrick is a penguin. Pip is a penguin. All are one. All are dear to me. I hope beyond hope that the people here will look after him when I'm gone. I think they will. Terry will, at any rate. The others are men, I think. I cannot recall their names at present. I seem to remember that they, too, have a soft spot for Patrick-sausage-baby; Pip, as his name seems to be now. Soft, downy Pip with the big eyes and big feet, whose little scufflings I can hear if I focus hard.

248

'No, Pip, leave Veronica's slippers alone!'

What is he doing with my slippers? I want to see but it is too difficult to open my eyes and turning my head would be an impossibility.

A sigh tries to work its way through my lungs but can't. Even breathing shallowly is like dragging a hacksaw through my innards.

It's a great shame I never sorted out that legacy thing for the Adélies. I should have looked into it earlier. I have got it wrong, yet again. I suppose my whole inheritance will end up going to my grandson now. It isn't what I wanted at all. I wanted it to go to a worthwhile cause.

Words come at me again, filtering through the cloud of regrets. 'Veronica, I'm sorry about everything.' Her voice sounds lumpy and miserable. 'I'm really sorry you came all this way and we were . . . we were the way we were. You seemed so steadfast, so strong, I just didn't realize . . . I had no idea it might come to this. You were a challenge to us, sure, but you were also a breath of fresh air, and I may have been alone in this but . . . personally I liked you. I liked you very much and I wanted you to stay.'

I wish she'd stop talking about me in the past tense. It isn't at all polite.

'And then when you were so into the penguins I felt that, in spite of all our differences, I'd found a kindred spirit.'

She's getting sentimental, clogged up with tears. I now understand something I never spotted before. Terry is lonely.

'Then when you told me your story, it almost broke my heart,' she continues. 'I wanted to reach back into the past and be a friend to you when you so badly needed it all those years ago. All those people who were horrible to you even when you were grieving for your parents. It was cruel, cruel, cruel. And you were so young. And taking away your baby. It's . . . it's so . . . so wrong in every way.'

I'm not sure I can stand this much longer.

Suddenly there's a clatter at the far end of the room.

'Oh Patrick!' Terry cries, 'I mean Pip! What on earth are you up to? Oh, Veronica, you should see him! He's gone and climbed into the wastepaper basket, with just his head sticking out the top. He looks so funny!'

38

Patrick

Locket Island

I'M HERE.

Me, Patrick. Here, Antarctica. Unbelievable.

It was quite a journey. I managed to get a last-minute flight, but it was squashed and boring and seemed to go on for fricking ever. The last bit, though, the bit by ship, was epic. All those floating icebergs, all different shapes and sizes. Some were like blobs of cream cheese, some were like wedges of white bread. Some were sharp as teeth, some grained and splintered like broken glass catching flashes of sunlight. The wildlife was crazy, too. Seals slouched on the rocks, massive birds wheeling overhead, penguins shooting in and out of the water or standing in troops along the edges. Giant humpback whales one time, too. Still pinching myself.

And now I'm at this field base thing. Granny V is hanging in there, thank God. It's miserable seeing her like this. She's sort of acknowledged my presence through her eyes but she can't speak or anything. I don't know if she recognizes me or not. Hard to say.

I've found out some more about what happened from the scientists. She snuck out on her own, they said – something they'd never have let her do if they'd known about it, especially seeing as a blizzard was in the offing. Not your massive mow-everything-over-in-its-path type blizzard that you sometimes get out here, but pretty bad. Bad enough that they were majorly panicked and rushed out at once with their first aid kits. Bad enough that when they found her, slumped on the ground, they were worried they wouldn't get her back to the base alive. Bad enough that the helicopter plus medic couldn't come out for another four hours.

They did get her back to base, though, and did good keeping her warm and stuff. The doc, when he finally got here, diagnosed her with hypothermia and a lung infection. She was given a massive shot of penicillin and prescribed antibiotics. There was talk of trying to fly her back to a hospital in Argentina but she screamed when they tried to move her. The doc then decided it was better to leave her to rest. Implying the RIP type of rest? He asked them to try and contact Granny's family anyway. So here I am.

I bet those scientists are miffed. First they get an eighty-six-year-old who's spicy as a vindaloo and stubborn as a wild goat. Next she goes and gets herself dangerously ill. Then, on the ship that should have taken her back, they have me arriving instead – looniest grandson on the planet.

Mind you, they're a bit of a rum bunch themselves, these three snow-musketeers. In order of how much I like them, they are Terry, Dietrich and Mike. Terry is a cutie in specs. Straggly blond hair tucked into her hood. Little dimples every time she smiles. Sparky eyes, too.

'Oh, I thought, being a *Terry*, that you were a bloke,' I said first thing when she introduced herself.

'Everyone does,' she said with her dimply smile. 'Well, I might as well be,' she added, more to herself than to me. Not self-pitying, just kind of matter-of-fact. No way could you mistake her for a bloke looking at her, though. Man, no!

'I'm so, so sorry about your grandmother,' she said. All heartfelt. Blushing as if it was her fault.

'No worries,' I said. That sounded like I didn't care, so I added, 'She's a strong woman. Who knows, maybe she'll be hunky-dory.' That sounded flippant, so I said, 'You've done great. Thanks for looking after her!' That sounded inane, but I couldn't think what else to say so I shut up.

After we'd looked in on Granny they all showed me round their place together, the field camp building. It's quite big actually, bigger on the inside than it looks from the outside at least. Tardis-like. They've got a computer room (more of a cupboard really) and a sort of loo-cum-washroom and a kitchen that adjoins a room they call the lounge, which suggests luxury but it isn't. And – pretty amazing when you think of it – a bedroom each. There's even a bedroom for me. Well, it used to be a storeroom but they've cleared it out and found me a camp bed. Man, I'm glad I don't have to share a room with Granny. Granny's actually got a room-mate, anyway.

Weirdly, there's this baby penguin, the oddest, cutest creature you've ever seen, a little fluff ball with big feet and a massive personality. They call him Pip. Apparently he's been living at the field centre for a week and a half. The scientists accept his presence as if it's completely the norm. I have to say I'm finding it all a bit surreal. It's hard to get my head around the way they live.

'What made you come out here in the first place?' I asked Dietrich over a strong coffee after I'd settled in a bit. Dietrich is the boss-man, but nice with it. Kind of reminds me of Gav, but hairier and more foreign. (Mike is the I-want-to-be-the-boss man. Not nice with it. Doesn't remind me of anyone much. A younger Piers Morgan, maybe?)

Dietrich stroked his beard as he considered the answer to my question. 'Ah, you know. The thrill of scientific discovery. Fascination in the extremes of life, the way creatures can function on this level. Then there's the possibility of helping wildlife and the environment in some small way . . .'

'And you?' I asked Mike. Mike took a prolonged sip of coffee and eyed me, calculating his response.

'I am uniquely qualified for this job,' he said. 'It would be a waste not to make use of those skills.' Modest guy (not).

Terry rolled her eyes and gave an impetuous little sigh.

'How about you, Terry?' I asked. 'Why did you come out to Locket Island?'

'My dream job. I just love penguins,' she said simply, pushing her glasses up her nose.

I spent the rest of the afternoon at Granny V's bedside. I was thinking about the diaries and how I should say something soon, in case she popped her clogs all of a sudden. I've had time to think about it during the journey, but the words won't come. Gav would know what to say, and he'd say it in exactly the right way, but I'm pants at that sort of thing. So I just sat there like a mugwump. Maybe the fact I took the trouble to come out here is enough to make her feel vaguely better in some way. I'm hoping so.

Over dinner, Mike asked me a barrage of questions:

'So, Patrick, what do you do for a living?'

I wriggled in my chair. I get that Mike doesn't like me much. Terry's told me he's a bit resistant to anyone new upsetting the balance of the field camp. He's only just got used to Granny and now he's having to deal with yours truly. Well, tough, mate!

'I work at a bike shop on Mondays and I sign on,' I told him.

'Sign on? So the shop is your only job?'

'Got it in one.'

'Do you get your accommodation paid for by the state, then?'

How to make Patrick feel uncomfortable in one easy step.

'Mike!' Terry cried. 'Don't be so rude!'

Mike turned his fork around, weaving spaghetti on to it with precision. 'Sorry, I'm not meaning to be rude. I'm curious about our newest visitor, that's all. We don't exactly get many.'

'It's covered by the benefit, yes,' I inform him.

'You don't have a family or wife to support, I presume?'

'Nope.'

Mike curled his lip. I suppose it was a sort of smile. 'So what do you do all day in this bedsit of yours?'

'Oh, this and that. Telly. Mags. Plant-care. Nothing to write home about.'

After the meal, Terry came with me to Granny V's room.

'Sorry about the inquest,' she whispered in my ear.

I grinned. 'That Mike – bit uptight, isn't he?'

'Oh, he can come across that way, but he's all right once you get to know him.'

'Are you two together?'

'God, no! He's got a girlfriend back in London. She's quite high-powered, does stuff to do with organizing conferences for the corporate world, I think.'

'Oh,' I said. 'I'm surprised. I thought he was rather attached to *you*.'

She looked amused. 'Mike? Attached to me? Don't be silly!'

'Well, he can't seem to stop looking at you.'

She threw me a look of total disbelief and disappeared quickly into Veronica's room. I followed. Pip the Penguin was in his suitcase bed on the floor. He looked up at us. He seemed to register who we were and give his permission for us to tend to the patient, then laid his head back down.

Granny looked the same as earlier, lying on her back completely stationary. Her skin was covered in blotches and sagging all over the place. Her hair was sticking out in wisps over the pillow. She had grey circles round her eyes. Man, she looked sick as a dog.

Terry put her hand on Granny's forehead. 'She's very hot. Let's see if we can get some water down her. Could you . . . ?'

I tucked my arm behind Granny's head and carefully levered her up. I realized it was the first time I'd ever touched her. God, it felt sad, her being so fragile and everything. Her eyes flickered a little. My hand caught in something, a chain around her neck.

'What's this?'

'Oh, it's a locket she wears,' Terry answered. 'I thought it might be uncomfortable for her and tried to take it off, but she hit out. She made it quite clear she wasn't having any of it. I guess it must have some sentimental value.'

'I guess it must.' I didn't let on that I'd read about it in her diaries.

Terry held the glass of water to Granny's lips and we watched her take a sip or two, a lump moving slowly down her throat. She made a slight movement as if to say that was enough. I laid her head on the pillow again and gave her hand a little squeeze. It may be my imagination (it was kind of hard to tell) but I think she squeezed back.

'There you are, Granny V,' I said. 'Better now?' She didn't answer, of course.

I wondered how much of this she was registering.

It's not looking good. Not good at all.

39

Veronica

Locket Island

THE CHARMS OF DEATH are manifold. No more pain. No more stress. No more memories. No more having to make decisions. 'Tis a consummation', as Hamlet said (you will observe I remember with some accuracy my Shakespeare from my schooldays) 'devoutly to be wished.' To die. To sleep. It is rather appealing. Relaxing. And there's the added bonus of no more pain – have I said that already?

Because at this moment there *is* pain, intense and merciless. It seeps in and out of my body's pores, claws at my lungs and sears into every pocket of my heart like burning acid. I sincerely hope death will arrive soon.

My Antarctic companions will have a job getting my body back to Ayrshire for a decent burial. Or perhaps they won't bother. It may be that I'll get buried here under the snow. It may be that troops of penguins will wander over my grave. In their inimitable penguin way, they'll ignore my decaying presence and get on with the business of fornication, reproduction and defecation. They will themselves die around me in huge numbers. My soul can rise up and mingle with theirs. This is, of course, assuming I have a soul (which is debatable) and they have souls (which is also improbable).

I take a quick backwards glance at my life. At this stage there are supposed to be profound revelations, are there not? They don't seem to be materializing at all. My history imparts no great wisdom, no last words fine enough to go down for posterity. I can only think: well, what was *that* all about?

Patrick is here, Patrick my grandson, a large, ungainly presence at my bedside. Terry has put in my hearing aid in case any pearls of wisdom should issue from his lips. Patrick has indeed said 'Hello, Granny' to me but very little else. I couldn't reply, but I managed to flicker my eyelids to let him know I was aware of him. He seems incredibly gauche. He's sitting on a chair by the bed, holding something. I think it's a newspaper or magazine; it rattles in that sort of way. He sighs a lot, too.

I am baffled that he came. He must know I'm too ill to make any inheritance arrangements.

After a long period of silence I hear somebody else coming into the room.

'Are you two all right?'

Terry's voice is light and warm, designed to be comforting. My grandson's answer comes quickly. 'Yes. Fine, just, y'know . . . quiet.'

'Pip's been with me for the last hour, watching me do some tidying, but I've brought him back in for a bit. I thought Veronica might like him here. She seems to find his presence soothing. You don't mind, do you?'

'Um. No. No. He's very cute.'

'I need to shake out his bedding. Can you hold him for a sec?'

'Er . . .'

There's a slight scuffling sound then an 'Ow!' from Patrick.

'Maybe not,' says Terry. 'He doesn't know you yet. Hang on a mo. If I hold him and you stroke him gently, like this . . .'

'Are you sure he won't go for me again? That beak is sharp!'

'You scared him because you were grabby. See? He's happy now. He goes all gooey when his neck is stroked. Don't you, Pip?'

A brief pause and then she chuckles. 'There, he really likes you.'

I hear Pip's little cheep and sense he's asking to be put down.

'We'll let him wander around for a bit, shall we?'

'Won't he make a mess on the floor?'

'Nah. If he does I'll clear it up in no time. Not a problem.'

'Not, well . . . unhygienic or anything?'

'Well, I'd say if he makes Veronica happy he should visit as often as he likes, don't you think?'

'Yup. You're right. Um, Terry, yes. Quite right.'

Patrick's voice sounds abashed. You'd think he'd never met a young woman holding a baby penguin before.

Terry speaks again. 'Could you keep an eye on him for a mo? I'm going to get myself a cuppa. Would you like one?'

'Oh, er, yes. Cool. Thanks.'

I sense him sitting down again and hear a few pages of the magazine turn. Then Terry's footsteps at the door.

'Here we go. Tea for us. And I've brought this for Pip. It's his suppertime.'

A strong smell of fish permeates the room along with various clacking, cheeping and sucking noises.

Penguin-feeding in the presence of a dying eighty-six-year-old. If the dying one wasn't me, I'd laugh out loud.

40

Patrick

Locket Island
January 2013

THE OLD YEAR HAS gone and the new one has begun. Not that it makes any difference. Nobody was in the mood for celebrating. I've been here four days now and in that time Granny V hasn't eaten at all. She just lies there looking cross. I'm presuming that's not a good sign.

I feel like a spare part here. There's nothing I can do for her except sit by her bed, hoping she knows I'm there. Making moronic comments she'd probably pour scorn on if she could hear them, which I doubt. The scientists give me plenty of space. They're a busy lot anyway. Seems of vital importance that they go out every day and count penguins and tag penguins and weigh penguins and do other penguiny stuff. They're kind to me, though. Well, Terry and Dietrich are anyway. Mike tolerates me. That guy has issues. Looks down his nose at anyone who doesn't have a PhD in penguin studies.

I'm glad to have the company of Pip, the penguin. He's totally at home here. He sleeps a lot, eats a lot, runs round in circles a lot and gets under our feet a lot. And OK, I'll admit it: I sometimes talk to him. Call me crazy, but I actually find it quite a relief talking to a penguin. It's easier than talking to a comatose eighty-six-year-old, anyway.

According to Terry, Pip was called Patrick before I arrived. 'Veronica named him after you,' she said.

You could've knocked me down with a feather. Granny is a strange fish, no doubt about it. A seriously strange fish.

We've had the helicopter doctor in, the same one who came before. He prescribed more antibiotics and said she's comfortable and there's nothing else we can do for her except just being here. He says she'll know, even if she doesn't show it. She should either make a turn for the better or the worse very soon. He implied he didn't want to be called out again either way. We should just keep her warm and hydrated.

There's a plastic pot under the bed for emergencies. Terry is great and deals with the hygiene stuff. I did offer (I felt I had to) but wow, was I glad when Terry insisted! She says Veronica would hate any man to do it and I think she's right. My guess is that Granny hates everything about the situation she's in. Rough deal, being old and ill like that, especially when you're a million miles from home.

'You can't stay by Veronica's bedside the whole time,' Terry told me yesterday. 'It'll drive you mad. Anyway, she's stable for the moment. She can spare you an hour or two to see the Adélies.'

I have to admit, I was pretty keen to visit the colony. 'Well, if you're sure.' I flung on my fleece.

'Are you going to be warm enough in that?'

'Got two sweatshirts on underneath. But no, probably not. I'm not overly keen on cold like this.' Why do the wrong words always jump out of my mouth? That made me sound like a wimp.

'We keep a spare parka. That'll help.' She fetched me a jacket ten times thicker than the one I was wearing.

'Thanks.'

She looked down at my trainers. 'You're not nearly as prepared as your grandmother for all this. I think you'd better borrow Mike's spare mukluks.'

'Won't he go ape if I do that?'

'No, he'll understand.'

The mukluks fitted OK, and did help, to be honest.

The snow! I'd almost forgotten. The brightness hits you the minute you step outside. The landscape just swallows you up. The clarity. The sharpness of each breath as it hits your lungs. Man, it's quite something!

Up and over a great gleaming bank and there we were: penguin land. They were awesome, those birds. Thousands more than I was expecting, so you could hardly see the ground between them. Making a right old racket, too. Wild, waddling and wilful. Like humans but smaller and beakier and blacker-and-whiter and funnier. I swear, you couldn't *not* like those guys.

I kept saying dumb things like 'Wow' and 'Cool' and 'No way'. Some of the birds were curious about our presence and formed a little group around us. Us looking at them, them looking at us. Don't know what possessed me but I stooped down and gathered up a miniature snowball and threw it towards one of them, not hard or anything, just playful. It landed right at his feet. The penguin looked down in surprise then turned its gaze to me. Not hostile, but kind of puzzled. 'Sorry, mate,' I called to it. 'No offence. Just a scientific experiment – to see if it narked you or not. You did great, pal. Full marks for non-narkedness.'

I turned to Terry and pointed to her notebook. 'Better log that,' I told her. She laughed. 'You're funny,' she said.

As we went on I was half expecting the penguin to throw a snowball into my back, but he didn't.

A little while later Terry said: 'Patrick, I was wondering . . .'

'Yes, Terry?'

'About your grandmother, about Veronica. I expect you're very fond of her, aren't you?'

'Er . . . And that would be because of her warm and sunshiny personality?'

Terry chortled. She gets me. 'Well, you *did* come out all this way.'

'Yup. That's because . . . Well – it's complicated.'

Terry had this look like she couldn't quite decide on which words to say then just decided to say it anyhow.

'I suppose she told you all about her money?'

'That there's a ton of it? Yeah. Yup, she did.'

A slight pause. Terry studied the horizon. 'And did she tell you about her plans for her will? Her legacy?'

'Hell, no!'

Her voice went all quiet and I had a problem hearing what she said next. 'Veronica didn't actually have a will, from what she told me. She was planning on making one when she got back home.'

I was a bit surprised Terry was banging on about such a subject. She doesn't strike me as somebody who'd be majorly into money.

I shrugged. 'I guess we'll never know what her plan was.'

Terry marched on. 'I suppose not,' she declared to the frozen air.

Terry is first to come back from the Adélie colony today. She calls out 'Hi, Patrick,' then heads straight for the office.

When she emerges twenty minutes later I'm standing in the 'lounge', staring into space. You know how it is. Sometimes you just have to take a little break from the joys of Granny Veronica's bedside.

'God, I can't think of anything to say in the blog,' Terry confides. 'Veronica's become a real part of it, but I don't want to let on she's ill.'

There must be some great gem of wisdom I can offer here, but I can't seem to find it.

'Tricky,' I answer.

'It's probably best if I don't mention her at all. I don't want to lie and . . . it's all too upsetting.' She gulps and looks a bit teary. I'm wondering what's the best way to offer comfort. Might a hug be OK? It might, under the circumstances. But before I can make up my mind Mike and Dietrich come in, shaking the snow off their boots. The moment has gone.

After we've all had the inevitable how-was-your-day and how's-Veronica and how-are-the-penguins conversations, I broach something I've been wondering about for a while.

'Can I cook for you? I'd like to do something to, you know, say thanks for looking after Granny.' There's no way I can contribute any dosh, after all. There's no dosh to contribute.

Terry becomes smiley. 'Oh, that's very good of you!'

Mike becomes sneery. '*Can* you cook?'

'I'm not bad,' I reply, peed off at him. He clearly assumes I'm a complete waste of space. 'Not bad at all.'

'Ah, this is very good news,' cries Dietrich. 'Especially if you can come up with something we don't normally do. We're a bit stuck in the rut of frankfurter sausages, canned beans and pasta. *Gott*, we are sick of them all.'

'Can I see your store cupboard?'

'Yes. You're welcome, my friend. Follow me.' He takes me to the back room. It seems like they only ever use the tinned stuff and the packets of dried pasta, rice and ready-mix sauces. The only other thing that's been opened is a huge crate of peanut butter.

'We have the frozen stock, too,' Dietrich says, leading me to a lean-to out the back. 'Some meat, some veg – the ones that freeze OK. I'd steer clear of the cauliflower if I were you. It's putrid.'

I can well believe that frozen cauliflower would stick in the gullet. I notice some hunks of beef, though.

'That's not bad. From Argentina,' Dietrich tells me.

There's a box of frozen red and yellow peppers, too. I start to plan in my head.

An hour later the aroma of real food is wafting around: my beef and pepper goulash. It draws each of the scientists from their various corners of the building to the stove.

I dish up, piling the food high. I'd have liked to scatter it with fresh leaves of some sort, but fresh leaves aren't on the cards here. I've cooked masses, so there are seconds for everyone. They eat like vultures. I feel proud, I don't mind admitting it.

'There'll be plenty for tomorrow, too, if you don't mind having the same thing twice,' I tell them.

'Mind!' cries Terry with her mouth full.

'You can come again!' says Dietrich.

Mike doesn't say a word about the food but I notice how he gobbles it up.

'Like it?' I ask pointedly.

'Yes. Very good. Very good indeed. Thank you,' he replies stiffly.

Terry's Penguin Blog

3 January 2013

Here are the latest pictures of Pip the Penguin. Yes, we've decided to change his name because we currently have another Patrick (a human one) staying with us on the island.

Pip has bulked out a lot, as you'll see, and now he weighs 1,700g. He is a keen explorer and likes to discover new places to sleep. His latest is a wastepaper basket . . .

Life is busy at the research centre at the moment and I am a little short of time, so I'm just going to leave you with some more lovely penguin photos.

41

Veronica

Locket Island

DAD IS HERE, AND Mum, dancing together in the kitchen, the Lambeth Walk. Their footsteps clack loudly on the floor. The window is open and a vast sapphire sky stretches beyond it, blurry and fluctuating slightly. A gust of wind blows in and lifts both of them off the floor as if they're tiny twists of paper. I try to grab hold of them, chase them round. But they slip through my fingers like ribbons and sail out of the window again, dancing shadows sucked into the endless blue.

I hear a voice, calling. 'Ver-on-ee-cah!' First it seems as though the sound is coming from ahead of me, then behind. I spin round and round. Then it thunders down on me from above: *Get thee to a nunnery, go!*

Now I can see Janet, Norah and Harry. They are not quite real but seem like huge doll versions of themselves, leering at me, pointing mocking fingers at my swollen belly. They circle like wolves.

Norah lunges at me. I am bleeding, bleeding. But it isn't blood that is flowing out from my veins; it is strawberry jam.

Suddenly there are nuns, a river of nuns in black and white, flowing past. Each one is holding a baby out for me to inspect but snatches it away again before I can see if it is my Enzo. I can't handle this any more. I hurl myself into the river, screaming. The black-and-white flow closes over me. I wait to be trampled under the nuns' feet but . . . they are not human feet. They are webbed feet, soft and light. And I realize the nuns have sleek, tightly packed feathers and little stubby tails. They are not nuns at all. They are Adélie penguins.

Is it Giovanni, here with me? I can't see well but I think he is bending over the bed. He is about to kiss me. I try to speak his name but my mouth is too dry. He pulls back. There is no kiss, no touch. And no, I see now it isn't Giovanni. It is some uncouth young man with unshaven skin and messy hair who mutters and smells of fish. I don't know him at all. Or do I?

'Patrick!' somebody calls. It is a woman's voice, clear but coated in gentleness. 'I'm just heading out to the rookery. You'll be all right, won't you?'

'Yeah, no probs,' answers the man whose face is above me. I feel a hand placed on my forehead for a moment. Then a 'Blimey, you're hot!'

Is it Giovanni? The hair is a similar colour, and there's something about the eyes . . . But no. I'm sure it's not him, not as I remember him anyway. And my memory is as good as . . . as good as Hamlet's.

I move my lips again and try to speak but it's useless.

Patrick. That name is echoing in my head. I think there was a boy called Patrick. Yes, a boy who I'd hoped would be an oasis but he ended up being just another mirage in the thirsty desert of my soul. I grapple with fear once more. I have this unpleasant notion that somebody I once pinned my hopes on turned out to be an awful, dirty lout who smoked dope. The image in my head seems to match this man who is here now.

I can't focus very well. I'm trying to force my thoughts into order but they are a knotted mass. Wait . . . something is coming. The words *Patrick* and *grandson* are linked. But that is ridiculous! Patrick is a bird, a small fluffy penguin. I am sure of it. My grandson cannot possibly be a penguin.

42

Patrick

Locket Island

OH JEEZ! OH NO! Is this it? She looks grim. Her face is scrunched up like an old piece of tissue paper. Her mouth is oddly twisted. A rasping breath comes out then there's a horribly long interval before the next one. I lean over and stroke her brow. Her forehead is burning but her hands are cold as ice. Her rheumy eyes look up at me, blurred and confused. Pleading. But what can I do?

Man, I'm wretched. I don't want to be alone to witness this suffering.

I rush to the door of the hut and fling it open, hoping Terry has been delayed, but there's only brightness and silence. Terry has disappeared from view. She's with the penguins and won't be back for hours. The others left for the colony first thing this morning. Pip is dozing in his wastepaper basket. It looks like it'll be just me and the penguin with Granny at the end.

I hare back to her room. She's floundering like a fish out of water. I grab a cold, damp flannel and press it against her face. Her body shudders. Then falls back, limp.

'Granny, Granny, don't!' I gulp. I'm so choked up it feels like some reptilian creature is wedged inside my throat.

I don't want Granny to die. I'm feeling feelings I haven't had in years. A sudden violent need for family connection. A longing to know more about her. Shame at my behaviour the first time we met. Sorrow that I never got her to see how much I wanted to make up for it. Then there's the fact that she came to Antarctica. She came to *Antarctica*, to this weird, wild place at the end of the earth – I find that bizarrely moving. On top of that my mind is spinning with images from her diaries: young Veronica, all alive and fiery, ready to take on everything and everybody. So unlike now.

Her eyebrows draw together as if she's trying to work something out. Her mouth forms into a shape. I put my ear close, desperate to catch her words.

Her breath comes again in a series of shallow gasps. At last there is a single word, a hoarse, grating whisper. It is my own name: 'Patrick.'

At the sound, Pip, who has, Terry tells me, been suffering an identity crisis since his name was changed, rouses himself. He clambers out of his wastepaper basket and plops on to the floor. Then, with stunning power and energy, he catapults himself into the air and lands right on top of the bed. He clearly thinks Granny is calling him for a feeding session. Eager little guy. He topples forward on to the bedclothes then wriggles on his belly towards her face. Startled, her eyes open and focus on him. The two of them are almost nose to beak, beak to nose. It's as if they're locked in a soundless dialogue and I'm a mere bystander, looking on.

And I swear I can see Granny changing, undergoing a kind of transformation right there in front of me.

43

Veronica

Locket Island

I AM TIRED OF it all and ready to go. *For who would bear the whips and scorns of time . . . The heart-ache and the thousand natural shocks that flesh is heir to?*

Not me. Not any more. Nobody could call my life a success. Why make the effort to hang on to it any longer?

And yet.

When a cannonball of a young penguin propels himself on to your prostrate body and stares into your face with glittering eyes, you stop whatever you are doing for a moment, even if what you are doing is dying.

His body is warm and small and rounded, horizontally positioned over the blankets, just heavy enough to weigh gently on my chest. Right over my heart.

The world has been wobbling wildly for some time. In this moment it steadies and comes to a standstill. The room looks sharper and brighter and incredibly defined, as if somebody has drawn round everything with a pen. My head is clear. Moreover, all my pain has disappeared. I feel positively light and carefree.

Pip. The baby bird is Pip, I know that without a shadow of a doubt. Pip, my own beloved penguin. And the dishevelled man who is looming behind and above is Patrick, my own beloved grandson.

Beloved grandson? Have I gone completely crazy?

I must be hallucinating because now I see great, fat tears coursing down the man's face. I look at Pip again, seeking verification.

Is all that grief for me?

'Yes, that's right,' Pip answers.

I'm sure he spoke. Or maybe he didn't speak? No, there weren't any actual words out loud. Perhaps he spoke with his eyes. Yes, I think that's it. How very curious . . . I am beginning to realize a penguin's eyes can tell you many things if only you are willing to listen.

Thoughts bubble up from my subconscious but again, it seems as though they are transmitted to me through Pip. He is smiling with his whole body. 'So you're going to stay with us! You're not going to die now, are you?'

'Aren't I?' It seems rather a hasty assumption.

'No,' he replies without hesitation. 'I hope not, anyway.'

I am flattered; tickled pink in fact. 'You hope not?' It is a rare gift to be able to communicate with a penguin like this; inaudibly, without moving my lips.

'Look at it this way,' he suggests. I am intrigued to hear what he has to say. 'A while back you saved me,' he goes on, 'from certain death. You decided my life was worthwhile even though I'm only a penguin. So it's only fair if you let me decide whether *your* life is worthwhile. And do you know what I think? It's *definitely* worthwhile.'

It is rather nice to have a penguin tell you that.

'You've got a choice,' he continues, not moving his gaze but shuffling one flipper slightly so that it brushes against my cheek. 'And I'm asking you nicely if you'll do your best to recover. Because, personally, I'd very much like you to stay alive.'

'You would?' I ask, bemused.

'Yes! And so would this here man, your beloved grandson, a.k.a. Patrick.'

'Still harping on about Patrick?'

'Isn't that the point?'

I focus on Patrick. His eyes are still brimming with tears. I am very confused now about what is real and what is not real.

I transfer my gaze to Pip again. 'See?' he says. 'It's perfectly possible for somebody to love you, even though you insist on making it difficult for them. You don't have to be so alone.'

Am I imagining it or has a shaft of sunlight just fallen across the room?

'Please,' he says, 'live a little longer and you'll see.'

He is fading now, becoming dim and blurry round the edges. The extraordinary episode seems to have ended. Reality has resumed its course and I can feel pain flooding back through my veins. But those words keep reverberating in my head.

Live a little longer and you'll see . . .

44

Veronica

Locket Island

'Honestly, her face was completely changed.' It's Patrick's voice. 'She looked positively radiant. And she couldn't keep her eyes off this little guy.'

'That's interesting,' I hear Terry reply. 'It could be that she was experiencing that phenomenon that sometimes happens when somebody's close to death. It's a kind of euphoria. For some people it's like a tunnel of light. For others – well, I guess Veronica is pretty obsessed with Pip. It may have manifested itself differently.'

'Well, it was totally bizarre, whatever it was.'

'She seems to have rallied a bit, though, doesn't she?'

I am indeed managing to gather a few particles of strength. It's possible I'll live for another few days . . . it's even faintly possible I'll live for another few years.

At the moment I'm not in a position to appreciate life very much at all. But, bearing in mind what Pip said (or didn't say?) I'm prepared to give it another go.

Pip's presence is a balm. Even when my eyes are closed or he is out of my line of sight I can sense when he's near. Sometimes Terry lifts him on to the bed and he snuggles into the crook of my arm, savouring the warmth. Encourages me on with this survival game and keeps my old heart alive somehow.

My lungs feel like a tired, limp balloon that will disintegrate if any reasonable quantity of air is drawn inside. My muscles ache. My throat is lined with sandpaper. Speaking isn't an option. Neither is sitting up. My days are inordinately tedious. The only way I can entertain myself is to listen to what's going on around me. It's fair to say I'm doing more listening than I've ever done in my life before. Never have I concentrated on others in quite this much detail.

I do find kindness confusing. I am not in the habit of trusting it. I have always assumed that if people are good to me it's because they want something back. Usually, these days, the thing they want is money.

Yet now I question that. The people here around me on Locket Island have been kind in a way I wasn't expecting. I had presumed they all had an agenda, but perhaps they are simply being kind because it's in their nature.

Dietrich comes to my room fairly often. He doesn't waste time in small talk or ask how I am. He knows I can't answer. 'Mrs McCreedy,' he exclaims in a voice of eagerness. 'I am going to read you another chapter from *Great Expectations*. I'm sure you're going to like it.' He clears his throat and starts without further preamble. I am plunged into the story of a young boy full of hopes and dreams. The narration entertains me. It also has me reflecting on youth and how quickly it is eaten up; and how we are changed by our experiences. What sort of a person would I have been if my own youth had been different? If my parents had lived? If war had not introduced me to Giovanni or torn us apart again? If I had been allowed to keep my baby?

Pressure is slowly building behind my eyes, a liquid rising to the surface. It gathers in two hot pools then starts to spill down my face and on to the pillow. I don't try to stop it. I am powerless.

Dietrich reads on. I like his voice now. The Austrian accent has a gentleness to it. I like the way his voice strokes the words as he reads. Sometimes, when the story touches on love, he pauses as if he is thinking, too. He has a wife and children in Austria. I find I am keenly aware of how much he misses them.

Time passes; minutes, hours, days. It's impossible to keep track of them. Mike, Patrick and Terry are all even more frequent visitors than Dietrich. They appear in different combinations, each one with its own dynamic.

Mike's visits surprise me most. I know he's not fond of me so there must be some other reason for them. Does he feel guilty about how frosty he was to me at the outset? Or is he attempting to prove something to someone?

'Veronica, hello. I've dropped in to see how you are,' he'll start, settling himself on the edge of the chair beside my bed. 'The weather today is a little warmer, nearly 1.8 degrees C . . .' (this means nothing to me. I only understand Fahrenheit). 'We haven't got any sunshine, though. I am going out to the rookery shortly.' He fills me in on the most recent news from the penguin colony, keeping it factual. The penguin called Sooty is still sitting forlornly on its nest. More chicks are hatching every day. Many of them succumb to starvation or have their lives snatched away by predators. Others are thriving. I picture them in my mind's eye and hope that one day I'll be well enough to see them again.

Whenever Mike coincides with Patrick there are short, terse exchanges. Little barbed comments from Mike. Stubborn resistance from Patrick. One-upmanship of various kinds. When Mike coincides with Terry, however, I've noticed he takes on a softer, much gentler tone.

As I previously suspected, Mike is in denial.

Terry has no idea, of course. She considers herself to be unattractive, asexual almost, because she isn't a typical magazine-style beauty. She sees herself as something of a geek. She pours her energies into looking after Pip and looking after me. ('Please try to eat something, Veronica. I have mushroom soup. Pip, be patient. It'll be your turn in a minute.') She likes to feel useful. She doesn't even seem to mind the unsavoury business of emptying the chamber pot and ensuring my cleanliness by means of sponges and flannels. I submit as needs must, grateful to the girl for her sensitivity and discretion. If she is anywhere near as revolted as I am at my body's shenanigans she must relish the task very little. Mercifully she is skilled in hiding the fact.

My grandson is here the most. He evidently has nothing else to do. I simply cannot comprehend why he is in Antarctica. I find it difficult to believe he would have undertaken such a voyage just for me, and yet it seems this is the case. Although his company was irksome to me at the beginning, I am becoming accustomed to it. He talks much more than he did. Sometimes it isn't clear which of us he is talking to, Pip or myself. He rattles on about his attempts at cooking decent food from the basic provisions here. He tells us about the bicycle shop back where he lives. He talks of his friend ('mate') called Gavin ('Gav') and a little girl called Daisy who has cancer. He even, when he thinks I am asleep, talks about his foster families and his ex-girlfriends. Slowly more parts of his life unfold.

I keep my eyes tightly closed and I listen. Whether I was hallucinating or not, I can't forget Pip talking to me as I lay dying. I remember what he said about Patrick, and a word that slipped out from me and seemed to be reiterated by him: the word 'beloved'.

It may be that I'm only having a brief respite. But if I do live a little longer, there is no doubt about it: I'm going to have to review my opinion of everything.

45

Patrick

Locket Island

GRANNY AND I HAVE one thing in common, at least. We're both nuts about penguins. I never used to give penguins much thought, to be honest, but all that's changed. What is it about penguins? I don't know if it's their human characteristics or their quirky birdiness, but watching them is a total therapy. They make me laugh. They make me kind of mushy inside. They're so small, yet they're brimming with life. It's a beautiful thing.

The scientists take a lot of their time at base writing up their notes. There's no TV and they're often using the super-slow internet, so I've started to explore the bookshelves. The novels mostly seem to be boring classics like Dickens and *Jane Eyre*. No crime or action stuff, except some stuffy old Agatha Christie and Sherlock Holmes. There's a ton of books about penguins, though. I've started on one of them. It's pretty interesting, actually.

'Your grandmother likes to be read to, you know,' said Dietrich the other day, seeing me turn the pages.

'Are you kidding?'

'Well, she seems to like *Great Expectations*. You can try her on *All You Ever Wanted to Know About Penguins*, if you think it's more her thing.'

'Thanks, mate. Maybe I will.'

So I do. I read penguin facts to Granny every day from the big volume. I plonk Pip on the bed and he settles down with us quite happily. Seems like he's fascinated to learn more about his species. Sometimes he looks cynical, as if he's saying, 'Well, that bit's pretty accurate, but that bit, mate, is complete bullshit.' Other times he plucks at the pages with his beak, trying their taste and texture.

A tiny hint of colour has come back to Granny's cheeks. She managed to gulp down some soup today, a spoonful or two of minestrone. She still doesn't speak a lot, but she did say this much, in a tone of great astonishment:

'You're a good chef, Patrick.'

I was chuffed. 'Why, thank you, Granny!'

She muttered something else so croaky I couldn't get what it was.

'What was that, Granny? What was that you said?'

'I said . . .' She cleared the phlegm from her throat. 'I said it must be the Italian in you.'

Of course! The Italian in me! I'd never thought of that.

Terry and I are out penguin-watching again. The snow is light and powdery, like sifted icing sugar. The sea is shining silver-blue, all decked out in its chunky jewellery of floating ice.

'So are you glad you came out here to Locket Island?' Terry asks as our boots creak along.

'No,' I answer, sticking hands in pockets, pulling the corners of my mouth down. 'It's been totally grim.'

She starts apologizing and saying what an upset the whole episode must be for me. I interrupt with a laugh.

'Terry, stop! It's not as if I've been majorly grief-stricken.' I tell her how I'd only actually met Granny on a couple of occasions, and what a fiasco that was. 'I *have* begun to like her, though,' I confess. 'Never ever thought I'd say that.'

'I'm so glad to hear it, Patrick.'

There's something about Terry: you feel you can tell her anything, totally anything. She'll be cool.

'I only came here because of one thing,' I admit. 'She sent me her teenage diaries. There was something about that gesture. And she had a bloody miserable past. So it seemed the decent thing to do was to come out here and be with her in her final hour.'

'What final hour?!'

We snigger happily. Looks like Granny's going to be around for a bit after all.

We've reached the colony. I look out at the acres of penguinyness and breathe in the heady stink of guano.

'Want to help me with some weighing today?' Terry asks. She shows me how to dive in and grasp a penguin, avoiding the jabbing beak and thrashing flippers; how to put him in the weighing bag before he's had time to think; how to get him weighed and set loose again. There's a definite art to it. I get myself pecked a bit and a few birds dive out of my grip and scuttle off before I've got control of them. It's OK, though. More than OK, actually. Man, I love it!

Terry does the weighing and recording, while I take on the role of Lord High Penguin-wrangler. I'm getting pretty nifty at it, though I say so myself. We laugh, how we laugh.

When we've done nine or ten penguins, Terry says to me, 'I've been thinking about Veronica.'

'Mmm?' This is what Gav does when he wants to encourage an opinion out of me. I want to see if it works with Terry. It does.

'She told me about her childhood. About the war. And about her parents and Giovanni and her baby.'

'Granny opened up to you?' Even Granny gets how cool Terry is.

Terry shrugs her shoulders. 'Veronica didn't talk about herself for ages. But one day it all came tumbling out.'

'Maybe these guys helped,' I comment, passing Terry a fat, bemused-looking penguin.

'Yes, I do think so.' She grabs the penguin and plunges him into the weighing sack. She makes the reading and jots it into her book. 'Veronica's been hurt again and again and again,' she continues. 'Everyone she loved disappeared. I think she's taught herself over the years to see the worst in everyone, to make sure she doesn't get attached. Because she simply can't cope with any more loss.'

'You may have a point there, Terry.'

She sighs. 'I can't imagine the pain of suddenly finding your baby has been taken away!'

'Taken away?'

'Yes, that's what happened to Veronica. When the nuns whisked him off and gave him to that Canadian couple – and she never even got to say goodbye.'

I gawp at Terry as what she is saying hits home. 'You mean . . . you mean she had *no choice*?'

'Didn't she tell you? Wasn't it in the diaries?' Terry's eyes widen in surprise. Then her mouth drops open as she sees I had no idea that's what happened.

'I thought *she* was the one who'd given him up for adoption, even though it seemed like she was fond of him. I get it now. God, poor Veronica! Poor kid!'

We share a moment of reflection. 'I guess it's as well you know,' Terry says at last. 'He was your father, after all. You do know he's dead, don't you?' she adds anxiously.

'Yeah, yeah. In his forties, mountaineering accident.'

She sighs again and her face takes on a philosophical kind of expression. 'Life's cruel, isn't it? Just when you've got over one thing, something else happens. So many people die.'

'Um . . . not wanting to be pessimistic and that, but I kind of think we *all* die,' I point out.

She darts a smile at me. It's cheeky and gobsmackingly beautiful. 'We don't have to do it yet, though, do we!'

'No,' I agree. 'We totally need to enjoy the time we've got.'

'Oops! Penguin!' We've been so engrossed chatting we've gone and left the fat penguin in the weighing sack. She empties him out and we watch him reel a little before scuttling off to join his mates.

We spend a while longer out there, weighing at least thirty penguins, and I enjoy every minute of it. It's fan-bloody-tastic, doing all this penguin stuff. I totally get why Terry, Mike and Dietrich are obsessed. It would be a tragedy if they had to stop the project.

My thick brain has finally cottoned on. That's what Terry was trying to tell me when she was going on about money that time, but she was too delicate to spell it out. Granny must have told her she was planning on leaving her millions to the penguin project, rather than yours truly. Terry's been guilt-stricken, I bet. Desperately needing the money for her beloved penguins but feeling it was my right to have it. Seeing both sides, because she would, she's like that. Assuming I care about the dosh.

And do I care? Well, look at it this way. I never even knew I had a Granny till a few months ago. And aside from paying Gav back for forking out on my travel here (which does worry me), I wouldn't actually know what to do with that kind of money. I'd probably fritter it on useless stuff. Video games, gym memberships, beer, bikes, fancy cooking equipment, etc etc.

No, Granny V is welcome to leave her millions to the Adélies. They need it a hell of a lot more than I do.

46

Veronica

Locket Island

'You have been kind to me.'

'Don't sound so surprised, Granny.'

I used to find the word 'Granny' toe-curlingly dreadful, particularly when applied to myself, particularly by him. However, I'm becoming quite accustomed to it. The boy has been generous with his attentions and gentle in all his ministrations.

'I confess to some degree of amazement,' I tell him.

I'm hunched up in bed, resting my shoulders and head on a mountain of pillows. Renewed health is surging through me. I'm still not up to much, of course, but it is an immense relief to breathe and eat properly once more. Patrick is on the chair beside me. He has just brought me tea. Terry is on the other side of the room, fixing a bright orange tag on to Pip's flipper. Now that Pip has started to go out, it's important we keep track of him. I'm desperately concerned about his safety. I have seen numerous penguins meet their deaths, and that first time I saw the chick dangling from the skua's talons is seared into my memory. I couldn't bear it if something should happen to our dear Pip. I try to put the thought out of my head. It's bad for my blood pressure.

'Tis better to have loved and lost than never to have loved at all. The phrase reels through my head. Where did it come from? I can't think. It isn't *Hamlet*.

When Pip is a little bigger he will have to go and live amongst his fellow penguins. Terry has pointed out that we can't carry on feeding him for ever and it would be wrong to do so anyway. He is not one of us; he is a penguin. He must be allowed to fulfil his penguin potential. He must make a life for himself away from us humans. In due course the whole colony will move seawards. The Adélies spend winter on the pack ice, where the air temperature is higher than on land. They find cracks in the ice to fish through. It is something we humans cannot teach Pip to do. He must learn along with his compatriots.

I switch my attention back to my grandson. If I study Patrick's face carefully I can perceive a little something of Giovanni in those eyes.

'I will admit my first impressions of you were not good,' I inform him. 'I was rather put off by your lack of cleanliness at the time. I am glad to note it has improved since.'

He bows his head in acknowledgement of this truth. 'Much obliged.'

'But the main problem for me was your drug-taking.' I'd like to know where I stand on this point. 'You seemed to be smoking cannabis when I arrived at your bedsit. I presumed you had an addiction.' I haven't noticed a trace of it since he arrived here, but it may be that he chooses to take his disgusting habit outside.

He considers. 'Well, I guess I was *semi*-addicted, if you know what I mean. I'm OK now, in case you're wondering. I only went back to dope because . . . sometimes things get to me. And at the time you decided to walk into my life my girlfriend had just run off with another guy and life was pretty darned tough, Granny.'

'I see.' I take a sip of Darjeeling. I am impressed. He has made it exactly the correct colour; neither too strong nor too weak.

I glance at Terry, who is gently pulling at Pip's tag to make sure it's attached firmly. She is half listening to the conversation at the same time.

'Since my arrival here I have reviewed my opinion of those who take cannabis,' I comment, 'thanks to Terry.' Had I been offered such a drug at a certain point in my own life I would doubtless have leapt at the chance. 'Addiction is a serious business, but we are all vulnerable at times. I myself am addicted to good quality tea.'

Patrick grins. 'Well, that's probably a much better addiction to have.'

Terry chips in: 'Can any addiction be good, though?'

'I'm beginning to suspect that some aren't so bad,' I answer. 'For example, your own addiction, Terry.'

She raises her eyebrows in surprise. 'What addiction?'

'Your addiction to penguins.'

'Well, I can't deny it,' she acknowledges. 'They do pretty much take up all my thoughts and energies.' She pulls Pip's beak play-fully. All three of us look at him with fondness. He sticks out the flipper with the new tag and waves it about a bit, testing if it still works. Then, quite satisfied, he folds his head over nonchalantly to the other side and starts preening.

Terry stands up. 'Well, there we are. I'd better take him out to the colony and introduce him to the other chicks.'

'Must you? So soon?'

'I'll bring him back, of course, but it's time to see how he gets on with his own species. We mustn't let him grow up thinking he's a human. And he's big enough to come outside for a proper walk now.'

'Can I come too?' asks Patrick, also standing.

'Of course.'

I start to struggle out of bed. 'What are you doing, Granny?'

'Coming with you.'

'No you're not!' Patrick and Terry chant together.

'You stay here and keep warm,' Terry adds.

I start to protest, but collapse back on to the bed. I'm physically incapable of a trip to the rookery at the moment, no matter how desperately I feel about it.

Patrick tucks the blanket around me, his big, gentle hands bringing some reassurance.

I reach out my own hand to Pip, who hops up straight away and rubs himself against it.

'You will look after him, won't you?' I urge, looking from Patrick to Terry and back again. 'Stay close to him. Don't let him near any skuas or seals. Or any aggressive adult penguins. And you'll bring him straight home if he looks hungry or lonely or unhappy in any way?'

'Of course we will, Granny.'

'And I want you to bring him here the minute you get back, even if you think I'm asleep.'

I won't be asleep. I shan't sleep a wink for worrying.

'It'll be fine, Veronica,' Terry insists. 'Trust us.'

It looks as if I'm going to have to.

Is that a sound at the door? Are they back? I seize my hearing aid and wedge it in, twisting the volume up to maximum.

'. . . like a mother seeing her child off to school for the first time.'

'Yes, bound to be tricky.'

'It's probably my fault for letting her get so attached.'

'Don't blame yourself. I know what Granny's like. She can be totally—'

'Hullo!' I roar. 'Is that you two? Is Pip with you?'

'Oh, hi, Veronica!' Terry calls back. 'Yes, we're just getting our boots off. Be with you in a minute. He's—'

I hear a scurrying and Pip's little face appears at my bedroom door.

'Pip!' I cry.

He shakes his flippers and waggles his head.

'You're all right! You're all right!' My cheeks are wet with tears. I am unable to stop their flow. 'Oh, silly me, showing such weakness!' I declare crossly as Patrick and Terry come in.

'Weakness?' Terry echoes. 'Nobody could call you weak, Veronica.' I drag my handkerchief out from under the pillow and dab my eyes furiously.

'It's totally OK to cry, Granny,' Patrick asserts, scooping Pip up and placing him on the bedspread. 'Crying has nothing to do with being weak.'

Terry nods. 'I agree. It's the opposite. Tears come when you've been too strong for much too long.'

'Never mind me,' I say tartly. 'Would you be so kind as to give me a full report on Pip's trip to the rookery?'

Pip was shy at first, they tell me, and he stayed very close to their feet. But soon his curiosity needed satisfying and he edged towards a cluster of chicks who were a similar age to himself. They were playing tag together. He didn't join in, but he watched the gang with fascination, edging closer and closer.

Terry takes out the camera and shows me a picture.

She chuckles. 'He's very wary of the adult penguins, but it's a great start.'

'He's a total hero,' added Patrick.

'Thank you for looking after him,' I say to them both, my voice slightly wobbly.

My grandson strokes Pip on the head. 'It was our pleasure, Granny.'

*

Would you believe it, Patrick has mended the generator! According to Terry, he went up the ladder to take a look at the wind turbine and came down muttering some gobbledygook about shafts, hubs and flywheels. Then, much to Mike's chagrin, he helped himself to some scraps of broken fencing and old sledge runners and patched the thing up. We are back to our normal supply of electricity. This means that Dietrich can listen to as many CDs as he likes, Terry can use the computer as much as she likes and I can have as many cups of tea as I like once more. I feel better at the mere thought of it.

'Strange, is it not, that my grandson, who has no qualifications whatsoever, can manage to mend the generator while you, with all your training, could not,' I pointed out to Mike.

'He's surprised us,' Mike sulkily acknowledged. 'But, in my defence, my skills are in biochemistry, Veronica, not mechanics.'

Bravo, Patrick!

I do wonder if there is something particular in the McCreedy genes: a spirit of enterprise, a need to push one's personal boundaries. I have experienced such a need several times in my life; for example, in coming to Antarctica. From the little I know of my son's life, I gather he experienced it too. His adoptive cousin told me in her letter that my Enzo (also known as Joe) was inclined to be stubborn and would never recognize his own limitations. He liked to stretch himself and loved wild places, which is why he became a mountaineer. Patrick has demonstrated a similar trait in coming out here and in climbing up ladders to fix things.

I confess, I do feel rather proud.

Now that I'm capable of conversing again, there is a matter I'd like to discuss with my grandson.

'Patrick, you say you don't remember anything about your father?'

He shakes his head. 'Nope. Nothing at all. You?'

'I remember changing his nappies.'

And I remember the feel of him, the warm feel of him, clinging to me with his tiny arms, my own darling little bundle of hope.

'I know you didn't give him away. I know he was taken from you, without you having any say in the matter,' Patrick declares.

Well, I should have thought that was obvious. If I'd had any say in the matter everything would have been very different indeed.

For a wild moment I wonder whether to open my locket and show Patrick the wisp of hair from his father's head, but I can't do it. At least, not yet. It would be too much. I content myself with the knowledge that Patrick has read my diaries. He knows I loved and treasured Enzo.

He knows a huge amount about me, in fact, and I know very little about him.

'Your mother . . . ?' I begin.

'Killed herself when I was six,' he says.

'Oh.'

I am so sorry to learn this. It is a tragedy indeed that anybody should go so far, especially when many others have their lives ripped away without the benefit of choice. And to leave a small boy alone in the world seems so wrong. But I realize my Enzo deserted the child Patrick, too. His own son. Why did he do that? *Why?*

'Do you remember, when you were little, if your mother ever talked about your father?' I ask.

'She never did. I can tell you this, though, Granny: I hated his guts! I blamed her death totally on him. Thought she did it because he'd left her in the lurch. But . . . I've been thinking about it a lot recently and I've realized it could've been something else. It may have been – you know – the way she was. Depressed as hell. Looking back, I can see that. Maybe he gave it his best shot but he just couldn't deal with her erratic behaviour – and that's why he left.'

I look at this shabby boy before me. I am in a state of wonder. He is remarkably willing to give the benefit of the doubt. He is extraordinarily forgiving. He is undeniably kind.

'Maybe one day, Granny – and this is only a suggestion – tell me to get lost if you like – we could go to Canada together and find out more about my dad, about his life.'

'I should like that very much, Patrick. Yes, very much indeed.'

Terry's Penguin Blog

9 January 2013

It's all about discovery at the moment. The penguin chicks are endlessly curious and venture further and further outside their nests – including our own Pip. He has now made a couple of trips to the colony and we're proud (and relieved) that he's beginning to make friends. He still appreciates his humans, though.

Here's a picture you've just got to love: Veronica reading a chapter of *Great Expectations* to Pip. He looks rather interested, doesn't he? He's been a great comfort to Veronica recently as she's suffering from a chest infection. Absolutely nothing to worry about, though.

You'll notice how much Pip has grown, and we can detect real feathers beneath his baby down. These feathers are the works, his proper and much-needed wetsuit.

Normally a young penguin's first encounter with the sea is a shock to the system. The juveniles will gasp and flounder in the waves, hurled and swirled about with no idea of their own abilities . . . until suddenly they go under and realize they can achieve amazing aqua-balletic feats.

Pip has already had several encounters with taps and basins. We'll do our utmost to ensure he is also at home with his fellow penguins before he takes the big plunge – which will be very soon.

47

Veronica

Locket Island

TERRY IS ALL SMILES.

'My last blog was retweeted eight hundred and forty-six times!'

Mike looks up from his notes and raises his eyebrows. 'You don't say?'

'I do say! It was that picture of Pip and Veronica with *Great Expectations* that did it. There's a load of lovely comments, too.'

'Wow! Well done, Terry!' he exclaims with unusual verve and generosity of spirit.

'And well done, Pip and Veronica,' she replies pointedly.

He nods in my direction by way of acknowledgement. I've finally made it to the lounge and am huddled up in a purple rug in my chair. It is evening and we're all planning on watching a film together. One of the shelves bears a small collection of flat boxes that are apparently DVDs (I haven't the faintest idea what that stands for). Terry has brought the computer screen in with her and deposited it on the table to be connected up to the DVD-playing thingamajig. Patrick is in the kitchen, preparing a 'dinner-on-laps' for us all.

Dietrich, meanwhile, is playing tug-of-war with Pip at the other end of the room. The rope between them is Dietrich's orange scarf. I'm not sure how this game started but Pip, who absolutely will not let go, has one end clamped firmly in his beak. Whenever Dietrich (who is on his hands and knees) pulls at the other end Pip's head ducks forward and he skates wob-blingly across the floor, flippers outstretched for balance. Then Dietrich lessens his grip and Pip hurriedly shuffles backwards to regain the ground he's lost. With the next tug from Dietrich, Pip decides to plop on to his tummy. Legs paddling frantically, he slithers forwards, dragged by the scarf. It is taut, growing longer by the minute.

'All right, then, little lad. You win,' chuckles Dietrich, resigning the prize to the victor. 'Please don't chew it to pieces though.' Pip gives a little hoot of delight. He pulls the scarf into a corner, loop by loop, and busies himself with the task of dissecting it.

'What's that you were saying about your blog, Terry?' Dietrich asks as he clambers to his feet.

'Big thumbs-up,' she answers. 'Eight hundred and forty-six retweets.'

Terry has told me about Twitter and tweets and retweets, all of which seem singularly pointless to me.

'*Mein Gott*, that's even better than when we had the *Plight of Penguins* coverage from Robert Saddlebow!'

'I know.' She emanates pride. 'Lots of new followers, too! It could even be worth dropping hints about how the penguin project is struggling for funds.' The mood in the room immediately plum-mets several levels from jovial to sombre. This happens whenever there's a reference to the demise of their project. Terry has confided in me that, in her new role, she has applied to the Anglo-Antarctic

Research Council for money but has come up against a brick wall. 'What do you think, guys?'

Dietrich scratches his chin. 'Well, we don't want to come across as grasping.'

'Perhaps,' suggests Mike, 'it would be best to put the emphasis on not just the Locket Island research but the fragile state of penguins – or even the planet – in general.' He turns towards me. I see passion smouldering in his eyes; see that, in spite of his cactus-like conduct, he really does care. 'Did you know that we're in the worst extinction period since the dinosaurs disappeared? Within a hundred years, half of all living species could be gone.'

Approaching the hundred-year mark as I am, I find this an alarmingly short time span. I shan't be around to witness the devastation, but still . . .

Half of all living species, gone. I'd thought that I, Veronica McCreedy, could make a difference, but I've begun to realize: it will take more than one old woman and her legacy of a few million pounds to save the Adélies and their environment.

'In the next fifteen to forty years, masses of animals will already be extinct,' Mike continues. 'Polar bears, chimpanzees, elephants, snow leopards, tigers . . . the list goes on.'

'Good God!' I exclaim. Such is my horror that I am feeling quite unwell again.

'What a sad legacy we're leaving for the next generation,' comments Dietrich. I know he's thinking of his own children. His eyes look misty.

'So what's the use of all this Twitter business?' I ask Terry. 'What on earth can those tweety people do?' I very much doubt that *they* would donate millions to conservation charities, even if, in some parallel universe that bears no resemblance to ours, they wanted to.

She's looking pensive. 'Perhaps I could blog more about that. I could throw in tips about how people might change their lifestyles:

what they buy, what they eat, the industries they support, the way they travel. Every little helps.'

I wonder if the situation is in fact remediable. In wartime, everyone made sacrifices for the common good. It could be done again if only enough people cared sufficiently.

I pick up litter with my tongs on the Ayrshire coast but I certainly do not give enough thought to these things. I must strive to get into better habits. When I arrive home, I shall tell Eileen my money is not to be spent on ginger thins from Kilmarnock Stores any more, although I am fond of them. Ginger thins, I recall, come in a cardboard box coated in plastic. Within that they are in a moulded plastic tray that is wrapped in a further layer of plastic. No doubt they have also unnecessarily been transported halfway across the globe. I am quite willing to sacrifice ginger thins for the benefit of the planet.

'The most terrifying threat to nature – and to all of us – is climate change,' Mike asserts. 'We have to put pressure on the politicians, because the only thing they worry about is the results of the next election. We must tell them over and over that our world is important to us.'

It certainly is.

'What could *possibly* be more important?' asks Terry with fervour.

'More important than what?' It's Patrick, staggering into the room with a tray laden with wine bottles, cheese sticks, multi-coloured dips and mini pizzas.

'Luxury!' exclaims Terry, suddenly all bright and breezy again. I'm not sure if she's answering the question or admiring the fare.

Mike shoots a look across at her that I can't quite interpret. He seems to be struggling with something. Then he stares at Patrick, perusing every inch of his face.

'What? What have I done?' asks my grandson. He plonks the tray on the table and looks questioningly round at us all. His eyes settle on Terry. She pushes her glasses up her nose and becomes a little pinker. She focuses on the food. 'You've only gone and spoilt us again, Patrick!'

'Looks great,' says Dietrich. 'And smells great. Let's get started. I can hear my tummy rumbling.'

Patrick passes round the cheese sticks. I twirl mine into a greenish creamy mixture and nibble on it. It is rather toothsome.

'So, which film have you decided on?' he asks.

'We haven't. We got distracted,' answers Terry. 'What do you fancy? We've seen them all before, so you and Veronica should decide.'

Patrick scans the shelf and reads a few titles out. '*The Return of the Pink Panther. Quantum of Solace. Mission Impossible. The Green Mile . . .*'

I prick up my ears. 'That last one sounds nice.'

'I don't think you'd like it, Granny. It's kind of . . . well, *not* nice. How about . . .' he considers '. . . *Vanity Fair?*'

'I should think that will do very well.'

The film is indeed thoroughly enjoyable, at least as far as I am concerned. There is much to be savoured in a good costume drama and the characters interest me. I notice Patrick shuffling in his chair and sighing a bit, however, and realize he has chosen it in view of my preferences, not his own.

I have managed a good breakfast today, including porridge and toast. The remains are by the bed on a tray. Now I am assailed by exhaustion again and in need of a nap. Patrick and Terry are by the door of the bedroom, talking in hushed tones.

'Shall we take Pip out again, then?' I hear Terry ask softly. 'I think he's getting restless.'

'Sounds like a good idea. Should we wake Granny though?'

They're standing close together. I can tell by their voices.

I fight off sleep in order to listen.

'No,' answers Terry. 'She'll only put herself through the stress of trying to come with us, and there's no way that's possible yet. Best if we just slip out.'

'But we'd better leave her a note, otherwise she'll freak out to find Pip gone.'

'You're right. Good plan.'

Patrick and Terry are getting on well. Could there be a whiff of romance in the air? Patrick doesn't give his feelings away, but I can discern a growing eagerness, like a tree beginning to leaf in the early warmth of spring. Terry cares for him too, that's obvious – but then Terry cares for everyone. She treats everyone as if they are special. She is quite the opposite of me.

I hear Patrick walk across to the wastepaper basket and lift Pip out. 'C'mon then, little blighter. You're coming with us today!' Terry and Patrick make cooing noises. I know they're caressing the chick, stroking his belly and chin. He'll be loving every moment of it. I slyly lift an eyelid to peek at them. They're like two parents fussing over a newborn baby.

I mull it over as they take Pip and move outside, closing the door quietly behind them. Patrick and Terry. Terry and Patrick. A quirky little duo. Pip and I have created a close connection between them. The more I ponder it, the more I am convinced of it: Patrick and Terry go together like a cup and saucer.

I'm hazy about how much time has passed. The calendar tells me it is still January. I know I've missed the date originally booked for my journey back to Britain. There has been talk of another ship arriving in a week's time and, as I am significantly recovered (they had a phone consultation with the doctor and he agreed), Patrick and I are supposed to depart on it. This is most unfortunate in view of the Patrick and Terry possibilities, which will simply not have time to come to fruition. There is no way Patrick will be permitted to prolong his visit, even if he wants to. He is neither a scientist nor a millionaire.

Terry and Patrick will inevitably be ripped apart.

That is exactly the kind of mean trick that Fate likes to play. I know, through long and bitter experience, how much strength is required to resist Fate when it is engaged in such brutality.

Patrick and Terry, however, are both too young and feeble-minded to realize this or do anything about it.

48

Patrick

Locket Island

MUCH AS I'M GLAD she didn't kick the bucket, it's still not exactly going to be fun accompanying Granny V home on the ship, plane and everything. At least I'm more used to her little ways now. I've just got to expect the unexpected, haven't I?

'I bet you'll be pleased to see the back of us,' I say to the guys. We're finishing breakfast and I'm wondering what to take through for Granny. There are some half-decent slices of bacon left and I'll brew her a pot of Darjeeling.

Dietrich smiles. 'It will be a relief that we don't have to worry about Mrs McCreedy any more, for sure. But it'll seem very dull without you both.'

'We'll miss your cooking,' adds Mike.

Deet winks. (Top man, Deet. I told him about Gav's daughter, Daisy, and he did one of his penguin drawings for her. I emailed it over to Gav yesterday.)

'We're used to changes here,' he tells me. 'In another few weeks the chicks will have their new feather coats and start heading out to sea along with their parents. That's when we'll begin to feel really sad.'

Terry fixes her gaze on the far wall. 'Every year you know it's coming, but it's always weirdly emotional.'

Mike sighs, picking up on her mood. 'It's going to be even worse this year, knowing it might be our last.'

He looks like he's got mixed feelings. He's got that girlfriend in England and if the project winds up he'll be able to go and live with her, maybe do all the marriage-and-children stuff. Still, I get the feeling he's in his element being independent and immersed in penguin business out in the ice and cold. His comfort zone is here.

I learned an interesting thing from Deet the other day. It was Mike who discovered Granny V lying in the snow that fatal day, although they were all out searching for her. It was Mike who did first aid and carried her back to base. Mike who, basically, saved her life. He's nowhere near as nasty as he makes out. He's just got this ton of chips on his shoulder, enough chips to fill three deep-fat fryers. But he's OK. I can even hold a pleasant conversation with him now and then.

Terry starts clearing away the dishes. She seems so sad; she cares for those penguins a lot. I want to suggest us meeting up in England if the Locket Island penguin project ends and she goes back there. It would be fantastic if I could spend some more time with her. I don't say anything, though. I don't want it to sound like I'm hoping the project ends.

When I go into her bedroom, Granny is up and on the chair, a rug over her knees. Pip is flopped on his belly asleep, moulding himself into her lap. Man, he looks blissful. Granny's gazing down at him, a fond smile on her face. I have to say, it's a sight that makes me glad I've got a granny. Even a bit glad she's stark raving bonkers.

She looks up at me. Her eyes flash with purpose. 'Now, Patrick. It's good that you're here.' She pats the chair beside her. 'A few practical things.'

I sit down. 'You seem a load better, Granny.'

'I am. I am a great deal better. In fact, I am pretty sure I shall live at least a while longer. Years, possibly. I might even be so generous as to give myself another decade.'

'Yay! I'm glad to hear it!' I leap up again, launch myself over and hug her. I can't seem to help it, even though she's hardly a huggy type of person. To my surprise she puts her arms around me and sort of hugs back, briefly. Pretty sure I didn't dream it.

The movement wakes Pip up. He hops off her knee on to the floor and starts preening his chest with his beak. Little scraps of fluff come off, revealing more of the new, sleek feathers underneath.

Granny is fumbling about in her handbag, which is beside her chair. Not the scarlet handbag (that one was attacked by a penguin) but a hideous bright-pink and gold thing. She pulls out a handkerchief, blows her nose loudly then looks me in the eye. 'Well, to business. I feel it is only fair to let you know that my intention is to make a will as soon as I get home.'

'Right-oh,' I say. Here goes.

She fixes her eyes on me. I never noticed before how many colours they are. Sort of slate-grey and sea-green but with gleams of pure gold.

'I decided a while ago that I'd make provisions to leave my entire inheritance to the penguin project,' she tells me.

I nod. I can't say I'm surprised. 'OK.'

'I have formed a particularly strong bond with the Adélies,' she goes on, 'and I believe it is essential to keep the species going somehow. If I can make a small contribution to help, I would like to do so.'

'Granny, you don't need to tell me this.' She thinks I must be well peed off not to get her money. I'm not, though. The important thing is that she's OK.

'These scientists, on the whole, know what they are doing and I trust them,' she goes on. 'I shall provide for them amply when I die—'

'Granny, stop it!'

'There's no point in mincing my words, Patrick. We both know it nearly happened. It will happen sooner or later anyway. In the meantime, I will supply the penguin team with a monthly stipend to keep them going.'

Just as I'd hoped. Sort of. But it means all three scientists will stay here on Locket Island for-bloody-ever.

'Terry will be pleased,' I say. It's true. She'll be ecstatic. She won't spare a thought for little old me back in the bicycle shop in Bolton.

Granny goes on. 'I shall provide amply for the future of the project with this one proviso,' Granny announces, 'that every year the scientists must save at least one orphaned penguin chick. To remind them that they have hearts.'

I laugh. 'You certainly like to make life difficult for everyone, Granny.'

She looks chuffed, as if it's a compliment.

Terry's sitting on the floor in the lounge, wriggling into her waterproof trousers. 'Chuck me the crampons, would you?'

I study them in mock horror. 'You could do some serious damage with those.' She takes them from me, straps them on, then waves a foot at me. The spikes pierce and slash the air. She cackles like a witch.

'Nice try, but evil doesn't come naturally to you, Terry.'

I scramble into my jacket and Mike's spare snow boots, which, to be fair, he's never commented on.

'You two going out together?' Mike, hovering by the door.

My hackles raise at his tone of voice.

'He needs to get out,' Terry says. 'Veronica's managing fine now.

I thought I'd take him up to the north end of the colony. He's never been there before and I guess it'll be his last chance. And we could see how Sooty's getting on.'

'Want to come?' I ask Mike.

'No. I'll leave you to it. I have guano analysis to do.'

We fetch Pip from Veronica's room. Terry says we need to expose him to the colony all we can. He'll have to go back and make a life for himself there pretty soon. Sometimes we leave him in the 'creche', which is the name they give to a bunch of kiddo penguins left together while their penguin parents go out fishing. Pip's getting braver and braver. He trundles around with the other chicks, plays chase and hop-the-puddle and so on. Every time we take him out we have to promise Granny we'll keep an eye on him. I don't know how she's ever going to part with that penguin.

Terry and I walk slowly. Pip follows a few paces behind us, like a waddly kind of puppy. Today it's not actually that cold, just kind of bracing. The snow is patchy. In some places it's gathered in blobs like marshmallows and in others it's tissue-thin, with sharp spikes of grass and rounded pebbles showing through.

'I hope you don't regret coming out here,' Terry begins. 'If we'd known Veronica had such tenacity, we never would have summoned you.'

I look up at the sky. It's a porridgey colour and looks kind of pixelated.

'Terry, it's all good. You did the right thing.'

'Did I? I'm never sure.'

Granny's told her and the others that she's going to be funding the Locket Island project from now on. They were so grateful they didn't know what to say. Even Mike. It's a bit awkward though, isn't it, all this generosity stuff?

'Please believe me when I say I never asked Veronica for anything,' Terry urges. 'I really didn't expect her to hand out all this money, even though she'd mentioned something about her will. You don't think I've been exploiting her, do you?'

Terry just has no idea how great she is. 'Jeez, Terry, no! If anything, it was the other way round! You've always been true and honest and good and . . .' It's my turn to stop mid-sentence. I look at her and everything goes a bit weird. I don't know what's happened, why the atmosphere is different. Normally we're completely at ease in each other's company.

I rush on, gabbling: 'You've helped me get to know Granny V more than anyone else could. You're the only person she warmed to, the only one she opened up to. She didn't even open up to her carer, Eileen, in all those years.'

This is important. I see now how much I want Granny V in my life. Both my mum and my dad abandoned me, they left me in different ways. But my granny – well, she *found* me, didn't she? It took her a while, but she did it.

We've reached the top of the slope and the sun has edged out from behind the clouds. In the distant locket-hole lake there's a pale pathway of sunlight stretching across the water.

'Getting to know Granny has been one hell of a revelation,' I tell Terry. 'Maybe it was crazy of me to come all the way out here, but I'm glad I did. If I'd stayed in Bolton I never would have seen all this!' I wave my hand round at the scene: the jags on the horizon, the coloured splatters of lichen covering the rocks, the colony of penguins spread out beneath us, its own busy metropolis of life, love and pain.

'Besides, if I hadn't come to Antarctica I'd never have met . . .' I stop myself and know that my eyes are flicking towards hers, wondering if it's possible she could be feeling the same. No clues in those eyes. But how shimmering and deep they are . . . Man, you could drown in those eyes. I look away quick before it happens. I turn right round to face Pip, opening my arms out wide as our flippered friend struggles to catch up.

'. . . I'd never have met this little guy!'

I whisk him into my arms. He lets out a squeak of surprise. I roll on to my back in the snow, lifting him above me. I hold him in a mock flying position, his stubby feet sticking out behind, flippers arcing outwards. A gurgling sound comes from Pip's beak, as if he's laughing too. Terry swings the camera off her shoulder and points it at us to catch the moment. 'Hey, I love it!' she calls. 'Great mix of glee, childishness and human–penguin affection. Nobody could fail to be touched by it.' She dashes over to the other side to try and get another shot but trips over a stone. The jolt forces a sharp cry from her mouth and sends her sprawling to the ground.

'Are you OK?' It was quite a thump as she landed. Is she hurt? There's a moment of silence.

I set Pip down. Terry's head is twisted, her face is down in the snow. She doesn't move. The quickest way to reach her is to roll, so that's what I do.

I pull her round towards me. Her glasses have been knocked sideways. I carefully remove them and lay them beside us. She's smiling. No, she's laughing. There is just whiteness, Terry and me, her face close to mine, her mouth close to mine. Under mine. Our bodies are separated by layers and layers of weatherproof clothes but our lips meet and press together.

She can't speak for a while. When her lips are free again, she answers my question. 'Yes, Patrick. I'm very OK, thank you.'

49

Patrick

Locket Island

CIRCUMSTANCES JUST KIND OF collided in that moment and there wasn't a thing I could do about it.

But . . . hey! Result!

We carried on walking until we were in the middle of the penguin colony. Every so often she stopped walking and put her mouth up to be kissed. It felt a bit public with our audience of small tuxedoed gents, who weren't shy about staring at us. But when a girl like Terry puts her mouth up to be kissed by you, hell, what you do is you kiss it. And with each kiss I got more and more panicky about her expectations and how I wouldn't be able to fulfil them, but at the same time I wanted more of her. I wanted every bit of her, physical, mental, emotional, the whole shebang. If God had come up to me right then and said, 'Patrick, my son, you have two choices. Choice (A) I will grant you world peace, or Choice (B) you can stay with Terry in Antarctica for ever,' I swear I'd have plumped for staying with Terry in Antarctica for ever. I'd have said yes to that one straight off, no kidding.

After about the twentieth kiss, Terry said, 'This is going to be hard to hide from the guys.'

'Um, hate to disillusion you, Terry, but I think they already know,' I told her, sweeping my arm round at the thousands of beaked faces looking at us.

'Not the penguins, you wombat! The other scientists.'

'Do we need to hide it?' I asked. I was sort of in the mood of shouting it from the rooftops. Or iceberg-tops, or whatever.

'Yes, Patrick, we do,' she replied, as if it was a no-brainer.

'Terry, sneaking about really isn't my style.'

'Nor mine,' she said, 'but needs must.'

'Why must needs?'

'For starters, they'll worry. They'll think I might desert them and the work. They may even worry I'll go back to Britain with you.'

Why does the future always have to come busting in and spoil everything? Life always throws problems at you, doesn't it? Just when everything's going swimmingly, another problem pops up, and there you are, trying your darnedest to work out what the hell you can do about it.

I have – let me see – all of five and a half days' worth of a relationship with Terry left before I have to go back to the other side of the world with Granny.

'So this is it, then? This is all it is. A few kisses in the snow?'

'Kiss me again,' she said.

I obliged.

We clambered up another slope together, stepping over gullies full of snow and polished pebbles. The sunlight warmed our backs. The ramparts of ice all around glinted white, with glossy tints of green, blue and turquoise. Terry knew exactly where she was going.

'Look!' she said, pointing. The all-black penguin, Sooty, was there in front of us, on his nest. He had a kind of smug look about him, I thought.

'Still no sign of any eggs,' Terry said. 'He seems pretty determined, though. Who knows if he's found a partner or not?' She cares so much about these things. I like that about her.

As we scrambled back the way we'd come, I spotted a shiny seal sunning himself on a rock. He fixed us with a bland kind of gaze. He was all podge and flab and made me laugh out loud. But Terry said seals are the arch-enemy as far as Adélies are concerned. Not so much on land, but underwater they're lethal. A seal will hide under the surface of the sea and grab the unsuspecting penguin by the feet. Then it will shake him ferociously from side to side and beat his body against the ice until he's dead, a pool of red seeping through the white waters.

'Let's get back to Pip,' we both said at the same time. Maybe we'd been enjoying ourselves a tad too much.

Luckily Pip was doing fine. He'd stopped off at one of the penguin creches without our encouragement, a great sign for his future. He was happily running around with a gang of penguin chicks. It's such a relief that his social life hasn't been too hampered by his human upbringing. Just as well he's got that orange tag on his flipper, otherwise he could easily get mixed up with the others. Much as we love Pip, he does look pretty similar to the rest. His orange tag showed up well amongst the yellow ones of the other penguins.

Adults were returning to the edges of the creche, each calling to their young. The kiddos recognized the voices straight off and made a beeline for their own parent with stunning accuracy. No way were they going to miss any chance of a helping of regurgitated krill. Pip tried it on a couple of times with the bigger penguins, but nobody fell for it. They weren't going to waste their precious regurgitations on an intruder, no matter how cute he was.

'Sorry, mate!' I called out to him. 'You're going to have to come back with us until you've learned how to catch your own fish.'

Pip turned his head and surveyed me. I swear he understood every word. Anyhow, he came scooting towards us. When he reached us he leaned affectionately into Terry's knees. Then looked back at his buddies as if to say, 'Hey, guys, these are *my* parents.'

We stooped down to his level and made a fuss of him. A handful of baby down came off and floated away on the breeze.

After a while Terry pulled me up and put her arms around me. I held her close for as long as I could, feelings bubbling up inside me.

She let out a long sigh. 'This is so difficult. I . . . Oh God, I wish you could stay.'

Nice.

'You needn't call me God, though,' I said.

She aimed a playful kick at my shin. What I should have said was 'I really wish I could stay, too,' but it seemed a bit late for that now. So I drew a heart in the snow instead and put a T and P inside it. It was a goodish save. Terry seemed to like it anyway.

Pip was intrigued and bent his head down to look at my design.

'I know you think the P is you, but it's actually me, mate,' I told him. He wasn't impressed. He promptly walked all over the heart, blurring its outline and the letters inside it. Vandal.

'What are we going to do?' Terry said. I knew she meant our relationship. It was a good question.

'Enjoy these five days together, at any rate,' I suggested. 'Enjoy every moment we can snatch alone together. Snatch as many as we can.'

It's going to be one hell of a five days, with an ill grandmother and a penguin chick to care for and a cabin full of scientists with no room to manoeuvre at all, let alone indulge our new-found passion.

I took my gloves off and stroked her hair back from her face. Her cheeks were cool and soft. Her eyes looked a bit moist.

I had to ask. Man, I just had to. 'Sure you don't want to come back to England with me?'

The crowd of penguins faded into the background, their noise hushed for a moment. They all seemed to be waiting with me for her answer.

I felt it then: that sinking feeling. You know the one. Like when Tescos are doing a three-for-one offer on beer and you buy eight crates, only to discover, when it goes through checkout, that you've misread the sign. It wasn't beer that was three-for-one, it was the mini packets of peanuts.

I knew I shouldn't have asked. I should have guessed she'd never put me above the penguins.

'No, Patrick. Sorry. It's . . . No, I can't. Not now we know the project has a future. I just have to be a part of that. It's everything to me.'

All this was doing my head in. I somehow had to disentangle myself from Terry. I glanced at my watch.

'Hell, I've been out for hours. It's high time I checked on Granny.'

I zoomed back, super-speedy through the snow.

50

Patrick

Locket Island

WHAT THE HELL'S GOING on? I thought Granny was getting better, thought she was out of danger. Thought we'd be reminiscing about penguins on the flight back next week and everything would be cool. Seems I was wrong. She was back in bed and out for the count when I got back from the colony. She didn't wake up when the others came in later, either. Nor when we were feeding Pip, even though he was quite clamorous and noisy about it. We left her to sleep. I brought her in a light supper on a tray but the food was still untouched this morning.

Today she hasn't eaten a thing. Hasn't even been able to raise herself off the pillow. She's gone paler again and sort of glassy, sort of distant. Terry, Mike and Dietrich have been out on an all-dayer, so it's been deathly quiet. I took the big book and tried reading Granny some penguin facts. I've had no reaction from her at all.

It's nearly five when I hear the door and the voices of all three scientists arriving together.

'Guys, Granny's bad again,' I tell them, rushing to meet them. 'She's had nothing to eat all day, and she hasn't moved a muscle.'

Terry rushes straight to her room and I hear her saying Veronica's name over and over. She comes back, her face drained of colour.

'Patrick's right. I can't get her to speak to me. She seems really ill.'

Dietrich frowns. '*Gott*, no, I don't believe it.'

Mike becomes Action Man all of a sudden. 'We should try and get a doctor out again. I'll radio them straight away.' Mike is a good man to have around in a crisis. He hurries into the kitchen to pick up his radio and we hear his voice urging and a muffled voice asking questions at the other end. He comes back in looking exasperated.

'They won't come. They have an emergency on. So long as Veronica is comfortable and kept warm, they say there's nothing else they can do.'

'There's got to be something!' I cry. God, I hate this.

He shakes his head. 'They pointed out again that she's an old lady. They implied it would be best to let her go in peace. I'm really sorry, Patrick.'

He sounds like he means it, too. Terry walks straight up and puts her arms around me. I'll admit, that feels good. But I can't enjoy it. I can't bear to think that Granny's on the way out again, just when I thought we were over the worst. I'd let myself hope we'd be able to start from the beginning again. I'd make her my best ever lemon polenta cake, and this time I'd listen to everything she had to say instead of getting tied in knots about Lynette. Hell, Lynette! I don't care a bug's arse for her now.

I can't believe Granny's on the wane again, right when we were getting to know each other. I've got this weird feeling, like a realization slapping me in the face, hard. My life is never going to be the same again.

51

Patrick

Locket Island

MAYBE IT'S JUST AS well those medical people never came. They'd have been pretty peed off if they had. Granny was fading fast that day, but the next day she seemed much perkier. At least, she managed to slurp down some soup and exchanged a few words with me.

But then.

The next day it all went down the pan. She stayed motionless in bed, not eating, not responding. At death's door all over again.

She's like this human yoyo. It's driving us all insane. She eats like a horse one day and is all springy and energetic, then suddenly she droops and seems incapable of anything. Then, once we've resigned ourselves to an Antarctic deathbed scene, she sits up and says she's hungry and she's A-OK again. I don't get it. What the hell is going on?

'She keeps us on our toes, doesn't she?' Dietrich said to me after the third down and up in a row.

'Not half, mate,' I said.

I emailed Gav and told him about it. He emailed back, saying, *Hang in there, mate, just do the right thing.* And a message from young Daisy saying thanks for the penguin picture and a photo of her with it. I printed the photo out and showed it to Deet, who was chuffed. I showed it to Granny V, too and she totally seemed to perk up at the sight of it. Only to wilt again later.

Grief's a weird animal at the best of times. It's even weirder when you think it's a dead cert (pardon the pun) but then it disappears only to come hurtling right back at you. It's like this bungee-jump of emotions. You get jolted all over the place. It gives you this sick feeling in your stomach, makes you jittery and wobbly, plays havoc with your sleep patterns. I'm beginning to wish I had a spliff at hand.

Then there's Terry. I never reckoned I could hurtle headlong into such a ton of feelings so fricking fast. And she says the same about me. Even though we know it can't last, neither of us seems to be able to control it. We try being all sensible, try pointing out that we're reaching out to each other just for comfort . . . but I know and she knows (and she knows I know) it's a hell of a lot more than that.

There's this massive amount of pain ahead, sitting there waiting to pounce on me. I'm heading straight for it. Even if Granny does survive I'm going to be a wreck because of having to say goodbye to Terry.

Will Granny make it through? The ship that's due to take us home comes to Locket Island tomorrow, but to be honest I haven't the foggiest if we'll be on it or not.

52

Veronica

Locket Island

I HAVE ALWAYS HELD a nothing ventured, nothing gained philosophy. I confided in my dear Pip last night while the humans were at supper. Pip does like to be talked to and he listens to every word. He scratched his head with his foot in a most thoughtful way, and I am sure my devious plan has gained his approval.

Over the past few days my grandson and the scientists have fretted endlessly, sought medical advice via the radio and taken it in turns to watch over me. Dietrich has resumed reading *Great Expectations* and Mike has resumed telling me of the degrees centigrade outside.

Meanwhile, I count the days carefully. I monitor what I eat and what (with the help of my cosmetics bag) my appearance gives away. I watch. I listen. I've begun to realize that, when I make the effort, I am quite a shrewd judge of character.

Terry and Patrick do many of their shifts together. Innumerable meaningful looks pass between them and often, when they think I am asleep, they exchange whispered terms of endearment. Sometimes there are long silences. I am careful not to open my eyes but I am sure I can hear kisses.

Yesterday I built my strength up a little and now it is time to make another small sacrifice to further my cause. I shall not be partaking in any meals today. I take a cosmetic wipe from the packet on my bedside table and remove every trace of make-up. I consult the mirror. Yes, already I am looking so much less healthy.

We are due to leave this afternoon and, should there remain any molecule of doubt on the matter, it is time for my *pièce de résistance*. The others are at breakfast and have left me alone for a blessed ten minutes.

I climb silently out of bed and exchange my woollen tartan dressing-gown for my silky violet negligee, which, I believe, will provide extra dramatic effect. I then arrange myself with utmost care on the floor. My hair sticking out. My head twisted to one side. My negligee ballooning around me. I stretch my leg out slowly, and with my foot I manage to reach up and nudge the glass of water on my bedside towards the edge of the table . . . further and further . . . until it topples over the edge and dives to the floor with a thunderous crash.

There is a running of footsteps, a calling of 'Veronica? Veronica! What's happened?'

And then an 'Oh NO!', a *'Mein Gott!'* and a 'Fricking Hell!' all at once as they set eyes on me.

53

Veronica

Locket Island
Two and a half weeks later

I HAVE THE CONSTITUTION of an ox but there is a limit to what one can put one's body through. I finally stopped messing around and gave myself a chance to recover properly. My (though I say so myself) skilfully managed vacillating health achieved exactly what I wanted it to achieve.

We missed the ship back. Patrick has been kept here for far longer than he intended. Long enough not only for him to demonstrate his spectacular ability with technical issues, but also long enough for him and Terry to fall for each other, head over heels, in the awkward, all-consuming, good old-fashioned way.

My second but perhaps not quite so miraculous recovery is complete. I have ventured out to the rookery with the scientists, Patrick and Pip several times over the past two weeks. I am both joyous and emotional to observe how well my little chick gets on with his penguin mates. It may be my imagination, but I could swear he examines his human family in a new way, as if debating with himself whether we are massive, gangly penguins with strange markings.

All the chicks are substantially larger now and become ever more gregarious. The bustling community life of Locket Island continues. It nudges me into an awareness that I myself have learned much about community life since arriving here. And, like the penguins, however harsh conditions may be, I, Veronica McCreedy, am a survivor.

I must, however, get used to letting things run their own course here without my interference. So this morning I have stayed at the research centre to sort through my things. My thoughts turn towards home once again, to The Ballahays, to the opposite side of the world. Here, it feels as if home is the illusion, the faraway dream, while this Antarctic wilderness is the only reality. Soon it will be the reverse.

My day-to-day humdrum existence will resume. I will occupy myself with arranging roses for the dining-room table, ordering shrubs from catalogues and poring over the *Telegraph* crossword. I will walk along the coast path with my stick, handbag and litter tongs. I will have no need of thermals or mukluks. I will remonstrate with Eileen about dust and spiders.

Yet some things will never be the same. I have indulged in the company of thousands of birds whose *joie de vivre* has to be seen to be believed. I have lived with three scientists at the southern-most tip of the earth and witnessed their ways of operating. Perhaps even more surprisingly, I have embarked on the rather satisfying process of sharing thoughts and experiences with my long-lost grandson.

On top of all this I have had an argument with a baby penguin and consequently defied death – at least for the time being. These things change a woman. Even a very old and cantankerous one like me.

I am expecting Patrick soon. He promised he would be back

before the others in order to prepare lunch (a hearty stew, apparently).

I hear him at the door and ready myself. He has scarcely shed his coat and boots before I launch into the conversation I have been mulling over for the last six hours. I need to make sure I've said all that I want to say before it disappears from my head.

'Patrick, I believe you and I have outstayed our welcome on Locket Island by a considerable time. We shall soon be returning to our homeland. No doubt by now you must be utterly desperate to get back to Bolton?'

He sinks into a chair. 'I – er. Well . . . Um, yes and no. It's difficult.'

I am not going to pussyfoot around. I need to know.

'Difficult, is it? I see. And is this, by any chance, because of Terry?'

He performs what I believe is commonly called a 'double-take'. He sucks his breath in then lets it out slowly. 'Because of Terry,' he admits.

'I thought as much.' You can't fool Veronica McCreedy. I may be an ancient prune but I do remember what it is to love. I remember, too, the agony of parting. 'You'll never pull that girl away from her penguins,' I tell him. I am quite clear on this point, and Patrick needs to understand. 'It's her love, her life, her vocation. Even if you did manage to get her away, she'd hate you for it in the end.'

His shoulders droop.

'I s'pose.'

I scrutinize him. I'm beginning to understand how his mind works. I will need to approach this with some care, so that it does not appear I am robbing him of choices. 'Think, Patrick,' I urge him. 'Think. It doesn't have to be this way. There is an alternative.' If he comes out with it himself, I'll know he is in earnest.

'What? Like me staying here, you mean?' He shakes his head miserably. 'As if they'd let me. They wouldn't. They couldn't.'

He is completely oblivious to his own merits. 'They like your cooking,' I point out. 'And you mended the generator for them. You have practical skills that are most useful. You have, you tell me, become skilled in the art of penguin-wrangling. Moreover, you are extremely well informed in penguin science through your reading.' His eyebrows are slowly rising as I speak. I am becoming rather enthusiastic. 'An extra person such as yourself might prove to be quite an asset here. The research centre certainly has the space for at least one more. If you had a little funding . . . If, perhaps, you were to be sponsored privately by an individual . . .'

Patrick's eyebrows have lifted as far as it is geographically possible for them to go. 'What are you saying, Granny?'

I clear my throat and choose my words with care. 'Well, in view of the fact the scientists have put me up for far longer than they were expecting, and under extremely difficult circumstances, I feel that, on top of the funding to continue the project, I should like to contribute sponsorship for an extra researcher.'

He springs from his chair. 'You'd do that?' He reminds me of a big, bouncy breed of dog who has been offered his favourite toy.

'Only on one condition: that the extra researcher is you. Would you like to stay here if I could do that?'

He launches himself at me and engulfs me in a hug. It is the second time this has happened. I have immediately transformed in his view from a crusty old woman into a shining angel.

'Patrick, I beg you, please stop it!'

He obeys and backs off respectfully. I reach for my handkerchief and have a quick dab at my eyes. They do keep causing me problems.

Patrick has meanwhile started absorbing the implications of the plan. He sinks back into his chair. Now he looks dejected, like a dog who has had his favourite toy taken away. 'You're great, Granny, for having that idea. You're totally amazing. But it's not going to work. They've got their own little club here. They're proper, like, *scientists*. I'm just a bum. Even if you pay them, they're never going to let me stay.'

I fold up my handkerchief carefully and replace it in my hand-bag. 'I think you'll find that they are.'

'They are? How do you mean? As in they *are* going to let me stay?'

I nod my confirmation.

'You've spoken to Dietrich?' he gasps.

'I have. And he thinks it's a splendid idea.'

'He *does*?' The doggy enthusiasm is returning. The tail is wag-ging. Then, as another thought occurs to him, it plummets again. 'But Mike won't agree. He hates my guts.'

'On the contrary, Patrick. I've also had a consultation with him. He recognizes your value entirely. He was most insistent that we convince you to remain here and assist with the project.'

This is a slight massaging of the truth. He does not need to know that Mike required considerable persuasion from both myself and Dietrich.

I wait for him to ask. I don't have to wait for long.

'And . . . Terry? She's going to be the boss very soon. Did you broach it with her?'

The metaphorical tail is now suspended in mid-air. It is rather entertaining to watch the tension, anxiety and hope chasing each other across his face.

'I have not yet mentioned the plan to Terry,' I tell him. 'I thought it best to be sure of the others' support first. I thought she might worry about her own vested interest so much she'd make herself say no. I also needed to check that you were as keen to stay as I thought you'd be.'

'I am, Granny. I totally, abso-fricking-lutely, bloody well am!'

This is all working out most satisfactorily.

'You're amazing, Granny. I can't believe it.'

'Your bicycle shop man will manage without you?'

'Oh, Gav will be cool. He knows tons of other people who can take my place, no probs.'

'Excellent.'

'I owe Gav big time, though,' he adds, on reflection. 'And I'll miss him a hell of a lot.'

It would be gratifying if he would deign to miss me, too, but I refuse to allow myself any expectations on that count. I am pleasantly surprised, consequently, when he bursts out with: 'But how about you, Granny? I'd have liked to see a bit more of you, now that we've got together.'

Yes, very pleasantly surprised.

He stirs his mop of hair. 'You're not thinking of – you *can't* be thinking of staying here permanently yourself?'

The thought had actually crossed my mind. However, there are limits to my eccentricity. Besides, some degree of physical comfort is necessary at my age, I have realized. It was hard enough surviving the Antarctic 'summer'. I dread to think what winter is like on Locket Island.

'My role will merely be as a provider of funds as far as the penguin project is concerned,' I inform Patrick. 'I shall be returning to Scotland as planned.'

'Well, I'll come and see you whenever I'm in the right hemisphere,' he promises. 'And when I do, perhaps we can start on researching my dad?'

I nod, acknowledging our mutual need to know more.

We are both silent, turning over future possibilities in our minds. 'I have given a great deal of thought and attention to my own situation,' I tell him, once he has had a little more time to process his new prospects. 'I should like to make use of my rather splendid home more than I have done up to now. It can be a lonely place and could do with the laughter of children. Do you think that your friend Gav might bring his family to stay from time to time? I would particularly like to meet his daughter, Dora.'

'Erm, it's Daisy, actually.'

How trying that the girl should have such an unmemorable name. I shake away the annoyance. 'Dora, Daisy or whoever she is, do you think she would like to come and stay in my house some time? Inevitably she'd have to put up with my company, but it ought to be possible for her and her brother to conjure up for themselves something akin to fun.'

'Granny, I know they'd love it! You and Daisy will get on like a house on fire.'

That will be some consolation. I am dreading all these imminent partings. Saying goodbye to Pip will be the hardest because I know I will never see him again. I will not be able to make another voyage such as this. And let me assure you, the fondness one can feel for a young penguin knows very few bounds.

I am confident that Terry and the others will keep an eye on Pip while they can. But they won't be able to protect him from the multiple dangers at sea. With luck, he may outlive me. Penguins can, I'm told, live to be twenty years old or more. The Locket Island team may see him return year by year, and if they do I know they'll send news of him. I must be prepared for horrors, though. He's getting too big for the skuas, but leopard seals will take over as the most hazardous peril.

I must be strong. Maybe this Daisy girl will provide me with a new focus. I might even, conceivably, tell her something about my own life. I am beginning to think it is a good idea to tell people how you feel occasionally. At least, it is if you choose the people with care.

Patrick is still looking utterly electrified. There is another matter I was going to refer to. What was it, now? It has altogether flown from my brain, which is extremely frustrating. I know it was important.

54

Patrick

Locket Island

'You and Daisy will get on like a house on fire,' I tell her. It's so true. I can just see them together. A new mission will be great for Granny. She needs to care about somebody like she's cared for Pip all this time. It brings out the best in her.

There is a pause that goes on for some time while Granny ruminates.

'Your Terry,' she says finally.

Terry. That lovely word. That word which fills me with hope.

'She's one in a million. One in a million, do you hear?'

'No need to shout, Granny. I hear you.'

Granny frowns. 'You treat her right, else I shall come straight back to Antarctica – even if it's from the grave – and haunt you.'

Terry's Penguin Blog

6 February 2013

In penguin news there is much going on. Pip is well and happy and spending more and more time with his fellows. His feathers are scruffily emerging and he has a Mohican-style hairdo.

And you may remember the penguin we call Sooty? Well, I'm delighted to report that he has found a mate – a beautiful, bright-eyed penguin lady. When we last saw him he was looking very proud and just a bit surprised. And she looked totally devoted. Call me soppy, but I do find penguin love rather wonderful. Maybe it's too late this year for them to start laying eggs, but I feel sure they'll be happy together for many years to come.

55

Veronica

Locket Island

THE CHARMS OF LIFE are manifold, even for an eighty-six-year-old like me. If you will excuse my lecturing, I will expand a little: yes, life brings pain and problems in droves ('battalions', as Hamlet would say), but also, sometimes when you are on the very point of giving up, it delivers absolute delight. There may be surprises in the form of a grandson you suddenly discover you love, a group of scientists who care so much more than you thought, a girl who takes the trouble to understand. There may be revelations brought to you by a mass of stumpy, squalling birds. There may be new hope suddenly sprouting up in a heart that was convinced all humanity was bad, a heart that had grown sick of the world.

Life can be generous. It can heal that heart and whisper that it's always possible to start again, never too late to make a difference. It asserts that there are many, many things worth living for. And one of those things – one of the most unexpectedly joyful things of all – is penguins.

We look out to sea. A great grey ship stands in the bay amongst the icebergs. My suitcases are gathered around me.

A phrase from *Hamlet* ripples through my head. I have probably not mentioned it before but such is the strength of my memory that I can recall reams of passages from my childhood Shakespeare.

I murmur the words to myself: 'This above all: to thine own self be true.' Close on the heels of this phrase, my father's words come to me, the words that always made me take my litter-picking tongs when going out for a walk: *There are three types of people in this world, Very. There are those who make the world worse, those who make no difference, and those who make the world better. Be one who makes the world better, if you can.*

I remember his face as he said it, his warm smile and the smoke of his Woodbine making gentle wreaths around the kitchen. How I wish he and my mother had lived into old age, to guide me through the multifarious turmoils of life. How I long for them both, even now.

I turn away from the others with a lump in my throat and view the rugged features of Locket Island. Crags jut against acres of silky blue-grey sky. Gulls soar above the banks of snow and multi-coloured lichens. Meltwater streams glimmer and shimmer over the dark, volcanic rocks. I want to gather it all into my mind, to take it with me, at least in my memory. I stand here and breathe for a moment.

I haven't told Patrick that I've changed my mind about my leg-acy. I shall be making a will as soon as I arrive on the green shores of Scotland, but I shan't be leaving my millions to the penguin project after all. I shall be leaving every penny to my grandson. The choice of how to use it lies with him. I shall always worry about our planet and the dreadful things humans do to it, but there is a limit to what money can do. Sometimes you have to let the heart dictate what happens.

I trust Patrick. And if he goes off the rails, he has Terry, who I trust even more. I may be wrong, but I have my suspicions that the Adélie penguins are going to benefit quite substantially anyway.

It is time to say goodbye. There are various little men arranged at different points in the journey to help me and my suitcases on and off ships and planes. My luggage is somewhat lighter than on the trip out. It lacks the turquoise cardigan with gold buttons – that was donated towards a particularly good cause. It also lacks one scarlet handbag that was ruined beyond repair, and is lighter in both soap and Darjeeling tea.

Pip is here with us. I can hardly bear to look at him.

'Are you quite sure you don't want to stay out here in Antarctica with us, Granny?' Patrick asks.

I sense that the three scientists are making frantic signs at him behind my back, shaking their heads no doubt and drawing hands like knives across their throats. I am severely tempted to say: 'Yes, I've decided to stay here on Locket Island until my dying day.' But I'm not sure Mike would survive the horror. So instead I utter the truth: 'No. It's time I was heading home. Locket Island is for you young people. Sort out your futures and the future of the penguins and the future of the planet. This is no place for me, not any more. I require a lifestyle that includes limitless hot water and fresh vege-tables, an electric fire with fake flames and the choice of several good quality tea sets. I am also beginning to miss the evergreens at The Ballahays. Besides, Eileen needs me.'

Terry steps forward. 'You'll email us, won't you?'

'Email!' I think not.

'Granny doesn't do email,' Patrick explains.

'Maybe you should think about buying yourself a computer, Mrs McCreedy,' suggests Dietrich.

What an unpleasant idea. I frown. 'There is absolutely no way that is going to happen,' I answer. 'I will write proper letters to you using pen and ink. I am sure Eileen will be kind enough to transcribe them into her computer. And I will ask her to print out any replies you might send. And, of course, I shall ask her for a copy of your doo-dah, Terry.'

'You mean my blog?'

'Yes.' The word had escaped me for a moment.

'It won't be the same without you, Veronica.'

'Nothing will,' adds Mike, with a wink.

'We'll miss you,' Dietrich assures me, wrapping my hand in his.

Mike takes my hand next. 'Take care!' he says. 'You may not believe it, but I'm really glad you came.'

I look at him in astonishment.

Patrick and Terry each give me a hug, then they pick up Pip and hold him out to me. I let my fingers run through his feathers. There isn't much baby down left now, only a comical top-knot that waves slightly in the wind as he bobs his head.

I know I will never see this penguin again, this small, stubby friend who has made a world of difference. He presses his head against my hand in a gesture of affection, as if he knows it too.

I touch my locket as it hangs there under my many layers of clothes, the metal smooth against my skin. It is tightly packed now. In addition to the four strands that were there before there are two new specimens of human hair, plus a tiny tuft of fluff from a penguin.

My eyes are watering yet again, which is rather an annoyance. It seems to be becoming a habit.

I turn towards the ship.

Terry's Penguin Blog

9 February 2013

It's been all change at the field centre on Locket Island. The youngsters are now fully fledged and will soon take their first trip to the sea. They'll be nervous of the huge waves, but they'll go for it. They have a real feel-the-fear-but-do-it-anyway attitude. We'll be so sorry to see them go. Our own Pip will be among them. We've been gradually introducing him to the colony and he spends longer and longer with his fellows, which is a good thing and a relief.

Tempting though it is, we try not to see the penguins as little black-and-white humans. They are very different from us and very special in their own right. Pip is no exception and it is vital that he interacts with his own species and gets on with all those mysteriously 'penguin' aspects of life that we humans will never fully understand but can only admire. The months at sea will be full of new adventures for him.

We are all very proud of him, particularly Veronica.

Sadly, Veronica has finished her stay here. But we are delighted to welcome to the penguin team a new helper, Patrick, who is none other than Veronica's grandson.

Veronica has promised she'll carry on championing penguins from her home on the west coast of Scotland. It has been a real privilege to have her here with us. I can truthfully say we will never forget her visit.

56

Veronica

The Ballahays
March 2013

'Are you sure, Mrs McCreedy?'

'Quite sure, Eileen.'

She is wearing her nonplussed expression. Her hands fidget as she sifts through any plausible explanations she can think of for my erratic behaviour.

'Is it because of the penguins?'

'In a way, yes. You could say that the penguins changed everything.'

'In a *good* way?' she asks, uncertain.

'Indeed, yes. Most assuredly. You could even say that the penguins *saved* me.'

Her facial muscles relax. 'Oh, Mrs McCreedy. How lovely is that!'

I don't deign to answer. Instead I examine myself in the gilt-edged mirror over the mantelpiece. The Veronica McCreedy who looks back at me is as unsightly as ever, despite the generously applied lipstick and eyebrow pencil. Nonetheless, I am aware that a significant transformation has been wrought inside.

'So, just to check I've got this right,' Eileen continues, as if expecting me to deny the instructions I have given her. 'You want me to make up the beds in the two rooms overlooking the rose garden?'

'Absolutely. And Eileen, please be sure to give the dressing tables a thorough dust and polish. It is a good many years since they've been used.'

'Right you are!' She stops by the door. 'They may be noisy,' she warns.

'The dressing tables?'

'No, the children.'

'Humour me, Eileen, and give me the credit for having thought this through.'

Certainly, I am not keen on the equanimity of The Ballahays being disturbed by young children tearing about. But equally I have a strong sense of purpose regarding this Daisy and I need to meet her. As she is a mere eight years old, it would be unreasonable to expect her to come all this way without at least some members of her family. I have therefore, somewhat alarmingly, committed myself to putting up all four of them. I issued the invitation by handwritten letter and was reassured to receive a very polite and enthusiastic acceptance also by Royal Mail. I believe Patrick has been sending explanatory emails to his friend at the bicycle shop. It seems Terry's blogs have gained a small but select following in Bolton. I have gathered there is a bill to settle with Gavin, too. (I cannot bring myself to call him 'Gav'. I fail to comprehend why everyone these days insists on uglifying their name.)

Eileen fetches armfuls of clean sheets from the laundry. 'Don't worry, Mrs McCreedy. I'll come back and close the door once my hands are free,' she calls on her way out of the room.

'On no account trouble yourself, Eileen. The door can remain open.'

So that Pip can get in and out . . . but no. I have to keep reminding myself. Pip isn't with me. He is across the other side of the world. I can only hope with all my heart that he is alive and well. Do penguins remember? Will he ever think of me? I feel a little pang. I can picture him so clearly, his flippers outstretched in excitement, his new coat of black-and-white feathers agleam, determination burning in his eyes. Perhaps at this moment he is tobogganing across the snow together with his penguin friends. Perhaps he is deep under the blue-green waters, chasing fish. Or perhaps he is riding recklessly on the sunlit waves of a wild Antarctic sea.

I had forgotten how very small children are. The boy hides behind his father (who is on the bulky side) as introductions are made, but Daisy skips out in front. She is indeed a diminutive figure, dressed in yellow dungarees and a spotted scarf that clings to her skull. She has a purposeful and inquisitive air about her. There's a pallor to her skin which, added to her lack of hair, indicates the sickliness of the child, but it seems to have done little to diminish her levels of energy. She speaks fast and moves fast. A gabble of words flies from her mouth as she dashes past me into the hall. Her parents are full of shy apologies.

I make tea.

I have given some consideration to the issue of which tea set to use and have settled for the Coalport china. It is distinguished without being too threatening towards those who may not be accustomed to the finer things in life. Eileen, in her great wisdom, has taken it upon herself to bring cupcakes. They are quite horrendous, topped with gaudy pink and purple icing and miniature silver balls that pose a serious hazard to the teeth. I have displayed them on doilies, however, and supplemented them with a selection of caramel wafers and shortbread (*not* ginger thins). We take everything through into the sitting room on the tea trolley. Eileen passes around the cakes and biscuits whilst informing the gathered company that the weather in Ayrshire is not usually this bad.

'Do not be deceived,' I warn them. 'The weather is often considerably worse than this.'

'Although maybe not as cold as Antarctica?' Gavin suggests.

I acquiesce. 'Indeed, the climate of Scotland appears to have transformed itself. To my mind, it has become significantly milder since my travels.'

While we sip our tea, we talk of Patrick. I am able to reassure Gavin and his wife that my grandson has proved himself to be a marvellous addition to the Locket Island team. He is busy and, as far as I can tell, happy. Gavin asks many questions about Terry, some of which I am prepared to answer. I do not divulge how very smug I am feeling about the potential I have created there. As we talk, the children rapidly succeed in getting their faces smeared all over with pink and purple icing.

'Can we go and explore, can we look round the big house, please?' they clamour.

No sooner have I given permission than they are on the rampage, shooting about everywhere. I hear them shrieking at various discoveries, thumping on the stairs, whooping into the alcoves to try out the echoes. I try to rein in my horror.

Gavin and his wife tell me their offspring will calm down shortly and they have toys in the car which will keep them out of trouble for a while. The two of them then disappear out into the drizzle to fetch the aforementioned toys along with the rest of their luggage, Eileen trailing in their wake. The little boy, hearing their exit, nips out after them, roaring something incomprehensible about a 'robo-saurus'. I dread to think what that might be.

I observe that Daisy has meanwhile returned to the sitting room and is now tugging open all the drawers of the dresser. I'm terrified she will knock over the candelabra.

I lower myself on to the sofa and pat the place next to me. 'Come and sit over here, Daisy. There is something I want to talk to you about.'

'What is it, Veronica?'

Really, calling me by my Christian name when she is so tiny, I am so many years her senior, and she has only known me for twenty minutes! However, I let it go.

'I have a very important thing to tell you,' I repeat.

'How important?' She's going to take some convincing.

'It is important to the whole world,' I answer. 'It is important for the planet and for everyone on it. It is important to me personally. And – because you are the future, Daisy – it is important to *you*.'

I have her attention now. She abandons the dresser, dashes over and perches next to me.

'But I will only tell you if you are very still and very, *very* quiet.'

'I can do that,' she assures me, with some verve and volume. 'I can be still. Look.' She freezes in a comical pose. 'And I can be very quiet, too,' she whispers. 'Like a mouse. See.'

I let her wait for a moment. The silence is quite delicious. Her eyes are wide, hungry.

I shall enjoy this.

'Listen, Daisy. I am going to tell you all about penguins . . .'

Epilogue

Giovanni lies in the Naples hospital bed. He is hardly aware of the people gathered around him. He doesn't register that they are four generations of his family who have come to be with him as he draws his final breaths. His mind is filled with bright, mismatched fragments from the past.

Now the images circling inside his head are from the years he spent as a prisoner of war in the North of England. He homes in on that one particular year, the year he met the beautiful English girl. What was her name? Veronica, that was it.

Giovanni doesn't recall how the affair ended; he remembers nothing about arriving home after the war, confiding in his mother and announcing his plans to go back and find Veronica. His mother wouldn't hear of such a thing: Veronica, she insisted, had forgotten him without a doubt. He'd be so much better off marrying a lovely Italian girl, she said – and there was a suitable Italian girl who was eager to see him again. Giovanni had followed his mother's advice. He had sometimes questioned whether he'd done right, wondered if he could have made Veronica happy in the long term. Could it have worked? They'd both been so madly in love . . . but then they'd both been so young and so very needy . . .

Gradually his new life had taken over. He had produced a happy, riotous family of his own. Over the years they had given him countless headaches and unending joy, leaving little room in his thoughts for anything else.

But now, for a moment, Veronica steps back inside his head. A smile hovers on his lips. Her image is fresh and clear. Beautiful Veronica! Her eyes burn with determination as she strides through the Derbyshire countryside, her poppy-coloured dress blowing in the breeze. Veronica: true, headstrong and gloriously vivid. How she shines! No matter what life throws at her, she will defy the odds. Whatever she does, she will be extraordinary.

Acknowledgements

A massive thank-you to everyone who reads this book. You make it all worthwhile and it is my fervent wish that you enjoy every minute of it.

Many people have contributed towards *Away with the Penguins*. As ever, my heartfelt thanks go to my magnificent agent Darley Anderson and his team. Without them this book would never have been written, let alone read!

A million thanks to Sarah Adams and Danielle Perez, my super-skilled editors, for all their wisdom and guidance. They've made everything so much clearer and better. I've also benefited enormously from the editorial input of Francesca Best and Molly Crawford when the novel was in its early stages, and Imogen Nelson at its later stages. It is an immense privilege to work with both Transworld and Berkley. Thank you also to the brilliant marketing and publicity people (Alison, Ruth, Tara, Danielle, Fareeda and Jessica) for all your ideas and hard work. You've done me proud. I'm also indebted to the marvellous team at Penguin Random House Canada, particularly Helen Smith, who sent me an uplifting penguin book and a whole load of enthusiasm when I most needed it.

A special thank-you to Nia Williams for reading my first chapters when I was in panic mode and for giving me a big thumbs-up.

Without your constant encouragement I would have found it hard to carry on.

Penguins are amazing and they have made this story what it is. Massive thanks go to my dear friend Ursula Franklin, whose love of penguins provided me with the initial idea, whose penguin-themed books have helped me with research and whose photos of penguins are a wonder, delight and inspiration.

Living Coasts (Torquay) gave me the unforgettable experience of meeting real penguins up close. I've absorbed anecdotes from penguin patroller Lauren, and I've been lucky to meet Jason Keller, who generously shared facts about hand-rearing a baby penguin. Noah Stryker's book *Among Penguins* has been invaluable, and Noah answered my awkward questions about being a penguin researcher in Antarctica. Louise Emmerson from Australian Antarctic Division kindly supplied data about Adelie chicks. Thank you, a thousand times, all you fantastic penguin people.

Locket Island doesn't really exist, but I have done my best to capture the spirit of the South Shetlands. I am indebted to the British Antarctic Survey: their website includes many fascinating blogs written by scientists working in Antarctica. I have also reaped inspiration from the TV programmes presented by David Attenborough. WWF is another tour de force and I'd like to thank them for supplying information on Adelie penguins and for their Adopt a Penguin campaign. I can't help hoping this novel will inspire people to adopt penguins – or to do something else that chimes with them to care for our world.

For historical accuracy I've referred to numerous books and websites, but I've also been fortunate to talk to several people who experienced the Second World War first-hand, as well as hearing bits and pieces remembered by my parents. I'm grateful to the residents of Westerley Care Home in Minehead for sharing so many of their wartime memories with me. I'd also like to thank Mary

Adams for letting me read her memoir and for telling me about Anderson shelters and glycerin cake.

Thanks, too, to everyone who has contributed towards other areas of research, including Nia Williams (again), Ed Norman and Swati Singh. Any mistakes are my own.

I'm humbled and delighted that so many bookish people have supported my writing. Thanks to fellow authors Trisha Ashley, Phaedra Patrick, Simon Hall, Rebecca Tinnelly and Jo Thomas. Also to Lionel Ward of Brendon Books in Taunton, Kayleigh Diggle of Liznojan Books in Tiverton, Miche Tompkins of Appledore Book Festival, and Marcus and Stuart at Waterstones in Yeovil. And, of course, to everyone involved in Somerset libraries. You are all stars.

Thank you (and sorry) to all the friends who have put up with my strange ways and supported me, even when I was – as often happens – 'elsewhere'. In addition, I must acknowledge our Purrsy, who is always with me as I write, being purrsome and funny, giving his own kind of moral support, which helps enormously and which animal lovers will understand.

Most of all, thank you to Jonathan – for sacrificing your study to me and my mess, and for taking care of computer issues, logistics, bills, laundry, gardening and a million other things so that I can write. You have stood by me through everything, and it was you who made this possible.

HAZEL PRIOR lives on Exmoor with her husband and a huge ginger cat. As well as writing, she works as a freelance harpist. Her wonderful debut novel *Ellie and the Harp-Maker* is now available in paperback.

You can find Hazel on twitter @HazelPriorBooks

COMPETITION

Win a Meet the Penguins experience at a location near you!

Has reading AWAY WITH THE PENGUINS made you want to make friends with these wonderful waddling and waggling birds?

One lucky reader will win a Meet the Penguins experience for two!

For terms and to enter, visit www.penguin.co.uk/meetthepenguins
Competition closes 30/09/2020